HE DROWNED IN MEMORY

HE DROWNED IN MEMORY

ZACHARY GOLDMAN MYSTERIES
BOOK ELEVEN

P.D. WORKMAN

PD WORKMAN

ISBN: 9781774682517 (KDP Hardcover)

ISBN: 9781774682463 (KDP Paperback)

ISBN: 9781774682470 (IS Large Print)

ISBN: 9781774682500 (Lulu Paperback)

ISBN: 9781774682487 (Kindle)

ISBN: 9781774682494 (ePub)

ALSO BY P.D. WORKMAN

For the rescuers
and the lost

1

Zachary watched out the windshield as Kenzie drove back to her house. It seemed like a long time since he had been outside. It was very bright with all the white snow on the ground, the branches of the trees also covered with piles of newly fallen snow. It always looked so nice and clean right after a snowfall. Before all the dirt from the roads was kicked up and tracks and trails were stomped down by pedestrians.

Kenzie's car was warm, since she had driven it from home to the hospital to pick him up. It wasn't very energy efficient to heat the little red convertible during the Vermont winters. It lost a lot of heat through the canvas top. But Kenzie's "baby" was her pride and joy, and she insisted on driving it to the hospital even though she could have taken Zachary's white compact instead. She would drive her car through all but the worst of weather.

"Glad to be out?" Kenzie asked. She turned her head to look at him for an instant, her curly dark hair bouncing.

Zachary nodded. "Nice to get out in the fresh air… the hospital gets so stale, recycling the same air over and over again."

"I'll bet."

Zachary had lost track of how long it had been. Five weeks? Six? The days tended to all run together in the psych ward. It was hard to even keep track of what day of the week it was. But he was feeling good now. There was a lot of work to be done, but he tried not to feel anxious about it. He would be fine once he got back into the swing of things. He knew that from experience. Every year, he struggled to get through December, but he could see the light at the end of the tunnel once he was past Christmas. He could restart his life. He'd stayed in the hospital a little longer than he usually did because they had changed his med cocktail around to try to address his heightened obsessive behavior. It was always best to stay under supervision to ensure the med change didn't cause additional problems.

"Do you want to go out for dinner tonight?" Kenzie suggested. "A celebratory supper?"

Zachary's shoulders tensed. He had been anticipating a nice quiet night at home. Supper in the kitchen with Kenzie. Cuddling on the couch and watching an old movie. Maybe going through his mass of accumulated emails to see if he could put a dent in them so that it wouldn't take so long to tackle them the next day.

Kenzie glanced at him. "No? We don't have to if you're not up to it."

"I *could*. I just… was hoping to be at home tonight."

"That's fine." Kenzie smiled. "It was just a suggestion. I thought you might want to be out and about. Restless after being cooped up for so long."

"No. Maybe tomorrow or on the weekend. Tonight, I just want to be… *home*."

It was funny how quickly Kenzie's house had become home. He should probably think about giving up his apartment, since it no longer represented home for him. He really didn't need a separate place. He didn't have a lot of possessions, having become accustomed to living on very little in foster care as a teen. He would see if Kenzie could make some space for his files and the rest of his photography equipment, but none of the larger items like furniture meant anything to him.

There was no point in paying rent on a place where he didn't live anymore.

But it would be a big step. The last time he had moved in with someone and given up keeping separate residences had been when he'd moved in with Bridget.

Zachary turned his focus as quickly as he could to his business. He couldn't spend any time thinking about Bridget. Bridget was in the past. She had her own family and life, and he wasn't part of that anymore.

He would call Heather, his older sister, when he got home. She had been keeping on top of business calls while he had been away. It was the first time that he'd had a business partner to do that while he had been in the hospital. While Heather didn't do any fieldwork, she enjoyed doing skip tracing and some of the other computer work. She had taken over the accounting system for Zachary, entering expenses, reconciling the credit card and bank account, and chasing down delinquent accounts. Her husband was a bookkeeper and Zachary supposed she had absorbed enough from his work to know what she was doing and had someone to turn to if she had any questions about errors that needed to be straightened out.

"We'll stay in tonight," Kenzie confirmed. "I have a lasagna in the freezer. We can throw together a salad to go with it."

"That sounds great. After more than a month of hospital food…"

Kenzie chuckled. "You could probably use a little something to spice up your diet."

Zachary heartily agreed. It took an effort to gain back the weight he lost during his cyclical depressions, not easy with the bland meals they served in the hospital. He needed some real food. Lasagna sounded heavenly.

Walking into the house felt so right. Zachary took a deep breath and let it out slowly, trying to relax all his muscles. He had been a little bit afraid, in the back of his mind, that he wouldn't feel like he belonged there anymore. That he might have lost something during his absence. But everything in the house was just as it should be. Down to his computer on his mobile desk in the living room and his phone charging on the side table. He walked down the hall to put his duffel bag down in the bedroom, but didn't bother unpacking yet. That could wait. The only things in it were clothes. And he would probably want to put them all directly into the washer to get the smell and feel of the hospital out of them.

"This is wonderful." Back in the living room, he hugged Kenzie impulsively, pulling her close against him and reveling in how good she felt in his arms. He was home, and he was with her, and it would be almost a year before Christmas came around again. By that time, maybe with the new med protocol and individual and couple's therapy, next Christmas wouldn't be as bad. He would stay out of the hospital and just have a quiet Christmas at home with Kenzie.

"How is your mom?" he asked, remembering that she had been planning to visit Lisa Cole Kirsch over the Christmas holiday. She'd never really told him how that had gone.

Kenzie looked surprised. She considered the question for a moment, then gave a slight shake of her head. "She's fine."

Zachary studied Kenzie's face. Something felt *off*. But he wasn't going to ruin his first day home by pursuing something she didn't feel like talking to him about. Her parents had always been a sensitive topic.

As were Zachary's.

2

Z achary looked around the kitchen, frowning. Kenzie had taken the garlic bread out of the oven, and he had been planning to slice it for her, but when he reached for the place where the butcher block of knives used to sit on the counter, it was no longer there.

"Uh, Kenz...?"

Leaning over the lasagna in the oven to see if it was done, Kenzie turned her head to look back at him.

"Oh... drawer to your left."

Zachary opened the nearest drawer, then realized it was the wrong side, closed it, and opened the next one over. The knives were there. He chose the one he needed for the crusty loaf and closed the drawer.

"You moved them." He stated the obvious. Was he upset that she had changed something while he was gone? He wasn't sure. It was such a small thing, but it made him feel suddenly awkward, and he found himself looking around the kitchen for anything else that might have changed.

"Yeah." Kenzie lifted the lasagna pan from the oven and put it onto the stove top. She turned off the oven. "I thought it was best to have them out of sight. So if you're feeling bad..."

Zachary remembered how he had put all the knives in the fridge when he had been having thoughts of suicide. It had been too difficult having them out on the counter where he could see them all the time, even from the couch where he sat with his computer. And then later, when things had gotten worse, he had swept them all out of the fridge onto the floor as he wrestled the mental demons who whispered to him that if he just ended his life, he wouldn't have to keep suffering. His cheeks flamed as he thought about it.

But Kenzie didn't bring any of that up. She didn't see the need to lecture him on how he should control himself better or not overreact to his emotional state. He'd heard plenty of those lectures before, though not from her. He wasn't sure whether it was because of her medical training or just her personality that she seemed to understand better than most people. Zachary was silent as he unwrapped the garlic toast and cut it into thick slices. He licked garlic butter off his finger. He could have made his entire meal out of a crusty, warm loaf of garlic bread. Which, of course, Kenzie had known when she had bought it. Like everyone else, she was determined to fatten him up as quickly as she could.

They moved around each other, getting the meal ready. Zachary wanted everything to be perfect, so he stayed focused on what he was doing, concentrating hard on setting the table and putting out the bread and the jug of water, not doing a slap-dash job of it and forgetting something vital like the forks or plates. In a few minutes, they were sitting down together. They dug into the meal, making appreciative noises and enjoying their first chance in weeks to just sit down to a meal together.

"I should set up a time for us to go visit Mr. Peterson," Zachary suggested.

Kenzie nodded. She took a sip of her water. "He and Pat would love to see you. So much nicer to visit at their house than at the hospital."

There were always distractions at the hospital. Too many things that Zachary had to keep an eye on while he was talking to visitors. While he knew he needed to be there, he worried about whether the other patients would disturb his visitors. Someone might have a violent episode while they were there, a psychotic break, and threaten them. It wasn't the best place for an intimate family visit.

Mr. Peterson and Patrick Parker were the closest things to parents that Zachary had. Mr. Peterson—Lorne—had been one of Zachary's foster fathers for a few weeks when he first went into foster care at age ten. While Zachary had not been able to stay in the Peterson home for long, he and Mr. Peterson had kept in touch over the years. It was a couple of decades since he and his wife had divorced, and Pat, a somewhat younger man, had become his partner. They had been close to Zachary through all the intervening years, becoming his chosen family.

"I should call Tyrrell. Maybe he'd like to join us too."

Kenzie pursed her lips. "If you want to."

It seemed like an odd response. She had never been reluctant to have Tyrrell, Zachary's younger brother, join them before. She had been the one who had encouraged him to reunite with Tyrrell, and it had been amazing to have one of his biological siblings in his life again. And Tyrrell had introduced him to Heather, and then later to Jocelyn, their two older sisters.

"I don't think it would be too much," Zachary said. Meeting with a larger group *could* be overwhelming. Especially if one of the members of the group was Jocelyn. Sharp, bitter Joss. But just Tyrrell joining them wouldn't be too hard. Tyrrell was undemanding and easy to get along with. Zachary didn't feel like he had to always be on guard with Tyrrell.

Kenzie nodded. "If you can get him."

"Why wouldn't I be able to get him?"

Kenzie shrugged. She took a couple more bites of lasagna. "He hasn't been around the last little while. Hasn't answered any calls."

Zachary stopped, his fork in front of his mouth. "What? What do you mean?"

"Just that. He hasn't been answering phone calls. But maybe he'll answer you."

"Do you mean… today? He hasn't been answering calls *today?*"

"No. I mean… since Christmas."

Zachary frowned. "But you've talked to him since then, haven't you?"

"No. We've been concerned, but... I've been busy with work, and you, and... other things. I figure that he'll make contact again when he is ready. Until then... best to just leave him to sort things out."

Zachary felt like something had exploded in his brain. Tyrrell had stopped communicating? What had happened to him? He'd seemed fine the last time Zachary had seen him. Tyrrell was always cheerful, easygoing, reassuring to Zachary when he got upset or anxious about something. He was the strong one, what Zachary might have been like if it hadn't been for the fire and everything he'd dealt with jumping from family to family in foster care.

"What do you mean, 'We've been concerned?' You and who?"

"Heather." Kenzie poked at the lasagna that remained on her plate, staring down at it instead of looking into Zachary's face. "Tyrrell was supposed to go to the hospital with Heather and Joss on Christmas Day. But Tyrrell didn't show up. She tried to get him then, but couldn't get him to call her back."

"He's not talking to Heather either?" Zachary shook his head. "Aren't you worried about this? Don't you think it is serious?"

"I told you that we *are* worried about him. But there's nothing we can do if he doesn't want to talk to us. He's a grown man. He's allowed to decide who he talks to or doesn't."

"Has anyone gone to see him? Made sure that he's okay? Somebody has *seen* him, right?"

"He has gone incommunicado before. His ex-wife said that he'd gone off the rails a few times... he would disappear for days on a drinking binge. Not talk to anyone. Then come back and act as if nothing had happened and he couldn't understand why everyone was upset about it."

"Has she talked to him? What about the kids? Has he talked to Mason or Alisha?"

"No. He was supposed to have them on Christmas Day. But he didn't show up."

"Don't you think something is wrong?" he asked urgently.

"Maybe... it is getting to the point where I wonder if we want to have the police do a welfare check. But something like that really isn't up to me to do. It should be someone closer to him. His work, friends, neighbors… family."

"We *are* family." Zachary pulled his phone out of his pocket and tapped the contact record for Tyrrell. He listened to it ring, hoping that Kenzie would be wrong and Tyrrell would pick it up and everything would be fine. Maybe there had been some misunderstanding. He'd had a fight with his ex and hadn't wanted to pick up the kids, then had been too embarrassed to go with Heather and Joss and explain why he didn't have them. And he hadn't wanted to talk to Kenzie because she was an outsider. There could be perfectly logical reasons they hadn't been able to get ahold of Tyrrell, but he would answer Zachary's call.

The call rang through to voicemail.

3

———————————

Zachary waited for Tyrrell's outgoing message to finish. He wasn't going to hang up and not let Tyrrell know he was looking for him. Tyrrell would be able to see Zachary's name on his missed call list, but that wasn't good enough. After the beep, Zachary spoke.

"Hey, T. Listen… I'm out of the hospital and back home. I thought I might set up dinner at Mr. Peterson's—Lorne's—and you might want to join us. Kenzie says she hasn't heard anything from you lately, so will you call me back? Let me know either way. I want to make sure you're okay."

He paused, thinking about whether he'd said everything he should or whether he'd messed it up and should start over again. He couldn't think of what else to say, and he knew that before too long, the voicemail would hang up on him.

"Okay. So… give me a call. Bye."

He tapped the red button on his phone and stared down at it for a few minutes. Kenzie's fork touched her plate with a soft clink as she continued to eat. He looked up at her.

"What if something happened to him? What if something bad happened, and nobody bothered to find out?"

"I don't think anything has happened to him. His ex says that he's done this before. So even if they did call the police, the police would know that and probably wouldn't put any time into it."

"But just because he has gone on a bender before, that doesn't mean nothing happened to him this time. He could have been hurt or sick. He might have needed help." Zachary heard his volume rising and tried to lower it, but he was angry that no one had followed up. Tyrrell could disappear and no one even bothered to look for him? How could everyone sit around and just do nothing? "Bad things happen," he snapped at Kenzie. "With your job, I'd think you would know that!"

She gazed at him steadily. "I do, Zach. I realize that. But like I said, I didn't think it was up to me. Heather and Tyrrell's ex both knew what was going on. If they felt concerned enough about it, either one could have called the police or gone to check on him. But they both figured that he'd just fallen off the wagon. And you know..." She shrugged, uncomfortable under his gaze. "You know that when we were at the Lodge, someone had a fair amount to drink from the alcohol cabinet in our cabin."

Zachary felt a chill. He'd forgotten about that. So much had happened since then. Both while they were at the Lodge and upon their return. It seemed like it had all happened years ago. *Had* Tyrrell been drinking while they were there? They all knew that'd he'd had a problem with alcohol in the past. He didn't drink, not even a little bit on holidays. But things had been stressful at the Lodge. Had he slipped? They had asked him, straight out, and he'd said no. Zachary didn't like to think that Tyrrell had lied right to his face and he hadn't detected it. What kind of a brother was Zachary if he couldn't even tell when his own brother was lying or in distress?

"Do you think that's what happened? He started drinking when we were at the Lodge, and then... he just let it take over?"

"Maybe. We don't know what has happened before, or what might have been going on in his life at the time. We don't know what has triggered a setback before. But his ex-wife seemed to think that this is pretty normal. Not unexpected."

"But he's been so good for the time that we've known him."

"That's still not very long. It might seem like a long time since you reunited, but it's only been a year. That's not a long time when you're talking about addiction and sobriety. People fall off the wagon after decades of being sober."

"But he didn't just stop a year ago. I thought it was a long time ago. Years ago."

"He never said *when* to me. But with the way the kids were behaving around him... they remember him being different from now. You remember Alisha being afraid to tell him that she had gone vegetarian? There wouldn't be any reason for that if he was just calm and easygoing all the time. She's known him when he's been different, when that might have triggered a negative reaction. So he was probably still drinking within the past few years."

Zachary *had* noticed how the kids behaved around Tyrrell, but he had told himself that he was just seeing something that wasn't there because of the way he had grown up. Always afraid his father was going to explode. Or his foster fathers. He had been about Alisha's age when he had entered foster care.

But Kenzie had seen it too, which meant it wasn't just something Zachary had imagined because of his history.

"I need to do something." He fingered his phone, wondering if he should put a call in to the police right away. But of course, the Roxboro police wouldn't be able to help him. He would have to talk to the police in Riverbrook where Tyrrell lived. And it probably wouldn't do to just call them. He would need to go there and make a pest of himself. Look in Tyrrell's windows if he wouldn't answer the door and call the police for a welfare check while he was there to increase the urgency. "Do you think... maybe I should call Heather? Maybe she has heard something but just didn't have a chance to mention it to you yet. You've been busy with work and everything."

Kenzie nodded. "I have cookies and ice cream for dessert if you want some."

Zachary sensed she was trying to distract him. With his ADHD, it wasn't that hard, and maybe she was hoping that he would let it go for the rest of the evening. But he wasn't going to forget that his little brother was missing, that he could be in danger.

"No. I'm full. Dinner was really good," Zachary pushed his plate an inch away from himself. "Really hit the spot. But I'm full. And I should call Heather."

"Okay. Maybe we can have dessert later when dinner has had a chance to settle."

"Yeah. Sure. That sounds good." Zachary pushed himself away from the table and stood up. He could tell that Kenzie didn't want him calling Heather to bug her about Tyrrell, so it was probably best if he didn't do it while sitting at the table. It was probably rude to make phone calls at the dinner table but, with cellphones being so ubiquitous, stuff that used to be seen as extremely impolite was now normal, everyday behavior. He'd already pushed it once by calling Tyrrell. He wouldn't repeat it by calling Heather from the table as well.

"I'll… be back in a bit."

Since he didn't have a separate office or bedroom at Kenzie's house, there wasn't really anywhere private for him to retreat to. He decided to use the bedroom, since Kenzie was in the kitchen. It would only take a few minutes to talk to Heather, and then Kenzie could have her room back if she wanted it.

4

Zachary sat down on the bed and tapped Heather's avatar on his phone. It would be nice to talk to her again, though he wished the circumstances were different. He hadn't seen her since Christmas Day when she and Joss had visited him at the hospital. He appreciated the gesture, but it had been difficult for him. Now, at home, without other distractions, it would be easier to focus on Heather and to hear the emotions behind her words.

"Zachary!" Heather's voice was warm and full of enthusiasm. "You're back!"

"Yeah. I guess I am. How are you?"

"I'm just fine. I'm so happy to hear from you. Things are better?"

"I'm on a new med cocktail, and it seems to be working okay. Now that I'm out... I guess I'll really put it to the test. It's never quite the same, at the hospital and in real life. Different stresses, and some medications take a few weeks to reach full efficacy, so you aren't seeing the real effects of them until later on."

"Sounds complicated."

"It is. Be glad that you're not in charge of it. I can't imagine trying to handle the needs and prescriptions of multiple patients. It's hard enough for me to keep track of my own and figure out what is working and what isn't."

"Better the doctors than me. Have you had a chance to look at your email yet? I've been sending weekly summary reports, so that is probably where you want to start. Get an overview of what has been going on before you dive into all of the individual emails from clients and other contacts."

"I will. I haven't logged in to my computer yet. Just had dinner with Kenzie and found out about Tyrrell."

There was only silence from Heather.

"I can't understand why anyone didn't get the police involved," Zachary told her. "That's their job. Missing persons. If he has been missing since Christmas, then someone should have reported it."

"I don't know if he's actually *missing*, or if he's just not bothering to return calls. I don't really have any way of knowing what is going on in Riverbrook. Other than by calling his ex, and I really don't want to push my luck there. She wasn't too happy to hear from me before."

"What did she say?"

"She said that Tyrrell is irresponsible. That him not showing to pick up the kids like he was supposed to wasn't anything new. And that I should just stay out of it and let him work things out himself. He needs to take responsibility for his own life, not have someone coddling him and putting up with his sh—nonsense."

"But has she seen him at all? Has anyone seen him?"

"I imagine someone has. Not Lindsey, though. He's behind on child support and she says that he's probably avoiding her because of that."

"She hasn't looked for him?"

"No. And I could understand what she was saying about not enabling him or trying to take care of him. So I stayed out of the way."

"He could be hurt or sick. He could be dead in his apartment, and how would anyone know if everybody refuses to take any responsibility for him and find out?"

"You're welcome to try. But I don't have any desire to be around him if he's on a bender. And if he is dead in his apartment, I don't want to be the one to find that out either!"

Zachary opened his mouth to snap back at her that it wasn't

funny, then reconsidered. She wasn't joking. Since getting married, she had led a fairly sheltered life and was a bit of a hermit, preferring to stay home where she didn't have to deal with the rest of the world except by computer and telephone. She had dealt with enough abuse and trauma in her teen years. She deserved to live free of all of that nastiness as an adult.

Finding Tyrrell was Zachary's job, not Heather's. If he could take responsibility for finding out what had happened to Tyrrell on himself, he was happy to be able to help Heather continue to live the life she had made for herself, away from the ugliness of Tyrrell's addiction and where it might have led him.

"Okay," he told her in a quiet voice. "I'll take care of it. You don't need to."

There was another small silence.

"Thank you, Zachary," Heather said eventually. "I'm sure every-thing is okay… but I just don't want to be involved in it."

"That's fine. You don't have to. Tyrrell is not your responsibility anymore."

When they had been young, the little children had been the responsibilities of the older ones. Heather and Joss had been mothers to the little brood of Goldman children way before they were old enough to take on such a responsibility.

"Thanks. I'm sure he's fine… What are you going to do first?"

"I've left a message for him to call me. Maybe he will. I haven't talked to him since a couple of weeks before Christmas… more than a month ago. If he doesn't call me back, I'll drive down to Riverbrook and have a look around. See if he is there. Get the police involved if he isn't or if it looks like there was any foul play involved. Then… I don't know. It will depend on what I find out."

"What about the rest of the business? We've got a good amount of stuff backlogged that you should be starting on when you're feeling up to it."

"It won't matter whether I start now or in a few days. If they've waited this long, they'll wait a bit longer. If they can't… then it's better that someone else takes that on instead of me having to worry about getting something done in a hurry. Tyrrell is family. He comes first."

5

When Zachary got off the phone and went back out to the living room, Kenzie was still tidying up in the kitchen. He realized that he had left her with all of the clearing up, not even thinking about it in his concern over Tyrrell's disappearance. She had made most of the meal; the least he could do was help with the clean-up. He couldn't remember for sure whether he had even finished what was on his plate or whether he had just walked off, leaving half of his dinner behind.

"Sorry—I'm sorry, I didn't mean to leave you with everything." Zachary hurried into the kitchen and looked around to see what else needed to be done. "Is there anything else? Can I help?"

Kenzie sighed. "No, it's done now."

"I wasn't thinking. I'll do better. I'm sorry."

"I appreciate it. How was Heather?"

"How was she? Good, I guess…" Zachary wasn't sure he had even asked her how she was. He had just launched into his questions about Tyrrell and whether she had seen or talked to him. Two strikes against him already, and he had only been out of the hospital for a few hours. He had thought that his symptoms were under control, but if he couldn't even show any courtesy to the people around him due to his distraction, then maybe he wasn't doing as well as he had hoped.

18

"She hasn't heard from Tyrrell?"

"No. And she doesn't want to get involved. I guess Tyrrell's ex talked her out of doing anything. But I can't just let it go."

Kenzie nodded. "That's understandable." She closed the dishwasher, latched it, and pressed a button to start the cleaning cycle. She motioned toward the living room, and they both walked in and sat down together on the couch. Zachary was feeling awkward, unsure whether they were having a serious conversation or if Kenzie just wanted to cuddle and watch TV or had other things in mind. He watched her for any cues.

"You might want to ease into things a little more slowly," Kenzie suggested. "Let yourself get acclimatized first. It seems like jumping headlong into Tyrrell's problems might be a bit much when you're just out of the hospital. Maybe start with your emails and seeing what work Heather has done and what is waiting for you. Then maybe take a trip down this weekend to see Tyrrell on the way to the Petersons'."

There was logic to laying it out that way so that Tyrrell's bender didn't become central to his life, tying him up in knots when he wasn't ready to take on such an emotional job.

But Zachary was anything but logical. He *did* throw himself headlong into things after Christmas every year. He didn't wait to recover from his depression and regain his strength. He just threw himself back into his work and tried to catch up on what he had missed or gotten behind on. And he couldn't pretend that Tyrrell's disappearance didn't bother him and was something that could just be put off until it was more convenient to investigate it.

"Yeah, we'll see," he told Kenzie, "I'll think about that." It was better if she thought he was going to listen so that she wasn't anxious about him all evening and ended up not being able to sleep well before she went back to her job at the Medical Examiner's Office in the morning. She wouldn't know that he was starting his investigation until later the next day. By that time, he would be well into it. She would be able to see that he was fine and that investigating Tyrrell's disappearance wouldn't throw his recovery off the rails.

"Do you want to watch something?" Kenzie asked, nodding

toward the TV screen. "Or did you want some time to get work done?"

"Would you mind if I did my email while we watch something? I know that usually we don't do that, but…"

One of the things they had discussed in couple's therapy was to really be present when they were spending time together. Zachary needed to take a break from his computer and business and just spend time with Kenzie and pay attention to her. And it was something he worked hard on, making it a rule for himself that he put his computer away when it was time for them to spend time together in the evening or on the weekend. Zachary confined his work activities to Kenzie's hours at work as much as possible. Sometimes, surveillance jobs took him away from her during the evening, but he tried to keep them to a minimum.

"I think it's fine this once," Kenzie said slowly, as if she were picking her words carefully. "It's the first opportunity that you've had to log on. But… I don't want it to be something that gets you all wound up so that you can't sleep. If it's something that you're not going to be able to pull away from…"

"I think it will be fine. I've been doing pretty well lately."

"But you've been in a different environment. Staying on task at the hospital when you don't have access to a computer or your email or other distractions is not exactly the same as being home."

"No. But it should be fine. I'm not going to start working tonight. Just getting an idea of what work there is to be done." And he wouldn't even start on it the next day. He already knew he would be in Riverbrook.

Kenzie shrugged. She picked up the remote control for the TV. Zachary waited a few seconds, making it look like he was interested in the process of picking something to watch, and then reached for his laptop.

6

Zachary couldn't have said what movie they watched together. There had been so much email in his inbox after being away from his computer for weeks that he had done exactly what he had said he wouldn't and gotten so focused on it that he forgot everything else and probably hadn't given Kenzie any of the attention she had expected.

But he was true to his word and didn't start on his work. He didn't send out any emails, start any inquiries, or set up any new files.

Heather's advice to read her weekly email reports first had been a good one. He appreciated her doing that for him so that he had a sane, logical place to start. He vaguely remembered her saying once that her kids both had ADHD. She had clearly learned some strategies to help them deal with it.

But after reading through her reports and putting them into a folder to refer back to later, there was still lots of work to do weeding out all of the spam and the emails to do with inquiries that Heather had already taken care of and to pare the contents of his inbox down to what he would need to concentrate on once he had talked to Tyrrell and was ready to get back to work.

Before he knew it, he could hear the music for the movie's closing credits and, looking up, saw the names of the actors scrolling up the screen. He hadn't even been aware of most of them having appeared in the movie. He had only looked up once or twice while it was on, a dramatic fight or chase scene pulling him away from his email. He slowly closed the lid on his laptop and put it back on his table. He squeezed his eyes shut a few times to lubricate them. They were dry and scratchy after staring at the screen without a break.

"Good movie; what did you think?" Kenzie asked.

"Uh, yeah," Zachary agreed, forcing a smile and nodding. "Exciting."

There was a bowl sitting on his table where he had probably put it down. A cookie swimming in a pool of melted ice cream. Zachary picked up the bowl and held it close to his body so that when he picked up the cookie, the ice cream dripped back into the bowl instead of into his lap. He took a bite of the cookie.

"Mmm. These are good."

Kenzie was giving him an amused look. One that told him that she was completely aware of how lost he had become in his email review. She had probably tried to talk to him a few times and gotten no response. And the fact that he had no awareness of the cookie and ice cream until after the closing credits of the movie told him that he had been oblivious to her getting up and preparing the evening snack for the two of them and had ignored it when she gave it to him or put it on the table.

Zachary cleared his throat, his ears getting hot.

"Are you going to need some time to unwind before bed?"

He rubbed his jaw. "Uh, yes. I guess so."

"Anything I can do to help you relax?" She put her hand on his thigh, leaning in closer.

Zachary turned his body toward her and put his arms around her before kissing her gently. He was glad that he had put the computer away. Some other important things needed his full attention.

Before going to bed, Zachary took his new regimen of pills into the main bathroom. He arranged them on the shelf of the medicine cabinet. He disposed of all the old prescriptions so that he wouldn't get confused about what he was supposed to be taking. None of the bottles was full. He refilled his prescriptions often, rather than having enough pills on hand to make overdosing a temptation. It would be possible to do harm by combining several together, but that didn't seem to be as much of a problem for him when he was seriously depressed. It took too much mental energy to figure out what combination to take.

He reviewed the label of each pill bottle before he took each one. He had been on enough other cocktails that he was pretty familiar with everything out there. Still, the combination and dosages were new, so he wanted to ensure he got them right until they became ingrained as a habit. Then it would be more automatic.

Kenzie walked by in the hallway as he was taking his night dosages and stopped to talk to him. "So this new cocktail, you think it's good? Think it will help?"

Zachary nodded as he downed a couple more pills. "Seems to be pretty good so far. Not so nauseated in the morning, so that's good." He looked at the next bottle on the shelf and hesitated.

"Take them all," Kenzie prompted.

Zachary didn't like taking all of them every day. He preferred to judge whether he needed anything for anxiety or not. Whether he needed a sleeping pill. He would take his ADHD meds—a daytime prescription, not night—if he were doing something he knew he would need it for, but didn't like to take them every day. He looked at Kenzie sideways, gauging what her response would be if he told her that he didn't need to take all of them.

Kenzie raised her brows.

"I'm just thinking… it would be nice not to have to take a sleep aid tonight, since I'm at home."

"If you do that, you'll be up again at the crack of dawn. You need to make sure you're getting enough sleep for good mental health and to be able to focus on your work."

"But I'm in a good place already. The hospital enforced all that kind of thing. I just don't like the way they make me feel in the morning…"

"And don't like relying on an aid to get to sleep every night. I know. I just think that for the first few days at home, the transition, it would be a good idea not to vary anything. Once you're sure that you're stable, then you can start using a bit of your own discretion."

That was one of the few issues Zachary had with having a medical doctor for a partner. She was too sure that she knew exactly what he needed to do for his own mental health. That if he just followed medical advice, everything would be fine. While there was some truth to what she said, Zachary had been through the cycle of med changes enough times to know what he was talking about and how his body worked.

But he didn't want to have an argument with her the first day back. He had already come dangerously close to that with his comments about how she and Heather should have dealt with Tyrrell's absence. Even if they didn't *argue*, a discussion about meds right before bedtime was likely to degrade to obsessive thoughts and an inability to get to sleep.

He took the sleep aid without any further comment, short-circuiting any more discussion about which route would be best for him to take. Med discussions were fine in the morning, but not right before bed.

Kenzie nodded and walked the rest of the way down the hall to the bedroom. Zachary took the last couple of prescriptions and followed her.

7

As Zachary had expected, when morning rolled around, he felt groggy from the sleep aid. The prescription sleep aid was much stronger than the Benadryl or over-the-counter sleep aids that the drug store stocked and made him feel thick-headed for the first hour or two after he got up. But it had had the desired effect of keeping him asleep for almost seven hours, like a normal person. If the doctors were right and that helped him be healthier physically and mentally, he would have to put up with the adverse effects.

"Morning!" Kenzie rolled over to give him a kiss. "How are you feeling this morning?"

"Great," he lied. "I'm going to have a quick shower to wash away the cobwebs. You work today?"

"I work every day," Kenzie said with a shrug and a little laugh. She was doing better at getting off at least one day on the weekend. Or if she couldn't do that, at least working shorter hours on the weekend, but it was hard for her to tear herself away from her work sometimes. If Zachary's job had been dealing with dead people every day, he thought he would be happy to go home by the end of the day. "I won't be late, though," Kenzie promised. "Dr. Wiltshire knows that you're back home, and I told him I wanted to make sure we had clear evenings for at least the first week or two."

"So unless there is an emergency…" Zachary gave her an out, knowing that things often came up that were beyond her control.

"If there's a zombie apocalypse, then I might have to stay late. But I don't plan to."

Zachary rubbed his eyes and pressed hard on the bony ridge over his eyes, trying to ease the hangover-like headache, considering her answer.

"Wait, would a zombie apocalypse mean that there were more people in your morgue because the zombies killed them, or less because everyone was *undead?*"

"Uh… hmm… good question. I'll have to think about that one. I'll ask Dr. Wiltshire what he thinks." She grinned at the thought.

If she did that, Dr. Wiltshire might just send Zachary straight back to the psych ward. If that was something the medical examiner could order.

Zachary had never met or spoken with Lindsey, Tyrrell's ex-wife. Zachary and Tyrrell were both divorced, and they didn't talk much to each other about their exes. Tyrrell knew that Zachary's relationship with Bridget was fraught. Zachary fought against himself because of his obsession with Bridget even though he was now with Kenzie and worked hard on his relationship with her. He couldn't help that his brain kept going back to Bridget, replaying the things that had happened between the two of them over and over again, imagining what would have happened if they had stayed together, about if Bridget's newborn twin girls had been his instead of Gordon's, about what he would do if Bridget ever decided she wanted him in her life again. Which he knew wasn't going to happen, but he couldn't stop his brain from going there.

But Heather had Lindsey's name and contact details, so Zachary hadn't had to go searching for her himself. He called ahead, deciding it was probably best not to just show up on her doorstep. In addition to the fact that she probably wouldn't want a stranger calling, much less her ex's brother, he knew that she could be working. Showing up at her house without setting up an appointment first could result in his having to wait a very long time to talk to her.

Lindsey was clearly not excited about talking to him. She spoke slowly, with caution, considering her words carefully before she said anything.

"I suppose you can come over around three," she said finally. "I have to be home for when the kids get out of school. But there isn't really much to tell you. I can already tell you the whole of the conversation. Tyrrell is off drinking. Yes, he's done it before. No, I don't know where he goes to drink. He'll come back eventually. Maybe someday, he will hit bottom and be able to stay off the bottle for more than a few months or a year at a time."

"Okay, thanks." Zachary didn't bother addressing his questions to her over the phone. It would be easier face-to-face, where he could watch her reactions and hopefully discern when she was telling him the truth and when she was just hoping to avoid or end the conversation. If he were there with her, she couldn't hang up. And it would be a lot harder to get him out of the house. Not that he wouldn't go if she asked him to, but people found it difficult to do things they thought were rude, and she would be sure to think that kicking him out when he was just trying to find and help his brother was pretty harsh. She would be polite, even though she didn't want him looking for Tyrrell and didn't want Tyrrell back.

Driving on the highway was one of Zachary's favorite activities. The only time that his brain truly quieted and let him just sit and think. He imagined that was what the brain of a normal person felt like most of the time. His time on the highway was a rolling meditation.

And without Kenzie in the car with him, he could go as fast as he liked. He didn't have to get to Riverbrook in a hurry. It wasn't an emergency. He wasn't going to get more done if he got there faster. But he loved to drive fast down the highway, finding a clear lane where he could just fly for ten minutes without anyone pulling in front of him. Or navigating from one lane to the other to avoid the slower vehicles, like a real-life game of Frogger. Kenzie didn't like his speeding, so he always had to slow down to just above the speed limit if she were in the passenger's seat.

As a result, he rolled into Riverbrook much earlier than he should have. It would still be some time before he could go to Lindsey's house to interview her. He input Tyrrell's address into the GPS and navigated to his building.

The area of town was shabby. Not that any of it was upscale. It was a small Vermont town, similar to many others, where people lived in little bungalows or condo units, not mansions. Not big places like Bridget's new house with Gordon or the home that Kenzie had grown up in. Tyrrell's building was similar to somewhere Zachary would have rented. A small bachelor pad or studio apartment where he could sleep, watch TV, and conduct his business. Smaller than Zachary's current apartment. He reminded himself he needed to make sure there weren't any flyers sticking out from under his door. And he should talk to the manager about getting out of his lease.

He circled once, looking at the building and the neighborhood, before pulling into the parking lot. There were no visitor spaces marked that he could see. He found a curb with Tyrrell's unit number stenciled on it and pulled in. He walked into the building and found himself in the security alcove with a panel of buttons and a speaker. He looked for Tyrrell's name on one of the labels, but didn't find it. He located the button which should have had Tyrrell's name or unit number on it and pressed it firmly.

The speaker played a ringing-phone tone and, after the first three rings, Zachary knew that Tyrrell wasn't going to answer it. He hadn't answered or returned Zachary's phone call. Why would he let someone into his apartment? If he was there, he didn't want company.

It continued to ring, until eventually hanging up, an electronic voice informing him that the party he was trying to call could not be reached. It didn't seem to forward to Tyrrell's cell number. Zachary pressed it again, with the same results. He tried a couple of other buttons, but no one answered. It was the middle of the workday. People were either still at the office or had been on other shifts and were sleeping. Or shopping for groceries. Zachary looked at his phone and saw that he still had time to kill. He returned to his car, got in, and drove around the neighborhood, taking note of the grocery, convenience, and liquor stores.

He didn't see Tyrrell out walking anywhere, but he hadn't expected to.

Maybe Tyrrell was at a nearby bar. Or one in an adjacent town, if he didn't want to be seen by any of his friends or neighbors.

8

Eventually, Zachary managed to run the clock down until it was time to meet Lindsey at the house. He was at her curb a couple of minutes before the hour and waited until the clock ticked over to three o'clock before climbing out of his car and standing at her door.

It was a slightly nicer area. Lots of family homes. Mostly leased cars at the curb, four-doors and soccer mom vans. The sidewalk had been shoveled, but still had icy patches. Like maybe Mason had been the one to do the shoveling and had gotten distracted partway through the job or hadn't been willing to put in the work to do the harder sections. Zachary stomped the snow off his boots on the welcome mat at the front door and rang the doorbell. At least he didn't need to worry about waking a sleeping infant.

The woman who came to the door had a pinched white face. She was slightly taller than Zachary, which would help her to feel more relaxed and safer talking to him. She looked tired and quite possibly at the end of her rope. Not wanting to take the time to deal with her ex-husband's issues on top of her own.

But maybe if Zachary could find Tyrrell and get him operational again, that would be good for Lindsey. She might start getting child support money again. Having someone in her life who could take the kids every second weekend to give her some time to pamper herself or run errands without constant questions and interruptions from Mason.

"Hi. I'm Zachary." He waited for a moment, then offered his hand when she didn't say anything. "I'm sorry to be bothering you about this."

"Come in, I guess. Lindsey. Goldman. As you know."

Zachary nodded and followed her into the house, divesting his winter clothes.

The house smelled good. Clean and fresh. The smell of Lindsey's coffee hung in the area, as well as something else sweet. Maybe some leftover Christmas cookies warmed in the microwave? There was the kind of clutter that accumulated in houses with active children. It wasn't messy or neglected, just lived in. He got a good vibe walking in the door.

Lindsey sat down in the living room and motioned for Zachary to sit in a comfy recliner. Zachary settled in. He took out his notebook, which so far only contained Lindsey's contact information and a few observations Zachary had made about Tyrrell's neighborhood.

"I'll try not to take up too much of your time. Can you tell me when it was that Tyrrell dropped out of sight? When was the last time you saw him or talked to him?"

"Before Christmas. I couldn't tell you what day. A few days before Christmas or maybe a week. It was his year to have the kids for Christmas. Although, after what happened over Thanksgiving…" She looked at Zachary and shook her head as if it had been his fault.

He wasn't even the one who had planned the Thanksgiving vacation. That had been Kenzie. She had invited Tyrrell and rented a cabin with enough room for all of them. And it hadn't been her fault that they had gotten snowed in. None of the rest of the stuff that had happened had been her fault either.

"Yeah. Thanksgiving was interesting," Zachary agreed, hoping she would just let it go. "When was he supposed to pick the kids up?"

"Christmas morning, after they'd had a chance to look at their stockings. He was supposed to have a couple of days with them. I knew he was going to visit you at the hospital with Heather and Joss.

Kenzie was going to look after the kids while he was there, so that they didn't have to see you in the hospital."

Zachary nodded. He hadn't felt like the psych ward was a good place for the children to spend any time and he'd asked Tyrrell not to bring them.

"So… why didn't he just plan to pick up the kids later in the day?"

"Because I was going to my parents' house. He was supposed to pick up the kids before that so that I would be free to go."

"And he never showed up? Did he call or give any excuse?"

"None." Lindsey's mouth tightened, angry at the memory. Remembering how upset she had gotten while waiting around for him to show up and do as they had agreed. "I called him and left messages, and there wasn't any answer. I texted him. Nothing. Then Heather called, saying that he hadn't met up with them and wondering where he was. He hadn't called them to change his plans either. No one had seen him or talked to him."

"Did he call at all after that? So that you knew he was okay?"

"No."

Zachary swallowed. He made a couple of notes in his notepad, though he wasn't going to forget any of this basic information.

"Have you seen him anywhere? Seen any sign of him? Have the kids talked to him?"

"No."

"He just disappeared."

She nodded. "Exactly."

"Weren't you worried? Why didn't you file a report with the police?"

9

B ecause I've done that enough times before," Lindsey said, her voice bitter. "I told you; this isn't the first time he's dropped out of sight. This is what he does. Leaves everyone behind worrying about him, wondering if something awful has happened to him. And then a few weeks or months later, he shows up again, all clean and acting like nothing happened."

"You must have talked to him about that."

"Yeah, we had talked it to death. He always promised that he would never do it again. That he would always call me and let me know what was going on, even if it was bad news. Of course, he swore never to drink again, but if he did, he'd make sure that I knew he was okay. And that the kids wouldn't have to worry about him, wondering if their daddy was even alive."

Lindsey's voice cracked, and she grabbed a tissue from the nearby box. She dabbed at her eyes.

"Sorry. I should be a lot tougher than this by now. I can let Tyrrell go. I can let him find his own way, whatever way that is, and hope and pray that he'll find peace someday. But the kids... I hate how much it hurts them. No kid should have to go back to school wondering if his daddy is ever going to come home again."

Zachary swallowed and nodded. That was a pretty harsh experience for any kid to go through. His parents had been drinkers, often getting into knock-down blow-out fights at night after drinking all evening. His father hadn't taken off and disappeared, but one or the other of them was sometimes hauled off to jail overnight. He tried to imagine what it would have been like to have his father just disappear.

"Do you know where Tyrrell would go to drink? Does he have a favorite watering hole?"

"If he did, I would have told you that when you called, instead of you coming here. I'd rather not have to do this!"

"I'm sorry." Zachary's face heated. He knew that he was making things difficult for Lindsey. Tyrrell's disappearance was not her fault. She had divorced the man. She shouldn't have to still be responsible for him. "I just hoped that there was somewhere to start. Maybe a drinking buddy or hangout. Anything about his drinking habits."

"He was a closet drinker. For the longest time, I didn't even know he drank. He hid it, drank on the sly. Who knows how much of our marriage he was completely pickled. It would explain a lot. So I don't know. I don't know who he drinks with or where when he disappears like this."

Zachary nodded. It didn't look like he would be able to get anything else out of her. And he didn't want to extend the interview, causing her pain, when it wasn't going anywhere. "Okay. Does he have any friends I could talk to? And maybe his work number? Someone else might know more. Even though he hid his drinking from you, others might have known about it."

"He worked at K&L Construction. But I doubt he does anymore. He'll have lost that one by now."

"Has he lost a lot of jobs to his drinking?"

"Yes. He's not a reliable worker. Employers can't be expected to keep him on when he stops showing up. I don't know if he's ever been caught drinking on the job, but his... illness has certainly kept him from being able to stick with a company for more than a few months at a time."

"And friends...?"

"I don't know. You could start knocking on doors and have better luck than you would with any leads from me. I don't know who he talks to."

"How about… his best man at your wedding?" Zachary tried. Tyrrell must have had a best friend; someone he had wanted to be at his side for that event.

Lindsey rolled her eyes. "We didn't have a ceremony. He didn't have any family around. I didn't want to blow all of my savings on some big event. We just had civil union at the courthouse. No attendants, just us and a judge signing papers."

"What about Vince and Mindy?"

Lindsey blinked at him. "Who?"

"Our youngest siblings. They were kept together in foster care, so Tyrrell knew where they were. Why weren't they a part of it?"

"Oh. Right." Lindsey shrugged. "They haven't been that close. I think they kind of drifted apart when Tyrrell aged out of foster care. You know teenagers; they don't see the need to stay close. He emails them a bit. He was a lot more excited about being reunited with the rest of you. I guess you miss what you don't have. He had a relationship with Vincent and Mindy, so he didn't value them as much as tracking down the rest of his family."

"Do you have… their contact information?"

Lindsey raised her brows and shook her head. "No. I was never in touch with them. You'll have to track them down yourself." She gave him a wry smile. "Maybe hire a private investigator."

Zachary chuckled at this. "I guess so." He put his hands on his knees, preparing to rise. He had taken enough of Lindsey's time, making her focus on something that she wanted nothing to do with.

The front door slammed open and Zachary heard a burst of children's voices as Mason and Alisha arrived home from school. He smiled fondly. He'd enjoyed getting to know them at the Lodge during their Thanksgiving vacation. It had been fun to be around kids for a little while.

Mason came around the half-wall of the doorway and spotted Zachary sitting in the living room. "Uncle Zachary!" he crowed, and threw himself at Zachary.

Zachary caught him, laughing, and gave him a tight hug. "Long time, no see! How are you doing, buddy?"

"We just got home from school. We're studying a plant unit in science right now," Mason informed him, talking rapidly, "but I think it's stupid to do a plant unit in the middle of the winter! We should do it in spring when we can plant gardens and watch them grow! Don't you think that would be better? It's stupid to have it in the middle of the winter."

Zachary nodded. "Yeah. It would probably make more sense to have it in the spring," he agreed. He thumped Mason on the back and released him. "Hey, you'd better take off your boots. You're melting in here."

Mason looked down at his feet, then shot a look at his mother. "I didn't see! I was just saying hi to Uncle Zachary."

"Go take them off at the door," Lindsey told him tiredly.

"Sorry."

Alisha's approach was more sedate. She had remembered to take off her boots and other snow gear. She looked at Zachary shyly. He opened his arms slightly to offer a hug, but kept the gesture small enough that she could choose whether she wanted to or not. Alisha stepped forward and put her arms around him. Zachary gave her a little squeeze and let her go.

"It's nice to see you too, Alisha."

"Where is Auntie Kenzie? Did she come with you too?"

"No, she's working today. I just came to talk to your mom for a few minutes..." He trailed off, unsure what he should say about Tyrrell or the fact that he was missing or out of contact. From what Lindsey had said, they knew something of the situation, but he didn't want to make them feel worse. "I just got out of the hospital, and I wanted to make sure... that everyone was okay."

Alisha nodded soberly, her face very serious. "Are you feeling better now? Daddy said that you were feeling... very sad. But that you always do around Christmas."

Zachary nodded. "I'm doing a lot better now. Christmas is over and the doctors gave me some new pills to help me feel better. So you don't need to worry about me."

Mason stomped back into the room, now in his stocking feet. He'd shed his gloves and hat but was still wearing his heavy winter coat. "*We* were sad at Christmas too," he informed Zachary. "I cried."

Zachary ruffled his hair. "I'm sorry, bud. It must have been pretty hard for you."

Mason agreed. "Why does our daddy have to drink? Why does he keep doing it if alcohol makes him feel so bad? And makes him forget to come home or pick us up?"

Zachary looked at Lindsey. She just stared back at him, not offering any direction as to where he should go with the conversation. Zachary hugged Mason and pulled him up onto his knee to cuddle and try to explain it to him.

"Because he has an addiction. He doesn't want to, and he's trying to get better, but that means that he stills goes back to drinking sometimes, even though he knows it hurts him and other people."

"Are you here to find him and tell him to stop?"

Zachary nodded, chuckling a little. "Yes. That's about it."

"Good. I want to tell him that too," Mason said boldly. But then his little face crumpled, and he buried it in Zachary's chest. "But I don't like the way he is when he's drinking. He gets really mad. And mean."

Zachary rubbed Mason's back, tears prickling his eyes. "I'm sorry about that. Our daddy drank too. I don't know if your daddy remembers what that was like, but I do. It was pretty scary."

Mason nodded, his head bumping against Zachary's breastbone.

"I'll try to help him," Zachary promised. "The first thing is… I have to find him."

10

Zachary had already been by Tyrrell's apartment and hadn't seen anything helpful there, so he decided to check out Tyrrell's last known job before going back there. Eventually, he would need to get into Tyrrell's apartment to ensure he wasn't there, hurt, sick, or worse. But it seemed prudent to get to K&L Construction before they closed for the day, if he could.

A quick search on his phone gave the address of K&L. Riverbrook was not a big place, so it wouldn't take him a long time to get there. Tyrrell had been lucky to find a place in town that would hire him, especially if his work experience was as checkered as Lindsey had said it was. Zachary had expected to find that K&L was in another town.

The office was not very big. A prefab metal trailer with rough wooden steps placed in front of the door, on a small lot surrounded by a fence so that the company's heavy equipment could be locked up at night. A yellow bulldozer and a few other pieces of equipment were parked around the corner from the front door, and probably a few more were out on jobs during the workday.

As he approached the building, Zachary felt like he had been kicked in the stomach. The sensation was so sudden and powerful that he froze mid-step and stood where he was, trying to catch his breath. He looked around, worried, trying to figure out what had triggered such a strong sense of danger and unease. His stomach cramped, and he breathed shallowly through his mouth, trying to regain control.

There was nothing to be afraid of at the little construction company. He was sure that nothing had happened to Tyrrell there. Zachary just wanted to question them about the last time they had seen Tyrrell and if they knew anything about his problems or why he had dropped out of sight. There was no reason for him to be anxious, and especially not so anxious that he couldn't proceed.

He bent over, pressing his hands to his thighs to keep himself upright. He had no idea what had triggered the panic. He kept looking around, trying to identify the danger. He knew that his instincts, his animal brain, might have caught some danger that his logical brain had not yet processed. Or his anxiety might have been triggered by something completely innocuous, like when he walked into a room where there was a lit candle. Or sometimes, even an unlit one.

He still couldn't see anything that should have triggered his reaction, so he forced himself to take one step and then another, and keep pressing forward to the office. Turning away wasn't going to help him overcome the anxiety. It wouldn't help him advance his investigation into Tyrrell's disappearance either.

It wasn't until he walked into the trailer that his conscious brain finally started to make the connections his unconscious brain had already made.

Jose.

Going to Jose's place of work when investigating *his* disappearance. Jose had been an illegal immigrant who was a friend of Pat's, working for a small landscaping company. There was a superficial resemblance between the office of the landscaping company Jose had worked for and the construction company Tyrrell had worked for. They were probably nothing alike, but both had a small prefab front office with heavy equipment behind them in a fenced lot.

And, of course, the search for Jose had not gone well. He had been the victim of a serial killer. A killer who Zachary had also run afoul of, though thankfully he had been rescued before Archuro had been able to follow through on all of his plans. But he had still left a lot of scars, both physical and mental. Zachary's body had clearly connected the configuration of the landscaping office with what had happened to him later.

Understanding the trigger for his panic helped. This case would be nothing like the search for missing Jose. Nothing had happened to Tyrrell. He had just gone on a bender, like Lindsey said. There was no serial killer this time. Zachary would find Tyrrell and make sure he didn't need anything, maybe help him get himself into a detox program. And then he would go home, knowing that he had helped his brother all he could.

He stood there in front of the office for another minute, breathing slowly in and out and trying to calm the pounding of his heart. He could get through it. Dr. B assured him that the best way to get over the trigger for a panic attack was to face it and push through. It had worked for fire. It would work for other things.

After his breathing and heart rate had slowed to a more normal speed, he stepped up the rough wooden stairs to the door of the office, knocked a couple of times, and tried the handle. It turned in his hand, and he walked into the reception area. Again, very similar to the one at Jose's construction company. Nothing to be afraid of. There were probably hundreds of little industrial offices that followed exactly the same pattern. How creative could they get with such a small space?

There was a man at the reception desk, not a woman. That was different from his investigation into Jose's disappearance. A concrete difference that he could hold onto.

"Hello," Zachary said with a friendly nod, still finding himself slightly out of breath, like he had run up a flight of steps, but pushing ahead anyway. "I wonder if there is a supervisor or owner here that I can talk to about an employee or former employee."

"Who are you?" the man demanded in a less-than-friendly tone. He was tall and spare, gray hair cut close to his head.

"My name is… Zachary Goldman."

"Goldman," the man repeated. "Then I guess I know which

employee you're inquiring about." He shrugged. "You may as well just go back the way you came. You're not going to find him around here."

"I suspected as much," Zachary said with a nod, trying to look and sound as sympathetic as possible. "I wonder if you could tell me... what his last day was. When he worked last."

"Been a while. I'd have to check the computer."

But he made no move to do so, shuffling through the papers on the desk in front of him and initialing forms. Zachary shifted his feet.

"I'd appreciate that."

"Your brother left us high and dry." He glanced up from the papers to Zachary's face. "Brother?" he repeated, checking.

"Yeah. He's my brother. Though we haven't actually... known each other that long. I have been away, and I just got into town and found out that he kind of disappeared a few weeks ago. I'm trying to retrace his steps. See if I can track him down and make sure he's okay."

"Why? You think something happened to him?"

"No, probably not. But I'd like to make sure. And help him if there is anything I can do to get him back on track again."

"Nothing you can do for guys like that. They'll just keep messing you up as long as you let them. Need to leave him alone, let them deal with the consequences of their actions instead of bailing them out."

"I'm not bailing him out. I don't know where he is or if he's gotten himself into any trouble. But I need to find out."

"Suit yourself. You're not going to get anywhere."

"Does that mean you know what happened to him?" Zachary asked tentatively. "Did you hear where he went or what he was doing?"

"Out on a drunk, I assume. He told us when he started here that he was in recovery. Said he was on the wagon and working on emotional sobriety, whatever that means. He was a dry drunk. Sometimes we give guys like that a chance. See if they can keep things together." The man initialed a few more pages. He shrugged. "Obviously, Goldman couldn't."

"You don't know where he might have gone or any of his drinking buddies? Anything at all that gave you a clue where he might go?"

"Not my concern. I have a business to run. If he's going to go off like that… nothing I can do about it. He's going to have to deal with the consequences himself. He won't have a job if he ever shows up here again. But chances are, he won't. They never do."

"Did he leave anything here? Did he have a locker where he might have left any personal items?"

"Cleared it out already. Tossed anything that couldn't be reused. Kept the hardhat. Tool belt."

"He didn't have any papers? Photographs? What kind of things did you have to throw out?"

"Pay stubs, mostly. He hadn't worked here long enough to have accumulated a lot of personal items. And we discourage them from keeping them in their lockers. It's a business. We don't need them sticking up naked pictures of their girlfriends inside. Unprofessional." He shook his head. "I don't remember anything of interest in Tyrrell's locker. Sorry."

"Do you think you could look up what day he worked last?"

The man sighed. He raised his head again and studied Zachary closely.

"I *would* ask for ID. Shouldn't be giving out any personal information about former employees. But you look alike. He's not a scarecrow like you are, but his face is the same. His eyes. Real family resemblance there, isn't there?"

Zachary nodded. He and Tyrrell both had the same dark hair and eyes. Similar facial structures. They took after their father. "I have identification if you want it. Photo ID. And I don't need anything else, just the date he showed up last. And if he has any friends in the company…"

"Not really. I had him floating from crew to crew, hadn't assigned him anywhere permanently. If he'd made close friends, I would have kept him on the crew he worked the best with. But he didn't go out with anyone after work. Made a fuss about how he didn't drink anymore. Couldn't go to the bar for drinks after they knocked off for the day." The manager shrugged. "Don't imagine there's anyone here who could tell you where he went when he fell off the wagon."

"Okay." Zachary stood there, waiting. If the manager wanted him to leave, he would have to look up that date on the computer sooner or later.

The man shook his head and sighed again, then turned toward a narrow corridor that led along the side of the trailer to whatever office spaces he had carved out. "Wait here a minute."

Zachary let his eyes wander around the interior of the office while he waited. It was spartan, undecorated. No feminine touches. No inspirational posters or signs outlining the company rules or safety issues. Utilitarian. It was a few minutes before the man returned, an envelope in his hand.

"December tenth," he advised. "That was the last date he worked. Then he never showed up again. After missing two shifts, we terminated him." He held the slim envelope in Zachary's direction. "There's his final pay, if you find him."

"I probably shouldn't," Zachary said, not taking it. If he didn't find Tyrrell, what would he do with the check? Just keep carrying it around with him? He'd rather leave the responsibility with the company. They could mail it to his apartment.

The man twitched the envelope. "Come on. Chances are better that you'll see him than I will. You might as well take it."

"Well, I guess." Zachary conceded and took the envelope from him. He looked down at it, at "Tyrrell Goldman" showing through the window, and nothing else.

11

Zachary took long, slow, even breaths as he walked back to his car in the parking lot. Darkness was gathering and his car sat in a pool of light cast by a streetlight. He had made it through the interview without spiraling into a panic attack over the similarities between the investigations into Jose's disappearance and Tyrrell's. He had kept the memories of that case from flooding back, but couldn't hold them off any longer. When he slid into the seat of his car, he put his hands over his eyes and let go.

His brain replayed his investigations into Jose's work, the other immigrants he lived with, all crammed into a tiny apartment, and the men that Jose saw romantically. Blind to what had been in front of Zachary's face all along, to the man who was watching and stalking him. All of the questions and the driving curiosity that had led to him being taken to that cabin, where he'd been drugged and held and tortured.

"Hey, what do you think you're doing here?"

Zachary straightened with a shock, dropping his hands from his eyes, lids flying open to identify his attacker and protect himself. This time he would protect himself. He wouldn't be taken unaware.

He held his hands out in front of him. A heavyset, sweaty-faced man bent over, peering in at him.

"You can't just sit here," the man told him aggressively. "You're trespassing on private property. Get out of here."

"I was just... resting for a minute."

"You can't sleep here. Go find somewhere else. We don't need your kind around here."

Zachary blinked his eyes, trying to banish the flashbacks once and for all. He focused on the angry man's face, trying to stay fully present. "My kind?" he repeated, not sure what he was referring to.

"Drunks. Junkies. This is a business, not a place to crash."

"I'm not a drunk," Zachary said evenly. "I was just talking to the manager—" he tipped his head in the direction of the office he had just come from. "I was looking for some information on my brother. And then I was just—I had something in my eye. I was trying to get it out."

"You're already changing your story. First, you were resting, now you were washing something out of your eye. Go somewhere else, or I'll call the cops."

"Do you work here? At K&L?"

The man's eyes went to the office, then back to Zachary. "So you actually looked at the sign. So what, is that supposed to impress me?"

"I'm looking for my brother. If you work here... maybe you could help me."

"I'm not here to answer your questions. I have plenty of my own work to do. You worry about your own family and leave me to mine."

"Tyrrell Goldman. Do you know him?"

The man pursed his lips, looking at Zachary speculatively. "Goldman. Yeah, Goldman used to work here. You're his brother?" He shook his head. "Good riddance to bad rubbish, I say. And you look worse than him."

Zachary knew that with his dead white skin and cadaverous face, he didn't look particularly well. He did look like a strung-out drunk or junkie. The man couldn't be blamed for thinking that.

"I've been sick," he informed the man. "I've been through chemotherapy recently."

It wasn't a lie. But it wasn't exactly the full truth either. But it

45

would, hopefully, be enough to turn the tide in his favor. Not a junkie, but a man who was sick, maybe dying.

"Oh. Well, yeah, you look like it. So what are you doing here? Shouldn't you be… resting in bed?"

"Would you be resting in bed if your bother was missing?"

"If he was a piece of trash like Goldman, yeah, I would. I don't know why they bothered to hire him in the first place. Boss knew that he was a drunk. Should have known that he wouldn't be any good."

Zachary ground his teeth at Tyrrell being classified as "a piece of trash." He'd dealt with all kinds of bullying and name-calling growing up. People who thought they could get away with it because he was a foster child, because he was always in trouble and tried to keep his head down, because he was poor and they had power on their side. But ignoring name-calling when someone was denigrating him and letting this man call his brother undeserved names were two very different things.

"Don't call him that. You don't know anything about him or what he has been through."

"Oh, I'm supposed to care why he's a drunk? Everybody has a sob story. I hate the way everybody thinks they have the right to use their 'traumatic' pasts to excuse bad behavior. How we're supposed to feel sorry for all of the poor people and addicts because they haven't had the courage to pull themselves up by their bootstraps like everybody else. You think I was born with a silver spoon in my mouth?" The man gestured to himself. Greasy, five o'clock shadow, stained clothing soaked with sweat around the collar and armpits. "Me? You think that anyone ever gave me a chance just because I whined and made a big deal about how badly I'd been done by? No. I didn't have good parents. I didn't have money growing up. But I didn't become a drunk or an addict. I'm a hard worker. Been here a lot longer than Goldman, and I'll be here long after. Because I'm willing to put in the work, and he isn't. He uses it as an excuse to drink and just stop showing up."

"You don't know anything about it."

And to be honest, Zachary really didn't either. He and Tyrrell hadn't talked a lot about what had happened to each of them in foster care. They covered it in broad strokes—who they had been with and for how long—and left the rest unsaid. Tyrrell hadn't given Zachary any reason to think that he'd been abused in foster care, but that didn't mean that he hadn't been. Zachary hadn't told Tyrrell much about the abuses he had suffered either. He tried to bury it, not even to think about it himself. Tyrrell knew of Zachary's mental health struggles and the institutions he had lived in, but he'd never had much to say about his own alcoholism, implying that it was something he had overcome years before and that he was perfectly fine now. And Zachary hadn't bothered to pursue it, to dig down deep enough to find out his story.

"You need to move on," the sweaty man told Zachary, motioning for him to pull his car out. "I don't care what you were here for. You're just loitering here now, trespassing on private property."

"Did you know Tyrrell very well?" Zachary asked, turning the key in the ignition so that the man could see he was getting ready to go, as he had been asked. "Did you work with him at all?"

"He was on my crew a couple of times. But he wasn't a good worker, if that's what you want to know. He just skated by, barely putting thought into anything he did. Figured he was better than anyone else. He had a degree. He was supposed to be this smart, educated guy who was just stuck in a dead-end job because of his addiction. But he didn't know anything. He wasn't any better than anyone else he worked with. He was a lot worse."

Zachary was careful not to show his surprise at these statements. He'd expected the man to denigrate Tyrrell's work, but Tyrrell had a degree? That was news to him. Tyrrell had never said anything about it. Zachary would not have thought that he would be able to get through college with an addiction. Maybe his alcoholism hadn't come until later, when he was looking for a job, trying to put that education to use. Maybe it hadn't come until he'd failed at several jobs and realized that what he had earned through his hard work and study wasn't going to get him anywhere in life. That it had all just been a waste of time.

Zachary had wondered a few times whether he should go to college to upgrade his education. There were night school classes. He could attend programs while still working as a private investigator, as long as he didn't let any surveillance jobs get in the way of it. Money had been a problem up until he had hit a few big cases in a row. Now that he could afford it, he wasn't sure he wanted to. Wasn't sure it would actually get him anywhere in life.

"So, you had a problem with him. You didn't like him."

The man nodded in agreement. "Yeah. I didn't like him."

"What is your name?"

The man folded his arms across his chest. "I don't see how that's any of your business."

"Well, if it turns out that something has happened to him... it's always good to know who his enemies were."

12

Zachary returned to Tyrrell's apartment building. Tyrrell's marked space was still empty, of course, so he pulled into it. He went into the alcove with the call buttons again and pressed the one that should be Tyrrell's. No answer again.

He could see that there were more people home. More cars filled the parking lot than had been there previously. He could probably raise a few of Tyrrell's neighbors if he pushed the other buttons.

But would that help him at all? Would it help Tyrrell? If his neighbors were like his co-worker at K&L, they were probably indifferent and didn't pay much attention to Tyrrell's absence or presence but, if Zachary harassed them, they might target Tyrrell when he returned. Zachary didn't want to make things worse for him.

He pressed Tyrrell's button again, holding it down for a few seconds. Of course, that didn't make any difference. He hadn't expected it to. If Tyrrell hadn't answered it the first few times, he wouldn't answer it the next time because Zachary held the button down.

Zachary sighed.

There was no button for a manager. No indication if there were a resident manager to handle complaints. He hadn't seen a sign anywhere outside indicating where he could go or call for help, either.

P.D. WORKMAN

Eventually, he gave in and looked up the phone number for the Riverbrook police department on his phone. There was no point in dialing 9-1-1. The town was probably too small to have 9-1-1 service and, even if they did, he couldn't claim that it was an emergency when Tyrrell had been absent for weeks. Unless he lied and said he had reason to believe that Tyrrell was in imminent danger. And it wouldn't take the police long to figure out that he had deliberately lied and charge him for wasting police resources.

"Riverbrook Police," a woman announced, picking up after one ring. Was it a good sign that she didn't have half a dozen other calls backed up ahead of him, because someone would get on to the case quickly? Or bad because the Riverbrook police didn't have much experience?

"Hi. My name is Zachary Goldman, and I'm in Riverbrook because my brother hasn't been answering any calls, and I'm checking up on him. He's not answering his door, either. I'm worried something has happened to him. Could you send the police out for a welfare check?"

"How long has he not been answering calls, and why do you think there's anything to be concerned about?"

"I've been in the hospital, but the other members of the family have been trying to reach him since Christmas. I just talked to his employer, and the last time he reported to work was December tenth. That's a long time ago, now."

"No one has seen him since then?"

"No."

Not that Zachary had talked to a lot of other people and gotten dates from them. It seemed like most of the family hadn't been trying to reach him until Christmas Day. Had anyone even tried to contact him between the tenth and twenty-fifth? Or did he think that everyone cared so little that no one had even noticed his absence during those two weeks?

"What is his name? How old is he?"

Zachary gave her his information and all of the follow-up details she wanted.

HE DROWNED IN MEMORY

"We will try to reach him before coming out. You're at his home now?"

"Yes. Outside."

"Can you see in through the windows?"

"It's an apartment building. I can't see anything from outside and can't get into the building unless someone lets me in."

She got Zachary's phone number to call him back to report, and terminated the call.

Zachary left the security alcove and wandered around the front of the building for a few minutes, waiting. But he didn't want people to be concerned about a stranger lurking around the building in the dark, so he got back into the car and sat there, hoping that somehow, Tyrrell would answer the phone when the police called. But of course he wouldn't. He would answer a call from his brother before answering one from a number that had no identification or said Riverbrook Police.

Eventually, his phone rang and Zachary raised it quickly to his ear. "Hello?"

"Zachary. Where are you? I was wondering if you were going to be home for dinner."

It was Kenzie, not the police. Zachary looked at the time. He had been thinking about the time of day in terms of when he needed to meet Lindsey and when people would be arriving home from work. He hadn't thought once about Kenzie getting home and wondering where he was. He hadn't told her what he had planned for the day.

"Oh. Sorry, I wasn't thinking about it getting so late. No... I'm not going to be able to get home in time for supper. I'm sorry. I'm not quite back into the routine."

"No." She was silent for a moment. "I thought you would just be catching up on emails and communications with the people who had reached out to you while you were in the hospital. That you would be mostly at home for the first few days, until you got back into the swing of things."

He could hear the implied criticism. He was jumping into things too fast, doing things too soon instead of letting himself acclimatize to being out of the hospital. But he couldn't just sit still and wait. It had been different when he had been in the hospital after they had met two years before. He had been in a car accident then and had needed a lot of physical rehabilitation. It had forced him to take things more slowly.

"I'm not working, actually." Maybe that would ease her concerns, and maybe not. "I'm in Riverbrook. Came to see if I could talk to Tyrrell."

"You're in Riverbrook?"

"Yes. Sorry, I should have let you know I was going out of town. I didn't think about it. Or about the timing."

"So, are you even coming home tonight?"

"Yes, I'll come home once I'm finished here."

Zachary looked around. He would already be driving back to Roxboro in the dark. He didn't know how long it would take for the police to make it there and check on Tyrrell. Zachary would need to file a missing person report. Even if he were done in an hour, it would be eight o'clock or later before he got home.

And he wasn't going to be done in an hour.

"I'll get home as soon as I can, but it might be late. Sorry. I couldn't see Lindsey until she was home from work, so things got pushed back a lot later than I would have liked..."

"Well, Tyrrell is your brother, and if something has happened to him..."

"Nobody else is doing anything about it. I get why they aren't, but... I need to."

"Yeah. But you'll be back tonight for sure."

"Yes. For sure. As soon as I've finished dealing with the police."

"All right. I'll see you tonight, then. How are you feeling today? Has everything gone okay?"

"Yes." Zachary thought about the stress level at Lindsey's house and his panic attack in approaching the construction company office. All par for the course. He'd been able to keep from melting down. The meds were working. "I've been feeling okay."

"Have you eaten?"

"No. I'll grab something when I'm done here. Eat on the way back."

As long as he remembered. He missed more meals than he liked to admit. Between meds that dampened his appetite and being focused on other things, food seemed unimportant.

"Make sure you do. And I still have cookies, when you get here."

"Dessert. I won't forget that."

Kenzie snorted. "Right. Keep me informed, okay? Let me know if you find anything out and when you're on your way back."

A dark car pulled up behind Zachary's, headlights reflecting in his mirror, and sat right behind him.

Zachary agreed and, after goodbyes, terminated the call.

The car behind him laid on the horn. He looked at it in the mirror. It was not a police car. No flashing lights or markings. He looked at it for a minute, waiting to see what the driver wanted. Maybe it was the building manager or security, and they didn't like him sitting there.

He opened his door and stood up. As he walked over to the car, the driver rolled down his window. A man. Scruffy growth of beard. From what Zachary could see of him, a fairly big man. And he wasn't happy.

"Get out of my parking space," the man snapped.

Zachary looked back at his car. "Oh... I'm sorry." But he was pretty sure he had picked the right stall for Tyrrell's unit number. Maybe the man had an arrangement with Tyrrell. Maybe Tyrrell rented him the space and parked out on the street somewhere. Less convenient for him, but a bit of money to help offset the bills. "I thought... isn't this Tyrrell's parking space?"

"Who is Tyrrell?"

"My brother. In unit 201. I thought this was his slot."

"He's not in unit 201. I am."

"You are. Oh. I guess I got the wrong number. I'll move out of your way." Zachary paused. "Do you know what unit Tyrrell is in? We look similar. Dark hair and eyes, he's a bit taller than I am."

"No. Never met him."

Zachary headed back to his car to move it out of the way. There were still several open spaces, but he was afraid that the owners of those spaces would be getting home soon and he would just go through the same process again. He didn't want to irritate everyone in the building. So he parked off to the side, illegally, close to a group of parking stalls that were filled up, so that he wasn't blocking entry to anyone else. The resident of unit 201 pulled into his parking space and got out of his car. He shot an angry look in Zachary's direction.

Zachary walked quickly toward him. "I was just wondering... how long have you been in unit 201?"

"Just a couple of weeks. Why?"

"Do you know the name of the person who was in there before you?"

13

The man shook his head. "Why, you think it was your brother?"

Zachary took a deep breath in and let it out slowly. "I was told that was his unit. And no one has been able to get ahold of him. So… maybe. I don't know. Is there a manager or someone around? The police are going to be here, and if I have the wrong unit for Tyrrell, that could be a little embarrassing."

"The police are coming? Why?"

"My brother is missing. No one has seen him for weeks."

The man raised an eyebrow. "Well… sorry to hear that. I hope everything is okay."

He hesitated before patting his pockets and eventually coming up with a business card and a pen. He wrote a phone number on the back of the card.

"The manager is Gerald. At that number. He should be able to help you out."

"Thanks."

"Hope you find your brother. Good luck."

Zachary nodded and watched the man enter the building. He didn't try to catch the door and enter after him. His phone vibrated, and he pulled it out and answered the call identified as Riverbrook PD.

"Hello?"

"We tried to reach your brother by phone and were unable to get through to him. A car has been dispatched to the building and should be there in a few minutes."

"Thanks. I just got the phone number of the manager from one of the other residents—"

"You can give that to the officers when they arrive. That will be helpful, I'm sure. Is there anything else I can do for you?"

"I'm just wondering... about checking hospitals, the morgue, that kind of thing? If there are any unidentified patients or..."

"The police will deal with that once they have had a chance to do the welfare check. They know what they're doing. They'll help you out."

"Okay, thanks. I guess that's it, then. Thanks for your help."

She ended the call. Zachary didn't feel like getting back into his car, just to get out again in five minutes when the police arrived, so he paced around, keeping an eye out for anything unusual or suspicious, until a marked patrol car pulled into the parking lot. It wasn't like he expected to find any evidence of foul play in Tyrrell's disappearance. But he'd worked too many cases to take it at face value. Weird things happened. Sometimes the most vanilla of cases could turn out to be something much more complex and sinister than it appeared.

But that wasn't going to happen with Tyrrell. He was sure it was just what everyone else kept telling him. Tyrrell had fallen prey to his own addiction. And it was up to Zachary to find him and try to bring him back.

Two officers got out of the police car. One of them was looking at a notepad. "You're Tyrrell Goldman?"

"No, I'm Zachary Goldman. I'm looking for Tyrrell Goldman. I need to make sure he is okay."

The cop nodded. He was an older man. In a bigger city, a man of his age would not have been on patrol. He would probably be a detective or working a desk at the police station. Leaving patrol positions to the younger, more physically active officers. But in a small town like Riverbrook, he might have any rank and decades of experience.

"When is the last time you saw him?"

"Before Christmas. Early December. I talked to his work, and the last day he showed up there was December tenth." Zachary shifted his stance, feeling awkward. "I'm just looking into it now because I've been in the hospital. I didn't know that he'd dropped out of sight."

"What have you found out so far?"

"I don't know of anyone who saw him after that. December tenth. He was supposed to visit me on Christmas Day, had made arrangements with my sisters to come by, but he didn't show up and didn't answer the phone. He was supposed to have his kids for the holiday too, but he never showed up to pick them up."

The cop nodded, tapping his pen against his notepad. "Was he usually pretty reliable about that?"

"I think... he has been for the past year. But he has a history of alcoholism and goes off on binges sometimes."

"Thought I recognized the name." The cop nodded toward the apartment building. "You've buzzed him?"

"Yeah, there's no answer. And I think... this guy here..." Zachary pointed to the car that had pulled into slot 201. "I think he actually is living in the apartment Tyrrell was renting."

"They know each other? Or your brother lost it?"

"I guess he lost it. I got the number for the manager." Zachary handed the cop the business card with Gerald's number on the back.

He looked at both sides of it and then handed it to his partner. "Call him. Get him over here to talk with us in person."

The junior cop looked doubtful. "For a drunk?" He glanced at Zachary. "He's not going to want to come over here. Can't we just deal with him on the phone?"

"No. He will have to leave his beer and his TV and come here to talk with us. Tell us exactly what he knows and what happened to the subject's possessions if he turned around and rented the unit to another tenant."

The junior officer shrugged and walked away from them to make the call with the manager more private.

The older cop was studying Zachary. He looked away from the man's face and squinted at his name bar. Sergeant Fontaine.

"Do you live around here?" Fontaine asked.

"In Roxboro."

"You look familiar. Like I've seen you around here before."

"No. I don't live here." Zachary hesitated. "There was a case I dealt with a year ago that kind of made it to national news."

"A case?" Fontaine frowned. "Are you on the job?"

"On the job" meaning in law enforcement. Zachary shook his head. "I'm a private investigator. I was involved in a serial killer case about a year ago. You might have seen some of the coverage."

"Yeah. Yeah, I think I might have." Fontaine looked suspicious. "I thought you said this was your brother. Are you stretching the truth? Looking for someone for a client? I want to know the facts here. Don't try to snow me."

"Tyrrell is my brother," Zachary assured him. He patted his pockets and found his wallet. He showed his driver's license to Fontaine. "You see? Goldman. I don't have a client; I am looking for my brother because I'm concerned about him. Someone else should have gotten the police on it while I was in the hospital, but I guess they didn't feel like it was the right thing to do. So..." Zachary shrugged helplessly. "Now it's been weeks and the trail is going to be cold."

"Very," Fontaine agreed. His eyes went to his partner, who walked back toward them.

"Yeah, he's going to come, but he wasn't happy about it," the younger man said. "Like I said."

Fontaine rolled his eyes. "We don't do police work so that people will like us. We do what needs to be done."

The younger man still projected attitude as he stood there, waiting for further instructions or for the manager to show up. Zachary looked at his name bar as well. Moss.

Fontaine asked Zachary a few more questions while they stood waiting for the manager. Zachary was starting to get cold. He slapped his hands together, stomped his feet, and pulled his hat down snugly over the tops of his ears. When the manager, a sixty-ish, balding man, showed up, Fontaine motioned to the building. "Let's talk inside where it's more comfortable."

Gerald grumbled but agreed and led them all in, unlocking the door on the other side of the alcove. There were a couple of upholstered chairs and artificial trees in a lobby that was probably never used by the residents. Zachary didn't sit, but was happy to be somewhere warmer. The temperature dropped like a rock when the sun went down.

"We're looking for Tyrrell Goldman," Fontaine told Gerald. "He seems to have dropped out of sight. He lives or lived here?"

"Yeah, I'd love to find him too," Gerald said. "Didn't pay his January rent, and I had to come around looking for it. After knocking on his door a few times and talking to his neighbors, I entered his unit. Food rotting in the fridge. Air was stale; that door hadn't been opened in days. Left him a note to call me in case he did come back, but he didn't. Cleaned it out so someone else could rent it."

"Do you know what day it was when you went looking for the rent?"

Gerald scratched the back of his neck. "They're supposed to pay their rent a month in advance, the ones who use checks. So that I don't have to go looking for them at the beginning of the month and can just make one deposit. Most of them have automatic e-transfers set up; heckuva lot easier."

Fontaine nodded. "So, at the beginning of December, you were looking for the January check?"

Gerald considered again, shaking his head slowly. "Wasn't as early as that. I've got a lot to do the first week of the month, making sure that everyone is moved in and things are running smoothly. It would have been the second week, at least." He thought about it some more. "Had to advertise for a new tenant, get the place cleaned out and ready for him for January first." He chewed the inside of his cheek. "Maybe the middle of the month. Thirteenth, fifteenth, something like that. I can look up what day I sent a new ad into the paper if you need to know. But he hadn't been there for a while. The food was going bad."

"After the tenth."

Gerald nodded. "Yeah. Definitely after the tenth. I couldn't have got there much earlier than that."

"What did you do with Tyrrell Goldman's possessions?"

"Threw out most of it. Just crap, garage sale stuff. Nothing the next guy would want or that anyone would bother coming back for. I kept a few personal things, just in case he did, but there's not much."

"We'd like to see it, please."

"I have it in storage." Gerald cleared his throat, rolled his eyes, and eventually took out a ring of keys and led them to a back corridor where the apartment mailboxes and utility and storage rooms were located.

"Was there any sign of violence or a break-in in the apartment?" Fontaine asked. "Blood? Door wasn't forced? Didn't look like it had been ransacked?"

"No, none of that. Just like the guy walked out and didn't bother to come back. Maybe something happened to him, I don't know. But I think he just never came back."

He unlocked the storage room door and took them into it. There were several boxes on a shelving unit with names on them. He selected a cardboard banker's box with Goldman written on the end and pulled it off the shelf. "Like I said… there wasn't very much."

He handed the box to Fontaine. It had no lid, and Zachary tried to peer down inside, which wasn't easy since Fontaine was quite a bit taller than he was.

"Let's have a quick look," Fontaine said. He set it down on a folding table and started to pull items out and place them on the table. There were a couple of changes of clothing. A cheap laptop for web surfing or small office jobs. Charging cables. Some mail that had either been left in the apartment or had arrived after Tyrrell's disappearance and been thrown in on top. A largish brown envelope that contained some papers and photographs.

"Can I look at those?" Zachary asked.

Fontaine gave him a look, then started to lay the contents out on the table.

14

All of Tyrrell's accumulated personal possessions fit in that little box, except for what he might have had in his pockets. Zachary looked at the papers and photographs. Tyrrell's old marriage certificate with his and Lindsey's names on it, corners crumpled and dirty. Some family photographs—the children when they were born, lying in hospital bassinets. A couple of happy family shots. Other bits and pieces.

"Do you mind if I take pictures?" Zachary asked, taking out his phone.

"Go ahead." Fontaine shrugged. "All of this is going to go to you if your brother doesn't turn up anyway."

"Thanks." Zachary carefully framed each paper and took a picture of it.

He didn't see any sign of anything from Tyrrell's early life. No pictures of Vincent and Mindy or their foster parents. No awards or report cards from school. No prom photographs or even pictures of Lindsey and Tyrrell together without the kids.

If Lindsey had been telling the truth when she said that Tyrrell had disappeared like this several times before—and Zachary couldn't see any reason she would be lying about that—then he had probably lost any earlier possessions on other binges. Landlords and shelters wouldn't keep them for long. Tyrrell would lose whatever he'd owned.

"He hasn't called or left a forwarding address?" Fontaine asked.

Gerald shook his head. "No. I wouldn't still have this here if he had. That's the rental business, though; people just take off sometimes."

Zachary had worked other missing person cases and he knew it was true. Sometimes life just became overwhelming and people ran away. Teenagers weren't the only ones who took off, looking for a better life. But like teenagers, adults rarely found any happiness in running away. Most returned home within a week, maybe two. But one thing that Zachary had discovered was that they usually stayed close to home. They didn't take off on a multistate journey looking for the gold at the other end of the rainbow like in some budget TV movie. They tended to stay in the area they knew and still felt safe in.

So, where was Tyrrell? Where would he have settled? Did he already have another apartment where he had started fresh? Had he crashed at a friend's, as Zachary had after fire destroyed his apartment? A homeless shelter was a less-likely possibility, barely better than sleeping rough on the street. Vermont winters were cold. Homeless people moved inside during the winter as much as they could. Was Tyrrell squatting somewhere in an abandoned house or warehouse with other alcoholics and addicts? Zachary stared off into space, trying to put it all together. But he had very little to go on yet.

"Mr. Goldman."

He realized that Fontaine was talking to him again. "Sorry—what?"

"Do you want to come down to the police station and file a missing person report?"

"Yeah. I'd better do that." Zachary pushed the button on his phone to look at the time. He needed to get the report done quickly and get home to Kenzie. He didn't want her waiting up for him, or going to bed before he got home, wondering if something had happened to him.

Despite his hopes, things did not move quickly at the police station. They never did, even when he was working with the law enforcement officers who were his friends. The cops in Riverbrook didn't know him. They tended to be suspicious of the fact that he was a private investigator and had worked some cases that had blown up big in the media. They suspected his motives, thought he wasn't really Tyrrell's brother, thought that there must be more to it than a man who had just dropped out of sight. They insisted on dotting all of the I's and crossing all of the T's and going over everything three times, just to ensure they couldn't be accused of making a mistake or not doing their duty if *this* case should go public.

And there were forms. Zachary had known that there would be, but he hadn't actually made a missing person report before and was surprised at just how much they needed him to fill out. His learning disabilities made form-filling extra tedious. He had to write very slowly to form the letters so that they would be legible to someone who tried to read them later. He *could* print neatly, but it took about five times as long as his usual chicken scratch.

He rubbed his eyes and the muscles around them, strained with fatigue. It was a good thing that he'd listened to Kenzie and gotten in so much sleep the night before because, even with seven hours under his belt, he was fading.

"Sorry to take so long with this," a female cop told him in a brisk, unapologetic tone as she went through his forms a second time and asked additional questions, adding her notes here and there as he clarified certain details.

Zachary nodded. He told himself that it was good they were being so thorough. Maybe there was a chance that they would actually help track Tyrrell down, and he wouldn't have to do all of the work himself.

But he wasn't holding his breath.

"And your contact information is correct?" She read Zachary's phone number, email address, and postal address back to him. It reminded Zachary that he needed to stop by his apartment to make sure that no one had left him anything there. There was bound to at least be junk mail in his mailbox. It could really stack up over a few weeks. There shouldn't be anything urgent in the postal mail; everyone used email or phone if it were time-sensitive. But he should check, just in case.

"Yes, that's all right," Zachary agreed. He stood up. She hadn't dismissed him, but he suspected that if he didn't take matters into his own hands, they would keep him busy all night long. "I have to head home. I'll be available by phone tomorrow, and I'll be back here as soon as I come across anything that suggests where he might have gone. Just give me a call if you think of anything else."

"I'm not sure the sergeant has finished with you…" The woman looked at her wristwatch.

Zachary shook his head. "If there is anything else, have him give me a call. I'll have my phone on Bluetooth and can talk while I'm driving home. I need to get on my way before I'm too tired to drive."

"I suppose," she agreed grudgingly. "As long as we can reach you."

"I'll be doing everything I can to find my brother. If you come up with any leads or have any questions, I'll be right on top of it. I want to make sure he is okay."

15

It felt good to get out to the highway again. The drive was cleansing, as if he were showering off all of the accumulated grime of the day. Washing his brain of all of the anxiety and just immersing himself in the driving. His kind of meditation.

And then he was home. The outside light was on for him, and Kenzie was still up, though yawning.

"Come have something to eat," she told him, giving him a quick peck on the lips. "And tell me how your day went."

Zachary went into the kitchen, realizing that he hadn't remembered to stop for something on the way home. Kenzie had probably already guessed that. She started pulling dishes out of the fridge to put a plate together for him.

"You don't need to do that," Zachary objected. "I can fix something myself. Or maybe I'll just have cookies."

"You'll have dinner *and* cookies." She continued to prepare his late supper despite his objection. "You must be exhausted."

"I'm okay. Really. You're probably just as tired as I am."

Kenzie pushed the plate into the microwave, threw a cover over it, and started the microwave cooking.

"Were you able to find anything out about Tyrrell?"

"Not much. Lindsey says that he's done this before, just disappearing and making everyone around him worry, and then he shows up again later. So that's good news if things go the same way this time."

Kenzie nodded her agreement.

"I stopped by his workplace, but he didn't give them any kind of notice. Just stopped showing up. Same with his apartment. He didn't pay the rent and hadn't returned. It's already been rented to someone else."

"That was quick!"

"Landlord cleaned it out as soon as he knew Tyrrell hadn't paid for January and had left food rotting in the fridge."

"I'm not sure if that's legal. Tenants have rights. He'd already paid for December, right?"

Zachary shrugged. "It doesn't matter whether he cleaned it out in December or January; it all comes out to the same. Tyrrell walked out and didn't go back."

"So… do you have any leads?"

Zachary scratched the back of his neck. Kenzie took the food out of the microwave and put it on the table for Zachary, giving him a fork from the dishwasher. She started putting away the clean dishes while he took a few bites.

"I don't know. I have to think about it all… there's nothing immediately helpful, but maybe I can figure something out. I'll call the hospitals near there, see if they have seen Tyrrell or a John Doe that matches his description."

"They can't tell you anything under the privacy laws."

"No… but I can usually find something out." Zachary smiled like he did when talking to nurses and receptionists at the hospital. "I'm charming."

"They're just afraid that you're going to drop dead if they cause any stress," Kenzie returned. "You don't look like you'd stand up to a strong wind."

Zachary's smile grew, and he tried to mask it as he ate leftover lasagna. Maybe she was right. It was more because they felt sorry for him than that he cut such a dashing figure. "Anyway. If he's been there, I should be able to find something out."

66

"You should leave it to the police. They can actually talk to the hospital in conjunction with a missing person investigation. You filed an official report, right?"

"Yes. Of course. But I don't think they're going to do much about it. Tyrrell has already been missing for weeks. They missed their chance to do anything in the first forty-eight hours."

"That doesn't mean they won't investigate it."

"It means it won't be a high priority. There are a lot more cases they have a better chance of solving than a guy who disappeared weeks ago. They probably won't do much more than going to his employer to find out if they know anything about where Tyrrell went and if anyone he worked with was close to him."

"Which you've already checked."

"Yeah. Not much there. I can go back if nothing else pans out, actually talk to each of the employees who has worked with him. But the boss is probably right. He didn't make friends there. Didn't work on the same crew regularly. If he'd made a friend, he would have been sure to get himself put on the same crew."

"Mmm. Maybe," Kenzie agreed. "And Lindsey didn't have any idea where he would go? Who he might be with? Tyrrell must have had a few friends. He's an outgoing, friendly guy."

"She doesn't even have numbers for Vince and Mindy. She doesn't know where he usually goes when he's on a binge. No favorite watering hole."

"That's weird. It's so strange seeing Tyrrell in this light. He's always seemed so strong and down-to-earth. I never would have thought—I never did think—that he was still drinking. Or might go back to it."

Despite Zachary being the older brother, since being reunited he'd felt like Tyrrell was the older, more responsible one. He was bigger than Zachary, in better physical shape, and had a wife and two kids. He didn't act like he was down on his luck or still in the thrall of addiction. Everything he said and did gave the impression that everything was fine. He hugged Zachary, told him to eat more, told him that things would be better after Christmas.

"I thought it was far in the past too," Zachary agreed. "When he was a teenager, maybe. That he'd been fine as an adult."

"I guess people don't like to show their weaknesses. Even to family."

"I wish he'd told me more about it. I wish... that I'd asked. But I thought... it was just a part of his life that was closed now and that it would be painful to discuss."

Kenzie sat down across the table from him with a glass of water. No coffee so close to bed for her.

"I guess we're always finding out new things about people, even the ones we think we're close to. People we think we know everything about." Her tone was pensive.

Zachary stared at the food on his plate, not really hungry, but trying to will himself to eat more. His body needed it, whether he felt hunger pangs or not.

"I guess so," he agreed. He was still learning new things about Kenzie and her background. Her family and the things that had shaped their relationships. And as well as he had thought he knew Bridget, it had become evident in the last year that she was a different person from what he had thought. She wasn't as secure as she always pretended to be. And her mind could be changed. Even things she had been adamant about during the time they had been married, like never having children. It still hurt that she had not wanted children with him, but did with Gordon. Maybe that was just an indicator of how bad their relationship had been. How unsuited to each other they were.

"Mason and Alisha said to say hi to Auntie Kenzie," Zachary said, remembering the children.

"Did you see them? That's wonderful. How are they doing?"

Zachary looked from his food to Kenzie's smiling face. It was a moment before her expression changed and she wasn't thinking about Santa and presents, but about their father disappearing. Her expression sobered.

"Oh. Of course. I'm sorry. How were they holding up?"

"They're hanging in there. It's tough on them. I think on Mason especially. He's younger."

"Or maybe Alisha is just better about hiding it. With Mason, everything is all out there. He wears his heart on his sleeve."

"Yes. I'm sure it's hard on both of them." Mason was the one who had soaked Zachary's shirt with tears. But that didn't mean that stoic Alisha, standing nearby, had been any less crushed by her father's disappearance. And by the previous disappearances. Repeated betrayals. Thinking that Tyrrell valued his family less than a bottle of alcohol. Zachary's mind went to his own father.

"I don't think he was physically abusive," he told Kenzie.

"Tyrrell?" Kenzie's expression was guarded. "I don't know. Did Lindsey say anything about it?"

"Not really. She only talks about problems they had in their marriage in general terms. Said that his being an addict explained a lot. She didn't know he was a closet drinker, to begin with. But Mason and Alisha... Mason said that he's mean when he's drinking."

"Poor guy."

"Yeah. But I don't think it was physical."

"Verbal and emotional abuse still hurt and can have long-lasting effects."

"Yeah. I know." It was the words that stayed with Zachary after so many years. Not an isolated fight or beating. His mother calling him incorrigible. Reminding him it was his fault that the house had burned down. His fault that the family was breaking up. That she never wanted anything to do with him again.

16

It was a tough night. Zachary followed Kenzie's suggestions and still took a sleep aid before bed. But his brain was determined to stay awake, whirling around and around with worries and speculations about Tyrrell. Nothing would quiet them and, as he had experienced before, his OCD and ADHD brain easily beat out a sleep aid on a bad night. He got up and paced, not wanting to keep Kenzie awake with his tossing and turning.

By morning, he had decided to call Joss. He'd talked to Heather, but he hadn't spoken to his oldest sibling. And maybe she knew something that Heather did not know, even if it were just an offhand comment that Tyrrell had made at some point.

Any throwaway remark could be the key to finding him.

He wasn't sure what time she usually worked. He knew she worked at a restaurant and that she might work late shifts, so he tried to leave it until a later enough hour, after Kenzie was gone to work, before calling. Joss could be cutting enough when he didn't wake her out of a much-needed sleep.

"Well, look who it is," Joss said when she picked up the phone. "What's going on, Zachary?"

Straight to the point, no opportunity for small talk. Zachary shifted his phone to his other ear, awkward at being put on the spot.

"Hi. How are you doing?" he asked.

"About the same as ever. How about you?" She conceded to at least asking about each other's health. "I guess you must be home again now?"

"Yes. Got home a couple of days ago. I'm doing a lot better. Now that... it's the new year. And I had some med changes that seem to be working better. Hopefully."

"Good to hear. Don't like it when my baby brother is in the hospital."

"I'm your oldest brother," Zachary pointed out. "Not the baby."

"You're all still babies as far as I'm concerned. I changed your diapers, you know."

Zachary cleared his throat. "Err..."

"What is it?" Joss asked brusquely. "Why did you call?"

"I wanted to talk to you about Tyrrell."

"What about him?"

"Have you seen him at all since Christmas? Since early December, actually. Have you talked or texted or anything?"

"No. He dropped out of sight. Don't know what he's up to."

"I'm trying to track him down. Make sure he's okay."

"You're better off just leaving him alone. If he wanted you to contact him, he would have left you that information."

"Something might have happened to him. He couldn't predict that. It's been long enough. I can't just sit around waiting to see if he shows up again."

"Sure, you can. That's what everyone else is doing."

"I know," Zachary grumbled. "But I can't do that. I've dealt with missing person cases before. I know you can't just leave it and hope they return on their own. If he was going to do that, he would have done it by now."

"You're just making things hard for yourself. Why don't you go back to your own business? Get that up and running again. I'm sure you must have plenty of people to call back. You always seem to have cases on the go."

"Yes, and I'm going to do that. But... I can't just ignore Tyrrell disappearing, either. It's important. He's my brother."

"He's important to me too," Joss conceded, "I just... don't see how chasing after him is going to help anything. He obviously wanted to disappear. It's not the first time he's done it. So why not just leave the man alone?"

"We don't know that he's disappeared on purpose, unless you know something I don't."

Joss was silent.

"Well?" Zachary prodded. "How do you know he wanted to disappear? Do you?"

"Because that's what he's done before. It's an established pattern. I know you don't like it; you would like to think that he's not just running away or diving into a bottle, but it's exactly what he's done before. So why would it be any different this time? He'll come back on his own eventually."

"Just because someone has run away before, that doesn't mean that something bad couldn't happen to them. An abduction or an accident. Sick or hurt. He might not be able to remember who he is or what happened to him, so he's stuck as a John Doe somewhere."

"Amnesia?" Joss demanded. Zachary could practically see her rolling her eyes. "Come on, Zach. That's TV stuff. How many of the missing people that you've found had amnesia?"

Zachary cleared his throat. She was right, of course, but he didn't like to be forced into a corner. "None of them," he admitted. "But that doesn't mean it can't happen. Sometimes it does."

"Well, it's your own time and energy to waste. So... have at it, I guess."

Zachary didn't know what to say to that. Reassert that he was going to go ahead whether anybody approved of his actions or not? He wasn't going to change his position, and he was sure that Joss already knew that. She knew him and his stubborn single-mindedness too well.

"How is Luke?" he said instead, changing the subject.

Joss blew out her breath in a whistle. "Luke? Yeah... he's good."

She didn't sound like she meant it. Zachary closed his eyes. What had happened to the teen since Zachary had taken him to Joss? It had been a little less than a year ago, and Zachary thought Luke and Joss had settled in together pretty well. Both had experienced addiction and trafficking, and Joss was helping Luke to turn his life around and build a better future for himself. They seemed to get along together pretty well, despite the fact that Luke was so friendly and Joss so acid. Even though she could see the danger of the life he had been leading and Luke wasn't quite so sure.

"What's wrong? Did he have a relapse?"

Zachary could relate. He may not have a substance abuse problem, but he certainly knew what it was like to give in to his impulses and fall back into the old thinking and behaviors he had been trying to overcome. It seemed like for every advance, there had to be a relapse.

"Not yet, that I know of. But he's... less committed than he was. He talks a lot about people he used to know and what he liked about the life. It's been long enough to forget some of the worst stuff and to fantasize about what was good about it."

"What was good?" Zachary demanded. "How could anything about that life be good?"

"Drugs whenever you need them. Party life. Good strokes from your bosses when you're doing well. Belonging. Knowing the rules. Having everything... planned and scripted so that you don't even have to think about it. Lots of things."

"You can't let him get back into that."

"I can't stop him from doing anything. If I try to enforce arbitrary rules to get him to conform, he'll just run. You know that. He's got no reason to stay here if he's just getting grief."

"But he was doing so well. I didn't think..."

"Anybody can be pulled back into that any time. As long as they have a use for you. He's still young, has a lot of talent and potential."

"If he goes back, they'll kill him. They were trying to kill us when he and Madison escaped."

"If he goes back to them, they'll welcome him with open arms. Don't kid yourself. He's hugely valuable to them if he brings in new kids."

"But he knows what kind of life he would be leading. What kind

73

of life he would be condemning them to. He said that he couldn't do that anymore after turning Madison out."

"And he hasn't. Yet. That doesn't mean that he won't or that he isn't considering it. Madison is gone. She won't stop him from seducing others."

"Can't you talk to him?" Zachary demanded.

"I do. Plenty. But I can't make his decisions for him. That's not the way it works. He's independent. He knows how to live on the streets. He doesn't need me for anything."

"Except to help him beat his addiction and get ahead in life."

"That's not the way he's thinking about it the nights when he's missing it all. When he needs a fix and the companionship and reassurance that he's doing a good job. Then... it's just a long, hard, lonely night."

And Zachary knew how overwhelming those could be.

"Would it help if I talked to him? Do you think he'd listen to anything I said?"

"A teenager? Listen? Not likely. You can talk to him any time you like, but remember... he's traumatized. Normal kids are hard enough to convince that they don't know better than anyone else. A kid like Luke, he's divorced himself from the rest of the world. Don't expect to get anywhere with him."

"Like you don't expect to get anywhere with me?" Zachary asked softly.

"Nope," she agreed flatly. "You're going to do what you think is right no matter what anyone else's opinion is."

Zachary was afraid that she was right. Once he'd identified a course of action, it didn't really matter who tried to talk him out of it. Even changing his own mind was nearly impossible.

He hadn't called Joss for advice on what he should do; he'd already decided that.

"I told you before that you weren't going to be able to change the direction of Luke's life," Joss reminded him. "You did more than I thought you could... but in the end, there's nothing either of us can do to prevent him going back to the life he was living before."

"I guess. But I don't like to hear that."

"Nope. You never did like being told no."

Zachary didn't speak.

"The one I want you to talk to is your friend Rhys. Tell him he's playing with fire, and he's going to get burned. You don't want him getting into that life too."

"No." Zachary had met Rhys on another case, one that Bridget had gotten him involved in. He was a Black teenager, being raised by his grandmother, with an impairment in his ability to communicate. He could occasionally say a few words, but was mostly non-speaking, getting along with gestures, sounds, and a mixture of typed text and gifs on his phone. Like Luke and Zachary, Rhys had also been damaged by trauma, witnessing his grandfather's murder when he was a child—and that was just the beginning. Rhys was very vulnerable, and he had a crush on Luke. Kenzie had said that she had seen the two of them talking together when Zachary was in the hospital and they had both been by for a visit.

"No, he can't drag Rhys into this," Zachary said flatly. He couldn't let that happen.

"Then talk to Rhys. Explain it to him."

"Okay. I will."

"Good. I'd better get going now. I have other things to do."

"Do you have Vince's and Mindy's phone numbers?"

"Vince and Mindy?" Joss repeated, as if she couldn't believe what she had heard.

"I know that Tyrrell was still in contact with them. I thought he might have given you their information."

"No. Neither of them has ever reached out to me; why would I reach out to them? It's Tyrrell who wanted to meet everyone, get everyone together. He's the one who contacted me and Heather. And you. Then Heather reached out to you because of her... assault."

She stopped. Had Joss wanted to meet him? Tyrrell and Heather had arranged to introduce Zachary to Joss. But had that been their idea or hers? Joss didn't sound like she would reach out to anyone who hadn't reached out to her first.

"I don't have their information," Joss said flatly. "You'll have to find them yourself."

"Did Tyrrell ever say where they were? Are they even in Vermont?"

"Hmm. I think so. But I don't know if he told me that or if I just assumed. None of us had the money to travel. I worked my way around the country for a while, but... there wasn't any reason for me to stay in any of those places. They didn't have anything for me."

17

Zachary had a lot to think about as he drove to his apartment. He tried to immerse himself in his driving and not think about any of it, but that wasn't easy. He worried about Jocelyn. She acted tough as nails, but Zachary knew that under it all, she was just as vulnerable and scared as he had ever been. She had lived a hard life. A desperately hard, dangerous life that could have killed her many times over. She had lived with predators who used every means possible to control her and make her conform to their wills.

And yet, she was still Joss. Still the tough little girl who had helped to raise him. Had protected him as much as she could from their parents, keeping him out of their way. Making sure that he had food and clothes and didn't get bullied too much at school.

He wanted to help her and ensure that the second half of her life was happier and easier than the beginning.

Luke and Rhys.

There was another problem that was going to be a challenge. How would he convince Rhys to stay away from Luke and not let himself be victimized by him or the people he worked with? Rhys wasn't completely naive. He was the one who had put Zachary on to Madison's trouble with the human trafficking ring to begin with. But

Zachary had no doubt that he would let the stars in his eyes blind him from seeing what Luke was and what he could do to Rhys.

But Tyrrell first. Zachary was relieved not to have found him dead and moldering in his apartment. He could have died from alcohol poisoning. Or tripping over his own feet while drunk and cracking his head on the corner of the counter. Or passing out and drowning in the bathtub.

It seemed like months since Zachary had been at his own apartment. And he supposed it had been, but not as long as it felt like. The apartment belonged to his before-moving-in-with-Kenzie life. A time that was now separate and distant in his mind. And it was time to let it go. There was no point hanging on to it when he wasn't using it.

He let himself in the apartment door, picking up a sheaf of flyers and other junk that had been shoved under his door. Not as much as he had expected to find there, based on his past experience. He flipped through it to make sure that there wasn't anything important stuck between the sheets of newsprint and tossed it all in the garbage in the kitchen.

On the table was another stack of flyers and a couple of envelopes lying separate from them.

Who had been in his apartment?

Zachary took a quick look around to confirm that he was alone there, locked the apartment door, and sat down at the table. The apartment had been unsecured for a while when the police had kicked in the door, and then it had taken a few days to get it fixed, but since then, it had been sitting there empty. No one else should have been there.

He picked up the letters. One of them was addressed to "Resident," and, slicing it open, Zachary found a "message of hope" from a Jehovah's Witness neighbor. Or someone who said he was a neighbor. Zachary tossed it onto the pile of flyers and picked up the other one.

This one was addressed to him by name. But of course, it had not come through the postal system, or it would be in his mailbox, not inside his apartment. It had been hand-delivered, one way or another.

Zachary tapped it against his hand before opening it. It was light, just a single sheet of folded paper, probably. Maybe another JW message, delivered after his neighbor had figured out his name?

Eventually, he turned the envelope over and slid his finger along the top edge to open it. He drew out the paper and unfolded it.

The handwriting was messy. A lengthy, rambling missive that sprawled across the page this way and that. Difficult to make any sense of. Zachary looked at the bottom of the letter for the signature, frowning.

A single initial.

T

Tyrrell.

Zachary blinked several times in surprise. Tyrrell had written to him? Had he been in his apartment and left a letter on his table? When had he been there? Zachary had never given him a key. Had never given anyone but Kenzie a key. Had Kenzie let him in? And if she had, then why wouldn't she have told him that when they started talking about Tyrrell being missing?

Zachary returned his gaze to the top of the page and tried to decode the tangle of words and letters. He wasn't a good reader at the best of times, with typewritten letters arranged in a neat and predictable way. The mess of words and phrases of the letter would take time to unravel.

After making several different attempts, Zachary settled on a method, typing words from the page into the notes app on his phone as he figured each one out the best he could. He knew that he was probably only getting half of the letters right. Consequently, a lot of the words were either the wrong words or a string of nonsense characters strung together in his best guess that he hoped to work out later.

He was about to tap the next word into his phone when it rang, startling him. Kenzie's picture appeared on the screen. Zachary picked up the phone and held it to his ear.

"Kenzie?"

"Hi. I'm just taking a break, so I thought I would check in and see how you're doing."

She didn't usually check up on him. It was probably a reaction to his having been in the hospital. She wanted to convince herself that

P.D. WORKMAN

he was well and strong, and nothing was going to happen to set him
back again. She cared about what happened to him.

"I'm good. How has your morning been?"

"A beast. I needed to get away from it all for a few minutes. We've
got quite a backlog right now, and we're still trying to audit all of the
cases that people have brought forward after finding out about Nurse
Debbie. Everyone wants their case reviewed…"

"That's a lot of cases."

"Yes, it is. I'm going cross-eyed looking for patterns and flagging
which ones Dr. Wiltshire should have a look at. What are you
working on?"

"I'm at my apartment. Thought I'd better make sure everything
was okay here."

"Yeah, good idea. Things could happen while you were gone."

"Were… you here?" he asked tentatively.

"Was I there? In your apartment? No, not lately."

"Did you bring Tyrrell by here once? To leave a letter for me?"

"A letter? No, what are you talking about?" Kenzie's voice got
louder and higher. "What letter? Is everything okay?"

"There's a letter here from Tyrrell. On my table. If you didn't let
him in, then how did it get here? Did he pick the lock? Get the
manager to let him in?" Zachary's anxiety was rising. He looked at the
apartment door to make sure that it was bolted and reminded himself
that it was secure, not like it had been after the police had broken
it in.

"A letter… on your table…" Kenzie's voice got distant. Remembering something. "No—that *was* me. I did go by your apartment,
but I didn't have anyone with me. The letter and some flyers had been
slid in under your door, so I picked them up and left them on the
table for you to look at later. I completely forgot about that. Sorry. I
should have let you know there was correspondence for you to
review."

"When?"

"When was I there?"

Zachary nodded impatiently. For a smart woman, Kenzie could
be extremely slow keeping up with his mental processes sometimes.

"Yes. When was this? When did he leave the letter? Before Christmas? After?"

"Uh… let me think for a minute. It was the day you were missing. You checked yourself out of the hospital and I was looking for you, didn't know where you were. So I checked your apartment, just in case."

Zachary breathed out slowly and relaxed his shoulders. That all made sense. Of course she had gone there to look for him. If he wasn't at her house, then where else would he be? Not where she had expected him to be, that was for sure.

"So that was before Christmas."

"Yes. A couple of weeks."

"That would make it… sometime around December tenth?"

"Yes. About that. I can look it up for you later if the exact date is important."

"No, I guess not."

If Kenzie had found it the day that he had checked himself out of the psych ward, then it had been left there *before* Tyrrell disappeared.

"Are you sure? You sound upset. What does it say?"

"I'm still figuring it out."

"Figuring it out?"

"You know how you say that my handwriting in my notebooks is chicken scratch?"

"To say it is chicken scratch would be insulting to chickens," Kenzie quipped. "Especially when I know that you can print neatly when you have to."

"Well… it's sort of like that. So it's going to take some time to figure it out."

Kenzie chuckled. "Yes, if it's anything like your notebooks, you might need some training in hieroglyphics or code-breaking to figure it out."

18

After chatting for a few minutes, Kenzie had to get back to work and they said their goodbyes and continued with their own projects. Zachary went back to the letter and took a couple of minutes to figure out where he had left off. He grabbed a pencil from the kitchen drawer so that he could check off each word or group of letters as he transcribed them.

As he decoded the letter, Zachary's anxiety grew. As he had suspected from the start, it wasn't just a friendly holiday letter. It would have been nice if Tyrrell had left him a Christmas letter, knowing that Zachary wouldn't be able to read it until after he returned from the hospital, but then it would be there waiting for him. Something to warm his heart and know that someone had been thinking of him during the Christmas season even if he couldn't appreciate it then.

But, of course, that had not been the case. Tyrrell's words were dark and hopeless. Lindsey and Joss and the others had all assumed that Tyrrell had disappeared because he had gone on a binge, but as Zachary transcribed the words of the letter, he started to wonder if they had all gotten it wrong and Tyrrell's intentions had been something much worse.

Zachary,

This is a hard letter to write. I know things are bad for you
right now so we can't really talk and I don't want to make
things worse than they are. It has been a good year for me,
meeting you and getting to see Joss and Heather face to face
Thought I was on the right track and everything be good even
though divorce with Lindsey was final and I don't see kids
very often.

But everything is gone to hell When I see myself through
Mason's and Alisha's eyes I realize what a monster I have been.
Just like HIM. Thought I would be such a good dad but I've
hurt those kids so much. (not physically I never beat them
but they're afraid of me cause of yelling and stupid drunken
behavior) I thought I could still be a good dad and they
would forget all of that, but they remember and they
always will

And you and Kenzie were right about me drinking again. I
made my one year and I thought that was good and meant
that I'd be able to stay clean and sober forever they said not to
be complacent or I would slip up and I did and now it's all
too late and I know I can't be the person I want to be or could
be if I was sober

I'm sorry for everything. Wish I could take it all back. Wish I
could go back to being the person I was before I started to
drink. Before I was broken. Maybe when I was six, and you
were still there to tell me everything was okay.

But I can't I can only move forward and there is no future for
me. Can't be around the kids like this can't damage them any
further. I will be gone so that I can't hurt them or anyone else
any more.

Guess I am saying goodbye. I won't see you after Christmas.
Will stay until then because I don't want to cause you a
setback. But after that I will leave it all behind. I am sorry
again. Goodbye.

T

19

Zachary read the transcription on his phone screen and looked back at the scribbled words again, looking for some sign that he had misread it and that Tyrrell hadn't really meant the things Zachary saw on the page. Somehow, he had put his own spin on the letters he saw there and hadn't understood it. It didn't mean what he read there.

But he couldn't kid himself. He might have gotten a word or two wrong along the way, but the gist of the letter, the phrases he had put together, were all correct.

His heart was swollen and hurt with every beat. His stomach had that dropping, queasy feeling of an elevator lurch, only much worse.

With fumbling fingers, he found a pillbox in his pocket and downed a long oblong pill without water. He picked up his phone and the letter and walked out of his apartment and down to the car.

"I need to talk to Dr. Boyle."

Zachary had seen the polite receptionist many times before. He'd been seeing Dr. B at least twice a week, though, of course, he had not been at her office since he had admitted himself to the psych ward at the hospital. He couldn't remember the receptionist's name, though he was sure he should know it. A line creased her forehead as she looked at her computer screen. Her mouth smiled, but her eyes didn't.

"You don't have an appointment today, Mr. Goldman," she said pleasantly. "Did you think you had set something up?"

"No. I need to see her. It's an emergency."

Her eyes went over him, evaluating him carefully. She didn't argue, as he was afraid she would, and say that he would have to set up an appointment and come back then. In a day or two when Dr. B had a free appointment slot.

"Would you wait here for just a moment, Mr. Goldman? I'll need to talk to her."

Zachary nodded, relieved. He wiped at a bead of sweat dripping down his face. He must look a sight, like a wild man or someone with the plague. He felt like he could barely stay on his feet, yet he couldn't sit down and wait quietly, not with his heart hammering like it was. Not after reading Tyrrell's letter.

It was not long before Dr. Boyle came out with the receptionist. She took in Zachary's state with a quick glance and approached him.

"Elizabeth said it was an emergency, Zachary. Are you okay?"

He nodded jerkily, all of his muscles tight and his body coiled for action.

"Come with me. Let's see what I can do to help." She led the way back into her suite of offices, to one that they didn't normally use for their sessions. "Is this okay?"

It seemed a little unreal to be meeting with her somewhere different from usual, but Zachary could handle that, as long as she was there. She probably had another patient in her regular office.

"Do you want to sit?"

He looked at the chair and shook his head, too agitated to sit down.

"Can I take your pulse, Zachary? Is it okay if I touch you?"

He offered her his arm, feeling a little silly about it. Dr. B's fingers rested across his pulse for a second or two, and then she withdrew her hand.

"Wow. That's pretty fast. Are you having a reaction to your meds, or is it something else? I remember you had a bad reaction to one of the meds you were on when you were young."

"No, it's… something else." He fluttered the letter but didn't hand it to her, unsure what to say or do.

"Have you taken anything? Prescription or non-prescription?"

"Anxiety."

"Your anti-anxiety prescription?"

Zachary nodded again, feeling like a bird twitching its head all around to watch its surroundings. "Didn't think I could drive if I didn't."

Her brows went up. "You drove yourself here? I'm not sure that was a good idea in your condition. Get a ride or call an ambulance next time."

Zachary nodded. He probably wouldn't. But he didn't usually try to go anywhere during a panic attack, so it probably wouldn't come up again any time soon.

"What can you tell me about what's going on? Did something happen that upset you?"

"I got a letter." Zachary was holding the letter by the corner with his thumb and forefinger. He squeezed them tightly together, trying to feel the substance of the page between them. He could barely feel it, yet it weighed on his shoulders like a hundred-pound weight. "From my brother."

"From the brother you have met before, or the other one?"

"The one I met. Tyrrell."

"And he wrote you a letter?" Dr. B looked at the trifolded paper in Zachary's grasp. "I thought he lived close by. The two of you get together sometimes."

"Yeah. But he didn't want me to read it until I got out. Home from the hospital."

"He mailed it to your house?"

"Pushed it under the door at my apartment. Not where I live with Kenzie."

87

She raised her brows but didn't comment on his still keeping two residences. She had to know as well as anyone that he might sometimes need extra space, a retreat to go to if he felt overwhelmed.

"And the letter is not good news."

Zachary shook his head. He held it out toward her, letting her take it from him this time. Dr. B flattened it on the desk and sat down. She looked at the messy writing and frowned, eyebrows knitting as she studied it.

"I think..." Zachary unlocked his phone and slid it across the desk to her with his transcription of the note displayed. "It's hard to read, but I think that's pretty close."

She looked from his phone to the page a few times, then read through the note on his screen. She scrolled it up and down a couple of times, looked at the letter again, and then nodded.

"That must have taken you some work to unravel." She pushed both the letter and the phone back toward him. "You know that you're not responsible for Tyrrell or the choices he makes."

"What do you think when you read that? That he's going to commit suicide?"

"It's a possibility. But it could mean other things too. He might have been drunk when he wrote it and was fine when he sobered up. Maybe didn't even remember that he wrote it. He might find another way to reach out for help from a program or another family member. Call his sponsor, go into detox... there are a lot of options."

"But it doesn't sound like that, does it? It sounds..." Zachary licked his lips. His mouth was so dry he could hardly speak. "Hopeless and final."

"Maybe. That's one interpretation. Only one. Have you tried to call him?"

"He's missing." The lump in Zachary's throat grew hotter, making his voice crack and sound strained. "I've been trying to get him, but no one has seen him since December tenth. He didn't even wait until Christmas like he said he would. These things always happen..." He wanted to say, "before Christmas," but the words wouldn't come out.

Tears streamed down his face and Zachary wiped at them, embarrassed.

"Have you called the police to do a welfare check?" Dr. Boyle asked in a calm, even voice, making no comment about Zachary's messy display of emotion. That helped him to answer in a slightly calmer tone instead of breaking down further.

"I went to his place yesterday, called the police." He pulled a couple of tissues from the box on Dr. B's desk and pressed them to his eyes, trying to stop the stream of tears.

"And I assume they didn't find him."

"He's gone. No one knows where. He disappeared from work. Didn't pay his rent. It's been long enough that his landlord already rented it to someone else." Zachary sniffled and blew his nose.

"You've done what you can. If you've reported it to the police, then it's in their hands now. It's not any fun, but it's a waiting game now, until he shows up or the police find a lead."

Zachary shook his head impatiently. "The police aren't going to do anything about it. He's already been missing for weeks. The trail is cold. They aren't going to put any more manpower into it than they have to. Make sure he's not a John Doe in the morgue and talk to his boss about when he was in last. That's it. They aren't going to find him!"

"I know it's hard to just take a step back and wait—"

"I'm a private investigator. Finding missing people is something I do. I'm not going to just wait!"

"Seeing your reaction to this letter, I don't think that's a good idea. You need to think about your mental health and how an investigation like that would affect you."

"I'm going to find him," Zachary insisted.

Dr. Boyle studied him. "Why don't we take an intermission? I don't think you're in a good place to discuss this right now. You need some time to calm down, think about it, and see whether you can get some emotional distance. I think that this med regimen needs to be re-evaluated. You shouldn't be this close to a breakdown when you have been taking your meds and had an emergency dose of your anti-anxiety pills already. Have you been sleeping?"

"Yes."

"How much? Did you sleep last night?"

"Last night… maybe a couple of hours. But before that, seven or eight hours every night. When I was in the hospital and when I got home."

She shook her head. "Can you try some relaxation exercises while I finish up with another client? And then we'll talk again."

Zachary swallowed and nodded.

"You're going to stay here," Dr. B said firmly, meeting his eyes as she indicated the office. "I'm not going to come back here in five minutes and find out that you've taken off?"

Zachary hesitated. He didn't want to wait there. Dr. Boyle had confirmed what he went there to find out—that she also read the letter as a suicide note—and now he had to get on with the investigation. If Tyrrell weren't already dead, Zachary needed to find him. And if he were… Zachary needed to find him and bring him home in that case too. He wasn't going to sit around waiting for someone else to take responsibility for his brother.

"Zachary?"

He shook his head. "I need to go. Thanks for your help, but—"

"No, Zachary. No. Stay here. We're not done yet. We need to talk this through."

"I need to find him."

"Five minutes is not going to make any difference."

"Yes, it is," Zachary said sharply. He turned and took a step toward the door.

"You can't drive in this state. Call Kenzie to pick you up."

Zachary took another step. "I'm fine."

"If you leave here in an agitated, unstable state, I am going to call the police. They *will* pick you up."

"For driving?" Zachary challenged.

"For reckless endangerment. I'm telling you as your medical professional, you are not in a fit state to drive. If you get behind the wheel, you're putting the public at risk."

Zachary whirled around to face her again. "What?"

"Call Kenzie to pick you up."

Zachary clenched his teeth. "You can't do this. I'm fine. I'm under control. I'm not impaired."

She just stood there looking at him. Zachary clenched and unclenched his fists. "Let me go!" he insisted.

"Call Kenzie. I need to see her before I let you leave here."

"I'll walk. I'll get an Uber."

Dr. Boyle shook her head. Zachary was not going to be able to talk his way out of it. She'd gotten it into her head that he was too upset to drive, and she wasn't going to accept any other solution.

"Kenzie is working. I can't call her here to pick me up. She'll get fired!"

"I suspect that isn't true. If she is in the middle of something she can't leave, then you can chill here until she can."

"I'm calm." Zachary tried to arrange his face and relax his body so that she would believe him. But did he really think that she would believe he was no longer upset about his brother and the possibility that he had killed himself? Even if Zachary could make himself look calm, she probably wouldn't believe that his distress had cooled that quickly. He would need to go home with Kenzie. Have a quiet night. Convince everyone that he was back to normal again and perfectly capable of investigating Tyrrell's disappearance, just like he had been.

"That's good," Dr. B said. "I'm glad that you're calming down. Maybe with a bit of visualization and relaxation, you'll be able to process these feelings and think more logically. But right now, you're not being logical. You're running into a situation without thinking it through. You're not thinking about the consequences of your actions and, until you do, you are not going to be making good choices."

"You're not being fair." He was a grown man. He wasn't a child or a hotheaded teen anymore. He was a man fully capable of making his own choices. He had proven to her and Kenzie that he could judge when he needed medical intervention and when he didn't. And right now, he didn't need her jumping into his path and preventing him from moving forward.

"Give Kenzie a call and find out when she can be here. Then we'll talk. I'm going to go deal with my other client..." she looked at her watch, "If he's still here. And then I'll be back. And Elizabeth will be watching, if you think you're going to sneak out of here as soon as I'm occupied."

She looked at him, waiting for a response and, when Zachary didn't protest this, walked by him and out the door. She closed it after her and went to speak with her other patient.

20

Zachary paced back and forth across the office. He regretted having come to Dr. B for her opinion of the letter, believing that she could help him to get into Tyrrell's mind and figure out what he would do, what Zachary's next step should be. He knew Tyrrell, and Dr. B didn't. He should have kept it to himself.

But he also knew he was teetering on the edge of a breakdown, as Dr. B had observed. Not entirely in control of his emotions, though he was trying hard to get a handle on things. He still had that sick, plummeting feeling and was afraid that all he would find at the bottom of the elevator shaft was Tyrrell's dead body.

He took several deep breaths. He would have to call Kenzie, however much he didn't want to. Dr. Boyle wasn't going to be satisfied with anything else. Maybe it was unfair but, as more than one foster parent and social worker had told him, life wasn't fair, and he would just have to deal with it.

He walked slowly back and forth, trying to at least calm the tears and the hot lump in his throat so that he wouldn't sound like he was crying when he called Kenzie. He didn't want to panic her or to make her drop everything to deal with his problems, putting her own job in jeopardy. Dr. Wiltshire was a good boss, and Kenzie had told him about Zachary's depression and hospitalization. He had told Kenzie to take time off if she needed it. But saying that wasn't the same as being faced with the sudden absence of an employee he really needed to be there. What people promised and what they really found acceptable were often very different.

One more deep breath, and he touched Kenzie's number on his phone screen, then held the phone up to his ear. He held the phone a little away from his face so that his ragged breathing wouldn't be as loud.

"Hi, Zachary."

"Hey... how is your afternoon going?"

"My afternoon is going fine." Her fingers stopped tapping the keys on her computer. "What's up? Are you still at your apartment?" There was a new note of caution in her tone. Something had already tipped her off. Maybe just the fact that he didn't usually call her when she was working. Maybe over the lunch hour or when it was getting close to dinner and he didn't know whether she would be getting home in time, but not just in the middle of the day for no reason.

"No... I'm at Dr. Boyle's."

"I didn't remember you had an appointment today. Did you tell me that?" More key taps as she probably checked her calendar online to see whether she had forgotten about a scheduled appointment. Maybe to make sure that she hadn't forgotten about a couple's session, which she had done once before when she'd gotten too busy at work. "Zachary?"

"I... No. I didn't have anything scheduled. I came over because I wanted to talk to her about Tyrrell and this letter."

"Oh. Okay... how did that go?"

Zachary cleared his throat. It was closing up again, and he didn't want his tone changing as he spoke to her.

"I was pretty upset. I really needed her help."

"Uh-huh...?"

"And she... says that I can't drive."

"You can't drive?" There was confusion in Kenzie's tone. "Why can't you drive? Are you... impaired?"

"I'm not drunk. I haven't been drinking. Or taken anything else. Except an anxiety pill. She says I'm too upset."

"Oh. Okay. What does she want you to do? Stay there until you've calmed down? Catch an Uber?"

"She said you need to come pick me up." Zachary rolled his eyes and shook his head, hardly able to believe what he was telling her. It was *so* unfair and Dr. B was *so* off base this time. "She won't let me leave here without seeing you."

"Or what?" Kenzie gave a laugh of disbelief.

"Or she'll call the police and have them arrest me for… I forget. Putting people in danger."

"Oh." Kenzie blew out her breath, thinking about it. "Okay… can you give me about twenty minutes?"

"Yes. Of course. But don't rush over if it means losing your job. I can sit here all day if I have to," Zachary warned worriedly.

"I'm not going to lose my job. Don't worry about that. I should be about twenty minutes. Hang in there. You've already taken an anxiety pill?"

"Yes."

"You sound pretty good. I've heard you a lot worse."

"Yeah. That's what I told her. She's just overreacting."

"I take it she's not sitting there with you." Kenzie chuckled.

"No."

"Okay. Hang tight. I'll get there as soon as I can."

———

Zachary returned to the reception area for Dr. B's office. Elizabeth, the receptionist, gave him a warning look.

"It's okay if I sit out here to wait for Kenzie?" Zachary asked.

She nodded her assent and watched him walk over to one of the chairs to sit down. Once he was settled, she went back to her computer work.

But Zachary was still too agitated to sit down. There were a couple of other patients in the waiting room, and he didn't want to look like a crazy person. He should have just stayed in the office where the doctor had left him, but he'd thought he would be more comfortable in the waiting room where he was used to sitting and waiting.

Try as he could to hold the anxiety and restlessness inside, Zachary just couldn't do it. He bounced up out of his seat. Elizabeth's eyes immediately riveted on him, and he was sure she would reach for the phone to call the police if he made a move toward the door. But that wasn't what he intended. He paced the length of the waiting room and back, then repeated the journey another time. He'd hoped that he would be able to calm down again after taking a couple of laps of the room, but the agitation was not going away. His body was primed to run away. To escape the danger that was making his heart pound so hard and fast.

"Sorry," Zachary murmured as he walked past the woman who was waiting for her appointment.

She raised her brows, giving him a wide-eyed innocent look as if she had no idea why he was apologizing and that she hadn't been worried about his restlessness.

"I'm just waiting for a ride," Zachary explained. "She should be here any minute."

The woman nodded and looked down at the magazine she had open, as if what he did was of no concern to her whatsoever.

"Sorry," he repeated to the male patient who was also waiting. Not only was he making them nervous with his anxious pacing and Elizabeth's watchful gaze, but he had probably made Dr. B run later for the rest of the day's scheduled appointments too. Unlike many doctors, she actually seemed to try to stay on schedule, so a patient didn't have to wait two hours for a twenty-minute session.

Zachary glanced in Elizabeth's direction. He didn't meet her gaze, suspecting that if he did make eye contact, she would ask him to please sit down and wait for his ride without disturbing the other patients.

21

Eventually, the door from the hallway opened, and Kenzie stood there, smiling at Zachary.

"Your cab," she offered cheerfully.

But he could read her face better than she knew, and the tension around her eyes told him that she was worried about him.

Zachary took a step toward her.

"Dr. Boyle would like to talk to you before you go," Elizabeth said.

They both looked at her. Zachary wasn't sure which of them Dr. B wanted to see. Him, probably. She would want to gauge how much he had settled down during the time he'd been waiting for Kenzie.

"Dr. Kirsch," Elizabeth said. "She would like to see both of you. Would you wait for a moment? She's just finishing up with someone."

The two waiting patients gave Zachary poisonous looks. Another delay in their sessions. He'd already told them he was sorry. What else was there for him to say?

Kenzie entered the waiting room and looked at the chairs, then at Zachary standing at the far end of the room. She nodded to a chair, inviting Zachary to sit with her. He considered it, but didn't think he could sit. And he was going to have to sit down in the car for the drive home.

Then again, a car drive was usually relaxing to him, so maybe the ride home wouldn't be so torturous.

He walked over to where Kenzie sat down and stood beside her. She didn't tell him that he had to sit down to talk to her.

"You okay?" she asked.

He rolled his eyes. "I'm fine" was not an acceptable answer in their relationship. *Fine* was just a way to gloss over how he was really feeling.

"I want to get out of here," he said instead. "If we just go... they won't call the police if they know you're driving. Why do we have to wait?"

"Well, let's give it a few minutes. Dr. Boyle made time for you when you didn't have an appointment, so you should probably show her some courtesy and wait for a break in her schedule if she wants to see us for a few more minutes."

Zachary grumbled to himself. But she was right. Dr. Boyle had seen him when he'd been afraid he wouldn't be able to get in to see her. She had answered emergency phone calls when he had hit other crisis points. He should show her the courtesy of waiting until she'd had a chance to have her say, even if it was excruciating.

It wasn't an excessively long wait. A patient came out the door and Zachary drummed his fingers on the wall, waiting for Dr. B to come to the door to call him in or for Elizabeth to direct him to go in. Finally, the doctor came to the door and nodded, seeing them both there waiting for her.

"Zachary, Kenzie, this will just take a minute." She said it loudly enough that the other patients would hear and know that they would get in for their sessions before long.

Zachary and Kenzie followed her back to her office. The one they usually saw her in for couple's therapy. She didn't invite them to sit, but perched on the edge of her desk in an informal posture.

"Thanks for coming to pick Zachary up, Kenzie. I hope it wasn't too much of an inconvenience."

"No, of course not. It was fine. I just took my lunch break."

And now they could go home, and Zachary could get on the phone and start calling hospitals and jails and anywhere else that

Tyrrell might have ended up, either under his own name or as a John Doe. Maybe he couldn't drive back to Riverbrook now that Dr. B had decided he wasn't fit to drive, but he could still continue his investigation.

"I guess Zachary told you why I was concerned about him. Have you been talking about this case...?" Dr. B looked at Zachary, raising her brows to inquire whether it was safe to discuss it with Kenzie.

Zachary nodded. "Kenzie knows about Tyrrell. She's the one who told me he was missing." He paused. "I wish she'd told me sooner."

"You weren't in any condition to worry about him," Kenzie said. "We were trying to hold on to *you*."

"And what you found today?" Dr. B prompted.

"The letter." Zachary looked at Kenzie. "The letter from Tyrrell at my apartment."

Kenzie nodded understandingly. "What did it say?"

Zachary didn't say anything. Dr. B didn't give any details.

"Zachary was very upset. He made a good choice in taking his meds and coming to see me. Although driving was not a good choice, under the circumstances."

Kenzie looked at Zachary, one eyebrow raised.

"I didn't hit anything," Zachary said. "Or anyone."

Dr. Boyle shook her head. "No. But you could easily have gotten into an accident, considering your state."

"I'm calm now. And Kenzie is here to pick me up, so I don't see that we need to go over it again."

"If I took your pulse now, it would be normal?"

Zachary scratched his cheek. "No," he admitted. "But I can't control that."

"No. And that means that adrenaline is still pumping through your body, and your body and your brain are primed for action. We have seen how badly a panic attack can affect you. No one wants you in the car when that happens."

"If I was going to break down, I would have already."

"Maybe. I think that your medication level has prevented that from happening yet. But we don't know if that will hold. With the doses that we've got you on, I was really hoping to at least reduce the frequency of flashbacks and panic attacks."

"It has. I've been fine. Everything has been stable for a few weeks."

"While you've been in the hospital. A therapeutic setting. Not in the outside world. You only got out yesterday, and we're seeing a huge spike in anxiety and agitation today. I don't think we've got it right. I'd like the hospital to run a few more tests. See where your vitals are right now. Check the levels of the various medications in your blood. Some brain imaging to see if we can tell what's going on. Keep you under observation to make sure that whatever this is will pass and—"

"No." Zachary shook his head. "No way. You want to know why I'm so upset? You don't think my brother committing suicide is enough reason for me to be like this? The meds are fine."

"Suicide?" Kenzie repeated, eyes widening. "Tyrrell?"

"That's speculation," Dr. B advised her. "Zachary is jumping to conclusions. That's my point. This level of agitation and emotion does not—"

"This level of agitation and emotion is exactly right under the circumstances," Zachary snapped, aware that his voice was too loud. He always spoke in a low voice in Dr. B's office. He didn't let himself get angry and explode.

"A drug reaction can make you more anxious. It can make you overreact in ways that you normally wouldn't."

"It's not a drug reaction!"

Kenzie's hand went up, motioning for him to stop and calm down. "Zachary, you're shouting—"

"I do not need to go back to the hospital for a drug review. I just got out!"

"If you're not going to cooperate and do it voluntarily..." Dr. Boyle started.

"You're going to commit me?" he demanded in disbelief.

Zachary wanted to scream at her. He wanted to tear the place apart, throwing her books and furniture around like a toddler having a tantrum.

Both women stood looking at him, eyes wide. Dr. Boyle with a flat, immobile expression, determined to do what she felt needed to be done. Kenzie looking shocked and overwhelmed, but not angry like Zachary felt. He was furious. He had come to Dr. B for help, and she was going to make him go back to the hospital. Back to the psych ward that he'd just left. A failure.

"I haven't been involuntarily committed since I was a teenager," Zachary growled.

"Then think this through. Would I be suggesting it if I didn't think there was reason to be worried? Yes, I agree that you have reason to be upset. But I'm uneasy about how quickly your behavior has degraded. I think we need to step back and review. Just a few days. Just to be sure that everything is okay, and you are stable."

"I wouldn't have signed myself out if I wasn't stable. The doctors at the hospital agreed. They were monitoring me. They talked to you. Everyone said I was fine with the new cocktail."

"And you were. While you were at the hospital. Let's just be absolutely sure."

"And if I don't agree… you *Title 18*."

She gave a little shrug and quirk of her head. If he forced her, she would make it involuntary. And then Zachary couldn't sign himself out. They had him for 72 hours to evaluate and decide whether he were a danger to himself or others. If he signed in voluntarily, he could leave when he wanted to. If they didn't see anything that indicated he was a danger, he could be out the next day instead of waiting for three. And who knew what those extra two days might mean to Tyrrell?

He swallowed and looked at Kenzie. Her eyes were still wide, and she swiped at a tear that escaped the corner of one. He hated what he had done to her; being hospitalized and Kenzie having to worry about whether he might harm himself. Worrying about whether he was ready to be released from the hospital. He had assured her that everything was fine and he was ready, and now Dr. B was saying that he had been wrong.

"Fine." Zachary swallowed again and licked his lips. "Fine, then. I'll go voluntarily."

22

Dr. Boyle said that she would call ahead to the hospital to give them a heads-up that Zachary was coming back in and to get started on the testing required. Going back to the hospital just ramped Zachary's anger and agitation level even more. They didn't normally do any extensive testing on a new drug protocol. They watched him for any obvious reactions, noted any behavioral changes, and had him self-report how he was feeling. If he felt good and wasn't showing any adverse reactions, it was a win. They didn't usually do blood tests unless he were on a drug that specifically required it. Brain imaging was something he'd only heard of being done for experimental drugs when they wanted to see what changes they caused in brain activation.

He couldn't believe that Dr. B would push it so far. She should be able to understand that he was simply worried about his brother and what might have happened to him.

Zachary remained stoic on his way out of the inner office, through the waiting room, and out to Kenzie's pristine red convertible. There was no riding with the top down in the middle of Vermont winter, but Kenzie didn't put her "baby" into storage while it was cold. The car didn't hold any heat with its canvas top and, when Zachary slid into the passenger seat, it was as chilly as if it had been sitting outside for hours, though Kenzie had just been driving it ten minutes before.

He pulled his seat belt across his hips and buckled it with a snap. Kenzie was slower getting into the car and getting herself buckled in. She looked at Zachary.

"Are you okay?"

"Obviously not."

"No. I know that. I mean… tell me what you found out about Tyrrell."

Zachary took a deep breath. At least *Kenzie* was concerned about the only thing that was important to him right now. "I'm worried… that he was planning to commit suicide."

She nodded gravely, her serious brown eyes meeting his. Zachary choked up and looked away. Without saying anything further, Kenzie started the car, played with the heater settings for a moment, and then pulled out.

Zachary tried to relax, to let the purr of Kenzie's car's engine lull him into a calmer and more centered place. But relaxing meant dropping the mask and, as soon as he released the superhuman hold on his emotions, the tears came again. He kept his face turned away from Kenzie and checked the glove box. He found a pocket pack of tissues conveniently stowed there, pulled a few out, and did his best to stop the flow. Kenzie didn't drill him with questions or tell him that he was being a baby like Bridget would have. She just drove to the hospital without comment. She stopped in one of the paid parking lots, away from the doors, and they sat there in silence for a few minutes. Zachary managed to slow the tears, but not to stop them.

"I shouldn't be crying," Zachary told her hoarsely. "I've got no reason to. Maybe it *is* the meds. Sometimes they make you emotional."

"I think you have plenty of reason to be upset. Don't beat yourself up about it. Is that the letter?" She nodded at Tyrrell's letter, still pinched between Zachary's numb fingers.

He handed it to her. Would she read it the same way as he had? Or would she say, like Dr. B, that there could be other interpretations? That it didn't mean that Tyrrell had been planning to kill himself.

Kenzie held the page close to her face and squinted. "You weren't kidding about the chicken scratch! This is *worse* than the handwriting in your notebooks. How could you read a word of it?"

Zachary pulled out his phone and unlocked it. Closing the phone app, Zachary again brought up his transcription of Tyrrell's words. He handed it to Kenzie.

She read through the transcription and, as Dr. Boyle had done, checked between the words on the screen and the words on the page to see if she could untangle the words as Zachary had. She rested her hands in her lap, holding them.

"Yeah. I can see why you found this so upsetting."

Zachary swallowed, the lump in his throat painful. "I'm not just *agitated by my meds.*"

"No. You're actually holding it together pretty well, all things considered."

He appreciated her words of support. He mopped at the tears on his face and in the corners of his eyes and got out more tissues to blow his nose.

"I can't take three days off for a med review. I don't *need* a med review."

"Let's see how much they can do today. It doesn't take long to do blood draws. You can talk to the doctor and explain the situation. The extra stress and emotion. Maybe he'll just want to bump up the dosages a bit and see if that's enough to help you handle the situation."

Zachary nodded.

"If you're admitting yourself, you don't need to stay the whole 72 hours. Just see how it goes. If you can get a nap in, maybe you'll feel better. A good cry and a nap can do wonders," she told him with a smile and encouraging voice.

"I'll sleep in the chairs while I'm waiting." They were bound to keep him waiting for a few hours. Even an emergency psych consult never really seemed to be considered an emergency.

Kenzie took her key out of the ignition and reached for the door.

Zachary stopped her. "I'll go in myself. You need to get back to work."

"I can come in for long enough to make sure that you get checked in and settled."

He shook his head. "I can do it on my own. You're on your lunch break. If you get right back to the morgue, it won't be like you missed any time at all."

"I *can* take the time. Dr. Wiltshire will understand."

"I'd rather you didn't."

Kenzie sat there for a moment, looking at him. He waited for her to say that she didn't trust him. That she needed to walk him in to make sure he got where he was supposed to and checked himself in. That he couldn't go off and investigate, breaking his promise to Dr. B.

"Okay," Kenzie said finally. She reached over and they hugged awkwardly across the center console. She pressed her cheek against his, kissed him, and murmured a goodbye in his ear.

They drew apart. Kenzie looked at the phone and the letter in her lap. "I guess I should hold on to these?"

"Yeah. Can't use my phone in there. No point in having it locked away. Maybe... you can keep it with you in case Tyrrell calls back. Or if Lindsey thinks of something..."

"Sure," Kenzie agreed, nodding briskly. "I'll do that. Take care, okay? I'll stop by after work, but I don't know if they'll let me visit. Or you might be busy with tests."

Zachary nodded. He popped the handle to open his door. "I'll see you tomorrow."

23

I t felt strange to be back in the psych ward again when he had just left there. He had left believing that he would not be back for at least another year. Maybe longer if he could get through the following Christmas. He didn't spend every Christmas there as an adult, not like when he was in foster care and had returned to Bonnie Brown every year, unable to tolerate being around Christmas decorations, candles, and happy families. Or worse yet, overstressed families fighting about Christmas decorations.

Zachary didn't like the hospital ward, but he didn't hate it either. He knew that if he couldn't handle things in the real world, or if his depression got too deep and he were considering harming himself, that they would watch him and keep him safe and provide the stability and support that he needed to get through the last few days or weeks before Christmas.

Just like taking medicine. He didn't look forward to it, didn't like it, but knew it was necessary to keep himself well and safe.

He normally found a certain amount of peace in the ward, in a place where there were rules and routines for everything.

He saw one of the nurses turn her head quickly as he approached, escorted by an orderly from the emergency room.

"Zachary?"

Zachary raised his eyebrows and sighed, giving her a grimace. "Hi again, Val."

"Did you forget something?" she teased. She nodded to the orderly. "Thanks, John. I'll take it from here."

John nodded and retreated.

"Dr. B wanted me to get checked out," Zachary explained. "She was worried about… a setback or a reaction to my new meds."

"Okay," Nurse Val nodded. "You can go right back to the same room. We haven't had time to rent it out to anyone else yet. What kind of setback?"

Zachary ran his hand over his face. "My brother is… missing. And he left me a note."

Nurse Val frowned. "The brother who visited you here? A suicide note?"

"It's… ambiguous," Zachary admitted. "He doesn't say straight out… but a lot of times, people don't."

"No, of course not. They talk around the problem. Use euphemisms. Pretend that if you don't name it, it won't happen. People act like if you use the word suicide, it might encourage someone to attempt suicide." Nurse Val shook her head. She studied Zachary's face closely as they walked toward his hospital room. She could see, Zachary was sure, that he'd been crying, his nose bright red and eyes puffy. Despite how kind she always was to him, he couldn't find a smile of appreciation and reassurance for her. She touched him lightly on the back for an instant, then pulled her hand back. "Well, I think you're doing pretty well under the circumstances. But the extra stress certainly could be more than you're ready for yet, just settling into this new cocktail. Would you like me to pass anything on to the doctor?"

Zachary shrugged. "Dr. B was going to call about the testing and follow-up she wants. Just…" he shook his head in frustration, "tell him I'm okay, and I'm not going to stay. Tyrrell needs me. I need to find him… wherever he is and whatever he's done."

Val nodded sympathetically. "Okay. Well, you know yourself best. I'll see if Dr. Boyle has sent orders over and we'll try to line everything up as quickly as we can. What have you taken today? Everything in your morning med list?"

"Yes. And emergency anxiety."

"Good. I'll note it down. Anything else? Alcohol? Over the counter? Recreational? Herbs?"

Zachary shook his head. "Nothing else." He rubbed his temples. Crying always gave him a terrible headache, and the panic attack and adrenaline rush that was now fading away made him just want to sleep. "But I could use a Tylenol."

She nodded. "I'll see if we can get you something. Have a rest here for a bit, and then we'll have someone lined up to do the blood work."

"Thanks." Zachary sat down on the edge of his bed. "Could you call Kenzie? Let her know I'm settled?"

She tapped the side of her head. "Already on my list."

Zachary did fall asleep, but not for long. He slept heavily and then woke up feeling groggy and hungover. He stared out the window, trying to estimate the time. It was afternoon, but didn't feel very late. Like he'd only been asleep for half an hour.

He didn't want to get up or move around, and he didn't have anything to do. He could go to the visitors' room to get a book or a pack of cards, but he didn't get any joy out of reading. It was just a chore. Something that helped to pass the time a little less slowly than lying in bed staring at the ceiling. Instead, he thought about his case, trying to divorce his emotions and analyze it logically.

If it wasn't his brother, what would his recommendation be to a client? Keep looking? Or had he exhausted all possible avenues of inquiry?

He hadn't memorized all of Tyrrell's letter, but tried to recall as much of it as he could.

The fact that Tyrrell had disappeared before his self-imposed Christmas deadline actually felt encouraging. If he had made and followed through on a suicide plan, then it should have been on the day he had picked. It didn't feel right to Zachary that he would switch to December tenth instead. Disappearing on or shortly after December tenth felt spontaneous. Like he'd been distracted from his plan or someone had pulled him away from it. But then where was he? In detox? It was a possibility. Zachary could follow up with detox programs when he got out. They might not tell him anything officially, but he thought he could talk them into giving away whether Tyrrell were there or not. He could ask Kenzie to check with other medical examiners in the state to see if they had any John Does matching Tyrrell's description. He thought she might do that for him. Or even as an official part of her job. Tyrrell had been reported as a missing person, after all.

He still had to check with the hospitals to see if Tyrrell had been admitted to one of them. Maybe he'd been in an accident and was unconscious or couldn't remember who he was. It didn't seem likely that he would disappear without at least seeing the kids for Christmas. They were important to him. Zachary had seen that when Tyrrell talked about them and when he'd brought them to the Lodge for Thanksgiving. He might have thought that he was the worst dad in the world but, as far as Zachary was concerned, that position had already been taken.

He hadn't done a deep dive into Tyrrell's social media accounts. He might find something there. A hint as to what he'd been considering after Christmas, a friend or two that might have an influence over him or know where he might have gone, clues as to his state of mind around December tenth.

And what about Tyrrell's email? He knew Tyrrell's email address and provider and might be able to guess at his password. It was likely to be one of the kids' names or his wedding date, or some combination of them.

There were still plenty of avenues left to investigate.

24

The staff wasn't happy when Zachary announced that he was checking out in the morning.

"Your blood work was fine," Julianna, the nurse at the desk told him, "But Dr. Boyle wanted some other tests run as well that we haven't been able to schedule in yet. And you should at least have one therapy session before you go to make sure that the doctor is in agreement that you are safe to be checked out."

Zachary shook his head. "I signed in voluntarily. I don't need a doctor's approval to sign out."

"But it would be good to ensure that everyone is in agreement that it is safe..."

"No one added any flags to my chart, did they? I've been calm. I haven't done anything to endanger others. I'm not having suicidal thoughts." He raised his brows. "You know I check myself in if I need to."

"But the other tests that Dr. Boyle wanted..."

"Call me when they're scheduled and I'll come back in for them."

Julianna rolled her eyes and gave him a frustrated glare. "Zachary..."

"Nurse Julianna," he said evenly.

"You took your morning meds?"

"Yes."

"And you'll come back if there are any changes? If you think that the medications are not doing their job or you have new symptoms?"

"Yes. I will. Or I'll call Dr. Boyle and see what she says."

"We would miss you if you never came back."

"I thought you didn't want me to come back. You want me to be well."

"That's not what I mean. I mean if you… *couldn't* come back."

Zachary nodded wearily. "I know," he agreed.

"You're going to need to sign some forms…"

"You sure you can't just use the ones I signed a couple of days ago?"

"No. The administrators would kill me. Especially since you got sent back after the last time."

"I didn't get *sent* back," Zachary corrected firmly. "It was voluntary. Just a check-in to make sure that my blood levels were okay."

She shook her head, knowing that it was because Dr. Boyle had insisted, that Zachary had nearly had a breakdown within two days of leaving. But Zachary wasn't going to let them derail him. He had a job to do. He wasn't going to sit around doing nothing in the psych ward until they finally admitted that he was fine.

It took time to sign all the releases that the legal department insisted on for liability purposes, but then he was free. Zachary walked out into the brisk, chilly air and took a deep breath of his second taste of freedom that week. It had been hard-fought and was all the sweeter for it.

But it was cold. January was not the best weather to be spending any amount of time outside. But Zachary did not have his phone and, therefore, his Uber app, and he wasn't going to wait around for a taxi. One would think that taxi service would be faster, now that they had competition in the driving business, but they seemed to get slower and slower instead of faster and more efficient.

Instead, he jogged to the nearest bus stop, knowing that in the early-morning rush, it would be arriving every fifteen minutes. He stood there, feeling the cold concrete through the bottoms of his thin shoes, stomping his feet to try to prevent his toes from going numb. It was twenty-five minutes before the next bus arrived, and his fingers were so cold it took forever to tease the change he needed out of the zippered section of his wallet and deposit them into the fare box. The bus driver had pulled out before Zachary finished, and he had to hang on to a pole while he deposited the rest of the coins.

The driver nodded. "Have a nice day."

Zachary sat down and watched out the window for his stop, waiting for his numb fingers and toes to start thawing out.

No one paid any attention to him. He blended in with the commuters, shoppers, and other riders. No one worried about his being an escaped psych patient or commented on his thin, unshaven face. People preferred not to look at those who were down on their luck, and three days' growth of whiskers was one of Zachary's best tools to make himself invisible. When he had been with Bridget—not that he had ever ridden on the bus with her, but when they had gone other places together—people had looked at them all the time, smiling at the pretty woman and probably wondering what the short, skinny, rough-looking man was doing with her. Bridget had never realized that people didn't smile at everyone the way they smiled at her.

He got off the bus close to Dr. B's office and went to find his car. There was, luckily, no ticket on it and it had not been impounded. Maybe Dr. B had told the security staff to leave it alone.

Even though the seat was cold when he slid into it, Zachary immediately melted into the bucket seat of the compact. It was nothing fancy. It was supposed to be just as nondescript as he was, in fact, but it was his and he always felt more at peace with the world when he was in the driver's seat. Maybe that was the only time he really felt like he was in control of his life. A car meant freedom.

He ran the engine for a few minutes, letting the heater do all of the work defrosting the windows instead of getting out to scrape off the frost. Eventually, when he could no longer see his breath and the

HE DROWNED IN MEMORY

front and back windows were both relatively clear, he put it into gear
and drove to the Medical Examiner's Office.

———

He hadn't called Kenzie to let her know that he had checked himself
out of the hospital already. How could he? She had his phone on her.
He could have borrowed a hospital phone or one belonging to a
nurse, but he hadn't wanted to chance a lecture from Kenzie about
how he was checking out too soon too. She'd been kind to him the
day before, not criticizing him for any of his choices, and he hoped to
keep it that way.

Instead, his old friend Martin Ash checked him through security
on the main floor where the police department was located, then took
the elevator downstairs. No one else got on the elevator, so he had it
to himself and there wouldn't be anyone else to demand Kenzie's
attention when he got there.

Her office was at the outside of the medical examiner's suite,
public facing so that she had to deal with inquiries and help people
fill in forms to make their requests for records while she completed
the rest of her work. But it was usually pretty quiet at the desk. Not a
lot of people requested records from the morgue.

His shoes were quiet, only squeaking slightly because of the
wetness from the snow on the sidewalks, so Zachary cleared his throat
as he walked toward Kenzie's desk to give her warning that someone
was approaching. He didn't want to startle her. She paused in her
typing and glanced in his direction. Then she smiled and pushed back
from the desk.

"Zachary! How are you doing? I wasn't expecting to see you this
early."

"I wanted to get to work."

Kenzie leaned across the desk to give him a quick hug and peck
on the cheek. "You must have been waiting for them to check you out
as soon someone got there."

Zachary shrugged. "Yes."

Kenzie patted her pockets, then bent over to open a drawer and paw through her purse. She pulled his phone out and placed it on the counter in front of him. "I guess this is what you came for?"

Zachary smiled, glad to see that she hadn't left it at home. He had asked her to keep an eye on it in case he got any calls, but he hadn't been sure if she would. He tapped the wake-up button and saw that it was fully charged and the only missed call was from Heather.

"It's been pretty quiet," Kenzie said. "I suspect Heather is still acting as gatekeeper."

Heather had taken it upon herself to redirect all business calls to herself while Zachary was in the hospital, helping who she could and explaining to those who needed fieldwork done that Zachary wouldn't be available until the new year. It was good to know that someone was looking after his clients, so they weren't all wondering why he wasn't picking up their calls.

"I'll give her a call and make sure nothing is urgent. But everyone is going to have to wait while I look for Tyrrell."

Kenzie nodded. He could tell that she was biting the inside of her lip, trying to decide what to say to him. He waited.

"How long are you going to take for that?" she asked. "What if you run out of leads?"

"I haven't run out yet. It will take... however long it takes."

Kenzie's lips pressed together and she nodded. She had probably had enough time to figure out that this was what was most important to him right now, and he wasn't going to be distracted from it by other jobs. "Well... good luck. I hope... that everything is okay."

"I don't know if this is something I can ask you, but... would you check with the other morgues and see if anyone has a John Doe...?" He didn't finish the sentence. Kenzie knew what he was asking. He didn't want to jinx it by saying the words. *A John Doe who matched Tyrrell's description.*

Kenzie pursed her lips, then nodded. "I'll make some time. I'll send out an email blast to everyone this morning, but you know that no one will bother to follow up today unless I call them. If it isn't marked urgent, they'll put it off."

"Thanks. It would be good to know... that he isn't in a cold room somewhere..."

Kenzie nodded soberly. "Yeah. It will ease my mind too."

She leaned forward to give him another kiss. "Good luck."

Zachary embraced her briefly, though it was awkward across the desk. "Thanks for everything."

It was comforting to know that Tyrrell's disappearance weighed on her mind too. He felt like no one else was taking it seriously. Someone should have reported it back on December eleventh. Or maybe the twelfth. It shouldn't have been another month before anyone responded to his absence.

He slid his phone into his pocket and headed for home to start investigating.

25

Zachary took a deep dive into Tyrrell's social media accounts, looking to see what his last posts had been on each platform, looking for any pattern or anything that might have indicated his state of mind or what had been bothering him. What had happened? Had he run away? Been in an accident? Been abducted?

He knew that the cops would say it was very unlikely that Tyrrell had been abducted. Grown men didn't get kidnapped. But it wasn't true. Jose and the immigrants hadn't just dissolved into thin air. They had been deliberately targeted, tortured, and killed. Being an adult and male did not make a person immune to violence.

Most of what Tyrrell had posted on his accounts had been jokes and memes. Fun stuff. Light. Nerdy. He had also posted messages of concern or encouragement to friends who had been struggling with the Christmas season or other challenges. Zachary copied down their names and URLs for future reference. He would follow up on them later. Tyrrell had also said how excited he was to see his kids over the Christmas vacation. The year before had been Lindsey's. She'd had them home all Christmas Day, and Tyrrell had only had a weekend visit, just like the rest of the year. His friends posted congratulations and encouraging thoughts about his being able to have them for Christmas.

What had kept him from them? What had happened to keep him away from the two kids he claimed were the most important people in his life?

He had been drinking at Thanksgiving. He had confirmed that in his letter to Zachary, had admitted that when they had asked him about the liquor in the cabin at the Lodge, he had denied drinking and said he was still sober when he was not. Zachary had wondered at the time but, when Tyrrell denied it, had pushed the unwelcome thoughts away and ignored the feeling of dread that had blossomed in his stomach. There had been too much else going on to spend his time worrying about whether Tyrrell was telling the truth or not.

Lindsey had said he was a closet drinker. He'd kept it away from everyone, including her, so Zachary couldn't be blamed for not seeing any warning signs. If Tyrrell's own wife hadn't known the difference, how could Zachary be expected to?

Tyrrell hadn't posted much between the Thanksgiving vacation and December tenth. As if nothing at all had happened, even though the murders and their rescue had been posted all over the news and social media.

Maybe because he didn't want Lindsey to be reminded about it or to know the full extent of what had gone on while they had been there. How much did Lindsey actually know about it? Had Tyrrell been trying to hide that too?

Eventually, Zachary decided he wasn't going to get anything else out of Tyrrell's public posts and turned his attention to email.

The first thing to do was to check to make sure he hadn't received any emails from Tyrrell while he'd been in the hospital that had gotten lost in the sea of emails he'd been swamped with. And that nothing had mistakenly gone into his junk mail folder.

But he and Tyrrell hadn't exchanged emails very often. Zachary preferred talking over typing and reading. He didn't find any emails that he had missed during December. The last thing he had from Tyrrell went back to November.

He went to the login page for Tyrrell's email provider. How many wrong passwords would they take before locking his account? He checked a few references before making any attempt. It looked like he was safe as long as he didn't keep trying from the same device, but cycled among trying to log in on from his phone, tablet, and computer. He typed a list of names and dates in varying combinations, then ranked them in order of likelihood. Unlike with most of the missing person searches he did, he knew something about Tyrrell and the way he thought, and that gave him an advantage. He typed in Tyrrell's email address and tried the first password.

Predictably, it failed. Zachary typed an *X* beside it and tried the next one. It too failed. He would try one more, and then switch devices. The list was long and, even though he had ranked them by likelihood, he found his eyes drawn down the list to a string that combined Mason's and Alisha's name with the year of Tyrrell's wedding. He typed it in. A circle spun on the screen, but it didn't immediately reject the password. He crossed his fingers, hoping that Tyrrell didn't have two-factor verification set up. He didn't have Tyrrell's phone or any other devices to confirm it.

Then the screen flashed and quickly resolved into an email inbox.

Cracked in three attempts—not bad! Zachary skimmed the list of email subjects. Lots of spam and advertisements. Not a lot of personal correspondence. Hundreds of emails sitting there unread. Tyrrell hadn't accessed his email in a long time. Wherever he was, he wasn't using his phone to keep up with what was going on in his email inbox. But a lot of people didn't check their emails regularly and, if Tyrrell was feeling bad, he might not have any motivation to look at it.

Zachary had a sense of deja vu as he started to scroll through the emails, looking for anything important. Just a couple of days before, he'd been doing the same thing with his own email inbox. Catching up with the life that he'd abandoned for several weeks. He wanted to be able to leave everything as he had found it, but knew that there was no way he would be able to find what he needed just by scanning subject lines. He set up a temporary folder and started dragging all of the spam and bulk emails into it in order to dig down and find anything that might be important. He watched for the names of family members. Heather, Joss, even Lindsey or the kids. And for names that might be repeated. Some emails had replies marked, and

Zachary switched to the sent folder to see the conversations Tyrrell had found important enough to reply to before his disappearance. He set up another folder and dragged all of Tyrrell's most recently sent emails into it. He worked through the recipient names and ran them through searches, pulling out any recent emails that Tyrrell had not responded to and dragging them into the same folder. He switched to Tyrrell's inbox again and continued to work his way through it, dragging most of the emails into the bulk folder he had set up.

Following this protocol, it wasn't long before everything that had been sitting in Tyrrell's inbox was sorted between the two folders. He went to the important folder and set up subfolders, dividing the emails into correspondence with family, friends, and vendors or services. The family and friends folders were quite small. Zachary read through each email thread carefully. He stopped when he had read partway through one thread, looking back up at the top to see who the contact was.

Vincent.

Zachary stared at it for a moment, trying to process it.

Not Vincent Goldman, but Vincent Miller. But the email exchange sounded like a couple of brothers talking to each other. Someone in a pretty close relationship, anyway. Could Vincent Miller be *their* Vincent? Their little brother?

Zachary searched for Goldman in the sender field, and saw mostly emails between himself and Tyrrell. There were a few with Joss, but they were pretty sparse. Maybe she preferred to communicate by phone, as Zachary did.

He searched for Miller and, as well as pulling up conversations with Vincent Miller, there were also conversations with Mindy Miller. There was no way it was a coincidence Vincent and Mindy Miller had to be Vincent and Mindy Goldman. They had apparently taken on the name of their foster family. Maybe they'd even been adopted.

Tyrrell had never mentioned this to Zachary, and he himself still went by Goldman. Did that mean that he was estranged from his foster family? Did he go by both? It wouldn't do for Zachary to only search for Tyrrell under the name Tyrrell Goldman if he sometimes went by Tyrrell Miller. He scribbled a note in his notebook and continued to read through emails and perform searches, building a picture in his mind of the period of time before Tyrrell had disappeared.

He made some more notes. Then he clicked on Vincent's name and found a contact card that included Vincent's phone number. Mindy's had been set up as well. Zachary wrote them into his notebook, and then put them into his phone as well.

His little brother and sister. The ones that he hadn't seen or talked to since the day of the fire on Christmas Eve when he was only ten years old.

26

Vince and Mindy wouldn't remember him. Vince had only been four and Mindy two. Tyrrell could remember Zachary, having been six at the time they were separated. But his recollections were spotty, remembering one or two things about that night vividly, but not a lot about what things had been like growing up in the Goldman family. Vince and Mindy would remember even less, if they remembered anything at all. He was sure Mindy would have no recollection at all of her first family. She wouldn't remember anything about how Zachary used to help take care of her, coaxing her to feed when she wouldn't take a bottle from anyone else, changing her diapers, carrying her around on his hip to keep her quiet when their mother was trying to sleep. She had not been an easy, happy baby.

He had their phone numbers. He needed to call them and see if they'd heard anything from Tyrrell. If Tyrrell needed somewhere to crash because he'd lost the apartment, what better place than on his brother's couch? Or in his sister's spare room? Just because it wasn't mentioned in the email conversations, that didn't mean that Tyrrell had not approached one of them. If they saw each other face to face, there wouldn't be any need to mention it in an email. And if Tyrrell had needed a place to crash, it was more likely that he would call his brother or show up on his doorstep than send an email inquiry about it.

Zachary had never tracked down anyone in his family. He knew that he was the reason the family had been broken up. His mother had made it very clear that it was primarily his fault. She couldn't manage him while they'd been living in the house and, now that there was no home to go back to, she didn't want anything else to do with him. Mrs. Pratt had tried to talk her into keeping the kids, or dividing the kids between her and their father as they went separate directions, but she had been adamant. She didn't want anything more to do with them.

That had hurt Zachary worse than the burns from the fire.

The burns would eventually heal and not cause him further problems. But the pain of her rejection was something that would never go away.

He had not searched any of them up because he hadn't wanted to face that kind of rejection again. He didn't want to hear from his brothers and sisters that they didn't want him in their lives. He had left them alone, believing that he would never see any of them again.

And then Tyrrell had found him. Tyrrell was the first one who had reappeared in Zachary's life, giving him heartfelt hugs and slaps on the back, repeating over and over again that he couldn't believe it. Tyrrell had also searched out Heather, and they had been talking to each other for a while before Tyrrell arranged for the three of them to meet face to face so that Heather could ask Zachary for his help on her old assault case if she felt good about it.

And then Joss. She was the first one to show any bitterness toward Zachary. But he had quickly discovered that was pretty much her default outlook. She had a heart. The tenderness was still there, buried deep behind the hard-as-nails exterior. But she didn't show it often and didn't trust Zachary just because he had once been her brother.

Tyrrell had been in contact with Vince and Mindy all along. But he'd never suggested to Zachary that they would like to meet him, even just by phone or email. Why would they want to meet someone they didn't know, especially knowing his history?

But this wasn't about Zachary, it was about Tyrrell, and they had grown up with him and clearly cared about him and kept in touch. Zachary would just have to swallow his anxiety and self-consciousness and do what had to be done.

He tapped Vince's number into his phone. Maybe he should wait until a better time. If Vince worked regular hours, he would be at work, and Zachary didn't want to interrupt him there. But he could just as easily work evenings or nights. Without knowing anything about him, Zachary couldn't speculate on what his schedule was anyway. He had to start sometime.

It rang a few times, and Zachary was trying to decide whether to leave a voicemail message or not. Would that be weird? It would give Vince a chance to think about it and make a choice instead of just being ambushed. But if he weren't interested in talking to Zachary, maybe being ambushed was the only way that would work.

Maybe he was one of those people who didn't answer the phone if they didn't know the caller ID and it didn't matter how many times Zachary called, he would ignore it every time until he knew who it was.

"Hello?"

Zachary was startled. His brain stuttered, trying to get on script. "Uh... hi. I'm sorry to bother you, and if this is a bad time, you can call me back later. Or I can call you."

There was a moment of silence on the other end, probably Vince waiting for Zachary to tell him exactly who he was and what he wanted. Because Zachary hadn't exactly announced himself properly.

"Tyrrell?"

"No!" Zachary hadn't realized that his voice and Tyrrell's sounded similar. "This is—I'm looking for Tyrrell, actually—this is Zachary." It felt weird and incomplete for him to introduce himself by his first name. "Goldman."

But that was probably weirder.

"Zachary." Vince's voice went up in tone. He sounded so grown up. So much like an adult. Because, of course, he was, but, at the same time, he was still four years old in Zachary's mind. "How did you... well, I guess you're a private investigator, so you have ways of getting people's numbers."

"I got it from Tyrrell's email. I'm trying to find him... did he maybe crash with you?"

"No. I haven't heard from him in weeks."

"Do you know whether Mindy has?"

"I'll three-way her. Hang on for a minute."

There was a series of beeps, and Zachary was just listening to himself breathe. He had talked to Vince. And he was going to talk to Mindy. After so many years, decades of not seeing or hearing from them, he would have spoken to all of his siblings. The rush he got from the thought made his heart start pounding harder and faster, but it wasn't a panic attack. It was something else.

It felt good.

"You there, Zachary?" Vince's voice sounded in his ear.

"I'm here."

"Okay, we're all on. Say hi to Zachary, Mindy."

"Hi," a young woman's voice joined Vince's. She giggled awkwardly. "Hi, Zachary."

"Hi," Zachary echoed, holding on to the moment, breathing shallowly in case they might both disappear like the wisp of a dream if he were too loud. "It's nice to hear your voice."

"You too," Mindy agreed. "So... what's this? You're looking for T? Tyrrell, I mean?"

Zachary sucked in his breath, startled. "I call him T too. Umm... yes. No one I've been able to talk to has had any contact with him since December tenth. Did either of you hear from him after that? December tenth."

"No," Mindy said. "I tried to get him at Christmas and New Year's Day, but he didn't answer and didn't return my calls. I just figured he was... being Tyrrell."

"What does that mean?"

"You know... he drops out of sight for a while sometimes. Or gets distracted by a new project and forgets to call you back... Or he gets it into his head that we don't really want to talk to him. Never mind that I called him, so what makes him think I don't want to talk to him?"

"Oh. Okay. And Vince... you haven't heard anything?"

"No. Sorry."

"Do you go by Vince? Or do you want me to call you Vincent? I assume it isn't Vinnie anymore."

"Vince is good," he confirmed. "What about you? Always Zachary? No nicknames?"

"I prefer Zachary. Sometimes people call me Zach... and that's okay. I'll answer to it."

"Fair enough."

"If this is something that Tyrrell does sometimes—dropping out of sight—do you know where he usually goes when he does that?"

"I don't really know," Mindy said. "He drinks, you know. He's an alcoholic. But he doesn't like people to know that he does, so he... kind of hides out."

"I don't know who he drinks with," Vince agreed. "Not with me. I don't know any of his drinking buddies."

"Do you think... we could get together?" Zachary asked. He wanted desperately to be able to see them face to face. To see their facial expressions and body language, not just to hear the words they were saying. There might be other things he could pick up if he actually met with them. And to see his baby brother and sister after all of these years... "I don't know where you live. I can come to you if you're in Vermont or nearby."

There was silence for a moment. He didn't push the question, letting them think about it instead. He heard an alert bing on one of their phones and realized they were probably texting each other. Keeping him out of the loop while they discussed it. He waited.

"I suppose," Vince agreed. "You're all the way north, though. You don't want to come all the way here. How about meeting in Clintock? That's more central."

"We don't have to meet halfway. I enjoy driving. I don't mind coming to you."

"Clintock," Vince repeated. Maybe he wanted neutral territory. Not to invite a total stranger into his house. Not to tell him exactly where they each lived, though it wouldn't be hard to figure out now that he had their names and phone numbers.

Zachary nodded. "Clintock is fine," he agreed.

It wasn't where he preferred to meet. He had grown up there, mostly, and he'd had to go back when investigating Heather's case. It had been painful seeing the places he had lived, the places he had been bullied and abused. And where Heather had been hurt too. But it didn't hold the same kind of memories for Vince and Mindy. Maybe their memories were of family outings and ice cream cones. Pleasant, warm feelings.

"I don't know what your schedules are like. Is there a time we could meet today?"

"I could swing tomorrow," Vince said. "I'm already booked up today. Mindy? How about you?"

"We could do supper," Mindy suggested. "You still have to eat, don't you?"

"Supper today?" Vince made an indecisive hum. Zachary hoped that he would give in to Mindy's suggestion. He didn't want to have to put it off another day. Vince and Mindy were probably the people who knew Tyrrell best, other than Lindsey.

"It's Tyrrell," Mindy urged. "I've been worried about him too. Zachary is a PI. I'm sure he can find him."

"Well, okay," Vince conceded. "Supper, then."

He and Mindy tossed around a few suggestions and eventually settled on a restaurant they both liked.

"Is that okay with you?" Mindy asked him. "Do you like Chinese? Some people don't."

"It's fine. I'll see you there."

27

Zachary looked at the time on his phone after hanging up. He would have to head out before too long to be in Clintock in time to meet his siblings for dinner. He was going to be meeting his brother and sister for the first time in decades. He was glad Mindy had talked Vince into meeting the same day. He didn't know if he could have slept if it hadn't been scheduled until the next day.

He tapped the phone to call Kenzie. She picked up almost immediately.

"Zachary?" Her tone was sharp. She was obviously worried that something bad had happened. He'd had a breakdown and had to go back to the hospital again. Or he'd found out bad news about Tyrrell.

"It's okay," Zachary assured her. "I just talked to Vince and Mindy."

It took her half a second to connect who Vince and Mindy were. "Your brother and sister?"

"Yes. I found their numbers in Tyrrell's stuff."

"Wow! That's great. How did it go?"

"It was pretty short, but they both seemed... nice." Not angry like Joss. Neither one seemed to think that it was Zachary's fault they ended up in foster care like they did. Neither seemed upset about it.

They might not have reached out to Zachary, but they had been responsive enough to calling them. Cautious about letting someone new into their lives, but maybe that's how people who had been raised in good homes thought. They didn't just jump into new relationships without consideration. They thought about whether it was someone who would fit in their lives or not.

"I'm glad. This is a red-letter day for you."

If only it hadn't been because he was looking for Tyrrell. Just a call from Vince and Mindy because they wanted the chance to meet him.

"Yeah. I'm going to meet them for supper. I would wait and take you along, but I don't suppose you can break away from the office yet."

"You're eating now?"

"Driving. Soon. We're meeting in Clintock."

"Oh. Yeah, you don't want to be out there too late, then. No, you go ahead and meet with them yourself. I'll go with you next time. When it's just a social visit."

"Are you sure? I could ask them to change the time."

"No. Go ahead and do what you set up. You know that it's harder for you the more people there are. Unless you think you need me for moral support. But I'd rather stay out of the way."

Zachary was glad for the drive to Clintock. The highway driving soothed his racing brain and helped him to not obsess over what he was going to say to his brother and sister over and over again all the way there. He was calm and focused, even though he was still worried about what they would think of him and what he would say and if he would find out anything that would help with the investigation into Tyrrell's disappearance. It was a momentous occasion, a red-letter day, as Kenzie had put it. But it could go horribly wrong.

He was in Clintock before he was ready for it. And glancing at the time on his phone, he saw that he had misjudged how quickly he could get there. When he didn't have Kenzie in the car to slow him down and remind him not to go too much over the speed limit, he tended to go a little faster.

He drove around for a few minutes, remembering streets he had lived on, schools he had attended, and many of the other things that had happened there. He was glad he didn't live in the same town anymore or any of the others that he had spent time in as a child or teenager. He wasn't sure how he would keep from being overwhelmed with memories.

As it was, he still had to deal with memories of his life with Bridget. Maybe someday, he and Kenzie could buy an acreage or a house in another of the nearby towns to have more physical distance between him and Bridget and their shared memories.

Eventually, he didn't want to see anything else in Clintock, and he found the restaurant that Vince and Mindy had suggested. He wasn't sure if it was new or just new to him. It wasn't like he'd eaten at a lot of restaurants when he had lived there. Few foster families would dare take their kids out to a restaurant, especially not the type that Zachary tended to end up in, where they were experienced in dealing with children with serious behavioral problems.

He walked into the restaurant and looked around, but didn't see any faces that looked familiar. He assumed that Vince and Mindy would bear some resemblance to him, Tyrrell, Joss, or Heather. They all came from the same stock. A hostess approached Zachary, smiling. "Table for one…?"

He shook his head. "I'm meeting friends. I don't know if they're here yet, I think I'm still too early. Do you have a reservation for Goldman? I mean…" Zachary scrambled, trying to recall it. "Miller?"

She looked at the form in front of her. "For three?"

"Yeah."

"Come this way." She escorted him to a table and placed menus on it. "Do you want to order a drink now? Or wait for the others?"

"A water, please. I'll order something else when they get here."

"I'll have someone bring it to you." She smiled pleasantly and left him there to his thoughts.

Trying not to look like he was impatient, Zachary scrolled through his social networks on his phone, glancing toward the door every few minutes. While he didn't want to look like he was anxious, he also didn't want to look more interested in his phone than in meeting his siblings.

He heard the door open again and looked up. This time, it was a man and woman of approximately the right age, the woman with long dark hair and the man sporting a blond buzz cut. Zachary stood up, and they saw him immediately. Mindy pointed, and the two of them approached.

"Zachary?" Mindy asked, tilting her head to the side slightly as she studied him.

"Yes." Zachary put out his hand to shake, not wanting to force unwanted closeness on either of them. "Mindy, it's great to meet you. Vince."

Mindy shook, but then pulled him closer to put one arm around his shoulders, keeping her body slightly separated from his. "Nice to meet you, bro."

Vince kept it to a handshake, but nodded his head in agreement. "Yeah. This is… this is really something."

They all sat down. Zachary studied the two of them. He couldn't see the children they had been when they had been separated. Too much time had passed. With Tyrrell, he had recognized the eyes, still exactly the same as six-year-old Tyrrell's had been. With Heather, it had taken longer to catch a glimpse of the little girl he had known. Almost a teenager when they had been separated. Every now and then, he saw a spark of that little blond-haired gamine. Joss was nothing like she had been and nothing like their mother. Her face was prematurely old from smoking, drinking, and drug abuse. Sharp lines, almost anorexic, after being on drugs for so many years.

He closed his eyes for a minute and pictured Mindy, scrunched up in his arms as he fed her a bottle, coaxing her to take it, tricking her by getting her sucking on his finger and then sliding the nipple into its place. Of course there was nothing of that baby left in the woman seated across from him. He thought about Vince with a teddy bear or truck, following the older kids around, determined not to be left behind. The way he pursed his little mouth in determination.

There was just a shadow of that determination on his face again. Zachary smiled at him.

"You look a lot like Tyrrell," Vince observed. "But skinnier."

"Yeah. There's a resemblance."

"You don't look like me. Neither of you does."

Zachary nodded in agreement. He didn't know what else to say.

A waitress came over and took their drink orders. Mindy lifted her brows at Zachary's soft drink order. "Are you... 'on the wagon' too?"

"Not exactly. I don't drink much because it can cause problems with my meds. Some of them. Safer to just not have any."

Though he was hoping to share a couple of glasses of wine with Kenzie one evening and see how his night went. At the Lodge, when he had been out of his meds, they'd had a very pleasant time self-medicating with a couple of drinks. Nothing excessive, but it had definitely been better for their physical relationship than the drugs that tended to suppress his drive. His and Kenzie's intimate relationship had been turned upside down by the torture he had endured at the hands of a sadistic serial killer and the meds he needed to take to stay on an even keel.

"Zachary?"

He shifted his attention back to Mindy, blinking and shaking his head slightly. "Sorry. Trip down memory lane."

"It's a bit weird, isn't it?" she agreed. "Though... maybe more so for you. For me... I don't remember anything from before foster care, so it's like meeting someone that you always knew existed but have never met before."

"I remember you," Zachary said, nodding. "I remember feeding you and changing your diapers."

She got pink, laughing. "Well, isn't that great!"

Zachary chuckled. "All of the older kids helped with the younger ones." His own ears were burning, probably bright red.

"I don't know if I remember or not," Vince said, tilting his head to one side and then the other, looking at Zachary. "I mean, you didn't look like this, of course..."

"No. Heather says I look 'just the same,' but I think you can take that with a grain of salt."

"Unless you were a very ugly child."

"Vince!" Mindy elbowed him.

Vince grimaced. "I didn't mean you're ugly. I just meant that your face on a child's body…"

Mindy elbowed him again. They all laughed.

The waitress brought their drinks, and they browsed over the menu. But the two of them already knew what was good on the menu, and Zachary agreed on the approach of ordering several different dishes to share. That was always best at a Chinese restaurant.

Orders placed, Mindy looked at her brothers, growing more serious.

28

So, we know a little bit about you from what Tyrrell has said. I don't know if he's shared anything about us with you?"

Zachary shook his head. "He really hasn't done anything more than mention being in touch with you. I figured you wanted your privacy."

Vince and Mindy exchanged looks. Zachary tried to interpret them, to figure out if they were hiding something or if there were something they wanted to share. But he wasn't sure. Maybe a combination of both.

"It's probably more that Tyrrell knows us better," Mindy said. "Since we grew up together. He was really excited about finding you and told us everything he could, but he wouldn't have been excited about us since we were... the siblings he already knew. We were old news. He'd never been without us for long."

Zachary nodded. "Maybe that was it."

He suspected it probably went deeper than that, but it didn't matter. Now they were together and could find out about each other firsthand.

"You guys were all together growing up, right? And the two of you go by Miller."

They looked at each other and nodded. "Yeah. We always wanted the same name as our parents. They really did raise us, not... *your* mom and dad."

"Right. You probably don't even remember *them*."

"No. We were always with the Millers, so..."

They didn't offer whether the Millers had adopted them or whether they had just assumed their names. "But Tyrrell... he didn't change his name? I mean, I haven't ever seen his ID. I just assumed he went by Goldman. Doesn't he?"

"Yeah," Mindy agreed. "Tyrrell was always different."

More exchanged looks, communicating with each other without speaking, feeling out what they were going to tell Zachary and how they would say it.

"He had trouble from the time we were placed," Vince said. He drummed his fingers on the table. "I guess we all had issues. But Tyrrell was the oldest, had been with our bio parents the longest. He acted out a lot. Mom and Dad—the Millers—said that we had some trouble settling in too. We did a lot of the stuff that kids coming into foster care do... crying, throwing things, wetting the bed. But we still had each other. We hadn't lost everything. Tyrrell... he got in trouble a lot at school, talked back to the Millers and wouldn't follow their rules, no matter how many times they imposed consequences. Mom said he was really smart, but he acted wild at school. Made friends with the wrong kids. Got in fights."

Zachary had experienced a lot of disruption at school too. Being in a new place with new rules, trying to make new friends, being bullied. A lot of the stuff they blamed on him had really been started by the bullies. But the teachers and administrators didn't see what kind of people the bullies really were. Zachary was new and an obvious choice for the role of troublemaker. As much as he tried to behave at school and at his foster homes, he was always getting off on the wrong foot.

His learning disabilities and ADHD didn't help. High anxiety and what doctors later diagnosed as PTSD magnified everything. All of his worries, emotions, and reactions. Being constantly hypervigilant. ADHD meds helped him focus better and stay in his seat at school, but when he started rebounding from them at home around suppertime and before bed, the ADHD symptoms returned ten times as bad, right when he was supposed to be studying or doing his homework. He constantly fought, cried, or argued with his foster siblings, parents, and tutors.

"But they didn't take him away and put him into... Bonnie Brown or another home," Zachary said. "He was still allowed to stay with you?"

"They had him into programs all the time, but not residential. After school, weekends, holidays... they'd put him into another camp or group or therapy... or just respite to give the Millers a break. It was pretty tough on them," Vince explained.

"And him," Zachary pointed out.

"I guess. As kids, we didn't really understand what was going on, and I don't know how much Mom and Dad did. They didn't really know much about things like attachment and complex PTSD back then. It was all just... discipline. Tough love. Trying to... get him to settle down and be a part of the family."

"To break him."

Mindy held up her hands. "It wasn't like that. They love him and always just wanted him to be a real part of the family. But he didn't want to be."

"He *couldn't* be."

She shrugged. "Maybe you understand it better from his perspective than we ever could. When we were little, I couldn't understand why he was always mad and refusing to follow the rules and wasn't close to Mom and Dad like we were. Everybody kind of thought he was just a brat, or later, a rebellious teen. Our parents did everything they could, but he was sort of..."

"A lost cause," Zachary finished.

They both just looked at him. Even now, Zachary wondered how much they understood about how it must have been for Tyrrell. About how his brain chemistry was actually different from theirs because of the things he had gone through. That it wasn't a choice to be damaged. He just was.

"When did the drinking start?"

Mindy looked at Vince. Not about a shared secret this time, but calling on his recollections. He was older. He probably remembered it better.

"I'm not sure," Vince admitted. "I guess there was a lot of stuff going on that no one bothered to tell us because we were just kids. They wanted to shelter us from it. And maybe they didn't know when he started drinking until later on. It's always been something that he's tried to keep hidden."

"When he was a teenager?" Zachary suggested. "Drinking with friends? Or did he start raiding the liquor cabinet before that?"

Vince's lips pressed together and he shook his head. "I don't know. Really. Mom and Dad did have alcohol around, so he might have started with stealing from them. By the time we were teenagers, there was no alcohol allowed in the house. Not even cough syrup. So they knew then... but Tyrrell had already been in and out of a few different programs by then. Boot camps, that kind of thing."

Zachary nodded. He'd seen it happen. He had been in and out of Bonnie Brown from an early age; it was easiest to just send him back there, where they knew him and he knew and understood the rules and routines. There wasn't any point in trying those boot camp programs, which were mostly for kids who were with their biological families or long-term placements like Tyrrell had been. Kids with a family who really wanted him to be a part of it. Not kids who were throwaways, who it was easier to dispose of than to try to reclaim.

"But it wasn't all bad," Mindy said. "You know, he did really good in some of those programs. They got him back on track with school. He got his grades up and graduated and even went on to college."

"Yeah. I heard he had a degree."

"Did he tell you that?" Mindy asked. "He doesn't usually talk about it. Like he is embarrassed about it. Or doesn't think he deserves it."

"No, I heard it from someone else."

Mindy nodded. "Yeah. I don't know why he would never talk about it. He worked really hard to earn it. It wasn't like someone just handed it to him, you know. He got scholarships and bursaries, and he worked over the summer to earn money for tuition. We didn't have a lot of money, and he wouldn't let Mom and Dad pay for it.

Said to keep the money for us." She looked in Vince's direction. "To make sure that we could get a post-secondary education too. He was always really good to us."

Zachary smiled, his heart swelling at Tyrrell's generosity. "It was always up to the older kids to look after the younger ones."

The waitress arrived balancing a huge platter filled with smaller dishes. She smiled and greeted them cheerfully and set everything out on the table, pushing dishes and glasses around to make room for it all. They all dished up.

Mindy looked at the small servings on Zachary's plate. "I thought you said Chinese was okay. If you don't like it, you should have said so."

"I just don't have a very big appetite. Because of the meds. It's hard for me to eat much at a time."

"You could eat more than that," Vince countered.

Zachary shook his head. "This is a lot, actually. I might have taken too much."

They rolled their eyes at each other.

"So, what was it like?" Mindy asked. "Living with... our biological family? Your mom and dad and all of the kids?"

Zachary swallowed, looking down at the food.

29

Zachary took a deep breath and blew it out. He should have been expecting that. He had come to learn more about Tyrrell and to figure out the directions he should go to find him but, of course Mindy and Vince would be curious about the family they had come from. The home that had produced their rebellious older brother. The parents they had escaped.

"Well, I guess you know from whatever your social worker told you and how Tyrrell behaved that it wasn't the best home. Things were pretty tough. It was nice having brothers and sisters to play with and get help from. I missed that when I went into the system. Never had that connection again. But the rest of it... Mom and Dad got drunk and fought with each other. They were really strict and... disciplinarians. Mom had, I guess, postpartum depression every time she had a baby. Wouldn't want to get out of bed for weeks afterward, so we had to try to look out for you ourselves. I guess that's why we were all so close. We looked after each other. Tried to keep each other out of trouble."

"And then when they split us up, Tyrrell didn't have that anymore."

"No, I guess not. He had you, but he would have known that he needed to look after you. You weren't old enough to do anything."

Zachary looked at Vince. "You guys probably played together, though. You and T used to play together."

"Yeah, we did. I don't remember a lot, but I remember playing with cars together, playing cops and robbers running around outside, stuff like that. We got bikes when I was five and T was seven and were a menace to the neighborhood."

Zachary smiled. He remembered having a bike at home. It was probably one of the girls' cast-offs, but he didn't know the difference. Or maybe it had been stolen from someone else. He remembered the freedom of being able to bike around, riding to the park or the store or other places that had previously been out of range on foot.

Vince put down his fork for a moment, frowning. "Our social worker didn't say anything about any of that." He raised his brows at Zachary. "She said... that our mom was sick and couldn't take care of all of us. And our dad had to work, so he couldn't. That's why we were placed with the Millers."

Zachary stared at him, trying to comprehend this. "But... you knew about the fire. You knew why you were really put there."

"We knew there was a fire," Vince said slowly, "and that's why we didn't have a *home*. But that we wouldn't be able to go back, even when they rebuilt the house, because our mom was sick."

"She was... not sick. Not that way. Not like she had cancer or something. She was overwhelmed, I think, having to take care of six kids. And she and Dad drank. There was... lots of violence."

"So social services took us away."

"No. It was Mom." Zachary shook his head. "Tyrrell didn't tell you this? I talked to him about it."

"Tell us what?"

"About... how she broke up the family. She said that she didn't want us anymore. Couldn't handle us. Me especially." Zachary stared down at his plate. "I caused so much trouble. She said I was incorrigible. That it was all my fault."

Mindy leaned forward. "That *what* was your fault?"

"That we had to go into care. With me burning down the house..." There was a lump in his throat that was difficult to speak around. "That was the last straw. She didn't want anything to do with us."

Mindy and Vince were both staring at him, open-mouthed. Zachary felt sick. He had assumed they knew all of this. Their history. Why they had entered foster care in the first place. The social worker and their foster parents would have explained it to them. Tyrrell would have told them about the fire if they couldn't remember anything about it themselves. Especially after Tyrrell and Zachary had reunited and Zachary had helped fill in the gaps in his memory.

"You burned the house down?" Vince repeated.

Zachary closed his eyes. "Yeah. I was... I decorated the tree after everyone went to bed. Put out all of the other decorations. There were candles. Mom said we would light them on Christmas Eve, but they had a big fight... I thought she would be happy if everything was done, and everybody could have a... a magical..." He swallowed, unable to get the word *Christmas* out. "A magical day. Like on TV."

"So you lit the candles," Vince filled in.

"Yeah. Last time I ever lit a fire or handled matches." He took a drink of water, trying to irrigate the desert in his mouth. "Ever."

"We didn't know that." Mindy shook her head. "I always thought... it must have been electrical wiring or a lightning strike."

"No. It was me."

"That must have been awful for you. But no one was hurt. That was lucky."

Zachary nodded. He didn't push up his sleeves to show them the scars. Maybe one day, he would tell them that part.

"I can't believe that a mother would say something like that, though," Mindy said, shaking her head. "That's just... it's cruel. I can't imagine anyone saying that to their child. And she just... got rid of us? Like a litter of kittens?"

"I suppose we should be happy she didn't drown us," Zachary joked. But the joke fell flat. He knew it wasn't funny.

"Maybe our social worker didn't know what really happened," Vince suggested. "She might have gotten the story wrong. Misunderstood what had happened. Why we were in foster care."

Zachary chewed the inside of his cheek. "I thought... Tyrrell said that you had Mrs. Pratt. To begin with, anyway. Didn't you?"

"Yeah, that's right. Mrs. Pratt."

"She knew what happened. She was my caseworker too. She's the one Mom talked to. Told her that she didn't want us back. Mrs. Pratt brought her to see me at the—brought her to see me, to see if she would change her mind about giving up on the family. And she wouldn't, said that she didn't want to ever see us again. That we shouldn't be a family... that I should be in jail."

30

T hey were all silent, trying to reconcile the truths they had each grown up with.

Zachary immediately understood the fiction Mrs. Pratt had told the children. What benefit would there be to telling them that their parents simply didn't want them anymore? It was kinder to tell them a story that would make them feel better. A mother who was sick and unable to give them the care they needed. A father struggling just to make ends meet. Close enough to the truth.

But he wondered whether she had told the same fiction to the Miller parents. Had they thought they were getting children from a loving home devastated by illness? If so, it was no wonder they couldn't understand Tyrrell's behavior. Zachary knew that many of his issues stemmed from the abuse they had all suffered. They had grown up in a war zone, anxious about any raised voice, any hint of trouble. There had been physical abuse and neglect, money spent on alcohol and cigarettes rather than putting food on the table. The older children had tried to protect the younger children from the abuse they themselves had suffered, but were not always successful.

"I don't know what to think of this," Mindy said. "How could they not tell us any of this?" She bent her head and ate a few bites of her Chinese food as if it were a chore she had to do. "And..." she looked up at Zachary. "Tyrrell knew this?"

Zachary thought about it. What Tyrrell had remembered when he and Zachary had been reunited on Christmas Eve a year before. What things he had already known and what Zachary had needed to tell him or remind him of.

"He knew... some of it. Not everything. He didn't know what she said to me about not deserving to be a family. That was after we were split up. But he knew... that they fought. He knew that the fire was... because of me. He would have known that it wasn't because our mom was sick." He rubbed the space between his eyes that was beginning to throb with pain. "He was six. Maybe he believed what they told him. But he knew... to be scared. He knew about hiding when they fought. And about..." Zachary swallowed painfully. He couldn't get another bite of the restaurant food down. He took another gulp of water. "He knew about calling 9-1-1. And what would happen if the police came." Those things, he knew. He remembered Tyrrell asking, that last, horrible night if they should call 9-1-1. And Zachary had told him no.

Everything would have been different if he had said yes. Zachary probably wouldn't have had the opportunity to put out the Christmas decorations and to light the candles. Would his mother still have put them into the system if the house hadn't burned down? In another day? Another week? Or would they have stayed with her?

Sooner or later, he was sure that one of his parents would have killed the other. Maybe it was better that things had happened how and when they did. The little children got put into a loving home while at least two of them were still young enough to heal from the trauma. None of them had had to witness one parent killing the other. Or deciding to take out the whole family, as some parents had been known to do. At least Vince and Mindy had survived relatively unscathed.

Mindy reached across the table and touched Zachary's hand tentatively. "I'm sorry."

Zachary swallowed and licked his lips and tried to find something to say.

"I'm sorry that all that stuff happened to you," Mindy went on, "and that you had to explain it to us. I didn't mean to make you... relive something horrible."

Zachary shrugged as if it didn't matter. He used his knife and fork to cut pieces of meat and vegetables into smaller bits, so that it looked like he was eating, but he knew he wouldn't be able to get anything down.

There wasn't much more to say. Mindy and Vince had told Zachary about how they had grown up and how Tyrrell had coped in foster care. Zachary had told them more about where they had come from. What they had escaped, but Tyrrell had not.

Zachary had his notepad out and was jotting down the bits and pieces he had learned from them.

"So... T went to college and got a degree. In what?"

"Uh..." Mindy frowned, trying to recall the details. "Behavioral Science." She said it with an uptick in tone, as if she were asking a question. Vince nodded his agreement.

"Behavioral Science," Zachary repeated, trying to write it down but miserably failing in remembering how to spell 'behavior.' "So... what's that? It sounds like... FBI or something."

"They have a Behavioral Science Unit," Vince agreed, pointing at Zachary. "I used to tease Tyrrell about that, when he was going to school, and when he eventually earned it. Used to ask him if he was going to join the FBI."

"It's like... social work, addiction, psychology, that kind of thing," Mindy contributed, still frowning. Then she gave a little shrug and rolled her eyes.

Zachary raised his eyebrows at her. "Tyrrell studied addiction?"

"And passed with flying colors," Vince blurted, earning another sharp elbow to the ribs. He laughed and then looked away, maybe embarrassed by his own behavior. "I know, it's bizarre, right? I mean, he's learning this stuff at the college level, but it doesn't help him to overcome alcoholism himself? He needed it... but he couldn't use it in his own life."

"He stayed sober all the way through college," Mindy offered. "That's the longest he's ever gone. A few months, a year, and then he's off on a binge again. If he understands how it all works, why can't he use that?" Her voice was intense, filled with frustration at her brother's self-destructive behavior.

"Addiction is complex," Zachary said lamely. "It's not just about... choosing not to have a drink."

They were all silent, Mindy and Vince still pushing food around their plates and picking at what was left. Zachary had given up on his. He wrote down notes and questions, trying to see through everything Mindy and Vince knew about Tyrrell to the key that would lead Zachary to him. They had already told him more than once that they did not know where he went to drink or who he drank with. What further help was any of the rest of what they had told him?

"I'm glad that I found you," Zachary told his younger siblings. "Do you mind if... we stay in touch? Even though you have another family?"

"Sure," Mindy agreed, and they both nodded. "We've kind of left it all to Tyrrell. He was really the one interested in finding everyone, in making all of these family connections. But yes... I'd like to get to know you better."

"He was the one who found Heather and Joss too, right? Have you met either of them?"

"No." Mindy glanced over at Vince. "Not any of the others."

Zachary cocked his head, struck by the wording of her comment. Not "either" of the others, but "any" of the others. "Any?" he repeated. "Heather or Joss?"

Mindy nodded. "Or the others."

31

There was something in Zachary's ears, like a humming or a buzzing, only he couldn't identify what it was. He couldn't exactly hear it, but it blocked everything else out too, so he suddenly couldn't hear the buzz of conversation in the restaurant or anything other than the sound of his own heartbeat.

He stared at Mindy, trying to reconcile her words with what he knew. He had to make sense of it somehow. Mindy must have meant that the Millers fostered or adopted other children as well, and Tyrrell had been in contact with them, had been concerned about not losing touch with the other children he had grown up with.

Zachary tried to form words, but couldn't get them out. He took a drink of water. He could see Vince's and Mindy's mouths moving, their glances toward him, but he thought they must be communicating silently again. He swished a mouthful of water around his dry mouth, swallowed it, and cleared his throat.

"What others?" he asked.

"The other brothers and sisters."

"Tyrrell's? Other foster kids?"

Mindy shook her head. Her brows were drawn down in concentration, but they made her look angry or grumpy instead of studious.

She sighed and sat back in her seat. "I can't believe Tyrrell didn't tell you."

"Didn't tell me what? What other children are you talking about?"

Maybe Tyrrell had fathered other children with a woman other than Lindsey, and Mindy was talking about them. Tyrrell's kids. That would make more sense. Maybe Tyrrell was even shacked up somewhere with another woman. He was free from Lindsey; there was no reason he couldn't be. He might have other children that he hadn't told Zachary about.

But why wouldn't he have told his brother about them? He had been eager to tell him about Alisha and Mason. Keen to have Zachary meet them. If there were more, Zachary would have been happy to meet them too. He couldn't figure out why it would be a problem for Tyrrell. Even if they were older or the same age as Alisha and Mason, who was Zachary to judge? He wasn't the morality police.

Mindy scratched at a piece of dried food stuck to the table. "Tyrrell did one of those DNA tests. You know, where you can find out information about your ancestry, but they all connect to big databases now where everybody else who has had their DNA done—and has made it public—shows up. So you can find out that you have a third cousin in Russia or that your grandpa fathered a kid in Vietnam, or whatever."

Zachary's brain caught on Vietnam. Tyrrell hadn't been to Vietnam. No one he knew had served in Vietnam or even visited it. Certainly not anyone in his family.

"Well, you know, he did it so he could find out more about your family. The Goldman family. Where they were from and if he had any blood relatives around here. He was hoping that you or Jocelyn or Heather would have done yours, and it would be a really easy way to connect with you. Because you can just message each other and say, 'Hey, we both submitted DNA to this database, and you must be my long-lost brother...'"

Vince snorted. He was sitting back, arms folded. He clearly disapproved of Tyrrell having done what he had. Maybe as foster kids, they had been warned never to have anything to do with their biological family. Despite being told that they were in foster care because their mother was sick, maybe they had been told that Zachary didn't want to meet them or that their identities had to remain a secret if they wanted to stay with the Millers, or some lie like that. Or maybe Vince had divorced himself from his biological family, believing that he was better off with the Millers, and it was best not to ask questions or to dig into the past, in case he didn't like the answers he found there.

Mindy looked at Vince, waiting to see if he had something to say, but Vince shook his head and waited for her to continue.

"And none of you had registered in any of these databases, but there were other hits. Other people who had registered who showed up as brothers or sisters."

"How is that possible?" Zachary said stupidly. He knew all of his brothers and sisters. There had been six of them, and now he had been reunited with all of them. There were no more children in their family.

"Because your parents didn't stop having kids," Vince said, his voice hard.

"They stayed together? With each other?"

Mindy shook her head. "Not with each other. With other people. So there are half siblings. But… they are still siblings. Still biologically related."

Zachary tried to wrap his mind around this. It wasn't like it was the first time that the thought had occurred to him that his parents were still young enough when the family broke up that they could have had other children. As a kid, he had fantasized about having more family. If he couldn't be reunited with the brothers and sisters he knew, then there could be others. Or even just kids he got along with in his foster families. Kids who were more than just roommates or passing acquaintances, but who felt like real family, like Tyrrell.

But he hadn't thought seriously about it as an adult. His parents had to know what a mistake it would be to have more children. Hadn't their experiences taught them anything? His mother would understand that having another pregnancy would send her into the throes of depression. His father would know that he didn't want rug rats underfoot and throwing up on his things. Kids just made noise, fought with each other, and got in the way. He knew that he would rather spend his money on drinking than kids, so why would he have more?

"Why would they have more kids?"

Vince shook his head. "I didn't really think about it before. I mean, people do. They get together with someone new and decide to start another family. But... that was before I knew what you were saying... if they were such bad parents the first time, why would they go on and have more?"

"I don't know." Zachary shook his head in wonder. It was amazing to find out that he had more siblings than he had known about. But when he thought about the way they had lived before the fire, he was horrified. Why would his parents go on having other children? "Do you... know them? Have you met them?"

"No. We were happy with our family." Vince made a gesture that took in himself and Mindy, and maybe the absent Tyrrell as well. "We didn't feel like we needed to meet anyone else. It was Tyrrell. All Tyrrell. He was so determined to... find *everyone*."

When Zachary had first met Tyrrell a year before, Mr. Peterson had commented on the need of foster and adopted children to make biological connections, to feel anchored and to know where they had come from. Tyrrell had brushed this idea off without much comment, saying that his biological connection had been to his children. That he hadn't been as driven to find his siblings or his parents.

But his actions belied that statement. He was the one who had searched out Zachary. Who had searched out each of his siblings. Zachary was the private investigator. It would have been natural for him to track down his family members, to know where they were, even if he decided not to contact them. But he never had. Tyrrell had been the one to track them down and bring them back together.

"So Tyrrell has met them? All of them?"

"I don't know if he's met *all* of them," Vince said. "But he's met some of them. And there could be others... not everyone registers their DNA in these databases or makes it available for family matching."

"Do you know their names? Where they are? How old?"

Vince chuckled darkly. "As far as I know, they're all younger. But I don't know. I'm not sure Tyrrell would have told us if he found older siblings other than you three."

Mindy looked at a sparkling watch on her wrist. "I guess... we're going to be here a bit longer. You want to get coffee or a nightcap?"

32

It was much later than Zachary had expected before he was finally on his way home. He called Kenzie on Bluetooth once he got into the car, reaching her just as he merged onto the highway.

"Hey. I was expecting you home," Kenzie said. "I guess things must have gone pretty well if you were visiting this late. Were you there until the restaurant closed?"

Zachary laughed. "Actually, yes. And hopefully, I haven't had so much coffee that I have to make a pit stop on the way home."

"Well, at least you won't fall asleep at the wheel. How are you doing?"

"Okay. I'll tell you about it when I get home."

She didn't answer for a moment, then agreed. "Sure, of course. It will be easier to tell me everything when we are face to face. But it was okay? You're not upset?"

"It was okay."

She probably didn't fail to notice that he didn't say he was not upset.

Zachary didn't think he was upset, but he wasn't sure what he was feeling. He was feeling somewhat unsettled. But he wasn't sure how to describe it or if there was even a word for the kind of stress and letdown and confusion and disappointment and excitement that he was feeling. It was all mixed together so thoroughly.

"Drive carefully. You're not too tired, right?"

"No, I'm not tired. I'm never tired while I'm driving."

"Well, not usually, but sometimes it does happen."

He knew that he'd fallen asleep when they had been on their way to the Lodge. Not while he was driving, though; Kenzie had already taken the wheel when he conked out. But she had noticed that he was too tired to be safe anymore. It was a good thing she had taken over before he drove off the road.

He cleared his throat. "That's different. I was still recovering."

"I know. And now you're just out of the hospital and on new meds and trying to get used to a new schedule. You could still have problems. Just pay attention. And if you start feeling like you might be too tired, pull over. Give me a call. I can come to get you. Or you can walk around or stop at a convenience store for more coffee. But don't just keep driving."

"Okay."

"Okay?" she persisted, wanting to hear it again, wanting him to be more emphatic in his response so that she knew he had really heard her and would take her advice.

"Okay. I will," he agreed.

"Don't forget, I've seen what happens to people who fall asleep at the wheel. And to the people who happen to be in their way."

Kenzie did have a slightly different perspective on things that could kill a person than the average girlfriend.

***

When he got home, he sat in his car in front of the house for a minute, reviewing the day in his mind. It had been a long day. Was he any further ahead than he had been when he had first started? Did he have any concrete evidence that would help him to find Tyrrell? There were directions for him to investigate, but he didn't know where any of them would lead him, and if they would lead him toward or away from Tyrrell.

He hoped that the others were right, and that Tyrrell's disappearance was just the same as his other disappearances, the results of a binge. But was it? Or had something different happened this time? If it was a binge, was it just the natural progression of falling off the wagon when he had been at the Lodge? And had it just been the stress of the things that had happened at the Lodge that had made him start drinking again?

Or was he just assuming that Tyrrell had started drinking again at the Lodge because that was where he had noticed it? It was entirely possible that he'd been drinking for days or weeks before that. He was a closet drinker. He had plenty of experience hiding it. At the Lodge, it had been different. Tyrrell only had one source of alcohol, unless he had also brought some with him. He couldn't go out anywhere to get more, so he'd had to consume what was in the liquor cabinet in the cabin. And that was what Zachary had noticed. If Zachary hadn't been looking for something to calm his nerves in the absence of his medications, he probably wouldn't have looked at the bottles and noticed how the levels had gone down and wouldn't have been tipped off to Tyrrell's drinking. Tyrrell certainly hadn't looked or acted drunk.

Zachary had shut off the car and was starting to get cold. He climbed out and walked up the front sidewalk and into the house.

"The conquering hero returns," Kenzie quipped, smiling at him.

She was in her cozy pajamas, a blanket pulled over her lap as she sat on the couch, either watching TV or doing something on her phone.

"Hi." He bent down to kiss her, then sat beside her, pulling her over to cuddle against him. She was warm and soft, and he loved the shower-fresh smell of her. "Sorry to be so late."

"You couldn't very well leave in the middle of the discussion. Then you would just have to go back again tomorrow or some other time to finish. I take it you must have found a lot to talk about?"

He noticed she didn't ask whether he had gotten any leads on

Tyrrell's disappearance. Being reunited with his younger siblings was important in and of itself, whether he'd gotten the information he needed or not.

But it was Tyrrell he couldn't stop thinking about. Tyrrell who needed his help. Or not, as the case may be. Was he just voluntarily missing? Part of the street population or living out of his car or a shelter? Was everyone else right, and Tyrrell would eventually show up on his own and act as if nothing had happened? Or was he being held against his will? Or worse, hurt or sick?

He leaned his head against Kenzie's. "Did you... have any time today to talk to the other morgues?"

She took his hand in hers and gave it a squeeze. "I would have called you right away if I had found anything. I talked to almost all of the Medical Examiner's Offices. I left messages with any of the ones I couldn't talk to directly. No one who I have talked to has had any John Does matching Tyrrell's description."

"Okay." Zachary blew his breath out. "That's good."

Of course, Jose and the other men that Archuro had killed had never shown up at the morgue, either. Because he had carefully hidden the bodies after he had finished with them. The medical examiner was still trying to identify the various remains that the police had managed to locate by searching Archuro's properties, the land around them, and Santiago's cemetery. Who knew how long that would take. Maybe most of them would never be identified. He had targeted undocumented immigrants. While Zachary had provided the police with a list of all of the men that John Mwangi had thought were the victims of the same serial killer, they didn't have pictures, DNA, fingerprints, or even good descriptions of all of them. Some of the killings went back years, and the friends or families of those missing men could no longer be identified and tracked down.

"It is good," Kenzie agreed firmly. Maybe she knew where Zachary's mind had gone. "So... did you have anything to tell me about Vince and Mindy? You said you would tell me about it when you got home. Unless you're too tired. Did you want to head to bed and talk about it in the morning when you are fresh?"

"No. I don't think I'll be able to get to sleep for a while yet. I need to unwind first."

"And take your meds. Maybe you should take them now so that they have time to start working before you go to bed."

Zachary shrugged, but didn't get up to get them. It was probably a good idea, but he didn't like changing his routine. He was used to taking them right before getting into bed.

33

He started at the beginning, telling her about meeting Vince and Mindy and the discussion that followed in pretty much the order that had taken place. He told her about Tyrrell as a child and youth, the trouble he'd gotten into, and the lies that the social worker had told.

"If that's what she told their foster parents too…" he trailed off.

"Then they didn't have a hope of giving Tyrrell the support he needed," Kenzie finished. "They didn't have a clue why he was behaving the way he was."

"Maybe it wouldn't have made any difference. Maybe they didn't understand trauma and attachment back then and would have approached it the same way whether they knew the reason for his behavior or not. But…"

"They had at least a vague understanding of the effects of abuse on a child. Maybe not as well as they do now, and maybe they didn't have all of the same therapeutic choices as they do now. Still, they would have at least had some understanding of the fact that he was scared and traumatized instead of just being… bad. A wayward child in need of correction."

"Yeah. But who knows. Maybe the parents knew everything, and she only kept it from Vince and Mindy so that they wouldn't feel bad about their biological mother not wanting them."

"That would be pretty crushing," Kenzie agreed. With her arm around Zachary's neck, she stroked his head and face. "I'm sorry that was something you had to deal with. On top of the fire and your injuries, in addition to being taken away from them, you had to deal with your own mother's cruelty. Face to face, not just told to you by someone when you were old enough to understand."

Zachary shrugged, not wanting to talk about that pain. He had told her about it before. He might not have talked much about how it had affected him, but she was an intelligent woman with a medical background, and she had seen how damaged and dysfunctional he was.

Kenzie waited. Not forcing him to tell her about his feelings, just waiting to see what else he had to tell her. Dr. B had encouraged them to get comfortable with silence. With leaving open spaces in the conversation so that they each had a chance to contemplate and offer something new without feeling like they were being interrogated. There were things he didn't want to talk about, but there were also things he wanted to share, that he hoped she could help him to process.

"There's something else. Tyrrell was the one who wanted to find the rest of us. He's the one who tracked me down, and Heather and Joss."

"Sure. He seemed like it meant a lot to him. And I know it meant a lot to you too, even though you weren't the one who went looking for him."

Zachary never could have looked for the others. Not when he knew how his actions had ruined their lives. It was good that Tyrrell's disappearance had forced him to reach out to Vince and Mindy. If they weren't interested in searching out their other siblings, it might have been a long time before they were reunited with Zachary. Like the TV shows he had seen where adoptees from the same family were reunited at seventy or eighty years old.

"He did one of those DNA searches to see if he could find us through their DNA matching database."

"But he didn't really need to do that. Not that many Zachary Goldmans in Vermont."

"Vince and Mindy said that… he found other siblings."

Kenzie turned to look at him, surprised. "*Other* siblings? You don't mean Heather and Joss, I gather."

"No. My mom and dad apparently… had more children after they broke up." It was easier to say that they broke up than that they had dissolved the entire family and put them into the care of the state. It made it sound more normal.

"Oh, wow. How many?"

"I don't know. Vince and Mindy weren't interested in meeting them. Only Tyrrell. I don't know how many there were or from which parent. How many were in the database, or how many he contacted."

"Because there are probably kids who hadn't sent in their DNA either."

"Yeah. It could be one of these cases where a dozen or more kids are scattered across the state. Or the country. Who knows."

"You could have some interesting family reunions!"

"You're telling me." Zachary nodded.

"So, how do you find these other siblings? I assume you're going to. Do you have to submit a sample to their database? I guess that would take weeks to get results, and you wouldn't want to have to wait that long. Can the police get access to the results?"

There had been a lot of stuff in the news about whether it was ethical for family DNA search companies to provide information to the police when they asked for it. Whether they needed a warrant and what kind of information they would be required to provide. And there had been legislation passed in some states, including Vermont, about whether the police were even allowed to use familial DNA in an investigation.

"I don't need to go to the police with it," he told her, hoping that it was true. "I have access to Tyrrell's email account, so I should be able to see who he was in contact with. I didn't know before to look for anyone but Vince or Mindy. I've already started to sort through some of his emails, but haven't gone back any farther than December. These siblings he found must have been before that. Maybe even before he found me, because I think he did the DNA search in hopes that it would lead him directly to us. Me and Heather and Joss."

"So he might have been in contact with them for more than a year. He never mentioned it to you?"

"No. Maybe he thought I would be upset. Or jealous. I don't know. But if he has another family... maybe they know something about where he is."

Kenzie nodded slowly. "You sometimes hear about bigamists who have two separate families that don't know about each other. I guess it could be the same with birth families and foster families... and other biological families. Tyrrell could have two completely different lives. He may not have been comfortable with letting them cross over."

"It's just weird. Because they're my family too. Or biological relations, anyway. You would think..."

"You never can tell what is going on in someone else's mind. Maybe he thought that if one family rejected him, he would still have the other. Maybe he has secrets from them. And secrets from you."

Zachary nodded. "I just wish he'd said something. I feel kind of... like the kid who doesn't get picked for a team at school. By his best friend."

Betrayed. Why would Tyrrell not have shared that part of his life with Zachary?

34

Zachary took his meds and did his best to get to sleep. He could feel them kicking in, but his brain didn't slow down enough for them to take effect. He realized that he was just waiting for Kenzie to fall asleep so that he could get up and log in to his computer to do some more research into Tyrrell's disappearance. He'd already made up his mind that he wasn't going to sleep. Finding Tyrrell was more important. Saving him from whatever force was keeping him away from his family.

But what if the thing that was keeping him away from his family was more family? How was Zachary supposed to judge which was more important?

What did it matter which Zachary thought was more important? The decision wouldn't be up to him. It was up to Tyrrell. If he didn't want to be with the siblings he had grown up with, but instead wanted to spend his time with the others he had found, Zachary wouldn't have any say in it. It was out of his hands.

He couldn't know whether that was the case until he found Tyrrell and talked to him face to face. If Tyrrell didn't want to talk to him, at least Zachary would find out at that point.

Kenzie's breathing was long and even. Zachary lay listening to it for a few minutes, both to make sure she was fast asleep and would not wake up when he got up, and to see if her regularly paced breathing would convince his brain that it was time for him to go to sleep too.

But he felt like bugs were crawling under his skin. He couldn't keep lying there any longer. He needed to get up and do something. He slipped out of bed and grabbed his clothes, pulling them on as he made his way to the living room so that he was nearly dressed by the time he got there. He pulled on his socks as he waited for his computer to finish waking up.

He didn't look at his own email inbox, but went straight to Tyrrell's. He first checked on any mail that had arrived since he had looked at it last. There was a good amount of spam, as there had been before, and Zachary just dragged it out to the appropriate folder. He half-expected there to be an email from Vince to Tyrrell, warning him that they had told Zachary his secret. But apparently, it hadn't occurred to Vince to do so, or he knew that Tyrrell wouldn't be checking his email. Or maybe he realized Zachary would see it before Tyrrell. Zachary had told him that was how he had gotten Vince's contact information.

There wasn't anything personal in the inbox after Zachary finished going through all of the spam and bulk mail. No one expected Tyrrell to be there. No one thought that he would return their emails.

That probably meant nothing. Just that email wasn't Tyrrell's preferred mode of communication. It wasn't Zachary's. It was much quicker for him to deal with people by phone than reading and writing emails.

He searched for "DNA" and ended up with a whole raft of emails from multiple companies regarding his DNA profile and matches with relatives. Zachary looked at the status line. *1-50 results of hundreds.* He rubbed his temples, trying to figure out how to process that many emails. Did that mean hundreds of different matches? Hundreds of people they were related to? He couldn't even comprehend that many relatives. He had grown up in a family of eight. And then he had lost them all. The prospect of having hundreds of relatives was overwhelming.

He clicked on the most recent "You have a new match" email,

hoping it would give him some idea of how to proceed. Would it say right in it that the person was a brother or a sister? There was little information in the email, just pointing him to an online account for the DNA database company. He clicked. At the login page, he filled in Tyrrell's email address and the password he had used for his email login. It didn't work. Rather than trying more passwords, he just clicked on the "forgot password" link, filled in the email address again, and clicked Send. There was a ding in Tyrrell's email, and Zachary opened it and clicked on the new email from the DNA company. He clicked a link, set the new password to be the same as Tyrrell's email password, and got in.

There was a button for DNA matches up at the top, and Zachary clicked it. The screen refreshed and then filled with row after row of names. They appeared to be sorted by priority, putting Tyrrell's closest DNA matches at the top, with more distant relatives farther down the page.

Up at the top were several rows with "possible sibling" listed as the relationship.

A couple of them had photos attached, and Zachary stared at the strangers who, according to their DNA, were blood relations. Maybe his brothers and sisters. He clicked, and the profiles were scanty, with no family trees attached. There were a few with Goldman as their last name. Zachary wasn't sure what his mother's maiden name had been. Had he ever known it? Back when he was in school and still living at home, he might have. But if he had, it had been lost during the inter-vening years, when he had passed through so many different families and each had, in some way, overwritten another piece of his past. The mental space required to remember the details of a new family and to find some way to relate to them had made him lose track of his own family, at least the less important parts of it. He kept his siblings' faces and names carefully protected, but extraneous details about his parents and about extended family members, if he had ever known of any, were gone.

There didn't seem to be any email addresses or phone numbers attached to the DNA match records. Had Tyrrell recorded them somewhere else? In his contacts database? Zachary opened his contact list and searched for the names of the siblings, but they did not appear on the list. If Tyrrell had connected to them, it must have been another way. Zachary returned to the DNA company and found an inbox in the top right corner. He clicked on that and found a long list of contact names down the side, some of them bolded with numbers of unread communications beside them. Zachary clicked on one randomly.

A conversation threaded down the page, only the headings of the first few messages visible. "Are you there?" and "You haven't responded," at the top. Zachary clicked on one of the emails farther down the page, expanding it. A conversation between Tyrrell and Jason Tooley. There were details confirmed between them about Berk Goldman, Tyrrell's and Zachary's father. And apparently, Jason Tooley's as well. He was younger than either of them, which was as Zachary had expected. A child his father had produced after the family dissolution. He couldn't help being a little bit relieved that Jason hadn't been fathered while Zachary's parents were still together, though he couldn't say what difference it made. He already knew the kind of person his father was. It didn't make any difference whether he was adulterous or not. What mattered was the way he had behaved and treated his children before the family had been broken up.

Zachary backed out and clicked on another conversation. Tyrrell and Mary Smith Burns making arrangements to meet each other.

To meet. So, Tyrrell had gone on to meet at least some of the siblings.

Zachary didn't know why the feeling of betrayal was so strong. The other siblings, Mary Smith Burns and the others, were just as much Zachary's blood relations as they were Tyrrell's. Why wouldn't he want to see them and maybe learn something? To make as many personal connections as he could. The larger his support network, the better.

He stuffed the feelings down. It was exciting, learning that he had a larger family than he had thought. Maybe, like Vince and Mindy, they were less damaged than Zachary had been. Normal people without the same issues as he and the older kids had. And Tyrrell. Why did he have to be afflicted with alcoholism? It wasn't fair, after all he had been through with his biological family and having such a difficult time settling into a foster family, that he'd had to deal with addiction as well. Not just a few scrapes as a teenager, as Zachary had hoped at first, but ongoing problems.

Zachary didn't want to contact the siblings through the DNA website. He didn't want to pretend to be Tyrrell and he didn't want a record of his investigation inside of Tyrrell's accounts. He would put everything back to the way that it had been when he found Tyrrell. Other than the new password on the DNA database login. But it was easy enough to forget a login password. Or for the company to say that you needed to set a new one because of a data breach. If Tyrrell tried to log in, he would hopefully just think that he had forgotten a password or hadn't recorded that he had changed it. Since it was the same password as Tyrrell's email, he might even cycle through several common passwords that he used and hit on it. If not, he would just do a password reset, and everything in his account would be as he had left it.

He wrote down each of the names of the new siblings, and birth years if they were available. Where available, he saved their pictures to his hard drive to upload them into an image search engine and find their social networks.

He was a private investigator. It wouldn't take him long to find contact information for each of them outside the limits of the DNA database.

35

Zachary awoke later on the couch, one of the throw blankets pulled around him. He blinked blearily at Kenzie, who bent down and kissed him on the cheek.

"You got some sleep?" Kenzie asked, though the answer to that was obvious.

Zachary straightened his body out, stretched, and sat up slowly. He rubbed his neck, trying to massage away any cricks from sleeping in such an uncomfortable position.

"I guess it all caught up eventually," he admitted, and covered a yawn. "The sleep meds. I couldn't settle down, but I must have closed my eyes at some point..."

"And zonked. You were snoring to beat the band. Thought I had a saber-toothed tiger in my living room. It's probably too soon to ask you how you're feeling this morning."

Zachary nodded. It took him a while to feel human after he woke up in the morning, then to analyze his body and determine whether he felt better or worse than any other day.

"If you're still tired, why don't you move to the bed? You'll be a lot more comfortable."

"I won't go back to sleep now."

"You sure? You were still pretty deep under, for you. Don't overextend yourself. You were up late."

"I'm sure. Want to make some calls this morning, catch people before they get too busy."

"Just be careful. Sorry, I don't mean to be a nag. Just want to make sure you're taking care of yourself."

"I'm fine." He met her eyes. "The trip back to the hospital was unnecessary."

"Okay. I'll leave you alone. You're the best one to know your own limits." She put up her hands, indicating her surrendering of the issue, and turned toward the kitchen. "I'm putting on some coffee. Do you want it before your shower?"

Zachary noticed belatedly that she had already showered herself, damp curls still clinging around her collar. That meant it was quite a bit later than he usually woke up. The effects of the sleep aid or his body adjusting to his new, out-of-the-hospital activities. He would prefer to just wash his face, comb his hair, and slap on some deodorant to jump back into his work, but Kenzie's mention of a shower was probably a subtle nudge that he was noticeably in need of one, so he'd better not skip it.

"I'll have half a cup before."

Kenzie nodded and measured grounds into the hopper. The machine would make single cups, travel mugs, or a full carafe, and they generally went through a full carafe in the morning. They waited while it brewed, making small talk. Kenzie didn't bring up Zachary's siblings, letting him think about it and be in control of whether he wanted to talk about it some more. They ran through the usual pleasantries about sleep, the weather, and the newest bodies in the morgue. Zachary drank a full cup of coffee instead of a half and headed for the shower.

"I'll probably be gone when you're out," Kenzie advised. "Have a good day. I'll see you tonight."

"Okay, see you then."

"Date night, if you can swing it."

"Is it?" Zachary thought about the week and realized it was

Friday. "Right. I'll try not to get stuck doing anything that will make me late."

He should probably put date night in his calendar, if it wasn't already there. Something to remind him that he had a commitment that night. He tried to keep it all on his phone, but sometimes even when he had an appointment reminder, he didn't pay any attention to its noises and vibrations. They needed to make an ADHD phone that would actually reach out and shake *him* when he had to be somewhere.

His shower was brief, though he did stand under the spray for a while thinking about the discoveries he had made the previous day and night and planning out how to follow through on it all. When he got out, Kenzie was gone as predicted, on her way to work or maybe already at the office. She had a better temperament for office work. She was good at showing up at regular hours, following a routine when she got there, and keeping Dr. Wiltshire and the rest of the support staff on track. Zachary didn't really mind the idea of dealing with dead bodies. For him, they were the key to solving some of the really difficult cases. But the rest of Kenzie's work, the administrative stuff, and the years of school it had taken for her to get there, that would have done Zachary in.

He sat down at his computer, pulling on a shirt and then sipping another cup of coffee. The first order of business was to see if he could catch Rhys before school. Zachary looked at the time and decided that it would still be too early for any classes to have started, so he sent Rhys a message.

Hey, can we meet later today? After school?

Three dots appeared on the screen almost immediately as Rhys composed his answer. A brief reply, a thumbs-up that the two of them getting together would be fine. More dots appeared, and then a large, red, capital *Y. Why?*

"Just want to see how you are. Glad to be out of the hospital now."

Rhys sent back a gif of an adorable kitten asleep on its back, limbs splayed out. Affirming how relaxed and happy Zachary was about getting out of the hospital, Zachary assumed.

Just like that, Zachary confirmed back. Though it wasn't exactly the truth. He wasn't sure he'd ever been as relaxed and happy as that kitten. If he had been, he'd clearly been well-drugged at the time. *OK. Will come by after school. Fourish?*

Rhys posted a ticking clock and *c u*

Zachary turned to the next job at hand, which was to get back in touch with the cops in Riverbrook and see if they had made any progress on the investigation. Which he assumed they had not. They would have far more urgent things on their list than following up on some cold, voluntary disappearance. But if he harassed them enough, they might do some basic work on the file just to get him off of their backs.

He looked up the number for the Riverbrook Police Department and tapped it to put the call through. It was answered by the receptionist or officer of the day. "Riverbrook Police Department."

"Hi, I'm looking for Sergeant Fontaine. Is he available?"

"Not sure if he is in right now. I'll put you through to his number."

Zachary waited while it rang. Fontaine probably wouldn't answer, even if he were at his desk. After a few rings, however, there was a click and a brusque, "Fontaine."

"Sergeant Fontaine, it's Zachary Goldman. Tyrrell Goldman's brother? The missing person?" He knew that Tyrrell was probably not first and foremost in the cop's mind, and Zachary's name had probably been long forgotten.

"Ah," Fontaine said. "We haven't really had much time with the case yet. I'm afraid I don't have anything to report back to you."

If it had been a fresh case, the abduction of a child or a senior wandering off, they would have been right on top of it, with plenty of investigation done in the first twenty-four hours. But an adult not identified as high-risk who had been missing for weeks? That was a different story. Just about everything else would take precedent over it.

"I know this is not the only file on your desk," Zachary said. "And I don't want to be a pest, but I wanted to keep up on what you're doing and what I can do from my end."

"Just leave it to the police. There isn't anything for you to do other than to let us know if your brother calls you or shows up again."

"I'm a private investigator," Zachary reminded him. "I'm going to keep investigating it as long as I've got a direction to go."

Fontaine gave a growl. "We are not in the business of cooperating with private investigators."

"No. I'll do my thing, and I'll let you know if I come across anything that might be helpful to the case. But it's best if we're not duplicating efforts. Have you been able to check with the hospitals, or should I call them?"

"Yes, we've been in contact with the hospitals. Goldman hasn't been admitted. No John Does that match his description."

"And he hasn't shown up in the morgue. I already have confirmation of that."

"How would you know that?"

"I have a contact."

"We haven't had confirmation of that yet, but if you have, then go on."

"He doesn't show up in your system? As being arrested?"

"No. Though he does have a record. You know that, don't you?"

"I know he's been a missing person before," Zachary said cautiously.

"I'm not talking about being a missing person. I'm talking about his arrest record."

"Oh. No, I wasn't aware of that. Is it recent?"

Who knew how many times Tyrrell might have been arrested as an older teen. If he'd been rebellious and doing alcohol and drugs, he could have a lengthy record. Though Zachary thought he must be back on track again at that age, for a while at least, because he had gone to college and earned that degree. And since college? How many times since then had he been on the police department's radar?

"Nothing in the past year," Fontaine said carefully, obviously watching how much information he gave Zachary. "But there have been... a number of incidents."

"Are they all for the same thing?"

A pause while Fontaine considered this as well. "More or less."

If Tyrrell had been arrested for anything, it was probably DUI or disorderly conduct. So if Fontaine said they were all more or less for the same thing, Zachary figured he was safe in assuming they all had to do with his substance abuse issues.

"Okay, thanks. That's good to know. But he's not in the system right now..."

"No. No one that we have been in contact with has any idea where he might have disappeared to. But... there's no hint of foul play."

"He might be voluntary," Zachary agreed, "but we won't know that until we find him. Are you able to make inquiries about whether he's been admitted to any of the detox or drug rehab programs in the state?"

"That would be a lot of work, with probably little return. If he were in rehab right now, you would probably know about it."

"Maybe." Or maybe Tyrrell felt too guilty to tell anyone. Or he didn't know if it would "take" and didn't want to get anyone's hopes up.

In truth, Zachary doubted Tyrrell was in any kind of rehab program. The letter didn't make it sound like he was going somewhere to get better. It sounded like he was giving up on sobriety or having anything to do with his family. Fontaine was right; it probably wasn't worth the time it would take to make all of those phone calls.

"Have you checked Tyrrell's license plate?" Zachary asked, remembering a note he'd jotted down the night before. "See whether he has any parking tickets or if it's in impound? If he has a bunch of parking tickets from the same place, that might show where he goes to drink..."

"It hasn't been ticketed or impounded recently. I haven't examined the historical tickets. Might be worth looking into if he has a place he always goes. I'll have someone look into it later."

"Okay... well, thanks for putting up with me. I have a few leads to check out... it turns out that there are some other family members he'd found through a DNA search. Maybe one of them will know something."

Fontaine grunted. "Sure. Let me know if something comes up."

36

Zachary had the list of siblings in front of him, with the contact details that he had managed to pull up for each of them. It wasn't surprising, he supposed, that someone who put their DNA into a public database and used their legal name for their username was easy to find on social media and in phone directories.

Jason Tooley was the sibling trying to contact Tyrrell to find out why he had suddenly gone quiet. He seemed like the best bet for Tyrrell to reach out to. He wasn't apathetic about finding a new DNA relation, unlike Vince and Mindy.

He supposed that Vince and Mindy didn't need to find biological relations as much because they had grown up with each other. They always knew where a biological sibling was and could talk to each other whenever needed. Even though he had grown up in the Millers' home, Tyrrell had not felt like he belonged there. It sounded like he had spent a good amount of time separated from them, put into some program or respite care. He remembered their biological parents well enough to not feel like the Millers were his "real" parents and had missed the other siblings. Even though Zachary wished Tyrrell had been happier, he couldn't help feeling more warmly toward him than to Vince and Mindy because he had not forgotten Zachary and the older girls. He hadn't been satisfied with arrangements like the youngest children.

He took a few deep breaths and tried the first phone number beside Jason Tooley's name. It almost immediately went to a recorded voice saying that the number was no longer in service.

That wasn't an unusual event when trying to find someone based on information that was several years old. Maybe nothing saved to the internet was ever completely lost, but that didn't mean it was all correct or that nothing had changed. That was why Zachary always searched out all of the phone numbers he could the first time around. It was faster to assume that one or more of them would be wrong, and having to conduct repeated searches was not as efficient as getting the whole list of numbers the first time if he could. He went on to the next one on the list.

"Hello?"

"Hi. Is this Jason Tooley?"

"Yeah. Who is this?"

"My name is Zachary Goldman. I think you've been in touch with my brother, Tyrrell Goldman? Have I got the right Jason Tooley?"

"I'm the only one I know of. Yeah, I know Tyrrell. What's your name?"

"Zachary."

"Zachary. Yeah, he's mentioned you. What's up? Is everything okay with Tyrrell?"

He sounded young. Younger than Zachary had expected. He had unconsciously been envisioning a man around Vince and Mindy's age. But of course, that was wrong. They had not been conceived until after the fire. After his parents' break-up.

"I'm actually looking for him. I was hoping that maybe you had seen him and he had crashed on your couch. I guess not."

"No. Why would he come here? He's got a place of his own in River-whatever. What do you mean you're looking for him? You guys are in touch, aren't you? He sounded like you were pretty close."

Zachary sensed there might be a little jealousy in Jason's tone. Wondering why Tyrrell was so close to Zachary? Thinking that Tyrrell was spending more time or energy on his relationship with Zachary instead of his relationship with Jason?

"I haven't seen him for a while. I've been in the hospital. And it turns out that while I was in the hospital, he kind of dropped out of sight."

"Did you call him?"

"Yes." Zachary rolled his eyes. Why was that the first thing everyone asked him? Of course he had called. Tyrrell wouldn't be missing if he answered his phone. "I've called him, and there is no answer. A number of us have called him. And I went to his work and his home. He hasn't been to work since early in December, and his apartment has already been rented to someone else."

"They took his house?" Jason asked in surprise.

"Well, he had an apartment, not a house, and yeah… he stopped paying rent and didn't show up. Left food rotting in the fridge. The landlord cleaned it out and rented it to someone else."

"Sheesh." Jason blew out his breath. "You think he's okay?"

"I don't know. That's why I'm looking for him. I need to make sure he's all right." Zachary hesitated. "He left a letter for me while I was in the hospital, so I didn't get it until I was out. And he sounded pretty down. I'm really hoping that… it wasn't a suicide note."

"He wouldn't do that, would he? Tyrrell wasn't depressed. He was always up."

"You can't always tell. With some people, it's obvious when they are depressed." Zachary couldn't help thinking of the image of himself that looked back from the mirror as December approached. Drawn, pale, with dark bags under his eyes. But that wasn't what everyone was like. Some people hid it well, clowning around and cheering for everybody else while they were dying inside. "I didn't know that he was having trouble either. I thought that he might have started drinking again, but I didn't realize… how he was feeling about it."

"He was drinking?"

"Yeah. Started again sometime before Thanksgiving."

"I thought he was cured of that. He said he didn't drink anymore."

"He'd been sober for a year, or about that. But that doesn't mean it's permanent. People slip up. Fall off the wagon."

"And some people never get on it in the first place," Jason inserted, a non sequitur. Was he referring to himself? Someone else in his life? It certainly sounded like an observation of something he'd had close experience with.

"That's true," Zachary acknowledged. "So…" he wasn't sure where to go from there. "I guess that means you didn't know that he was off the wagon or where he went."

"No, man. I didn't know anything about it. Just that he'd stopped responding to me online. I didn't know if that was because he was busy and hadn't signed in lately, or if I'd said something. Maybe one of his *other* siblings had talked him out of it, said that he shouldn't be communicating with those of us… born on the wrong side of the sheets."

The antiquated expression made Zachary chuckle. Was Jason a reader of historical fiction? Or watching Downton Abbey or one of those other TV serials?

"I didn't even know about you until now," Zachary said. "I was talking to Vince and Mindy. They're the ones who told me about Tyrrell submitting his DNA. I… had no idea that either of our parents had more kids after the family was split up. I guess I thought that since they'd failed at parenthood the first time, they wouldn't have any more."

"Yeah."

Zachary cleared his throat. "So, do you have contact information for any of the other siblings? I don't know whether you grew up as an only child or whether you have other brothers or sisters growing up with you?"

"Yeah, I had a couple of sisters. There are others… but I haven't met everyone yet."

"Could I get their phone numbers and email addresses? Do you know if Tyrrell kept in contact with either of them?"

"I think it was mainly me, but the others might have been messaging him now and then too. We mostly called or texted. Going through that DNA site was awkward. You had to always be logged in, and you don't get a notification when there are new messages. I went back there a couple of times, though… When he stopped, I thought he might have lost his phone."

"I wish that was all it was."

Zachary tried to think of what else to say to Jason. He'd said all that he had planned to. Jason didn't have anything else for him. But it seemed rude to just end the conversation there when he'd only just met the other man. He wanted to explore more.

"You don't know anything about where Tyrrell would go or who he drank with, do you?" Zachary asked. "I guess if you figured he was sober, you didn't know any of that."

Jason made a noise of hesitation. "He didn't talk about that. I just thought it was in the past."

"Yeah. I always thought that it was longer ago. Like when he was a teenager or something. I didn't realize that it was so recent, or that he hadn't had any longer sober periods…"

"I knew he was drinking a year or two ago. I remember that. But I thought he was done with it." Jason sighed. "I guess not. It isn't that easy."

"No."

"Listen… you want to get together? I'm not sure if the girls will want to meet, but I think it's cool… having these other siblings. I always wanted a different family, and here I had one all along."

"Sure, yeah. I wouldn't mind getting together. I'm kind of busy with this investigation right now, but… maybe getting together to talk would trigger something. One of us might remember something that didn't seem significant before."

"Worth a try, right?" Jason asked, perking up. "You wouldn't like to overlook a clue if one of us holds the key to finding him."

Zachary didn't say anything.

"Sorry," Jason said, "that makes it sound like it's all just a big joke, and I didn't mean it that way. I'm just… excited about the possibility of getting together. I didn't mean it to be disrespectful of Tyrrell."

"It's okay. Where are you? Do you want to set something up for later today?" Something twigged at the back of Zachary's brain. He was going to ignore it, but it nagged away at him, and he eventually tried to figure out what it was. "Oh... I have a commitment later on today. So maybe late today or tomorrow would be better. I'd better stick around here until I've met with... a friend."

He couldn't forget the appointment with Rhys. Not after he'd reached out to him to set it up. Zachary pulled up his calendar on the computer screen and saw that he hadn't added the meeting with Rhys. If he wanted an alarm to remind him to get off of his butt and get moving, he'd better add it in. He quickly added the appointment and then tuned back in to Jason.

"Sorry... I just had to write something down. Do you want to do it late today or tomorrow?"

"Maybe it better be tomorrow. I can see if the girls are free too, if they want to come. Where are you? Where do you live?"

"Roxboro."

"Oh, we're not far away. We could meet there. You got a favorite bar?"

"Not a bar, but there are a few good restaurants. Steak house, buffet, Thai?"

"Steak house sounds good. Haven't had a good steak in ages. Everyone says red meat is so bad, but there's nothing wrong with having it now and then, right? Moderation."

Zachary nodded. "Okay. We'll plan on Old Joe's. I might bring my girlfriend along, if she is free. You don't mind that?"

"Might make the girls more likely to come if they know there will be another woman there. They get so twisted up about *men*, you know. Like every man has designs on them. If you've got your girlfriend there, they wouldn't have anything to complain about."

"I'll see if she's free. You can just call or text me after you've talked to your sisters."

"Our sisters," Jason corrected.

Zachary felt a flush wash over him, followed by goosebumps. He wasn't sure whether he was happy to know that he had all of these other siblings, or if it bothered him. It was weird, that was for sure.

37

It was hard to concentrate on other things, knowing that he would meet with even more siblings the next day. In the past year, he'd been reunited with all of his sibling group, including Vince and Mindy. And suddenly, he wasn't done at all. There were still more out there. Who knew how many more. It was exhilarating and anxiety-producing, both at the same time.

He spent some time looking over the other siblings in the database. How strange to have their similar DNA highlighted in colorful chunks, the computer telling him that all of those segments together meant that they were Tyrrell's siblings, and therefore Zachary's. Those were things that they had in common, whether there were any similarities in their looks or interests at all. Their DNA still told a story.

Some of them only had usernames that didn't give away their legal names, and they hadn't all responded to Tyrrell's requests for contact. So some of them, even though they had put their DNA into the system and even though the database had matched them up, had still decided they didn't want anything to do with their siblings. Why had they put their information into the system in the first place?

An alert sounded on his phone, and he looked down at it. He stared at the message for a moment before it made sense, and he closed his computer to prevent himself from being distracted by it. It was time to get ready to see Rhys.

His pondering then took a different direction. He had to forget about Tyrrell and his new siblings and the intricacies of DNA relationships and to focus on Rhys. He wasn't looking forward to the talk he needed to have with the boy.

Usually, he liked to visit Rhys. He liked feeling like he was helping and could understand Rhys when others didn't. Because they had both been through traumatic things in their childhoods and were both broken because of it. Communication with Rhys was difficult. He had stopped talking when his grandfather had been murdered. Rhys had been the only witness. He could say a word or two at a time, now and then, but most of the time, he struggled with even that. He used a mix of gestures, pictures and gifs on his phone, and a few typed words or letters here and there. Standardized communications systems, even those designed for those who didn't do most of their communication through speech, did not seem to work for him.

So it was rewarding when they were able to have a conversation. When Zachary was confident that he understood what Rhys was trying to express to him, and they could exchange something meaningful about their feelings and their individual struggles. Rhys knew about some of what Zachary had been through, about his depression and institutionalization from time to time. He knew about Zachary's feelings for Kenzie before Zachary could talk to anyone about them, even Kenzie herself.

And Zachary understood how devastated Rhys had been by the loss of his grandfather, one of the people who had been a parent to him when his mother had not been able to, struggling with her addiction and emotional issues. Now it was just him and his grandma, Vera. His mother was in prison and he only saw her occasionally.

The trouble with visiting Rhys was that Zachary couldn't tell whether he was home or not at a glance. Rhys didn't drive, so there was no car outside to give away if he were home. And Zachary preferred not to sit and visit Vera for an extended time while they waited for Rhys to show up. Vera was a wonderful grandma and was devoted to Rhys. Still, Zachary got the feeling sometimes that she didn't entirely approve of him. It was understandable, with what Rhys had been through and the complications Zachary presented. Vera was always polite to Zachary—offered him food, and called him when she felt like Rhys needed someone to talk to—but there was that little bit of hesitance that told him she had reservations about Zachary and about his playing too big of a role in Rhys's life.

Zachary parked the car and looked at the house. He took out his phone and typed a quick message to Rhys.

You home?

Dots indicated that Rhys was responding. Which probably meant that he was at home waiting for Zachary's visit. Zachary unbuckled his seat belt and prepared to get out.

A gif popped up on his screen. *Honey, I'm home!* the words across a cartoonized version of Lucille Ball.

Zachary got out of the car and made his way up to the door. Rhys opened it and stood there eating a burrito as he waited for Zachary. The tall, skinny Black boy's expression was neutral. Curious, maybe.

"You'd better have a plate!" Vera's voice floated out from the house.

Rhys grinned. He took another bite of the burrito. Before Zachary stepped into the house, Rhys shoved the entire second half of the burrito into his mouth before turning around to face his grandma.

Zachary tried not to laugh. His laughing could set off Rhys, and if Rhys started laughing with the burrito in his mouth, he could choke. That much food in his mouth was a serious hazard. So Zachary rolled his eyes up to the ceiling and refused to look at Rhys's face.

"Zachary, it's good to see you," Vera said pleasantly.

He looked at her, still studiously avoiding looking at Rhys. Was there more salt in her black, curly hair than the last time he had seen her? Zachary himself felt older. "Nice to see you again, Vera. How are you doing?"

"I'm lovely, thank you. Rhys, where is your plate?"

Rhys made a wide movement with his hands, shrugging questioningly. *What? I'm not eating.*

"Don't give me that! You're big enough to get out a plate when you're having a snack. You think I want crumbs or burrito sauce trailing across my carpet?"

Rhys shook his head and indicated the carpet, tidy and unstained.

Vera sighed. "Boys! I'll tell you, it's very different raising a boy than it was girls."

Zachary nodded politely. "Are you still eating, Rhys? Should we go into the kitchen?"

Rhys shook his head and motioned toward the bedroom instead. Zachary followed. "We'll just be in here."

Vera nodded, unconcerned.

In the bedroom, Zachary leaned up against the chest of drawers and tried to figure out how to approach the topic he was there to discuss. He'd been trying to script something out in his mind, but couldn't find anything that was comfortable. It didn't matter what he said, Rhys was not going to be happy with him and he wasn't sure how to express his concerns in a way that Rhys would listen to and respect.

Rhys sat down on his bed, stretching out his long legs and crossing them at the ankle. He made a motion toward Zachary, indicating he should start talking. He raised one eyebrow questioningly.

"How are you doing?" Zachary asked. "I haven't seen you since Christmas. Everything going okay?"

Rhys nodded, not smiling.

"School? Doing okay in your classes?"

He shrugged. Zachary knew Rhys struggled with his classes, especially those that required advanced language skills. He had accommodations so that he didn't have to give long paragraph answers or write essays. Still, Zachary imagined it would be difficult to convince an English teacher that he knew what he was talking about with his limitations. English Language Arts required more than just yes and no answers.

Rhys motioned back to Zachary with one hand. *You?* He motioned up and down the length of Zachary's body. *How are you?*

"Doing better," Zachary said with a shrug and a nod. "I always feel better once Christmas Day hits. They've been working on

181

adjusting my meds to see if something else will help me to… help me with some of the other symptoms. I think they're working pretty good. So far."

He decided not to tell Rhys about Tyrrell being missing and Zachary's investigation. That would take the spotlight away from Rhys and the issues that Zachary hoped to discuss. Rhys wouldn't know anything about where Tyrrell was. They didn't know each other. Maybe they might have run into each other at the hospital one day if both of them had gone to see Zachary. But Zachary couldn't remember both of them visiting the same day.

"So, I was talking to Joss…"

Rhys's face lit up. He smiled, waiting for Zachary to give him an update on Luke. Luke's physical recovery from a gunshot wound was not an issue. He had a scar on his head where the bullet had grazed him, which Zachary was sure Luke was probably proud of. Getting Luke clean and staying clean had been a much bigger deal. And Luke getting over the loss of Madison.

But he had seemed to be calm and in good spirits when Zachary had seen him last.

"I just wanted to talk to you about Luke."

Rhys frowned slightly and nodded for Zachary to go on.

"He's good," Zachary said. "But… you know, he still has struggles. He was with that trafficking ring for a long time, and they messed him up pretty bad."

Another serious nod.

"I wanted to say… that you need to be careful of who you talk to and hang around with."

Rhys pointed to the side, as if Luke, the subject of their conversation was standing there. *Luke?*

"Yes… you need to be careful of Luke."

Rhys folded his arms over his chest and shook his head firmly.

Zachary shifted, leaning a little closer to Rhys, wishing there were another place in the room for him to sit. "I like Luke. He's easy to talk to. He's friendly and charming…"

Rhys nodded his agreement, his eyes shining.

"But with the stuff he's been through, he can also be a dangerous person to know."

Rhys made an *X* with his hands and pushed them forcefully forward and then away from himself. *No way.*

"You know that he brought Madison into the trafficking ring. He was the one who turned her out."

Rhys shook his head and made a motion sweeping everything behind him.

"That was before?" Zachary guessed, making sure he was interpreting Rhys right.

Rhys nodded and made the motion again. He folded his arms across his chest once more.

"Just because we got him away from those guys… that doesn't mean it is over. It's hard to break away from a lifestyle like that. A lot of people just go right back."

Rhys's chin thrust forward. He shook his head and spread out his hands, palms up. *Why would he?*

"Because it's easier to take drugs and do what people tell you to do than to think for yourself and work hard for the things that you want. It's easier to have a relationship with someone because you were told to, and you were told what to say and do to keep them on the hook. And to have drugs and alcohol to take away any pain and regret you feel for what you are doing. Luke wanted to get out… but he also wants to go back."

Rhys shook his head.

"I know it's hard to understand. It doesn't make much sense if you haven't been in that life. But it's easier to be taken care of and not to have to think for yourself. When he does what they tell him to, he gets rewarded." Zachary tried to put everything that Joss had told him about it into words that would make sense to Rhys. "He gets drugs and money and gifts. He gets more seniority in the organization. They tell him what a good job he's doing and give him more of whatever it is that he wants."

Rhys put up his hands, palms up again. *So what?*

"What they want him to do isn't… it's not good for you. You can't just be friends with him if he chooses to go back. He recruits for the traffickers. Gets kids like you to hook for them. Gets them addicted to make them easier to handle. He knows all the ways to entice someone like you. He's been doing it since he was younger than you are now."

Rhys made the *X* again, then motioned from Zachary to the door. *Get out.*

"I'm not trying to hurt you or to accuse Luke of something. I'm trying to explain… why it's dangerous to be too close to him. I don't want him pulling you into this ring. You don't want that. You need to listen."

Rhys reached over and grabbed a basketball from the floor and whipped it at Zachary.

38

Zachary jumped to the side and the basketball smashed a lamp. The huge crash brought Vera running from the living room as fast as the older woman could run.

"What happened? Is everyone okay?" She looked wildly around the room and saw the shattered lamp on the floor, other stuff that had been on the dresser previously scattered on the floor in an arc. She looked at Zachary, brows drawn down as if she thought he was the one who had swept everything off in a fit of temper.

Zachary gave a slight shake of his head.

Vera looked at her grandson, eyes wide. "Rhys? What happened?"

Rhys pointed at Zachary and then at the door. Zachary turned his body toward it. "I'll go," he agreed. "I'm sorry," he murmured as he walked past Vera, embarrassed about the lamp. But it was best if he didn't stop to help clean up. If Rhys wanted him out of there, it was best that he leave before there were any more destruction. Zachary had said what he had come to say.

"Rhys. What is going on here?" Vera demanded, her voice strident. "You did this? You need to control yourself. You can't treat a guest this way. And breaking my things!"

There was a growl from Rhys. No words, just an angry noise of protest. Zachary reached back and touched Vera.

"Walk me out," he suggested.

She looked like she would argue, staying behind to discipline her grandson. Then she changed her mind and followed him. "What is going on? I want to know what's happening!"

Zachary spoke in a low voice as they walked down the hallway and out into the living room. "Rhys's friend Luke is having some trouble," he explained briefly. Rhys was not "out" to his grandmother, so he wouldn't say anything that might hint at Rhys's romantic interest in Luke, but she knew they were friends. "You know that before… he was involved in some criminal activities."

Vera couldn't help but remember the state that Zachary had returned Rhys to her in after the incident where Luke had been shot, which had triggered flashbacks for Rhys of his grandfather's murder. It had been a very difficult time, requiring intensive therapy.

She looked alarmed at Zachary's words. "I thought all of that was over. Luke has been very kind to Rhys. He hasn't been involved with those criminals again, has he?"

"Not yet. But he's having difficulty staying on… a straight path. It isn't easy to make big life changes and stick with them. And if he was to involve Rhys in any of that…"

"I won't let him. I'll ground him from having anything to do with Luke."

Zachary frowned, shaking his head. "I don't think that's a good idea. You see how he reacted to me telling him not to hang around with Luke." Zachary made a motion back toward the bedroom. "If you ground him or punish him for communicating with Luke, Rhys will run straight to him. And if Luke has gotten back in contact with these guys, it would be a very bad thing."

"Then what can I do? I can't just let him be involved with someone who is dangerous to him."

"Rhys already feels strongly about it." Zachary tilted his head back toward the bedroom. "He's too old for you to control him physically, to keep him in this house."

Zachary knew that Rhys was already skipping school and using his bus pass to get around town without Vera's knowledge. Behavior

Zachary had discouraged. But he couldn't physically prevent Rhys from making bad decisions either.

"Talk about what a nice boy Luke is. How charming. How much you like him. Invite him to come over if he is in town."

Vera's mouth hung open. "Why would I do that?"

"Because you don't want him to be the forbidden fruit. Make Rhys think about whether what you are saying is true. About whether he wants Luke to be around you. To be here in Rhys's safe place. I've done my best to explain why he shouldn't be spending time with Luke, so it's already in his head. Let him think about that."

"I can't let Luke come here. To know where we live and maybe tell those people where we are."

Zachary bit his lip. There was no point in explaining to Vera that Rhys had already been in contact with Luke over the past several months. Luke undoubtedly knew where Rhys lived and could pass that information on anytime he wanted to. The trafficking ring would not likely want to go in cold. They knew that Rhys and Luke were friends, and they would use Luke to get him to leave home voluntarily.

"Joss shouldn't even be bringing Luke into town. She did at Christmas, but I don't think she'll do it again. She doesn't want him to have contact with those old acquaintances either. So I don't think there is really any danger of Luke coming here if you invite him. But inviting him might be just what Rhys needs to see that he doesn't actually want Luke in his space."

Of course, Jocelyn didn't really need to drive Luke. The young man was perfectly capable of boosting a car and making the trip on his own or calling someone in the cartel to pick him up. They couldn't do anything about that risk. All Zachary could hope to do was to help Rhys see that Luke did not have his best interests at heart and that spending time with him could be a dangerous prospect. Putting Vera and Luke on the same side might help Rhys to realize that he didn't want his grandma near his Romeo, someone who could do Vera harm or use her as leverage.

"I don't know if I can do that." Vera touched Zachary's arm, looking for reassurance. "But... I'll do my best."

"Luke is a lost soul. He's been lost since his own grandma died, leaving him to people like that. Reach out to that part of him. Think about what it would be like for Rhys if you weren't there and he had to survive on his own. Luke is dangerous, but he's also a lost boy."

Vera nodded slowly, her eyes showing compassion. "I didn't know that about him."

"He didn't have the stability that Rhys has had staying with you. He was passed around a lot, subjected to abuse. His grandma was the only one who really cared about him, and when she was gone, he was alone."

"Okay." She swallowed and nodded. "I'll do what you say."

Zachary nodded and left.

He hoped that he had said and done the right things and not made things worse. He hoped that they would be able to keep Rhys safe from the predators.

39

For a few minutes, Zachary just sat in the car outside Rhys's house, resting his forehead on the steering wheel. His anxiety over having to talk to Rhys about Luke and the adrenaline rush from Rhys throwing the ball at him and smashing the lamp left him feeling drained and shaky. While being hit by the thrown basketball would not have seriously injured him, even if it had hit him in the face, Zachary's body and primitive brain had still reacted to Rhys throwing something at him in anger. He had still perceived it as an attack. And having been attacked, abused, and beaten in the past, his reaction was probably overblown.

Knowing that didn't stop it. He still needed to give himself the time to calm down and relax. He wasn't in any danger. He didn't need to escape.

Eventually, he turned on the radio and let the music flow over him for a while. He hoped that Vera and Rhys were not watching him out the window, but there was nothing he could do if they were. He wasn't prepared to drive. After listening to the music for a while, he tapped his phone and called Kenzie.

"Medical Examiner's Office."

"It's Zachary."

"Oh, hi, Zach. How are you doing?"

"Good. Just thought I'd see how your day is going."

"Well, none of the patients have registered any complaints," she joked. "But it's pretty dead down here today."

Zachary smiled, enjoying her banter. "If only they weren't all so cold," he offered. He could have done better, but he'd worn out all of his best dead body humor already. He needed some new material. "You'll be able to make it home for supper tonight?" he asked.

"Date night tonight. I'll be on time. How about you? How is your day shaping up?"

"Good. I… made contact with one of the siblings that Tyrrell was DNA matched with. Jason."

"Jason. And what was he like? You managed to reach him? Or left a message."

Zachary nodded. He started to feel excited about it again, the nervous anticipation of meeting another sibling or siblings that he had never even known existed flooding in to replace the anxiety and panic that he'd felt from the visit with Rhys.

"Yeah. He was interested in meeting me. Tyrrell mentioned me, I guess, even if he didn't tell me about all of *them*. We're going to set something up for tomorrow night at Old Joe's. Maybe him and his two sisters, and you. If that's okay."

"That's not going to be too much at once? Maybe you should just start with Jason, and then meet the others another day, so it isn't as overwhelming."

"No. They should come together. Give each other moral support. It will be okay."

"Are you sure you want me along?"

"Yes. I already asked him if it would be okay, and he thought it would be more comfortable for the sisters if you were with me."

"Okay." Kenzie's voice was warm. "That will be a real treat. You're turning out to have quite a big family, for someone who once told me that he was an only child."

Zachary flushed at the memory. It was easier to tell people he didn't have any brothers or sisters than to explain the whole story to them, telling them about the fire and about being split up and put

HE DROWNED IN MEMORY

into foster care. Easier if they thought it was just the usual. An only child. A man who happened to not have any family.

"Seems to me you told me you were an only child too," Zachary reminded her.

It was, after all, easier for her not to have to explain about Amanda, who had died. Less painful.

"I'm sure that's not the case," Kenzie said, chuckling. "But your fib was obviously bigger than mine. Five times bigger. And now with these three more…"

"It's not a lie if I didn't know about them."

She laughed. "Well, I should be getting back to work. I'll see you in a couple of hours."

"You bet. See you then."

Date night. Even though he had put it into his calendar, it had been chased out of his mind by the other events of the day. He should do more than just show up for supper and help decide what they were going to do for the evening. He should do something to actually show her what she meant to him.

Kenzie got home, yawning as she came in through the door from the garage and starting to remove her coat and winter things by the hooks and mat that constituted her mudroom. She stopped and looked into the kitchen.

"What's going on in here?"

She finished hanging up her coat and kicked off her boots and walked the rest of the way into the room. Her eyes went from the flowers in a vase on the table to the flickering tealights along the counter.

"Well, look at this. Is it Valentine's Day already? Did I forget a special anniversary?"

"No," Zachary couldn't dial down the big grin that was stretching his face, pleased with her reaction. "I just thought I should show you… I thought that we should have a nice time together. Really put some effort into it."

He pulled out her kitchen chair and Kenzie seated herself. Zachary poured ginger ale into each of the champagne flutes.

"The last couple of months haven't exactly been a walk in the park for you, but you've been so patient and supportive through it all. I want you to know how much I appreciate you," he told her.

"Well, you're definitely off to a good start. This is lovely." She raised her glass. "To us!"

Zachary raised his glass as well. They each sipped their drinks. Zachary put his down. "This is as far as I got," he said, his face warming. "I didn't make any dinner or order anything. I thought... we could discuss what we wanted and order in. Just relax while we wait for it. Unless you want to go out for something."

"No, this is awesome. What do you want tonight? Any preferences?"

Zachary considered. He always told Kenzie no, to just get whatever she felt like. Which meant that he made her responsible for dinner, and maybe she didn't like always having to be the one to decide. With the new medications Zachary was on, he felt different. He wasn't as nauseated in the morning and the new meds didn't seem to suppress his appetite as much. He wasn't quite hungry, but he was thinking of food and what would be nice.

"I don't know if pizza goes with flowers and candlelight..."

Kenzie looked surprised. "Sure, why not? We don't have to go with fancy French cuisine or anything. I like pizza."

"Pepperoni?"

"How about half vegetarian and half pepperoni?"

Zachary nodded his agreement. "Works for me. I thought you liked pepperoni."

"I do. But I want a choice. Something a bit fresher too."

"Okay." Zachary pulled out his phone and started tapping their order into the delivery app. "Sorry, I know it's no phones at the table on date night..."

"Doesn't count if you're ordering food."

"Good."

Kenzie watched him for a minute. "I'm going to change while we wait. I won't be long. If we're going to relax, I'm going to go all out."

She stood up. She moved to the counter, the opposite direction from the bedrooms, and looked down into one of the jars of flickering tealights.

"Artificial," Zachary acknowledged. "I'm not ready for open flames."

"Fine with me. They look very romantic. And they won't burn out if we take a little interlude partway through the evening and adjourn to the bedroom." She waggled her eyebrows.

Zachary grinned. He watched her sashay out of the kitchen and waited for her to reach the bedroom.

"Oh, Zachary!" she exclaimed.

He chuckled and followed her to the bedroom, where he had strung clusters of white twinkle lights and strewn more jars of tealights.

40

They cuddled on the bed, on top of the covers in the warm room. Zachary had pulled on pajama bottoms and a t-shirt which he never actually slept in, so that he would be prepared when the pizza delivery man rang the bell. Kenzie hadn't dressed, but had pulled a robe around herself and cuddled against his side, her head on his arm. She was close to sleep, her breathing long and deep.

Zachary enjoyed the warmth of her body and the room and the comfort of skin against skin contact. He had missed her while he had been in the hospital. He had spent many long, lonely nights wishing he was at home again but knowing he needed to be there for his own protection. Of course, he could have checked himself out, just as he had when he'd gone down to the NICU to check on Bridget's twins.

But the reason he had checked himself in was because of his suicidal thoughts. He wasn't going to try to tough it out at home or to put Kenzie through the stress of knowing he was a danger to himself and she was the only one there to put herself between him and a suicide attempt. He needed to be where the medical staff could help him twenty-four hours a day. Where there was someone to call on when it got to be too much. Kenzie couldn't be there all the time and she wasn't a psychologist. There was nothing she could do but hope he didn't try anything.

He stroked her dark, curly hair, letting his eyes close, waiting for the pizza to arrive.

There was a buzzing from his phone. Zachary turned reluctantly to get it. The pizza guy saying he couldn't find the house or had been delayed? Jason calling to set up a time to meet the next day? He didn't want it to be anyone else. Unless, of course, it was Tyrrell.

At the thought, Zachary's heart started to beat more rapidly. He knew that it wasn't going to be Tyrrell, but with the thought lodged in his brain, he couldn't get it out. He reached for his phone and pulled it to him, turning it to look at the ID on the face of the phone.

Medical Examiner's Office

Zachary's throat felt suddenly strangled. His thoughts jumped to the idea that he had actually picked up Kenzie's phone instead of his own. He knew it wasn't, but his brain immediately started floundering around for an explanation other than the one that immediately came to mind.

He sat up and put the phone to his ear. "Hello?"

Kenzie shifted, groaning. "Who is it?"

"Is this Mr. Zachary Goldman?" asked the voice on the phone.

"Yes."

"I have your name on this file as a point of contact when remains were positively identified."

Zachary gripped the phone more tightly. His eyes burned. A lump swelled in his throat and he couldn't swallow.

"What remains?" he asked, the words coming out in barely a whisper.

Kenzie propped herself up on her elbow, turned toward him, looking alarmed. She put her hand on his arm.

"We have positively identified the remains of Mr. Jose Flores."

It took a long time for Zachary to process the words. *Jose.*

Jose, not Tyrrell.

Jose.

It had been nearly a year since Jose's disappearance and the arrest of his killer. Zachary had assumed that identifying the various remains that were discovered on his land and nearby would be the work of a few days or weeks, not something that was just happening months later.

"It's Jose," he repeated, wanting the caller to confirm this again, and to communicate it to Kenzie. "Not Tyrrell. Jose."

There was a pause before the male voice on the other end came to him again. "Yes, Jose. I don't have a Tyrrell here."

"No," Zachary agreed. He let out his breath. "No, Tyrrell hasn't been found."

"Okay, then," the man said, still sounding confused. "So... these remains have been positively identified. Will you be claiming them?"

"Uh... maybe. I'll get back to you. Can I get your name and number?"

The man gave his information, grumbled for a moment, asking Zachary to get back to him as soon as possible because they couldn't keep holding remains for long, then hung up. Zachary flopped back, his back landing on the pillows but his head thwacking into the wall. He winced, but he didn't even care. All that mattered was that Tyrrell was not dead. They still didn't know what had happened to him. But he wasn't on some medical examiner's table.

"Jose?" Kenzie asked. "Pat's friend?"

"Yeah." Zachary rubbed his eyes, thinking about it. He would have to call Pat and Lorne to give them the information. He had made sure that he was the one on the contact sheet so that he could break it to them gently. Pat especially. He had been the one who had been closest to Jose. He had been the one Zachary had taken the case for. He had hoped to help alleviate Pat's concern. He had been hoping for a different resolution. That Jose had returned to his wife in El Salvador. Even that he had been apprehended by ICE and detained, but safe.

But what he had found was that Jose had been one of the victims of a serial killer who had been killing gay immigrant men for a very long time. They had known for some time that Jose was one of his victims, but with the identification of his remains among those that the police had recovered from on and around Archuro's property, now they had the proof.

"Should I even tell him?" Zachary pondered. "It's just going to make it worse. He's going to have to go through all that grief again, and you know how depressed he got. Can I just... not say anything?"

He knew the answer, but he needed someone else to tell him. He didn't have the fortitude to make himself do it without her help.

"No. We have to tell them. And Pat will be okay. Yes, he will be upset, but he has already grieved Jose. He already knew that he was one of the victims. This will just mean... that Jose can be laid to rest. They'll know what happened to him and where his remains are." Kenzie pushed her hair back from her face with both hands. "Will they bury him here? Or send him back to El Salvador?"

"To his wife, I guess. We need to make sure that he's... home."

"And *is* that with his wife? He left her behind while he came here. Had relationships with other people. Will she still want him back?"

"She doesn't know all of that. Only that he came here to work and then bring her and the kids over when he could save enough money."

Zachary started to think of the logistics of getting the body back to her. How was that done? And what kind of shape would it be in after so many months, even if it had been refrigerated for that long? He had no idea how to deal with such a thing. He looked at Kenzie. "How do we do that? How do we send it back?"

She squeezed his arm. "The easiest way is cremation here and shipping the cremains home. Much easier and cheaper. And his wife won't have to deal with... well, you know."

"Okay. So I'll tell them to do that. Or is that just assumed anyway?"

"You can tell them that. But let's do this one step at a time. You're getting a bit ahead of yourself."

Zachary grimaced. "That's because I don't want to do it."

"I know. But you need to. Don't spend your time fussing and being anxious about it. Just do it without thinking about it any more."

Zachary let out his breath, knowing that she was right. If he put it off, it would bother him all evening. He wouldn't be able to enjoy his time with Kenzie or to sleep when the time came. He would just get more anxious and upset about it until he couldn't handle it anymore.

He looked over at Kenzie. "I'm going to video call. You might want to get some clothes on."

"I think Pat and Lorne can handle seeing me in my robe."

He eyed her, wondering if it were really appropriate. It wasn't like they would be able to see anything, but... "And if the delivery guy comes while I'm on with them—which he will—do you want to be answering the door in your robe?"

Kenzie gave a teasing smile. "Are you saying you *don't* want me flashing the pizza delivery man?"

Zachary snorted. "At least then you wouldn't have to tip him..."

Kenzie laughed. She moved away from him, sliding her feet off of the bed to go get her pajamas on. Zachary knew he didn't need to be worried about her answering the door in some lacy, barely-there thing. Kenzie liked to be comfortable. In the winter, she liked wearing soft, warm flannels. Nothing that would give the pizza guy any thrills.

He took a couple more deep breaths and brought the phone up to face level and tapped the icon to video call Mr. Peterson. Lorne. The foster father who had been there for him ever since he was ten, even when he hadn't actually been Zachary's foster father.

Lorne answered after a few rings, staring intently at the computer for a minute to make sure it connected. He smiled, his round face cheerful as always. The white fringe of hair around his head was neatly trimmed and he wore a comfortable t-shirt. "Zachary! Good to see and hear from you! I was glad to hear that you were out of the hospital. How are you feeling?"

"Good. I'm glad to be out of there, and I think these new medications work really well for me. A few weeks before it reaches full efficacy, but it's working well now."

"Excellent. Good to hear it. They're always coming out with new medicines that work better..."

Maybe someday they would find a drug that could keep Zachary from getting depressed before Christmas. Maybe eventually... he could be almost normal. Except that all the pills would rattle when he walked.

"Is Pat there?" Zachary asked. "I'd like to talk to you both together."

Lorne called over his shoulder for Pat to join him. Kenzie sat on the bed and scooted over to Zachary, putting her head against his so that she could see the screen as well.

"Hi, Lorne."

"Hi, Kenzie." Lorne lifted his brows and gave a teasing smile. "You two are looking very comfortable. Do you have news for us?"

Zachary shook his head soberly, not wanting Lorne to get his hopes up that they were engaged or had some other special announcement to make. Lorne's smile disappeared, understanding that it was not the kind of news he was hoping for. He looked anxiously over his shoulder as Pat arrived.

Pat bent down to see the computer screen and fit into the camera frame. He was younger than Mr. Peterson, still broad and muscled across the chest, someone who took care of his health and his body. Getting more distinguished looking with some gray in his dark hair around his temples. Zachary had taken to calling Pat his stepfather. It was the closest he could get to describing the relationship they'd had since Pat and Mr. Peterson had become a couple.

"Zachary, Kenzie, so nice to see you. How is everything?"

Zachary clenched his teeth and steeled himself for what he had to say. "Can you sit down with us for a minute, Pat?"

Pat looked at Lorne uncertainly, then pulled a chair over from the other side of the office. It was an awkward space to fit both chairs into, but Zachary wanted him sitting for the news. He didn't want to take the chance that Pat would take the news badly and faint or collapse.

"What is it?" Pat asked. "What's going on?"

"I just got a call from the Medical Examiner's Office... He called about Jose's remains."

Zachary's eyes prickled as he saw the color drain from Pat's face. Lorne pulled him closer, a comforting arm around Pat's shoulders, pressing their cheeks together.

"It's… Jose? They found him and… identified him?"

"Yeah. I don't have any details. If his was one of the bodies they collected from Archuro's property or somewhere else. All I know is, he's been identified now. You don't need to wonder anymore."

Pat put his hands over his face. Zachary expected him to start sobbing, but he didn't. He just held them there, breathing, processing what Zachary had told him.

"Thank you for calling, Zachary," Lorne said softly, rubbing Pat's back. "I'm glad that you were the one to deliver the news."

Zachary nodded, unable to think of what else to say. He should say something comforting to Pat. Something about how Jose was at rest now. He was in a better place. Archuro would go away for the rest of his life for the terrible, depraved things he had done and for killing so many men.

But how could any of that be a comfort to Pat? Pat knew that his friend had died under the most terrible circumstances. They had known for months, and now they had confirmation that it was true. That wouldn't make him feel better.

Pat sniffled a few times and pulled his hands from his face. His expression was still one of grief, but he didn't look as devastated as Zachary had been worried he would. He actually did look as if he was a little relieved by the news. A little more at peace.

"Yes, thank you, Zachary. It is a terrible thing… but it's better to hear it from a friend."

The doorbell rang, and Kenzie gave the two a little wave and went to get the pizza.

"I'm so sorry," was all Zachary could think of to say.

"I know." Pat nodded. He swallowed. "So I guess…"

"Kenzie says what they usually do is cremate the remains, and then ship the ashes. It's easier that way. And… his wife won't ever have to see what he did to Jose."

Pat nodded and scratched the back of his neck. "If it's ashes… then maybe it would be okay to spread a few here, too. Just a little. So that… part of him stays in America."

41

It was difficult to get back into the "date" mindset after the calls with the Medical Examiner's Office and with Pat and Lorne. The pizza was hot, and the tealights still twinkled throughout the house. Zachary still felt the warmth and satisfaction of intimate time spent with Kenzie. But the happy mood was gone.

He did his best to focus on the smell of the pizza and how good it would taste, and he gazed at Kenzie in her charming flannel pajamas, but nothing that either of them did could negate the tinge of sadness that remained with them for the rest of the evening. Kenzie seemed to feel it too. Even though she smiled and joked, her eyes were sad, and she was obviously also unable to put Jose's death out of her mind.

The investigation of Jose's death and all that went along with it had been dark days for both of them. It had taken a lot of months to get past the damage Archuro had caused to their relationship with his assault of Zachary. The remnants of that encounter were something Zachary knew he might never be able to shake. It would always cling to him and be a barrier to intimate relationships.

But they did their best to pretend and buoy each other up throughout the evening, and went to bed late, which should have made it easier for Zachary to fall asleep.

Immediately after the assault, Zachary had found himself unable to do much but sleep. He had said that it was just because of his body's need for extra rest in order to heal, but a great deal of it had to do with his brain being unable to process all that had happened, not only with Archuro, but at various times in Zachary's past, incidents that he had previously been able to shove into a hidden room in his brain to forget about them. But Archuro had opened that door and let them all back out again, and it was just too much to deal with.

As he lay in the dark, cuddled up close to Kenzie, the feelings flooded back. Teddy's touch, his threats, and the torture. Other voices from the past; people who had been bigger and stronger than he, in positions of authority, taking advantage of a vulnerable child or teen who had no way to defend himself.

Dr. Boyle had given him relaxation exercises and ways to anchor himself in the present, but she had said that the best thing for Zachary to do was to process those memories. To discuss them in therapy, write them down, or find another way to acknowledge them and get them out. Outside of his head, they would die in the light of day.

But it wasn't day, and Zachary's thoughts were blacker than the night. He tossed and turned, trying to find a more comfortable position. But he knew that whatever position he was in, he still wasn't going to sleep. He was still going to be haunted by those memories all night long.

Kenzie's hand landed on the back of his shoulder. Zachary flinched away, surprised by her touch when so many bad things were writhing in his brain. She felt his tension and rubbed his shoulder and back gently.

"Are you awake?" she whispered.

Zachary took a deep breath in and out. "Yes."

He tried to relax his muscles, but his skin was crawling. The nightmares were too close to the surface.

"Are you okay?" Kenzie shifted her position, sliding her body up against his. She kissed his cheek. "Hey."

"I can't... turn it off."

She stroked his hair and nuzzled him. "You can't turn off your brain?"

"Yeah."

"Did you take your sleep aid tonight? It's probably not a good night to skip it."

"Yes. I took it."

"What about anti-anxiety?"

"I'm not having a panic attack." Zachary was aware that his tone was terse. He didn't need Kenzie telling him what to take and when to take it. He was in charge of his own body and his own medication regimen.

"But you are anxious, aren't you? That's why you're so restless and having trouble controlling your thoughts?"

Zachary didn't say anything. Kenzie rubbed his back again. "Sorry. Just trying to help. I don't mean to interfere."

"It's okay."

Her touch was soothing, now that he was expecting it and was talking to her, rather than being locked into those memories, alone in the darkness.

"Do you want to get up and talk? Is there anything I can do that would help?"

"No." He snuggled in to her, appreciating the warmth of her body, even through the flannel pajamas. "Just... being here."

"I'm not going anywhere," she assured him.

But in a few more minutes, she was asleep again.

When Kenzie got up in the morning and wandered through the living room area to get herself some coffee, she didn't make any comment about Zachary being up already or ask him how much sleep he had gotten. And that was good. She already knew that he'd been having trouble the night before, but they didn't need to talk it through. It didn't need to be the constant focus of their morning conversation.

"We're on for tonight?" Kenzie asked after pouring herself a mug of coffee from the waiting carafe. "Old Joe's, right?"

Zachary nodded. "Yeah. I'm not sure of the exact time yet. Probably seven or so. Jason and the others will need time to get here. And I assume they work. But I have no idea if they work shifts or banker's hours."

"Good. That gives me time to get back here after work and to change and relax for a few minutes."

"Probably. I don't know exactly what time yet."

"Got it. Are you looking forward to meeting them?"

Zachary thought about it. "I guess. Of course. They're family, so of course I want to meet them. It's sort of a strange situation, but I always like watching those reunion shows on TV, where they search out adoptees or whatever and reunite them with their siblings or birth parents. I know it won't necessarily be like that, but..."

She was studying him over the brim of her cup, watching his face. "But you've always wanted to be reunited with your siblings. So even if they're not the siblings you knew about, you're still eager."

Zachary nodded. "Yeah. Exactly. But... I'm also nervous. I know I don't always present well." He rubbed the whiskers on his chin. He needed to shave before they met. Shower, shave, fresh clothes, all the things that normal people did when trying to make a good impression. "What if we don't like each other? Or they resent me for... something?"

"How did Jason sound on the phone?"

"Good. Friendly. He wanted to get together."

"And did he tell you anything about his sisters? Or about how they would feel about getting together?"

"He didn't say much about them. But he's the one who suggested that they would like to meet me too." Zachary tried to replay everything that had been said. "He thought it would be a good idea for you to come around, so that they didn't feel anxious about meeting a man."

Kenzie nodded. "It can be a bit intense, as a woman, meeting a man face to face without some... backup. They have each other, so that's good, and they have their brother to balance things out. But having a girlfriend with you makes you... safer. Like I'm vouching for you and you won't be trying anything."

"They're my sisters. I wouldn't come on to them." Zachary gave a shudder at the suggestion. That was just creepy.

"You didn't grow up with them. They haven't a clue what you're like or what you might do. And there is sometimes a romantic attraction between genetic siblings who didn't grow up together. Sometimes, you see it in the news, siblings marrying each other before they find out they are related. It's been studied."

"I am not going to be romantically attracted to them."

"No." Kenzie smiled as she brought her coffee mug up to her mouth for another sip. "You're not."

He liked the way that she said it. A little possessive and commanding. There was no way she would let him go to any other woman. He stared at his computer screen, trying to focus on something else to head off a blush. But he was sure she could see his burning cheeks and earlobes getting red.

42

Zachary wasn't sure how he had gotten all the way through the day with all the worry and anticipation. He plugged away at his email and did a few low-level jobs for his actual business. Things he could get done in a few minutes or an hour and get the invoice out to the client. That made it feel like he was accomplishing something, even if they were just little things. A good way to ease back into his job.

He looked over his notes on Tyrrell in between jobs. He scanned his notepad pages and uploaded them to the cloud so that he would have them wherever he was and couldn't lose them if something happened to his physical notepad or computer. He transcribed a few notes or avenues to check. Although Fontaine had said they hadn't found any recent parking tickets for Tyrrell, he didn't know how far Fontaine had looked. Just in town? In the surrounding areas? What if his car had been left or ticketed somewhere outside Fontaine's jurisdiction? They had checked hospitals and morgues all across the state. Might as well look for his car too. Cars could be driven into the lake if the ice cover were not too thick, or left in long-term airport parking but, other than that, there weren't a lot of ways to get rid of one without documentation. Even car wreckers expected proof of ownership, and why would Tyrrell wreck his own car? More than likely, Tyrell's car was where he was, or close to him.

He called a few of the detox programs Tyrrell might have been able to get into without significant up-front costs, and asked for Tyrrell as if he knew Tyrrell was there.

"Tyrrell Goldman, please."

"Excuse me?"

"Tell him it's his brother, Zachary. I need to talk to him urgently."

That was usually enough to earn him a pause while they checked their log-in records to see if there was, in fact, a Tyrrell Goldman registered in the program.

"I'm sorry, there's no one by that name here. Are you sure you called the right facility?"

There were no confidentiality laws preventing a facility from saying someone wasn't a patient. Only if they were. If Zachary ran into one who told him that they couldn't disclose whether Tyrrell was there or not, then Zachary would know that he'd hit gold. Then he could either leave a message and hope that they passed it on and Tyrrell called him back, or go into phase two and show up at the facility. He was even more convincing face to face. If Tyrrell were in a program, Zachary would eventually find him. But he had a feeling that wasn't the case. Tyrrell had already been missing since before Christmas, and most of the programs Tyrrell was aware of were no more than thirty days. A six-week or three-month program was a rarity, especially for a state-funded facility. And Zachary doubted that Tyrrell had saved up the money to get himself into a more expensive program. Not with a casual construction job and paying child support. Zachary had seen where he lived. It wasn't high-end.

When Kenzie made it home, he finally pulled back from work and phone calls looking for Tyrrell. They both got showered and changed, and Zachary shaved. He studied himself in the mirror. Not that much better without the stubble, unfortunately. The partial beard helped to disguise how thin and gaunt his face was. Without it, he looked like he was starving.

Maybe they'd give him a discount at Old Joe's since it would look like it was the first time he'd eaten in a month.

"You're fine," Kenzie commented as she walked by the bathroom door and saw him peering at himself in the mirror. "Nobody cares what you look like. They want to get to know who you are."

"I know." Zachary busied himself with cleaning up the counter and his razor. "I just... wish I looked more like Tyrrell."

Kenzie grimaced and reached through the doorway to put a hand on his arm for a moment. "Maybe it's better if you don't. This way... they get to know you as your own person, instead of thinking that you are so similar to Tyrrell."

"Yeah."

He wouldn't mind being mistaken for Tyrrell's twin, though. He would like to look better, to be less damaged and more outgoing and friendly. He would like to be more comfortable in his own skin.

But that was an illusion. Tyrrell clearly hadn't been comfortable in his own skin. Things had been far different from what they appeared to be.

They got ready and, having a few minutes to kill, had another drink of the ginger ale in the fridge, now going flat. Kenzie glanced in the sink and saw the dishes there.

"Hey, you actually had lunch!"

"Yeah." Zachary chuckled. "I actually remembered to eat."

"Good for you. I'm sure that helps to fuel you through your afternoon. Keep up the energy levels."

"Or makes me want to sleep."

Kenzie shrugged. "I doubt it was anything heavy enough to make you want to sleep. Leftover pizza?"

"Yeah. A full slice of the pepperoni *and* a half slice of your vegetarian."

Kenzie raised her brows. "Does that mean you didn't pick the toppings off of the vegetarian?"

Zachary shifted his feet and took another sip of the ginger ale. "Not *all* of them."

He was good about eating things he didn't like. In foster care, he had quickly learned to chew and swallow whatever families put in front of him, no matter how weird or unpleasant it might be. He might not be able to avoid conflicts with foster parents because of his ADHD and other issues, but he could prevent disputes over food. But at home, when he had the choice, he could pick the toppings off of the vegetarian pizza if Kenzie were not there to see it. That was one of the few positives of eating alone.

Kenzie looked at her phone. "Okay. We shouldn't get there too early if we leave now."

Zachary felt like a dog let off the leash at the dog park. He was raring to go, but was being as cool about it as he could. Now he wanted to run, to speed all the way over to the grill and meet these new family members.

"Did you want to take your car?" he asked Kenzie.

"Well..." She looked him up and down. "I wouldn't mind. If you're offering."

"Sure. You can drive your baby."

Kenzie led the way into the heated garage where her car was waiting. No need to wait for it to heat up once they got outside. No frost to scrape. No sliding into freezing-cold seats. Zachary settled into the passenger seat and closed his eyes, trying to keep himself calm.

At Old Joe's, Zachary looked around at the other patrons curiously, looking for faces that were familiar. He hadn't ever seen Jason or his sisters before, but there was still the strong chance that they would look like one of Zachary's other siblings.

There was a group of three standing near the door, conversing. All tow-headed, younger than Zachary, a man and two women. They looked like they were from the same family. Not particularly like Zachary or Tyrrell, but maybe close to Heather, some of her facial features. Maybe something around the eyes.

"Jason?" Zachary asked.

They turned and looked at him.

"Zachary Goldman," Zachary offered, putting out his hand. "Is it Jason? Or have I just made a fool of myself in front of strangers?"

"Well, we are strangers," the man said, putting his hand out to take Zachary's. "But as luck would have it, yes, I'm Jason. And this is Margot and Celia."

Zachary shook hands firmly with Jason, then offered his hand toward Margot and Celia as well. "Hi. And this is my girlfriend, Kenzie Kirsch."

The girls seemed more warmly disposed toward Kenzie, smiling at her and nodding and greeting her. They decided not to leave Zachary hanging, and shook hands briefly.

"This is so weird," Margot observed.

Zachary tried not to stare at them. He wanted to drink in their features, to memorize every bit of them. Still, he knew it was inappropriate to keep looking at them. Like Kenzie had suggested, they might perceive him as a stalker or threat, when he was just interested in their faces.

"We have a reservation," he told the hostess who stepped up to greet them. "Goldman. Party of five."

She looked at her seating chart and nodded. "This way," she agreed, grabbing enough menus for them all and leading them over to a table. Zachary wished for the intimacy of a booth, where he wouldn't feel so exposed. But the booths were not wide enough to fit more than four of them into the bench seats. He shuffled around with the others until he could sit in the chair that gave him the best view of the room, then pulled out the one nearest at hand for Kenzie.

"This is nice," Celia said, looking around. "I haven't been here before."

"They really do have great food," Kenzie offered. "It's been a couple of months since we were here last, but we like to come here now and then for a treat."

How long had it been since Zachary had taken Kenzie there to treat her? He wasn't sure when the last time had been. Before the psych ward, of course. Before their vacation to the Lodge. Before the virus protocol. A long time ago. So much had happened. It was easy to lose track of the relationship, even though they went to couple's therapy and had specific things to work on. Sometimes it was nice to just go out to dinner together. He should get out more often and try to show Kenzie a good time.

"Zachary?"

It was Jason who was trying to get his attention, but Zachary looked at Kenzie instead. "Sorry, what? I was... remembering something."

She raised her eyebrow at him, telegraphing concern, then nodded. "Jason was just wondering whether we live here in town."

"Oh, yeah," Zachary looked back at Jason. "We are. It's good; everything is nice and convenient."

"It's a nice little town," Jason observed.

Zachary wasn't sure whether he was supposed to inquire after where Jason and the girls lived. He decided to leave it alone. If they wanted to tell him more about where they lived, that was fine. But if the women were leery about being stalked or pursued, maybe it was best that he just leave it alone.

Assuming they didn't know that he was a private investigator and already had most of their contact information.

"How long have you two known each other?" Margot asked, pointing to Zachary and Kenzie in turn.

"It's been about two years now," Kenzie said, looking at Zachary for confirmation.

"Yeah, just a little over that."

"How did you meet?"

Zachary looked over at Kenzie, waiting for her to tell the story.

"Well, I work for the Medical Examiner's Office," Kenzie said slowly. "And Zachary came down to fill out a form for some records. We just... something clicked, and we started seeing each other."

"And you've been together since?"

"Off and on," Kenzie said carefully. "It's not like we moved in with each other that day, but we started going out together, exploring, getting to know each other. Not like some TV romance where the couple falls in love the instant they lay eyes on each other. Real life rarely looks like the movies."

"You're telling me," Celia said with a laugh. "I'm still waiting for Prince Charming to come and sweep me off my feet."

Kenzie shook her head. "Don't wait around. See people. Get to know them."

"I know, I know. I'm just joking."

"Relationships take work if you're going to stay together. Both people have to be willing to put the time and energy into it."

43

S peaking of relationships…" Zachary scratched the back of his neck, hoping that the segue wasn't too abrupt. "I was interested in hearing about you meeting Tyrrell. And some more about you guys. Your history together."

Jason looked at his two sisters, then took on the explanation. "Well… you know that we were all registered with the DNA database."

"Yes, right."

"That was Celia's idea." Jason pointed at her.

"Well…" Celia took a sip of her water. "I figured that it was cheaper than getting paternity tests done. We could all just do the test, pop it in the mail, and when the results came back, we would know for sure who our father was. And whether we even all had the same one."

"You weren't sure?"

"Who can be sure of anything? If you believe what you see on daytime TV, half the mothers out there have no idea which man fathered her child. Which is… pretty sad. They all kind of make up their own story about what happened, even if half of it is complete… fiction. They like that guy, so they say he was the father. Or they don't like that guy and want to tell stories about him. Or they want to hit someone up for child support, so they pick the richest guy for that..."

"I guess. Did... your father live with you?"

"No, not most of the time," Jason said, shaking his head. "He'd come back every now and then and crash for a while, but he was usually gone again in a few days, maybe a week."

"To be fair, he was in prison for a fair length of time," Margot pointed out.

They all exchanged looks, but no one laughed like it was a joke.

"What was he in prison for?" Zachary asked. He'd never thought about the possibility. He'd honestly never thought very much about Berk at all. After the family had broken up, Zachary supposed he assumed that his dad would go on pretty much the same way as he had. Maybe going to jail sometimes when he got in an altercation. But he had always gotten out again pretty quickly.

"Manslaughter," Margot said, when no one else answered. She looked at Zachary. "You never knew that?"

"I never saw or heard about him again after we were split up. We were put into foster care, and I knew he could never take us, probably never wanted us. So..."

"He never talked about you guys," Jason said, leaning forward. "We never had any clue that he'd had another family. I guess he figured that since he wasn't in contact with you anymore, he didn't need to mention it."

"Who knows what he thought?" Zachary shook his head. "The family was gone, so I can't see any reason he had to talk about it. It wasn't like he had walked out on our mom."

"Like he did with ours. She made me so crazy. I don't understand how she could be happy every time he came around again. Kids are supposed to love their parents, but I got so tired of her taking him back," Margot said, shaking her head. "I hated it. I just didn't want anything else to do with him."

The others shrugged and nodded, apparently having similar feelings about it.

"When she finally said she was done with him, I was so glad to have him out of our lives. I don't know why she kept it going for so long. If that happened to me now, and some man kept coming back like he could just walk out of and back into my life… I couldn't do it."

"But maybe that's because you already saw what that was like," Celia put in. "You don't know what it was like before we were born or when we were really young. And you don't know much about what happened before that, what her family was like. Maybe she thought that when he came back, things were going to be different."

Margot shook her head. "The first time or two, maybe. But not over and over again. She should have figured it out a lot sooner."

They fell silent.

"Maybe it was the money," Jason suggested. "Maybe she thought she needed that, so she would put up with him disappearing, as long as he helped to keep food on the table."

"Are you kidding?" Celia said scornfully. "He never paid her any child support."

"But he paid for stuff when he came home. Went grocery shopping, paid bills, fixed her car. That's a lot for a single mom."

"Not enough," Margot declared. "I would never put up with a man just for money."

Zachary didn't remember his father coming and going like that, but had he? Or was that a new behavior he started with a new relationship? Zachary could remember specific things that had happened when they were younger, but not a chronology. He had no idea whether his father had been home every night or if he only came by now and then.

He had been there often enough to produce six babies. Assuming they were all his.

Zachary thought his dad had been there every day. At least, the days when he wasn't in jail.

He brought the conversation back around to the DNA testing. "So Celia thought it would be a good idea to see if Berk was really your dad. Of all of you."

They nodded. Celia gave a little shrug. "I never imagined finding other siblings. I just wanted to see that we all had the same paternal

DNA. It wasn't because we wanted anything from him. I just wanted to know… where we came from."

Zachary nodded.

"So we all did," Jason said. "Celia paid for it all, just bullied us into submitting our samples."

"I didn't bully anyone," Celia argued.

"Well," Jason gave her a teasing smile. "Maybe bully is a bit strong. She *strongly encouraged* us to submit our DNA. Gave us each a test collection kit and wouldn't leave until it was done."

Zachary smiled at that. Celia was apparently a very single-minded person.

"They all came back, and you confirmed that you were all siblings. But then you looked at the other results?"

Celia shook her head. "No, at first, it was just us. And people that we knew in the extended family. And more distant stuff that we didn't. But over time, other people add stuff to the database. When Tyrrell submitted his, I got a notification in my email inbox. 'You have a match.' I didn't think much of it, figured it was just another third cousin. Until I pulled it up, and it said 'sibling.' That was just bizarre."

"I can imagine," Zachary agreed. He felt like he might have somehow slipped into a parallel universe. It was a strange feeling, finding this alternate family who had lived a totally different life from his, the two never crossing paths.

"Jason and Tyrrell connected, and they talked and met a couple of times before Celia and I felt like it was safe to meet him," Margot said. She swirled the ice cubes in her cup. "We didn't want to meet him if he was like Dad."

Zachary nodded understandingly.

"It was on… it was during a sober period," Jason said, grimacing. "Tyrrell was great. We really clicked, got along together. He was excited to meet the girls. Showed us all pictures of his kids. Margot has kids too. Not as old as Tyrrell's."

Zachary smiled at Margot. More nieces and nephews. He would be excited to meet them, when Margot felt comfortable letting the two parts of her life mix.

"Tyrrell is a good guy," Zachary said. "We were only reunited a year ago, but... he means a lot to me. He always has, but meeting him and being able to talk to him again, that's been amazing. He's helped me to meet our other siblings too, my... full siblings that we lived with before... everything happened."

"You've met them all now?" Celia asked. "I thought you hadn't met the youngest ones yet. Tyrrell said he didn't think you were ready."

Zachary pressed his lips together, thinking about it. What had he done to make Tyrrell believe he didn't want to meet the other siblings or wasn't prepared for it? He had done well with his meetings with Heather and Joss. And Joss—she wasn't easy to get along with. If Zachary had been planning things out, he wouldn't have introduced Joss before Vince and Mindy.

"I met them just a couple of days ago. After Tyrrell's disappearance."

"Oh," Jason nodded. "That's what happened. What did you think? Did you get along with them too?"

"Yes. They're nice people. Didn't grow up the same way as I did, in foster care and institutions. They just grew up in one family, and it seems like they were treated well. So they're... more normal. Having that stability growing up makes a big difference in outcomes."

Jason cleared his throat. "You mean the difference between what you went through and what they did? Or Tyrrell and them?"

"Both, I guess. Tyrrell was lucky to have the Millers take them all in so that he could stay with Vince and Mindy and grow up in a more stable home than I did... but I guess a lot of the damage had already been done. He was six, old enough to remember what had gone on in his bio home. We always tried to protect the younger kids, but... he'd already experienced a lot of the... bad stuff."

Jason and his sisters exchanged looks with each other. Zachary looked away, admiring the furnishings and decorations at Old Joe's, even though he'd been there many times before. He looked at Kenzie and she gave him an encouraging smile.

"So... what was he like to you?" Jason finally asked. "Your father."

44

Zachary took a sip of his water, mouth dry as cotton. He tried to remember whether they had ordered drinks or their dinner yet. He thought that they had done both, but there was still just water on the table. Had everyone picked water, or were they still waiting for their drinks?

Under the table, Kenzie gave his leg a squeeze. She didn't say anything to him out loud, but he knew she was concerned about him and about how difficult the discussion was going to be.

"Things were... pretty bad. Growing up in that house, I knew that we were different than our friends. But since that was what I had grown up with, I didn't really realize how abusive and dysfunctional it was until I'd been in a bunch of other families. Learning from friends and foster siblings and social workers what was really normal and what wasn't."

Jason nodded his understanding. The girls were staring at him. Zachary wondered whether they were expecting him to cry or to blow up. While they tried to look relaxed, he could see that they were tense, coiled for action. Ready to defend themselves or flee from the situation if things went bad. He looked away from them again. He didn't want them to see him as confrontational or threatening.

"He and my mom fought a lot. Not just arguing, but actually

beating on each other. Cops would get called and when they showed up, one or both of my parents would be bloody."

Margot's eyes widened. "He would beat up on our mom. But she didn't fight him. She'd run away outside or lock herself into the bathroom. She'd tell us to hide and stay out of his way."

Zachary let out his breath, sighing. Was it better that his mother had fought back? He knew that Berk wasn't always the one who started the fights. Sometimes it was her. And she did not try to keep the children out of the way and protect them. She was just as likely to whip them as he was.

"We had... both of them. I don't like to talk about my mom... I always wanted to go back home, to show her that I could be better than she thought I was. I guess I loved her, but looking back, I don't know why. She was... she was abusive too. Verbally and physically. I guess... she thought it was the only way to handle six kids. Physical discipline." His throat was tight and hot. He took another drink, trying to cool it.

"Traumatic bonding," Kenzie suggested. "You depended on her for your life. You had to love her. To want to please her. It was a matter of survival." Her eyes were compassionate. As he'd said, he didn't like to talk about his mother and, even in therapy, he had avoided talking about her in front of Kenzie as much as possible. She knew about the things his mother had said when she had refused to take Zachary or the other children back after the fire. But he had not told Kenzie that she was physically abusive as well. Not in so many words; but Kenzie had probably figured out that much.

"I guess." Zachary shrugged. "Everybody loves their parents, right? That's what we're taught. That's what the media is always saying. No love like a mother's. Mom and apple pie. All of those... ideals."

"Not everybody loves their parents," Celia said darkly. "I hated him. I hated every minute he was with us. If the DNA testing had shown that he was not our father, I would have been so happy."

"Sorry." Zachary wasn't sure what he was apologizing for. Berk's abusive behavior? Zachary talking about how everyone was supposed to love their parents? But something had to be said, and he couldn't think of anything else to fill the silence.

"Well, he wasn't with us all the time," Jason said with forced cheer. "We were lucky he was such a deadbeat. And for the time he was in prison. Let's hear it for manslaughter charges!"

"What happened, do you know?" Zachary asked. He tried to push down the uneasy worry that Berk might have killed one of his children. Not one of Jason's full siblings, clearly, or he wouldn't be joking about it. But what if there had been another family? He knew that parents could kill. He'd known that from a very young age, and the fact had been impressed upon him recently with Ben Burton's case and the discovery that his abusive mother had killed her other son. "Who did he kill?"

"I don't really know anything about it," Jason said, looking at the girls to see if they had any thoughts. "I got the feeling it was maybe a bar fight?"

"That or a DUI," Margot said, shaking her head. "I don't know if we were ever told any details. But I definitely got the idea that it was something to do with drinking. So maybe our mom said that he'd had too much to drink and had killed someone, and we were just left to fill in the details ourselves."

Zachary could look up the details if he wanted to. He wasn't sure he wanted to know. "So he was away for a few years because of that?"

"Yeah. Three or four years, I think," Jason agreed. "It was a nice break. We kind of had a normal life during that time."

"And then when he came back, that was when Mom finally decided she'd had enough," Celia said.

They all looked at each other, a current running among the three of them. Something about it raised the hair on the back of Zachary's neck. He looked at each of them, analyzing their expressions and body language for an inkling of what had happened that they didn't want to put into words.

"What?" he asked finally. His eyes were drawn to Margot. She was the one who seemed to want to talk about it the most. He could feel her outrage, a boiling anger beneath the surface. "What happened?"

Margot exploded, calling Berk names, her volume and vehemence attracting stares from most of the restaurant patrons around them. The conversations going on in the restaurant ceased and everyone was silent, waiting to hear what was going on. There was a single laugh, somewhere on the other side of the room.

Jason gave Margot a look, but didn't tell her to mind herself. Celia put an arm around her sister and pulled her close. "We should... maybe we should go to the powder room," she suggested.

Margot looked furious. Not ready to be silenced and to behave like a lady. Celia squeezed her. "Come on. Let's just take a break. Splash some water on our faces."

"Where are our drinks? Didn't we order drinks?"

"I'll ask," Jason said. "You guys go ahead."

Celia managed to get Margot to her feet, and they headed toward the restrooms. Jason looked at Zachary and Kenzie and gave an embarrassed shrug. "Sorry..."

"No," Zachary shook his head. "It's fine. We've all got our triggers and hot buttons. I didn't mean to push."

"Probably best to get it out in the open in the beginning," Jason said philosophically. He looked in the direction the girls had gone, making sure that they were out of the way and weighing his words. "He didn't just hit them. The girls. When he came back after prison... it was worse. I don't know if it was because they were older and looked more mature, or if something happened to him in prison... or just being away from any *company* during that time. When Mom realized what was going on, that was the straw that finally broke the camel's back. She told him to get out and never come back unless he wanted to go straight back to prison. She'd call his parole officer, and he'd be back in prison and facing new charges."

"And even on the inside, they don't look on pedophiles too kindly."

"No."

"She didn't report it to the police?"

"No." Jason sighed. "She's an avoider. Would rather not have to deal with any of the fall-out. Says it was for the girls, so they wouldn't have to testify in court, but I think it was mostly selfish."

"They could still report it if they wanted to." Zachary nodded toward the back hallway where the two sisters had disappeared.

"They don't. They take after Mom. Just want to forget about it. Though you can see... it's not as easy to forget about as they would like."

"No." Zachary was an authority on that subject. "It's not."

"Did he do that to your family too? The older girls?"

"I don't know." Zachary thought back through the mists of time. It was hard to remember a lot of specifics from that long ago, especially since he had closed off as much of it as he could. If Berk had been molesting the older girls, would Zachary have been aware of it? Probably not. It would have been kept quiet, behind closed doors. He thought about Joss's bitterness and experience in being trafficked, and Heather's vulnerability to the foster father in the home she had been placed in. Both were consistent with a history of sexual assault. "Maybe. Neither of them have ever said anything to me about it, but... it's possible."

He felt nauseated at the thought of his father doing that, and his mother letting it go on, if she had been aware of it. And he felt immediately guilty, as if he should have been able to do something to prevent it. He should have been able to protect his sisters. He should have at least tried. But he didn't think that he had known about it. He had only known about the physical abuse, what he could see in front of him. What he had experienced himself. That had never been hidden.

Jason nodded. "I didn't really know what was going on at the time, or what the fighting was about. But then... he was gone, and I found out little bits over the next few years. Wish that I could have done something about it. That I had known at the time. I just thought that if he wasn't hitting anybody, it was all good."

Jason waved down a waitress walking by. "Hey. We ordered drinks, if you could check on those. And our dinners? We've been here a while."

She looked at him for a moment, then nodded. "Sure. I'll check."

45

Margot and Celia returned from the restroom as the drinks were delivered to the table. Margot appeared to have settled down, but Zachary could see that her eyes were red-rimmed and puffy. He looked away from her, not wanting to draw attention to the fact.

He didn't know if he should say anything about what Jason had told them. He had a feeling it wouldn't go over well if he said that he understood what she had gone through. The circumstances were different, and he couldn't know exactly what she felt like or if she had felt the same way as he had when he was assaulted in foster care or later by Archuro.

"Sorry," he said briefly, "that this is so hard for you. I didn't mean... to cause anyone grief."

"Not your fault," Margot said stoically, looking remarkably like Joss when she pushed him away, refusing to let him get too close. "It happened and it's my thing to deal with, not yours."

"I know, but... I don't want you to feel bad around me. To associate me with that stuff. We'll have a nice meal, talk about good times instead of bad..."

"Build a positive association," Kenzie contributed.

"Yeah." Zachary nodded. "Like that."

Margot rolled her eyes, not impressed with the suggestion. But she didn't argue. Talking about more positive stuff instead of focusing on what had happened to her at the hands of their father was clearly a better idea than immersing herself in the negativity, so she was willing to change the subject.

"You have kids?" Zachary asked her. "Why don't you tell me about them?"

"Yeah, I have two boys," Margot admitted and, though she didn't smile, he could hear in her voice that this was a preferred topic. She picked up her phone from the table next to her, unlocked it, and tapped it a few times, then handed it to Zachary with a picture on the screen. Two boys sitting on swings at the park. Both tow-headed and smiley, mischief sparkling in their eyes.

"Oh, they look like a going concern," Zachary observed, smiling.

Margot nodded, her face softening and the lines around her eyes lightening, even if she didn't give him a full smile yet. "Yes, they're always into something. But they are the light of my life. I don't know where I would be without them."

Zachary showed the picture to Kenzie. She smiled and had a sip of her drink. "What cuties. About four or five?"

"Yeah."

"Can I look at some other pictures?" Zachary asked, finger poised to swipe through the photos.

She held her hand out for her phone and took it back. She tapped and swiped through a few photos, then handed it back. "You can look through that album."

Zachary browsed through the pictures, holding the phone so that Kenzie could see them too. They laughed at pictures of the two smiling children amid big messes, going to the zoo, and sitting on the couch at home, arms wrapped around each other.

"Your mom must be in love with them," Zachary said. "They're her only grandchildren?"

"Yeah, as far as I know."

Zachary raised his brows. "Oh…?"

"After diving into the world of DNA relatives and finding out how many people are discovering deep dark secrets when they start researching their ancestral DNA… I'm not sure I'm willing to believe anyone with anything in regard to procreation." Margot looked at Celia, and they both shook their heads and rolled their eyes over the stories they had discovered. "As far as I know, we're Mom's only kids, but that doesn't mean she couldn't have gotten pregnant in high school and given the baby up. Or donated eggs. Who knows what else. But as far as I know, Bailey and Uriel are the only grandchildren that Mom knows about."

Zachary chuckled. "I guess nothing is as straightforward as we would like to pretend. We've lived in a society that was once so strict about marriage and out-of-wedlock babies, and is now so open about it… Secrets on one end and multiple relationships on the other…"

"It's weird," Celia agreed. "It's like nothing in this world was really what you thought it was."

They all thought about this. Zachary handed Margot's phone back eventually. "They're wonderful," he said. "I love kids."

"You don't have any of your own?"

"No."

"As far as you know," Celia said.

Zachary opened his mouth to argue, then shrugged. "As far as I know," he agreed with a shrug. He rolled his eyes a little at Kenzie, so that she would be the only one who saw it. Trying to communicate with her that he had not been indiscriminate in the past. She knew about Bridget and that she hadn't had any children with him. He hadn't had any other serious relationships. But he had to agree with Celia that sometimes things happened. A night when he'd had too much to drink and didn't remember much about what had happened when morning came around. Situations where he'd been taken advantage of in foster care. There was no way he could account for every possibility.

"Tyrrell has the two; I guess he told you about them. And Heather, she has two, plus one that she gave up for adoption who she was just reunited with recently."

"Tyrrell mentioned that," Celia said. "That's pretty cool too. I guess since he marked his information as private, he won't show up on our charts, but if he hadn't, he would show up as a nephew."

"The family keeps getting bigger." Zachary smiled. He took a drink, trying to hide the smile in case the others didn't feel the same way he did.

Celia smiled, but it was reserved. Not sure yet how she felt about having more relatives. And maybe with what they had gone through with their father, that was understandable. It would make it harder to trust anyone who was related or claimed to be. What if they had inherited that violence or those other proclivities from him? He could see why Jason had said it was a good idea if he brought Kenzie with him. It made him seem safer. Someone else to keep an eye on him and give references for him. Attest to the fact that he was an okay guy.

"And the two of you?" Zachary looked from Celia to Jason and back. "Do you have any plans to start a family? Anyone special in your lives?"

Celia shook her head firmly. Jason gave a shrug. "No one yet."

The waitress arrived with their steaks and deposited them around the table. "Can I get you anything else?"

"Ketchup?" Zachary suggested.

He didn't look at Kenzie, but knew that she rolled her eyes at that. Ketchup with steak and potatoes would have been sacrilege in the household she had grown up in. They'd probably eaten steak blood-rare and paired it with some special wine, and maybe baby asparagus or something else fancy.

Jason let out a loud guffaw. "You see?" he demanded, pointing at Margot. "I'm not the only one!"

"I'll bring you a bottle of ketchup," the waitress promised, smiling at them but not joining in on the laughter.

"You like it with ketchup too?" Zachary asked.

"I know. It's totally wrong. It means I'm a completely uncultured redneck. But it's my steak!"

"What you do with your steak is your own business," Margot told him. "I just wish we didn't have to see it."

The waitress returned quickly with the ketchup, putting it between the two men.

46

Zachary leaned back, putting his hand over his stomach. Way too full. It hadn't been the flavor of the steak or the ketchup, but the company that had made him keep eating when he'd already had enough. He caught Kenzie and Jason both eyeing his plate.

Jason raised an eyebrow. "Not to your liking? Didn't you get enough ketchup?"

Zachary shook his head. "I don't eat very much. This was actually a lot for me. I'm stuffed."

"You're stuffed. You barely had half the steak and hardly touched the potatoes. Even Celia ate more than you did."

"He's telling the truth," Kenzie said. "I was actually surprised that he got that much down. Usually, his servings are about the size of a four-year-old's."

Zachary scratched his neck, grimacing and feeling his earlobes getting red. "Kenzie...!"

"I'm not going to lie to them. Or have them thinking that you're not enjoying the meal, which you obviously are."

"Yeah, but... a four-year-old? I eat at least as much as a five-year-old."

She laughed, and the others joined in.

"I guess… before we go our separate directions, I had a few more questions," Zachary said. It might not be the most graceful conversation shift, but it would have to do. "About Tyrrell, you know. I'd really like to be able to find him."

Jason, Margot, and Celia looked at each other.

"I wish I could help you, man," Jason said. "But we really don't have any idea. Tyrrell… we visited a little, off and on, but he wasn't a best friend or anything. He didn't tell us what he was doing or where he was going."

"He told you about me and the others."

"Yeah. But how does that help you?"

"Maybe he told you other things about his life too. You just don't realize that it could be anything important."

"Like what? His favorite vacation would be to go to Disneyland? You going to fly to Disney to see if you can find him there?"

"It might not be anything like that. It might just be… someone he mentioned a few times. Someone he drinks with. A favorite childhood memory. Maybe where he went to dry out the last time he went into a program. I've only known him a year and… I guess he didn't tell me any of that kind of thing. I knew that he'd had a problem with alcohol, but I didn't realize it was so recent. I never asked him anything about it like I should have."

"We're in the same boat, Zach. I'm sorry. We just didn't talk about that kind of stuff. And when it became obvious that he still had a problem with the bottle, we kind of backed off. None of us wanted to have to deal with that. Not after Dad."

"He never talked about anyone else? Only us kids? And his own kids? Lindsey?"

"Yeah."

"Well, and *him*," Margot contributed.

Zachary shook his head, having missed the reference. "Sorry, who?"

They all looked at each other, no one eager to be the one to answer. Zachary frowned and ran the conversation back in his mind, trying to figure out what he had missed.

"Who do you mean? His brothers and sister, and his kids, and who?" He remembered they had talked about Heather's adopted son. Was that who Tyrrell had mentioned? Another family member that he was eager to meet?

Jason pushed his empty plate away from himself an inch. He lifted up his empty glass and swirled around the ice cubes melting in the bottom.

"Berk."

Zachary blinked. "Berk? He talked about our dad?"

Jason nodded.

Zachary supposed that made sense. He was the common tie between them. That was a subject that Zachary had thought to bring up as well. Comparing their experiences with Berk, what he'd been like as a father.

"Yeah, Berk," Margot said and called him a couple more foul names, but didn't get loud and attract attention like she had the first time. "Tyrrell thought... that he couldn't be as bad as we were making him out to be. That we remembered wrong, or our mom had made things worse, poisoned our minds against him."

Zachary rubbed the place between his eyebrows that was starting to get sore. He knew he was holding himself too tense. The atmosphere of Old Joe's, which had seemed to be warm and inviting before, was starting to feel hot and oppressive. A bead of sweat ran down his back.

"Why would he think that?"

"Because he couldn't remember as much about how things were when he was a kid as you do. He was younger, and in between, that stupid social worker told him lies about Berk. That he was poor and couldn't afford to take six kids or some nonsense like that. She didn't tell them what it was really like."

Zachary groaned and shook his head. "If he wanted to know, I would have told him. He never said he wanted to know anything about him. And I... don't talk about it. I thought he knew."

"Well, he didn't, so he thought that we were lying, and Berk was the one telling the truth. He thought we had been manipulated by our Mom. *Tyrrell* was the one who was manipulated."

Zachary nodded. "I know. Sheesh. If I'd known that he was

talking to anyone about it… I didn't even know about you; he didn't mention you. I didn't know that Dad had gone on to have other kids. He must have driven you crazy, repeating what the social worker said."

"It wasn't the social worker so much as him," Margot declared.

Zachary was having trouble making sense of the conversation. Every time he thought he had the thread, he lost it. Something was going on that he wasn't catching. He turned his head to look at Kenzie, wondering whether she were as lost as he was. Was one of his meds clouding his thought processes? Or maybe he was having a stroke. If he were having a stroke, Kenzie would notice, at least. She'd know what to do.

Kenzie gave a slight shake of her head, indicating she wasn't following it either. Zachary was relieved. The problem must be that the siblings had a sort of a shorthand between them. They knew what they were talking about, but it had to be explained to someone who didn't grow up with them and didn't already know what they did.

"He believed what *Berk* told him," Margot told Zachary in a tone that indicated she thought he was an idiot.

Zachary frowned at her, trying to process what she had said and what had already been said. Something was not computing.

yrrell was talking to Berk?" Zachary finally said, dragging the words out with difficulty. "Tyrrell was…?"

"Yes," Margot agreed, nodding vigorously. "Tyrrell was talking to him. Believing all of the nonsense that Berk was filling his head with. That everything had been fine when you guys were with him. That we were just making things up or exaggerating them because our mom filled our head with lies about him. Poor Berk was the victim, being unfairly maligned."

Zachary cupped his palms over his eyes, blocking everything out. He tried to force it to make sense, but he couldn't. What they were telling him didn't make any sense at all.

"When… where… how was Tyrrell talking to Berk? Where…?"

"I don't know where they met." Margot made a noise, blowing this off. "What does that matter?"

Zachary dropped his hands from his face. "You're saying that now, this year, Tyrrell saw Berk. Face to face? He was talking to him?"

"Last year," Jason corrected. "He was in contact with Berk even before us, so… two years… maybe more, I don't know."

"Why?" Zachary was flabbergasted. He couldn't figure out why anyone would want to see an abusive parent again. Not as an adult, anyway. He had wanted to go back home to his parents when he had been a child, before he had understood that not all parents were like that and really understood how much permanent damage they had done him. But as an adult, Tyrrell had to know that going back to Berk was a mistake. There was no reason for him to do it. No reason at all to go back to the man who had been so abusive.

The siblings looked at him. They had no answer to his question. Zachary covered his eyes again, grinding his fists into them, trying to push everything else out and to think about Tyrrell and why he would have ever wanted to see Berk again.

Tyrrell hadn't been able to remember everything about the home he had come from with the same clarity as Zachary. Just as there were things Heather and Joss remembered much better than Zachary. Tyrrell remembered their parents fighting the night of the fire, but maybe he didn't remember that there had been a physical fight. Maybe he didn't remember that was how it was all the time, with the two of them arguing and hitting, and the children also targets if they happened to get in the way or do something to raise the ire of either parent. Tyrrell had been six, and the older siblings had protected him from the abuse as much as they could. He didn't remember the worse stuff, or had blocked it out. He had been put into the Millers' home and maybe not gotten any therapy until after his behavior got so bad as a teenager. If Mrs. Pratt hadn't told his foster parents all that he had been through, they wouldn't have known what to do, wouldn't have known where the behavior came from.

As the years had passed, Tyrrell had decided to make contact with his family. And he had gone directly to DNA. Zachary and the others weren't in the database of the company that Tyrrell had gone through, but Jason and the girls had been. Tyrrell had contacted them and...

Zachary had to rewind. He was missing a step. Tyrrell had contacted Berk *before* meeting Jason, Margot, and Celia. How? Had they just happened to run into each other? Had Tyrrell's need to search been triggered by running into Berk by accident? Or had Berk sought him out?

Zachary hadn't gone back that far in Tyrrell's email. He had looked at the most recent matches and followed them back to Tyrrell's account with the DNA company. But that wasn't the only DNA matching company. Not by a long shot. They were getting more and more prevalent. And Zachary hadn't even checked the top three or four in the industry. He had stopped at the one nearest the top of Tyrrell's email inbox and assumed that Tyrrell would only have submitted his results to one database. Who would submit their DNA to more than one company?

"Did Berk show up in the database when you guys submitted your DNA tests?"

"No," Celia said, her tone crisp. "Like I said. It just showed that we were all siblings. And there was some extended family. Not Berk. But there were some Goldman relatives, so we knew that he was our father, not some other boyfriend."

"But he wasn't in there himself."

"No."

"Would Tyrrell have submitted tests to a bunch of different websites? That doesn't make any sense, does it? They all have pretty much the same thing; you wouldn't need to do more than one…"

"Zachary." Kenzie touched Zachary's arm, encouraging him to lower his hands from his face so he could see the others. He rested them on the table in front of him, closing his eyes for a moment to try to center himself, then opened them again.

Jason shook his head. "The others are probably a lot more conversant in this than I am, but the databases are all different. They have different pools of results, because there isn't one place where you can add your DNA to all of them simultaneously. And different companies have different tools on their websites. Not just different matches, but constructing DNA of ancestors based on their descendants, browsing genomes, finding out health risks, all kinds of things."

"So you do tests for all of these different companies?"

"No," Celia explained, "You do it once, and you download a copy of your raw genome. Then you can upload that to all of the other websites. You don't have to pay for a whole bunch of different test kits. Just the one."

"If Tyrrell met Berk before he met you… then he must have submitted his to a different testing company to start with."

"Yeah." Jason looked at the others, nodding, and they nodded in turn. "He must have. I hadn't thought about that, but it's the only way it makes sense because Berk didn't show up on our results."

"And Tyrrell contacted him… before he contacted you or any of us."

"Yes. We tried to explain to him what Berk was really like, but he wouldn't listen. Or he would seem like he was, but then the next time he talked to him, he would come back with all of this nonsense again."

Zachary looked at Kenzie, his throat starting to constrict. She recognized the panic in his eyes.

"It's okay," she assured him. "Focus on me. Deep breaths."

"I think it's Zachary's turn for the powder room this time," Margot said dryly, earning an elbow from Celia.

"Do you need to take a break?" Kenzie suggested. "Walk away for a few minutes until you can calm down?"

Zachary shook his head, embarrassed at putting on such a display in front of his new siblings. He took a sip of his water, forcing himself to swallow even though it felt impossible. The cold water helped, and he took a couple more gulps, then looked around for the waitress. Kenzie tried to flag one down.

"Some more water, please?"

The waitress murmured in passing that she would be back with it in a few minutes. Kenzie pushed her water glass toward Zachary. She had been drinking wine, so her water glass was still mostly full, though the ice had melted. Zachary gulped down the top half of it.

"Just breathe," Kenzie encouraged. She put her hand on his back, between his shoulders and, when Zachary didn't object, she rubbed, trying to loosen the tension he was holding there.

"Maybe we should call it a night," Jason suggested, watching Zachary.

Zachary shook his head.

"Give it a few minutes," Kenzie advised. "I think he can manage."

Celia and Margot whispered to each other. Zachary couldn't tell what they were saying. They were probably talking about him. About what a wreck their brothers were, Tyrrell with his alcoholism and Zachary with his obvious emotional problems.

"You don't drink?" Jason asked, his eyes on Zachary's water glass. Everyone else but Celia had ordered something else to drink. Only Zachary and Celia had stuck with water.

Zachary blew out his breath slowly and tried to answer. "Sometimes, a glass. But not..." He coughed and looked at Kenzie to help answer the question, not able to speak naturally yet.

"He can't take alcohol with some of his meds," Kenzie explained. "If he knows or thinks he will need to take one of them later, he won't drink." She patted him on the back. "He's very good about it. A lot of people just go ahead and mix them anyway, which is *not* a good idea."

"How come he's on medication? Is he sick?"

"ADHD, anxiety, depression," Zachary said, "stuff like that." He tried another sip of water. The constriction in his throat was gradually relaxing. "Most of the time... not this bad."

"Don't know why meeting three siblings you never even knew existed before would cause any anxiety," Celia joked. "Or, you know, talking about your abusive father."

Zachary nodded gratefully. "Yeah. It's... just a little stressful." He took a couple more deep breaths, trying to alleviate the feeling that he wasn't getting enough oxygen. Kenzie rubbed his back in soothing circles. "I can't believe... Tyrrell would be in contact with Berk. That he would believe anything he said."

"Yeah. Welcome to the club," Margot agreed. "I mean, I get it that he was pretty young the last time he saw him, but..." She shook her head. Obviously, she felt that Berk's behavior should have left an impression on Tyrrell, no matter how young he had been. He should have remembered enough to know that Berk was not a safe person to be around and that he was lying about his past.

"I'll talk to him when I find him," Zachary promised. "Explain it to him."

"And what makes you think he will believe you?"

Zachary's heart sank. He shook his head. "He has to. I need him to listen."

48

Zachary was glad that he had offered to go to the restaurant in Kenzie's vehicle, so there was no question that she would be the one driving home. He was not as enervated as he was when he had a full-blown panic attack. Still, the evening had defi- nitely been stressful. He was exhausted and just wanted to be by himself and go to bed. But at the same time, his anxious brain was trying to work through the new revelations about Tyrrell and his connection with Berk, and everything else he had learned about Berk that night.

Kenzie drove most of the way home in silence, checking in with him only one time to ask if he was okay. Zachary nodded and stared out the window.

"Just thinking."

When they got home, he didn't know what to do with himself. Hands in his pockets, he paced across to his usual seat on the couch, but he didn't feel like sitting down to use his computer or watch TV, and he turned around and paced back into the kitchen. He wasn't really hungry. In fact, he was pretty full from the steak dinner, but he went to the fridge anyway, looked for anything interesting, then looked through the cupboard. Of course, he didn't actually want anything to eat, so this was pointless.

Kenzie watched him pace down the hallway to the bathroom, decide that he didn't need anything there, and then return to the living room.

"You want to talk, or just go for a jog?" she asked lightly.

Zachary intended to tell her that he didn't feel like talking. He had done enough visiting that night and needed time to process it. But as soon as he opened his mouth to tell her he didn't want to talk, the words started to tumble out.

"I never even thought about him being alive. He was out of my life and I never wanted to see him again. I just... shut him out of my thoughts altogether, like he was dead and buried. I never thought to ask Tyrrell if he'd had any contact with him. Why would he?"

"Considering that in your mind, he was dead and buried."

"Yes. And... he was abusive. You don't go back to people who were abusive."

"But people do," Kenzie pointed out. "That's part of the cycle of abuse. Like Jason and the others were talking about tonight. Their mom kept taking him back, even though she knew he was physically and emotionally abusive."

Kenzie looked like she would say more, but kept her mouth shut. The fact that she held herself back meant that she had been about to say something that might hurt Zachary or make him more upset.

Bridget, of course. Who was Zachary to criticize Tyrrell for going back to his abusive father when Zachary had spent years at Bridget's beck and call, even knowing how verbally abusive she was? He had craved her attention, even if it was negative. Dr. B had suggested that Bridget might be an emotional surrogate for his mother. That Zachary wanted her attention, and he had unconsciously assigned Bridget to fill that role. The mother he could never please. The wife he could never please. The ex-wife. The ex-mother.

He shook his head at this and didn't try to address it directly. Kenzie was right to see the parallel. He was not one to talk about it being illogical to go back to an abuser.

"But... Berk. I can't understand it. What is he getting out of that relationship? He didn't just go back to see him once. Not from what they said. He kept going back."

"I don't know," Kenzie said honestly. "I can't imagine doing it myself. But I would have to guess… he's confused. Vulnerable. Trying to fulfill a dream."

Zachary nodded. He paced back and forth between the kitchen and living room. "I'm going to have to talk to him."

"Tyrrell? You want to talk to him about it? Get him to explain how he's feeling?"

"No. Berk. My dad. If he and Tyrrell have been talking to each other… he might have an idea about where Tyrrell would go. T's been keeping this whole thing a secret from me for a year. He has this whole other life. Two other lives that I never knew anything about."

And more. Tyrrell had his life with Mindy and Vince and his foster parents too. Zachary had at least known about them, but Tyrrell had kept everyone but Zachary and the older girls separate, had never let their lives overlap. He had all of these families, but had any of them given him what he was looking for?

"There are more matches in the DNA database as well," Zachary said. "Other sibling matches. I contacted Jason first because he had been trying to follow up, had been trying to get in touch with Tyrrell. I thought he was the closest, the one who would know best where Tyrrell is."

"It must feel so strange. I mean, first of all, to discover them through this DNA database. But also strange that Tyrrell would be so eager to contact them and then keep them secret from each other."

"It is, right?" Zachary thought that he had a pretty good under-standing of human behavior, even if he hadn't ever received any special training about it. He had lived with and observed so many different people in so many different circumstances. Sometimes his life or well-being had hinged on his being able to understand why they did what they did or what was likely to happen in response to his actions. Sure, he still failed. Usually, when he jumped right in and did something impulsively rather than thinking it over. He couldn't help that; it was part of his makeup. Part of his ADHD or PTSD. But when he was thinking and considering what to do next, he was usually pretty good at predicting other people's responses. "I would think that he would want us all to meet, to get along with each other. To all be one... big happy family."

Kenzie nodded. "I'm sure it is something that makes sense in his mind, even if it doesn't make sense to us."

"I have to find him," Zachary said, the steak dinner feeling heavy and solid in his stomach as he came to the realization.

"I know. We're all trying."

"No. Not Tyrrell."

Kenzie looked at him, frowning.

"Berk. I'm going to have to find my father."

49

Kenzie recognized the seriousness of the situation. She knew some of what Zachary had gone through as a kid. He hadn't told her everything. Nowhere near everything. But he thought that he had told her enough for her to understand that his home had not been a happy place. She had just listened to Jason and the others talking about how abusive Berk was to them and had heard Zachary confirm that it had been the same for him. She had to understand that the very last thing Zachary wanted to do was track down his father. If there were any way around it…

"That will have to wait," she said sensibly. "You can't track him down tonight, so you don't want to get yourself all wound up in trying. Let's have a nice evening together. Let you unwind and clear your head. Get a good sleep tonight. Then you can worry about your next step tomorrow."

Zachary was actually glad for an excuse not to begin the search. It seemed like the worst thing anyone could have asked him to do. He wished there were some other way around it. But Kenzie was offering a reprieve for the evening, anyway. He would do much better with it, mentally and emotionally, if he were fresh and well-rested. Things would go much better.

"Okay," he agreed. He took a few breaths and paced back and forth. "What do you want to do?"

"What do you feel like? Watch a movie? Cuddle? Work out your energy some way other than pacing back and forth?" She lifted an eyebrow.

Zachary laughed. "I don't think I'm up for much more than cuddling tonight. I'm too... My stomach really isn't feeling very good. I shouldn't have eaten so much tonight."

"I was glad to see you getting more than a few bites down. Sorry that it's making you uncomfortable, though."

Zachary held his hand over his stomach for a minute. "I think it's more than just the dinner. I think probably... I'm a little anxious."

"I think probably you're a lot anxious."

He shrugged and nodded. "Yeah."

"That's okay. Cuddling would make me happy, if that's what you want to do. Do you want to take something for the anxiety? You managed to head off an attack at the restaurant, but if you're still feeling anxious, maybe you should do something about it."

"Not yet." While Zachary didn't want to suffer through the physical discomfort and chattering brain that anxiety brought, he didn't want to take something to combat them, either. He wanted to be able to think. Not slowly and methodically like a scientist, but the way he knew his brain worked when he was not medicated—on hyperdrive, going through all of the possibilities. His daytime meds were wearing off and if he didn't need to take his night meds for a couple more hours, he had a window of time during which he could just let his brain run and see what solutions it came up with. If the anxiety didn't eventually start to fade on its own, he could take something before bed and see whether he could calm down and relax enough to sleep.

Kenzie didn't argue. He could sense her disapproval, but she was trying very hard to let him be in charge of his body and medications and not interfere just because she was a doctor and thought she knew what he should do. Or because she cared for him and wanted to eliminate as many of the symptoms as possible. She didn't understand much about how he could sometimes use his neurodivergence to his advantage.

"Let's put something on the TV for a while," Zachary suggested. "That will help distract me."

Partway through the movie, Zachary's phone buzzed. He looked over at it, where he'd left it on his computer table so that it would not be in his hand and distracting him from watching the movie and paying attention to Kenzie. He was sure that he had put it on Do Not Disturb so that he wouldn't be interrupted by any calls or texts. And he only had a few exceptions to his Do Not Disturb function. He glanced at Kenzie.

"Didn't you switch it over?" she asked.

He nodded. "I'm sure I did."

"You'd better see who it is, then."

Zachary picked up the phone, his mind immediately flying to what might be wrong. Although he knew that no one on his important contacts list had anything to do with his father, other than Tyrrell, Zachary's brain immediately jumped to the possibility that it was one of the DNA siblings, either the ones he had contacted or ones that he hadn't, who wanted something from him or were angry about his searching for Tyrrell and deciding to search for Berk.

But of course, they were not on his exceptions list. If they did call him, they would be funneled to voicemail, and he could catch up with them later. The name on the caller ID was Lorne Peterson.

Zachary swiped the answer call slider. "Mr. Peterson?"

"Lorne, Zachary," his patient voice reminded. "Calm down. I didn't call because something is wrong."

Zachary took a deep breath and let it out. He looked at Kenzie, who was also looking worried, and shrugged. He lowered his voice to something that he hoped didn't sound quite so panicked. "Sorry. Hi. How are you?"

"We are both doing just fine. What's got you so worked up?"

Zachary didn't feel like taking him through the whole case, so he just shrugged it off. "Nothing. I just wasn't expecting your call. It startled me."

2

"Didn't mean to cause any concern. Pat and I were wondering if you and Kenzie would be able to make it down for dinner and a visit on Sunday. I don't know what Kenzie's schedule is like. Sorry I didn't call sooner, but..."

Zachary covered up the mic on the phone to speak to Kenzie. "Sunday dinner?"

She nodded.

"Sure, that looks okay," Zachary agreed. "Would Pat like us to bring anything? A bottle of wine?"

"No, no. We'll handle everything this time. We're going to have a small gathering in the afternoon. A little memorial ceremony. Just a few people in our circles who knew Jose and wanted to... mark his passing."

"Oh. Sure, of course." Zachary thought about the people he had interviewed while he had been looking for Jose. He had run into some interesting characters, most of whom he really didn't want to meet up with again, even on Pat's turf. "Um... who are you having?"

"Not anyone you met, I don't think," Lorne said. "Some of the men we go to events with. Musicals. Performances."

"Not... Santiago?"

"No, no," Lorne assured him. "And we're not using any of his facilities. Just a little garden ceremony. Oh—Eric Naylor will be there... he is sometimes part of our group. Are you okay with that?"

Naylor ran a high-end second-hand clothing store, which is where Zachary had interviewed him. Not the kind of place where people went thrift shopping, but somewhere they could get a deal on a big-name brand without burning through thousands of dollars. He had not been particularly helpful to Zachary during his investigation, but Zachary didn't think he would be too uncomfortable around him. He, at least, hadn't shown any interest in Zachary. Nor was he a physically intimidating man; slim and fussy with long, tapering fingers.

"Yeah, that should be okay. I'd be fine with him."

"Okay, good. We'll have the ceremony in the afternoon when it is warmer, about three o'clock. Dinner later in the evening, so you'll have time to decompress in between. And dinner will be just the four of us."

Zachary nodded. "Sure. Sounds good. We'll be there."

"You haven't... found out anything about Tyrrell yet, have you?"

"Some new leads... but nothing concrete yet. I have... something to follow up on tomorrow. Maybe it will break the case." Zachary wasn't ready to give him any details yet about his biological family. That was too much. Something that should be saved for a face-to-face meeting. And since they would have one within a couple of days, he wasn't really holding anything back.

"That's good news. I'm glad you're making progress. We consider Tyrrell part of our extended family."

"Oh." This brought a quick tear to Zachary's eye, and he tried to blink it away and stay calm. "That's really nice. Thank you."

"Your family is our family. We'll see you Sunday, then. Take care."

"You too. Take care."

50

Zachary's active brain hadn't come up with anything brilliant while he was watching TV with Kenzie. He didn't feel like he was anywhere closer to understanding Tyrrell and the choices he had made about his family. He didn't have any brilliant insights into contacting Berk, but it should all be pretty straightforward. There must be contact information in Tyrrell's email system somewhere. And even if not, Berk Goldman was not a common name and it wouldn't be hard to run a few searches and find out his last few addresses. Since he had a prison record, he might even have to report to a parole officer or keep his address up to date on the sex offender registry. Just because Margot's and Celia's mother hadn't reported him for assaulting her daughters, that didn't mean that he'd never been caught and held accountable for another sexual assault. Someone else might not have been satisfied with just having him out of her life.

Taking an anti-anxiety pill and sleep aid before going to bed made his waking in the morning groggy and slow. He had breakfast with Kenzie, mostly just staring blearily at his food while she ate hers. After seeing her off to work, he opened up his computer and started to poke around to see what he could find. Kenzie wouldn't likely be gone all day. Usually when she went in on the weekend, it was just for a few hours to catch up on things or help Dr. Wiltshire with something urgent. Even though the Medical Examiner's Office was only supposed to be open on weekdays, they frequently used the weekend to clear any backlog. And Zachary really didn't mind that. They would have Sunday off together, and that would include a highway drive, which always made him feel more relaxed.

He was right, and it only took a few well-placed searches to find fairly comprehensive contact details for Berk Goldman. Zachary transcribed everything carefully, then looked at it again.

It might be easier and more efficient to try calling Berk on the phone rather than driving out to look for him in person. But that also gave him the option to hang up if he didn't want to talk to Zachary. Whether he knew anything about where Tyrrell was or not, he might very well want to avoid any kind of conversation with his oldest son. He would know that Zachary wasn't exactly likely to be bringing him any flowers.

He looked back at Berk's contact information again and decided that a personal visit was in order. The last thing he wanted to do was to see Berk face-to-face. But the thing he wanted most was to find Tyrrell, hopefully safe and sound, and that had to be a higher priority than avoiding his own discomfort with seeing his biological father again.

Overthinking would keep him from acting, so he gathered his notepad, phone, and keys and forced himself to walk out to his car and get on his way.

Snow was blowing across the highway, making the winter driving a little more treacherous than usual. Zachary drove a little more slowly than he usually would have without Kenzie in the car and lost himself in the meditative state that highway driving usually produced for him. He was able to ponder a little on what he would say or do when he met his father, something he hadn't been able to do without significant anxiety the night before. Rather than his anxiety increasing as he approached the event, it started to subside.

Berk Goldman didn't know Zachary. Not anymore. He had

known Zachary, the little boy. The little boy he had been before he had entered the foster care system. Before growing up and starting his own business and marrying and having adult relationships. He didn't know anything about the adult Zachary. And if Berk were threatening or unhelpful, it wasn't the end of the world. What was he going to do? He might say that no, he hadn't seen Tyrrell and didn't have any suggestions for Zachary as to where to find him, but so what? He wouldn't be any further behind than he already was. And just maybe, he would be able to get further ahead on the case.

The address that Zachary had found was for a small, rundown fourplex. There were children's toys and engine parts in the yard. One of the units in the fourplex had newspaper taped up all over the windows. Another had a dead, brown Christmas wreath with a red ribbon on the door. And Zachary wasn't sure whether it was actually that year's wreath.

He knocked on the door of Berk's unit several times but was unable to raise any answer. Berk might have been at work, but Zachary hadn't seen anything during his computer searches to indicate that Berk was working. More than likely, he was delinquent on the rent on the fourplex but was squatting there until the landlord was actually able to have him physically removed. It could be remarkably difficult to get a non-paying tenant out of a place. In the meantime, he wasn't likely making improvements to the interior.

Zachary went to the door closest to the children's toys and rang that doorbell. He could hear it ringing inside. In a few minutes, a woman came to the door. She had frizzy brown hair, freckles, and a skinny, mussy-haired child on her hip who was crying about something and squirming to get away.

"What is it?" the woman demanded fiercely. "Don't you know better than to be ringing doorbells in the middle of the afternoon?"

"Uh…"

"You woke her up!" She indicated the child in her arms with a jut of her chin. "Meggie, shut up! Stop that!"

The toddler continued to cry, squirming again to escape.

"I'm sorry. I didn't mean to cause any trouble. Hey, Meggie, it's okay. You can go back to sleep…"

"Go back to sleep?" the woman slapped her forehead. "You think a kid goes back to sleep after they get woken up? Grab a brain, why don't you?"

"I'm sorry…"

"Who are you? What do you want? You'd better not be selling anything, or I'm going to call your boss and read *him* the riot act. Then what do you think is going to happen to your cushy job?"

Zachary wasn't sure how door-to-door sales in the winter would count as a cushy job, but decided there was no point arguing it. "I'm just looking for one of your neighbors," he started, gesturing toward Berks' door.

"Then go ring his doorbell! What are you doing harassing me?"

"I'm just wondering whether you have seen him lately. It wouldn't make much sense for me to hang around here if he's moved out."

"Who?"

"Berk Goldman, the man in unit C." Zachary gestured. "Taller, heavyset guy. Sixties. Lives by himself, as far as I know."

"Oh, that old pervert? Yeah, he's still there. Sit on his doorstep for as long as you like, but don't be ringing my doorbell!" She started to shut the door, but Zachary put his hand out, stopping her.

"Sorry—just wondering if you know, does he have a job or is there somewhere he might be hanging out?"

"How do I know?"

"You might see a work truck? Or he might go out at the same time every day?"

She stared at him blankly.

"No? Is he usually here in the day? You sound like you've noticed him."

"Sometimes he's here during the day. I don't know. Sometimes he's sopping drunk and can't find his own door. What a loser!"

"He lives alone?"

"I told you that, didn't I?"

"No. I was just checking. Does he drink somewhere near here? Or do you know where he picks up his liquor?"

Zachary had looked for empties behind the fourplex, hoping to get some idea of where Berk did his buying or drinking, but without success. If Berk saved his empties rather than throwing them into the trash, then they were inside.

"Get lost," the woman sneered, forcing the door towards the shut position, "or I'm going to call the cops. You're trespassing."

So much for her suggestion that he could sit on his father's steps all day. He suspected that if he did stay there for any length of time, he would be explaining himself to the police. They wouldn't take kindly to his loitering around even if he was a private investigator and the subject's biological son.

Zachary did one more scout around the house, but didn't ring any more doorbells. There didn't appear to be anyone home in unit B. And he suspected that if he bothered the resident of the house with the newspapered windows, he would likely as not be greeted with a sawed-off shotgun.

51

Zachary used his phone to search for the closest bars, pubs, and liquor stores. If Berk was known for being a drinker and was sometimes so intoxicated that he "couldn't find his own door," then he probably didn't go far to drink. He would be known at all of the closest establishments or would have one "usual" place he hung out. He wouldn't be driving far with a habit like that.

The closest bar did not open until the afternoon. If Berk were out drinking rather than working, that wouldn't be his preferred watering hole. Zachary continued to scroll through the list and consider the pros and cons of each location. Somewhere close by, not too high-brow, open long hours. Probably near a convenience store where Berk could pick up cigarettes, a bottle to take home with him, and any other necessities. He had no idea whether Berk was into gambling or pool. Probably not. He probably didn't care about any of the other amenities. Other than girls. Berk would probably be somewhere he could watch women, if not pick them up. Not necessarily a strip club, where the drinks were sold at premium prices and he would get kicked out if he got sloppy drunk, but somewhere that either women would frequent or there were waitresses with skimpy outfits.

The first couple of places Zachary went, the bartenders and other staff shook their heads, not recognizing Berk's name. He was not active on social media, so Zachary didn't have a picture of him and could only give the most general description, not having seen the man for decades and only guessing how he might have changed as he aged.

Zachary went to the pub that was next on his list, though it wasn't the most promising location. More of a British vibe, no cute waitresses, as far as he could tell from the pub's reviews.

Despite it still being morning when he got there, the place smelled dank and sour. Beer and bodies and deep-fried chips. Zachary waited inside the door for a minute for his eyes to adjust to the dimness.

There were a few dedicated drinkers there already. It was quiet, just murmurs of conversation. A few TV monitors hung in the corners of the ceiling, but it was too early in the day for there to be anything interesting on. Poker games and rugby reruns; no one was watching them or even appeared to notice that they were on.

Zachary scanned the room, but there was a heavy lump in his stomach, his subconscious brain having come to a conclusion before he was able to look at any faces. His eyes stopped on a man in a back corner who sat facing the door. He had a glass and a bottle on the table in front of him, working through the whiskey at his own pace so that the wait staff didn't have to keep refilling for him. His face was vaguely familiar. Not the same man as Zachary had known decades earlier, through a child's eyes. More lined, with deep creases running from the edges of his nose to the corners of his mouth, everything turned downward, looking mean and angry.

Berk hadn't lost his hair, but it was peppered with gray, as was the stubble on his face. He was broader than Zachary remembered, with a beer gut straining his shirt. He was sitting down, so Zachary couldn't compare his height to that of the man who had towered over him as a child, but he assumed that he would seem shorter now, since Zachary was taller.

Zachary swallowed and walked across the pub toward Berk. The man's watery eyes lifted from his drink as they caught the new movement. For a moment, he just stared. Then he swore.

Zachary walked up to him, but had no idea what to say. Hello?

Introduce himself? Demand to know where and when he had last seen Tyrrell? Nothing seemed appropriate, either too impersonal or making him feel vulnerable. They just stared at each other.

For an instant, Zachary was flooded with memories. All different scenes from his childhood replayed through his mind in a flash. Happy times, anxious times, being hurt and terrified and trapped. Heather had reminded him once of how it felt to be caught in Berk's crosshairs. That horrible, terrifying feeling of anticipating the violence of a punishment. How his father had been God in their household, ruling with an iron fist, meting out whatever consequences he saw fit for their disobedience, for a bad report from the school, or just for crossing his path at the wrong time or knocking over a glass.

But now, he was just a man, and Zachary was having difficulty reconciling the two images. The raging father who had ruled his life and the drunk sitting in front of him, not even bothering to get to his feet.

"Hey, you ready for—" A man coming out from the back hallway where the restrooms were stopped speaking when he realized that someone was standing there who hadn't been there when he had left.

Zachary belatedly noticed the other glass on the table and a mess of coats and outerwear in a jumbled mess on one of the chairs. He turned slowly, his ears attuned to that voice, knowing as he turned around who he was going to see but still not believing it.

52

Zachary!"

Zachary stared at Tyrrell, frozen. Tyrrell's voice was shocked, disbelieving. They both just stared at each other.

Then Tyrrell's face broke into a grin. "Zach, my man! I can't believe you're here!"

He rushed forward and enveloped Zachary in a hug, pulling him close and thumping him on the back. Happy as Zachary was to see him alive and unharmed, he struggled immediately to get out of Tyrrell's grip. The other man stank and he was holding on too tightly. Zachary didn't want to be touched in that pub. Not by anyone. He jerked back and wrenched himself out of Tyrrell's grip.

Tyrrell looked surprised by this reaction. He smiled uncertainly and held one hand toward Zachary.

"Zach. Hey. It's me."

Zachary shook his head. He looked from Tyrrell to Berk and back again.

"Oh, yeah!" Tyrrell exclaimed, once again enthusiastic and eager. He gestured toward Berk. "This is our dad! Can you believe it? Berk Goldman!"

Zachary nodded. "Yeah. I remember."

"Come sit down with us. Have a drink. It's good to see you."

Zachary wanted to do anything but sit down there and talk to the two of them. He fought off the emotions and memories that threatened to engulf him, struggling to anchor himself in the present. The pub was too dark and too warm. It was too quiet, and he felt like everyone's eyes were on him. The floor was sticky. He couldn't seem to move from the spot.

But he had come there looking for Tyrrell. He wasn't going to just turn around and walk out of there again. He had spent a week trying to track down someone he loved who might very well be dead, and the roller-coaster of emotions ranged from fury at Tyrrell, to relief, to mourning the way Tyrrell had fallen. The way that Tyrrell had turned out not to be the man that Zachary had built him up to be. He wasn't strong and whole and healed, with everything going for him and his life put together, aimed at a bright future.

He was broken and imperfect, just like Zachary was.

All because of the man who sat there looking at them, taking another swallow of whiskey.

"Sit down!" Tyrrell urged. "Come on. Sit down with us. This is just amazing, isn't it? Did you ever think you would see him again?"

"No." Zachary swallowed and shook his head. "No, I never thought that I would."

Nor had he ever wanted to. Apparently, unlike Tyrrell.

Tyrrell moved past Zachary to the table. He picked up the coats from the chair beside him and put them on the fourth chair. "There. Come sit here." He pulled on Zachary's arm. Not hard, forcing him to go. Just a tug, encouragement, invitation.

Zachary finally moved, his stiff joints moving rustily, not wanting him to sit down in that waiting chair. He landed in it and, for a moment, just sat there, feeling disoriented and lost in space. He focused on the feeling of the hard chair. The movement of the air from the ventilation system. The background music, so quiet that he hadn't noticed it until then. Maybe the staff didn't even realize it was on. Or maybe the music was coming from somewhere else, inside of Zachary. *Santa Baby*. Why would they still be playing Christmas songs in January?

Tyrrell resumed his seat and again slapped Zachary on the back in a hearty, friendly way.

"Dad, this is Zachary! I told you he was a private investigator. Should have guessed that he would find us here!" Tyrrell laughed, pleased with himself. He picked up the bottle and poured more into his glass. He waved to one of the waiters. "Another glass!"

"No. Just water," Zachary insisted.

The waiter looked at him for a moment as if this were a bizarre cocktail he'd never heard of before, then shrugged and went to fetch a glass of water.

"Water," Berk growled. "No son of mine should be drinking water! Man up and have a real drink."

Zachary shook his head. He tried to answer Berk out loud, but couldn't. Tyrrell took a couple of gulps from his glass.

"This is so cool. All three of us together now. We just need Vinny, and then it will be all of the Goldman men together again!"

"Will it?" Zachary said. "What about Jason? And any others?"

Tyrrell snorted and covered a laugh with his hand as if his secret had been discovered and he was trying to hide his embarrassment. "Oh—you know about Jason?"

"Found him while I was looking for you. And how many others are there?"

Tyrrell shrugged and waved his hand around. "Who knows? Half the state could be populated with them!"

The thought of Berk traveling all over Vermont impregnating unsuspecting women and molesting young girls made Zachary sick. He didn't understand how Tyrrell could think that it was funny. But then, he was drunk. Everything was probably funny to him in this high-flying state.

Berk didn't give any answer about how many of his progeny might be scatted around the state, but he smirked and gave a careless "What are you gonna do?" gesture with his free hand.

The waiter came over and placed a glass of water in front of Zachary. Ice cubes floating on top. A wedge of lime balanced on the rim of the glass. Nice presentation.

Zachary nodded. "Thanks."

He had a sip of the water. Just tap water. Plenty of chlorine. Zachary wanted to drink to moisten his dry mouth but, feeling so heavy and nauseated, he didn't want anything in his stomach. He put the glass back down and squeezed the lime wedge to squirt a few drops of juice into the water to counteract the taste of the chlorine. He stared at the glass, watching trickles of lime juice descend into the water and diffuse into it to become indistinguishable.

"How did you find us?" Tyrrell demanded.

Zachary felt a surge of anger overtake the other emotions. He grasped hold of it and let it lead him into the conversation. "How could you do that? Disappear and leave everyone behind. Let everyone think that you were dead. That you'd killed yourself. You left your house, your job, your *children*!"

Tyrrell's brows dipped down, demonstrating sadness. "You don't know what it's like, Zachary. My life isn't like yours."

"I have things better?" Zachary demanded. "Stuck in a psych ward for weeks? A hair's breadth from suicide?"

Tyrrell waved this off with a careless gesture. "You have Kenzie."

Kenzie. Zachary couldn't argue that she wasn't the best thing in his life.

"And I have an ex too, just like you do. If you cleaned yourself up, you could look for someone else. Make space for someone like Kenzie to come into your life."

"Your ex." Tyrrell rolled his eyes. "She's got money. Try an ex who demands child support all the time. I don't even have enough to live on, and I'm supposed to give her money too?"

"They're your kids! You're lucky to have them! Do you know what I would give to have kids?"

Berk chuckled. "Havin' kids isn't exactly hard. Unless you're... not a *man*."

Zachary opened his mouth, furious, but nothing came out.

What *was* wrong with him? Bridget had said no to kids. But he could have insisted. He could have at least tried to talk her into it. Gordon had apparently managed to do it. The two of them now had newborn twins. Two precious little lives that Zachary would have done anything to protect from harm.

And what about Kenzie? They had never talked about children. Zachary knew that she wasn't ready for kids now, not as she was trying to get established in her career and to move up the food chain, to someday be a medical examiner with a morgue of her own and people working under her. But would she want kids in the future? Or had he ended up with a second woman who never wanted to have his children?

How could Berk end up with children by half a dozen women all over the state, and Zachary kept picking women who didn't want any?

"You need to assert your dominance," Berk told him, eyes glittering. "You don't ask. You tell her. You take what is yours. None of this wishy-washy politically correct 'talk it out' crap. Are you a man or a mouse?"

Zachary shook his head. He wasn't a predator. He would never be like that. He would never be *that* kind of a man.

Berk eyed him, waiting for him to say something, and had another sip of his drink.

"It's a different world today," Tyrrell whined, not exactly standing up for Zachary, but maybe defending his own weaknesses, "It's a lot different from when you were younger. Acting like that now... would just get us thrown in jail."

Berk shrugged. "Ain't that different than it ever was. But you're going to let that stop you? You don't change the world by being meek and mild. If you want the world to accept men being men, instead of these scraggly little hipsters that are showing up everywhere now and the so-called men in business suits preaching their kind of politics, then you have to act. Get out there and say what you want, instead of sitting at home, complaining that no one is giving you what you want."

Tyrrell nodded, accepting this. Looking as though he agreed with it on some level. Zachary shook his head. This wasn't the Tyrrell he knew. That wasn't the kind of person Tyrrell was at all.

"You have two wonderful children," Zachary told him. "Don't forget that. Don't run out on them. Do you know how much they want you to come home? To know that you're safe? What kind of a

Christmas do you think they had, wondering whether you were alive or dead?"

"I can't go home to them," Tyrrell pointed out. "I don't live there. Their mom does. And if she wants to raise two kids by herself, she's welcome to do that. She doesn't want me around. So fine. I'm not around anymore. She can do it by herself. She can do everything by herself."

Zachary just stared at him. Tyrrell drank down a few swallows and reached for the bottle again.

"They'll get over it," he growled. "I got over losing my family, didn't I?"

Zachary blinked and shook his head. "No, you didn't. You never did."

Tyrrell didn't argue the point. Maybe even so deep in his cups, he realized that Zachary was right. He had spent the last few years chasing family. His father, the siblings he had known before the fire, the siblings he never knew he had and were new to his life. He just kept adding more and more people, looking for that feeling of a family. He had confessed to Lorne Peterson that the reason he'd wanted children was to feel like he had a family. A complete little unit.

But that had not worked out. Tyrrell had gone badly off the rails.

He might not be able to mend fences with Lindsey, but that didn't mean that he couldn't still be a part of Mason's and Alisha's lives. The law allowed him that. Lindsey hadn't snatched the kids and run to the other side of the country to live under assumed names until they were grown. They were still there, with Tyrrell taking them on weekends and every other holiday.

53

Zachary saw Berk watching something behind him and turned to look. He didn't like sitting with his back to the door, but the seat Tyrrell had cleared for him was in the wrong position, and he wasn't going to sit next to his father.

Looking out the front window of the pub, he saw something he hadn't noticed before. A school field across the street. A class of girls ran around the field, despite the winter temperatures and the snow on the ground. Most wore long track pants, but a few showed off bare legs under shorts. Everything coordinated in the school colors. A private girls' school? No wonder Berk had chosen that location and sat facing the window.

"You're disgusting," he told Berk, the words popping out of his mouth before he was even aware of them.

Berk chuckled and seemed to be completely unoffended. Zachary looked at Tyrrell.

"You want to be like that? Like him? You think he is some kind of role model for you?"

Tyrrell rolled his eyes. "So he likes to look at the girls. He's not a bad guy."

Jason had warned Zachary that Tyrrell didn't remember what Berk had been like when they lived with him.

"He is," Zachary told Tyrrell in a lowered voice, though unless Berk was mostly deaf, he would still be able to hear what Zachary was saying. "I get that you don't remember what it was like at home, but believe me, this is not a guy you want to pattern your life after."

"You can't believe everything people tell you. I believe what I can see with my own eyes." Tyrrell gestured to indicate Berk. Clearly, he was just an inoffensive older man. A drunk. Not someone who went around harming anyone. He'd had wilder days when he was younger. Tyrrell had too. He'd been put through programs and was now older and wiser than he had been as a teenager. People changed.

"You did see it with your own eyes. You just don't remember. How he used to whale on us? How he and Mom used to have knock-down, drag-out fights until the neighbors called the cops and carted one of them off to jail? How he put drinking and all of his desires over putting food on the table for us? You saw it. Don't let anyone tell you any different."

Tyrrell shook his head, bemused. His eyes were glazed and far away.

"You're not remembering right either," Berk told Zachary. "I don't know who's filled your head with all of that nonsense. It never happened."

"The hell it didn't! I remember!" Zachary jumped to his feet. The table wobbled and his glass fell over, spilling water over the tabletop and down to the floor. Zachary set it upright again, forcing himself to handle it carefully when he would have preferred to throw it across the room. At Berk's head. "I was there and I remember what it was like. Not because anyone told me that was what happened. I *remember!*"

Berk just shook his head, looking amused. "That's the problem with all of these therapists and headshrinkers. They implant false memories. They ask you if your parents ever hurt you or did anything to you, and then they put the images in your head, making you think that it really happened. When it never did."

"No." Zachary looked at Tyrrell. "You told me you could remember the night of the fire. You said that you remembered *Santa Baby* being on the radio before I put you back to sleep again. When you were awake because they were fighting so bad and you wanted to call the cops."

Tyrrell cocked his head slightly as if trying to catch the notes of the song. Replaying it in his head and thinking about the circumstances surrounding it.

"Come on," Zachary insisted. "What do you remember?"

"Whatever was planted there by the cops and the psychologists," Berk said, his eyes still on the window behind Zachary. "Because neither of us did anything to hurt you kids. Zachary is the one who burned the house down. Why don't you ask him why he did that? He's the one that hurt everyone, destroying our home so that we had no place to live. Farming the kids out to foster care because there was no way for us to house them all."

"No," Zachary snapped. "That is just a lie. No psychologist told Tyrrell what to remember. He remembers what really happened, don't you T?"

"I... I don't know," Tyrrell said. "I remember the song. I remember us talking. About the snowman. You said we would build a snowman taller than me."

Zachary nodded. That was what they had done the morning after they were reunited. They had gone outside and built a snowman. Not taller than their heads, but it was something that had re-cemented their relationship as brothers. A shared memory and the completion of that promise from decades before.

"You *were* fighting," Tyrrell said slowly, looking at Berk. "You and Mom... over... something about Christmas. The decorations?"

Zachary opened his mouth to answer, then closed it. Tyrrell needed to remember on his own, not to have someone feeding it to him. Seeding his memories, as Berk had suggested.

"The tree," Tyrrell said, remembering. "Putting up the tree. Getting it decorated. Right?"

Zachary nodded.

Berk ran his fingers through his hair, making it stand up slightly. "Who doesn't argue over decorating the Christmas tree?" He chuckled. "You can't go by those Christmas romance movies where everyone works together to create a perfectly coordinated Christmas tree and then puts the star or angel on top in some lovely ceremony. That's just crap. It doesn't happen that way. The cords are tangled and half the lights don't work, and it's figure it out or go to the store to get more. And we didn't have money to buy more. They were all cast-offs as it was. Then you've got the kids underfoot, grabbing at everything and trying to put all of their favorites on the tree, and fighting over them and getting bloody noses. All of these stupid paper crafts from school that don't belong on a tree in the first place." He swore and rolled his eyes. "Whoever thought of Christmas trees should be shot."

As Zachary remembered it, the bloody noses hadn't been from the kids fighting with each other over tree ornaments.

54

achary fell back into his seat. At the mention of the paper crafts from school, he couldn't help remembering the different Christmas shapes cut out of paper with scribbles on them that he had carefully placed on the tree after everyone else had gone to bed. He'd made sure that there were ornaments created by each child on the tree in roughly equal numbers. He had spaced them around the tree, tucked them between branches, and done his very best to create that lovely Christmas-tree vision that he had seen in dopey Christmas movies on the TV.

And the paper crafts, when they had caught fire, made the whole thing go up like a torch. He saw it blazing, saw the curtains catch fire, saw dropping embers fall to the carpet and start it on fire. All around him, everything in the room had been burning. Black smoke filled his eyes and lungs, and he couldn't find his way out of the room. He had yelled his throat raw, trying to wake everyone up and get them out of the house. He had tried to squeeze himself under the couch, wrapped his arms around his face to try to create a breathable pocket of air and keep the flames from reaching his face.

"It's okay," Tyrrell said. "Zachary. Come back. It's okay."

He pulled Zachary's fingers from where they were clamped around the table and pressed a cold glass into Zachary's hand. He gulped, trying to douse the flames that singed his throat. The firemen had come. They had rescued him from the burning room and taken him to the hospital for treatment. And he had never seen his home or family again.

The drink would not put out the flames, went down hot itself but, within a few seconds, the flashback was starting to dissolve, the panic to recede. Zachary drank more, trying to wipe it all out. One day he would be able to talk about it without flashing back. Dr. B assured him of that.

One day.

"You okay?" Tyrrell sat with his hand hovering over Zachary's back, as if unsure whether he should pat or rub it, or if maybe that would make things worse.

Zachary needed to know that he was real. He grasped Tyrrell's other arm on the table, feeling the warmth and solidity of it. Not a fleeting vision. Something that was actually there in front of him. He hadn't imagined finding Tyrrell. He was right there.

"I found you," Zachary murmured. "I did. You're here."

"I'm here," Tyrrell reassured.

Berk watched them with distaste. "What a pansy! What a complete nut job I have for a son."

Zachary shook his head and let the words flow by him. What did he care what the old man said? He had not chosen to meet him again. The only reason he had searched for him was to find Tyrrell. And it had worked. He had found his brother safe and sound.

"He's not a nut job!" Tyrrell snapped back. "Do you have any idea what he's been through? He could have been killed in that fire. And then you and Mom abandoning us? How could you do that to us? How could you put us in foster care and not even care what happened to us?"

Berk shrugged, smirking again. He looked out the window, across the field, at the girls, who were now huddled in a group, getting instructions from their teacher or coach. "That was your mother's doing. Nothing to do with me. She's the one who arranged for it all. She could have taken you if she'd wanted to." His eyes left the window to focus on Zachary again. "But with one like this, why would she do that? Always in trouble. Always the first one to stick his hand in the oven or punch out a window. It's a wonder it didn't happen earlier. And the rest of you were nearly as bad. It was only a matter of time before you all followed his example. As soon as you could walk, you were all getting in trouble. The older girls…" He licked his lips. "They were different. More mature and put together. Didn't have all the issues you boys did." He rolled his eyes and swore at the memories. "Thought you must have had a missing chromosome or something. One of those things that make babies be born morons."

Zachary was reeling under his words. It shouldn't have affected him, after hearing how his mother spoke about him when she had come to the hospital with Mrs. Pratt, telling them both that she wanted nothing to do with Zachary anymore. That he was hopeless, incorrigible, a discard.

Tyrrell jumped to his feet, swinging his fists and shouting at Berk. Incomprehensible, but loud, disrupting everyone's conversations. Zachary struggled to get up and stabilize himself on his feet, but was too slow and wobbly to do anything about Tyrrell's attack.

Berk stood up and just shoved Tyrrell away from him, acting bored and unconcerned with his son's reaction. The bartender and one of the waiters hurried over to put a stop to the altercation. They pulled the wildly windmilling Tyrrell back, shoving him into the wall.

"That's one," the bartender warned. "You want to get kicked out of here?"

"I'm sorry!" Tyrrell started immediately to weep messily, tears flooding down his face, mouth open, ropes of drool descending to his shirt. "What's wrong with me? Can't I do anything right?" He swore and begged for God to strike him dead. Zachary wobbled over to him and touched Tyrrell on the shoulder, trying to calm him.

"T, T, it's okay. Chill. Let's get you out of here, okay? Let's get you back somewhere you can sleep this off. You'll feel better after that."

Actually, it was doubtful that he would feel much better, but he would at least be able to stay in better control of his emotions. Zachary looked at Berk. "Where is he staying? With you?"

Berk shook his head. "In his car. Drunk tank if he gets rousted."

Zachary thought about those searches he had asked Fontaine to do to see if there were any tickets on Tyrrell's car in other cities.

"Okay, okay. I'll check you into a hotel," Zachary told Tyrrell.

On the one hand, he wanted to take Tyrrell home, to try to get him to see the benefit of getting dry and starting over again. To have him under Zachary's roof so that he knew that he was okay. But he wouldn't do that to Kenzie.

The bartender touched Zachary's arm, shaking his head. "You're not driving anywhere. Not in this condition." He'd obviously seen Zachary's flashback or staggering to his feet and thought he was impaired.

"I'm not drunk. All I had was water."

But he knew that what Tyrrell had given him to drink and to pull him out of the flashback had not been water, and they would be able to smell the whiskey on his breath.

"I'll get a ride, then. Tyrrell. Come on. Come sit over here while we wait." He tried to pull Tyrrell toward the front door. They would grab the table closest to the door to get Tyrrell away from Berk and make a quick exit.

Tyrrell protested, trying to turn back to Berk, still weeping.

"Stop it. Come on. Come sit with me while I get us a ride and get you somewhere to stay tonight."

"I want to stay with my dad."

55

Zachary shook his head slightly in disbelief. He wasn't terribly impressed with this new, drunk version of Tyrrell. He wouldn't have talked like that if he'd been sober.

"You need to come with me. I've missed you. I haven't seen you since I got out of the hospital. You didn't even come at Christmas. I thought you were going to."

Tyrrell collapsed into a chair at the table Zachary guided him to. He immediately covered his face, continuing to sob.

"I should have come! I knew I should go see you! You would be all alone at the hospital." Tyrrell gasped and blubbered. Of course, Zachary hadn't been alone for Christmas. He'd had several visitors. Christmas Day was always a new revelation to him, a testament that he could start over again, despite the black despair and certainty of disaster that plagued him as Christmas Eve approached and darkness fell.

"So come visit with me now," Zachary encouraged. "You can tell me all about it."

He could see his car parked in the lot outside the pub. He glanced over at the bartender, wondering whether he would be able to get Tyrrell out to his car and drive off before they had a chance to figure out what he was doing and write down his license plate number. But he figured his chances of accomplishing that were pretty low. The bartender was watching him like a hawk as he dried glasses and, as soon as Zachary made for the door, he was bound to approach if he didn't see someone arriving to pick them up.

He sighed, irritated, and tapped the Uber app to order a ride.

"I couldn't come," Tyrrell explained. "I was feeling so bad, and Dad would have been alone for Christmas. I couldn't leave him alone, could I?"

"Instead, you abandoned your kids? They were looking forward to spending time with you."

"I did them a favor." Tyrrell sniffled loudly. "They don't need a dad like me. A dad who can't stay sober. Who is... abusive. They're better off without someone like me. I should spend the time with him," Tyrrell indicated Berk in the back of the pub. "I'm just like him."

"You're not like him. You're nothing like him," Zachary assured him. He leaned in, trying to look Tyrrell in the face. "I've seen you with Mason and Alisha. I didn't think that you were..."

"I've never hit them. I'd never do that. But... when I've been drinking... I yell. I get really mean. I'm impatient and I say things that..." he shook his head, "I can't forgive myself for."

Verbal abuse, Zachary could believe. He was relieved that the abuse wasn't physical. But at the same time, he knew how much words could hurt. It was still his mother's words, when she had told him that he wasn't wanted, that hurt him more than remembering what his father had done to them. The words had cut him to the quick and stayed with him for his whole life. The beatings had all blurred together and faded into the background.

"They still need you. You still want to spend time with your dad, right? Even after everything he did. Even though you haven't seen him for years. Don't make your kids miss you like that."

"I'm not... I shouldn't even be their father. I can't take care of anyone else. I can't even take care of myself. Look what a great job I'm doing. Living in my car. Spending all day drinking. How is that acting like a grown adult?"

"It will be okay. Things will look better in the morning. When we get you sobered up and can have a real talk, we can work on fixing things. Getting you better."

Tyrrell smeared tears around his face. He really was a mess. "I can't do that to my kids."

"Have you done any therapy? To help you with this?"

Tyrrell shook his head. "They always said that therapy was just an excuse or a bandage. That it didn't really help. The only thing that would help me was…" he let out a long, shuddering breath, "taking responsibility for my own actions and working harder. If I just… put my mind to it, I could do better."

"Who told you that? Your foster parents?"

Tyrrell nodded.

"Well, that's totally wrong. You can't just make up your mind not to have PTSD or addiction. You can't just decide that you're never going to have any issues again. Therapy can help. It can help you work through your problems, and you can even do family therapy with the kids to improve communication. Help them to understand what's going on with you and to give you guys strategies for dealing with each other when things get too hard."

Tyrrell bowed his head, just shaking it back and forth. Zachary rubbed his back.

"Come on, T. It's going to be okay."

"I'm a failure. A complete waste of space. I've never done anything for anyone. I wish I'd died in that fire."

Zachary had wished it himself from time to time over the years, when things got really bad and, looking back over his life, he wasn't happy with how little progress he had made and all of the people he had failed. But it struck him to the heart to hear Tyrrell, his baby brother, say those words.

"Tyrrell, no. That would have killed me. I'm so glad that you all survived, and that you hunted me down and met with me, and that I got to meet all the others. That's amazing. It's amazing how you have been able to find so many people to include in your family. I never would have. I had no idea."

"I know how you talk about him, and I'm exactly the same. I'm exactly the same as him."

"No. You're not. Do you hear yourself? I was there. I remember. He beat the snot out of us. Acted like we were only there to bother him. He killed someone and went to prison for it. And you talked to Jason. You know what he did to the girls."

Tyrrell wiped his eyes and looked up at Zachary. "What? What do you mean?"

"That he..." Zachary stared into Tyrrell's eyes, hoping for some recollection so that he wouldn't have to tell Tyrrell himself. Had Jason and his sisters *not* told Tyrrell? Zachary had had to worm it out of them. Maybe Tyrrell, with Berk whispering in his ear, poisoning his mind, had not been a safe person to reveal it to.

"That he abused the girls. Touched them. I don't know how far it went; I didn't ask. That's when their mom kicked him out."

Tyrrell turned his head to look at Berk, still sitting in the back of the pub, watching them or watching the schoolgirls out the window. As if he could tell by looking at Berk whether these accusations were true.

"No, he didn't! He wouldn't do that. No one ever said anything to me about that."

"Maybe because you wouldn't listen to anything else they told you about him."

"They're making it up. Half of that stuff they're saying they just made up. Their mother, she told them all kinds of things, and they're just repeating it. They poisoned him against Berk."

"Berk is poisoning you against the rest of us."

Tyrrell stared at Zachary. He shook his head, but didn't say anything.

"Then why won't you listen to what I'm telling you? You are not like him, and you don't want to keep hanging around him and letting him influence you. Look at everything you've thrown away! Things that you worked really hard for. Stop listening to him."

"You don't know what it's like."

"To be you? No. I don't know what it's like to be you. But I know what it's like to be me. I know what it's like to have a parent who beats you like that. Two parents who beat you like that. I know what it's like to lose your wife and any chance of having a family with her. I know what it's like to grow up in foster care, being used and abused by everyone who crosses your path. And to live in places you wouldn't sentence your worst enemy to. Places where you are a number and they'll drug you out or knock you around if you step out of line."

Zachary stared back at Tyrrell, willing him to hear and understand.

"I know what it's like to be your brother, T. And I still want to be your brother. I still want to see you, whether I'm in the hospital or you are. Whether you're managing your life okay or are hitting bottom. Just like you were there for me, right?" He touched Tyrrell on the shoulder. "You've been there for me. Let me help you too."

Tyrrell sniffled and sobbed. He grabbed a handful of napkins and tried to wipe his face and clean himself up. Zachary nodded and tried to help him. "We'll do a better job at the hotel. Where is your car? Is it close by?"

"Can't drive like this," Tyrrell pointed out sensibly.

"I know that. I just mean… to get you some clothes to change into… toiletries… whatever you've got in the car."

"Oh." Tyrrell sniffled and wiped his nose. He nodded. "It's just around the corner."

"Okay. We'll have the driver stop there so you can grab your stuff."

Tyrrell nodded, his head moving up and down in an exaggerated way like a bobblehead.

Zachary watched out the window for the arrival of their ride.

56

Zachary managed to find Tyrrell's car, though it wasn't exactly where Tyrrell thought he had left it, and to get what he figured Tyrrell would need for a night or two out of it. The Uber driver watched them with suspicion but didn't drive off and leave them there.

"He'd better not throw up in here," he said as Zachary maneuvered Tyrrell back into the car after getting his things.

He hadn't had a chance to suss out how drunk Tyrrell was when they had first climbed into the car. Now, after watching Tyrrell staggering around and hearing him make repeated weepy apologies, he had an idea what he was dealing with.

"We don't have far to go," Zachary assured him, hoping that Tyrrell wasn't prone to carsickness when he was drunk. Looking at his phone, he read off the address.

The driver nodded. "That the SleepEasy?"

"Yeah."

"We'll be there in five minutes." He sounded relieved, hoping as Zachary did that with only five minutes in the car, the odds of Tyrrell not being sick were pretty good.

Zachary concentrated on keeping Tyrrell upright and calm, reassuring him that everything would be fine. He watched out the window as they moved through town. He wanted to be far enough away from the pub that Tyrrell wouldn't get it into his head to walk back there and continue drinking with Berk, but close enough that Zachary could walk or Uber back once Tyrrell was asleep to pick up his own car. Tyrrell might get a ticket if his car weren't moved in the next twenty-four hours but, from what Zachary had seen inside the car, it wouldn't be his first one.

When they pulled up to the SleepEasy, Zachary got Tyrrell out of the car, thanked the driver and made sure to tip him well and give him a good rating on the app, and went to the front desk to book a room for the day. It was too early for check-in, and the manager at the desk eyed Tyrrell dubiously.

"Rooms aren't ready yet. They still need to be cleaned. And him…" he shook his head. "I don't think so."

"He needs somewhere to sleep it off. And he couldn't care less if the room has been cleaned or not. I'll pay for last night and tonight, if that would help. On *my* credit card," he assured the man.

"We can't really do that," he said, but he started typing information into the computer. "I've got a room in the back that wasn't used last night. But you pay for two nights."

"Yes. Sure."

The man looked at Tyrrell, swaying back and forth. "You're staying with him? You'll clean up after him?"

"Yes. I'll make sure nothing is damaged or left in a mess. You can put a damage deposit on it," Zachary suggested. "Like with a non-smoking room. Pre-authorize it on my card. If anything happens, you're covered."

"If I get complaints that he's disturbing any other guests, I'll call the cops."

"Of course."

He probably wouldn't. He would probably tell them to get on their way first, and only call the cops if they refused. It was best not to have police tromping through the hotel, attracting attention and making guests think there was something wrong.

"No alcohol in the room."

"Good grief. Absolutely not!"

The man at the desk gave a slight smile of amusement.

Tyrrell seemed to focus on this part of the conversation, however. He leaned on Zachary, breathing his foul, whiskey-laden breath in Zachary's face. He could practically feel the sting of the alcohol on his skin. "Zach, Zachy. I need a drink," he said urgently.

"No, you don't, T. You can have a nap. Then when you wake up… we'll start sorting this out."

"But bro… You don't know what it's like. I can't do that. It's too late. Let's stay down here at the lounge." He motioned to the dimly lit restaurant that was clearly not open yet. "We can talk over drinks."

"We need to go up to our room first," Zachary pointed out. "Put your clothes away."

"But…"

"Shh. Let me finish booking the room." Zachary pushed Tyrrell away slightly and moved his hands over to the counter so that he still had something to stabilize him. He shook his head at the clerk. "Let's get this done as quickly as we can. Put whatever deposit you want on my credit card." He pulled it out and handed it over. "Give me a room key. And when he's down," he jerked his head in Tyrrell's direction, "I'll come back and give you whatever other information you need."

The man nodded and worked away at the computer. He looked like he was getting used to the idea now and didn't think it was such a bad one. He prepped a room key while waiting for the printer to spit out its papers, then slid one of them across the counter to Zachary to sign the credit card authorization. He had included a hefty cleaning deposit. Zachary signed it without any objection and pushed it back.

"Room 220." The clerk handed him the room key. "Come back down when you've got him settled." He looked toward the big glass doors where Zachary and Tyrrell had entered. "Do you have a car?"

"I do, but it's not here yet. I need to go pick it up later. I'll give you the details."

"Okay." The clerk raised his brows. "Good luck," he encouraged, giving a small nod.

Zachary was pleasantly surprised by his change in attitude. "Thanks."

Zachary had intentionally picked a hotel that was not expensive enough to have a stocked minibar in the room. That would have been disastrous. There was a soft drink vending machine in the hallway on their floor, so Zachary purchased several drinks and filled an ice bucket for them. It would be important to keep Tyrrell well-hydrated as he sobered up to prevent as many physical symptoms as possible.

Tyrrell complained all the way to the room about needing to go to the lounge or a bar to get another drink or to return to the pub where Berk was to keep him company.

"He gets lonely," Tyrrell told Zachary plaintively. "He's an old man and he doesn't have anyone anymore. He likes to have someone to keep him company."

"It's not a good place for you to be right now. You can send him an email or text later on when you're feeling better."

"He shouldn't be there all alone. He likes it when I'm there with him."

"I'm sure he does," Zachary agreed. To Berk, Tyrrell would be evidence that he hadn't done anything wrong. If he had been such an awful person, then would his son have wanted to sit there keeping him company? If he was a bad person, Tyrrell would want to stay as far away from him as possible. But he clearly wasn't. It wasn't his fault that he'd been abandoned by everyone else and lived a lonely existence.

But once they reached the hotel room and Zachary suggested that Tyrrell sit down, he flopped onto the bed and closed his eyes. Within a few minutes, he was snoring loudly. Zachary watched him for a few minutes, making sure that he was sleeping deeply enough not to be bothered by anything happening in the room, and also making sure that he was on his side so that if he did get sick, he wouldn't choke.

He pulled out his phone and briefly browsed through his new emails, then gave Kenzie a call.

"Hey," Kenzie answered quickly. "I thought you would be home. Everything okay?"

"Are you back from work already?" Zachary looked at the time on his phone. Kenzie had put in half a day and had returned home, thinking that they would be able to spend some time together. And the next day, they had the memorial and dinner at Mr. Peterson's. He blew out his breath, trying to decide how to handle things. "Sorry... a lot has happened. I found him."

"Your father?"

"Yes, and Tyrrell was with him."

"Oh! That's great! I'm so glad that he's okay."

"Me too." Zachary hated to think of how many times he had wondered over the past few days if he would find Tyrrell alive or whether something had happened to him. Dead by his own hand, killed in a bar fight, kidnapped and killed by a serial killer, dead in a ditch somewhere. The possibilities unrolled in a long list. All the things that could happen to a person, especially to someone who was depressed, drinking too much, and didn't care. "So... I've checked him into a hotel. Going to try to sober him up today, stay over, and then see how things go in the morning. But we've got that thing at Mr. Peterson's tomorrow."

"Yeah. You told them you'd be there, and I think it's really important to Pat."

"I'll be there. I'm just not sure whether I'll have time to drive back to get you and then back to their house. I'm not sure how long it will take to get Tyrrell upright in the morning, and I don't want to leave him by himself. If I do, he'll just go back there and start drinking again. I'll have to bring him with me."

"Oh. I see." She sounded disappointed. They didn't like to spend all night apart. Zachary tried not to do too much night surveillance, so that, other than when he was in the hospital, he was at least at Kenzie's house, even if he couldn't sleep. It was comforting for him, and he assumed for her too. "Okay. I'll drive down and meet you at the house, then."

"Good." Zachary breathed a sigh of relief that she wasn't too upset about it. "I'll get there as soon as I can, but like I say, I don't know how long it will take to get Tyrrell moving."

"I don't hear him. He's there with you?"

"Sleeping. Passed out."

"This early. He must have really been tying one on."

"Yeah. I think… that's probably all he's been doing for the past month. Just… drinking all day with Berk."

"That's strange. They… get along?"

"Yeah. I know. I can hardly stand to be near him. Berk. But Tyrrell seems to think that they're buddies. That… Berk never did anything wrong."

"He was pretty young at the time of the fire. Wasn't he just five?"

"Six. Yeah."

"He probably doesn't have very many independent memories of Berk. Just whatever he's been told."

"And between the social worker telling them that he just couldn't raise them as a single dad and Berk telling Tyrrell that everything was just peachy when we were all together… he thinks that Berk was just a victim of circumstances. He doesn't think there's anything wrong with them hanging out together. Though he's gotta know what drinking does to him! He's gone a year sober, so he knows the difference."

"Addiction is a nasty disease. Tyrrell isn't thinking about it clearly and making logical comparisons and decisions."

"He's just trying to drown himself."

"More or less… yes."

Zachary sighed. "I'm sorry I won't be home tonight."

"Me too. But you need to take care of your brother. I get that. Do you think you'll be able to get him into a program?"

"I don't know. Right now… he's fighting me every step of the way. I'm hoping that once he sobers up, it will be easier."

57

Zachary hadn't planned to sleep away from home. Still, being used to surveillance and other jobs that took him away from home occasionally, sometimes unexpectedly, he was prepared. He had a "go bag" in his car with the essentials and, while he missed not having his computer with him to get some work done, he did have his phone, which would do in a pinch.

While retrieving the car, he made a few calls to the people who might care that Tyrrell was now home and safe. Most of them were less concerned than Zachary had been, assuming that he would show up again once he got himself straightened out. Lindsey thanked him coolly and promised to let the children know he was safe. Zachary couldn't bear to think of Mason and Alisha going to school each day, not knowing whether their daddy was dead or alive. They needed to know that he was alive, if nothing else. Hopefully, they would feel better knowing that Uncle Zachary was doing his best to look after him.

Tyrrell slept for several hours but, partway through the afternoon, was beginning to sober up. He moved around restlessly, snorting and asking Zachary random questions, and eventually propped himself up in the bed, his back against the wall, looking around.

"Where are we?"

"Hotel."

"This isn't some detox program?"

Zachary looked around the room. He was pretty sure that the detox programs Tyrrell could get into did not put that much money or thought into interior decorating. Even though it was an inexpensive hotel chain, they still had paintings on the wall, coordinated furniture, and a carpeted floor. Zachary assumed that detox rooms would be more like the institutions he had spent time in. Easily wipeable aluminum and melamine furniture. Tile floors. Plain white or green walls and acoustic tile ceilings. No artwork unless there was some mural painted by previous residents as part of their therapy. Such things made a good impression on donors and administrators.

"It's a hotel room."

"So I can go?"

"Where are you going to go? Back to the pub to start drinking again? At least spend a few hours with me sober and tell me about what's going on with you."

Tyrrell rolled his eyes and made a face. Clearly, being sober and talking about himself were two things he did not want to do.

"I missed you at Christmas," Zachary said. "I was expecting to see you. You were going to come with Heather and Joss."

"Yeah, I meant to… but things didn't work out that way."

"You said in your letter—which you could have given to me instead of sliding it under my apartment door—that you were going to wait until after Christmas to… do whatever it was you were planning on doing. Is this it? You just wanted to go off and drink yourself silly with Berk?"

"You don't know what it's like."

"Then tell me. I'm asking."

"I couldn't. Things happened. Just like with you, you wanted to be able to stay home for Christmas with Kenzie, but that didn't work out either."

Zachary nodded. That was the truth. He had hoped that he would be able to hang on, to tough it out at home as Christmas Eve approached. He had managed to stay out of the hospital the year before, with Kenzie and Tyrrell to lean on, but it had been close. He had hoped to build on that success but, instead, he had ended up crashing sooner than expected. With the virus and the anti-viral treatment protocol, his physical reserves had been wiped out, which had a significant impact on his mental and emotional state. Then going off of his meds while at the Lodge, and all of the stuff that had happened with Bridget and the twins—there had been no way. There had just been too much for him to deal with, and he had spiraled down into depression and suicidal thoughts much faster than expected.

"Yeah. You can't control life circumstances. Or mental health. Sometimes… things just happen and you lose control."

Tyrrell nodded eagerly at this. "Exactly," he agreed. "And it was just too hard. I couldn't deal with it all. I couldn't wait until Christmas. I just had to… escape."

"Your letter sounded suicidal. Were you? Or were you just planning to go see Berk all along?"

Tyrrell looked around the room again as if he expected something to have changed. He sucked his cheeks in, considering Zachary's question.

"I don't know. I was down, and struggling, but it was more… the temptation to drink than to kill myself."

"You really scared me. I thought that you were dead somewhere. No one had seen you. You hadn't been in contact with anyone or told them where you were going. The last communication I had from you… it sounded like you intended to commit suicide. I thought we had lost you."

Tyrrell thumped the mattress beside him with his thumbs. "It would have been better if I had. Then at least, this would all be over. I'd be done trying to fight it. To keep it from everybody. I wouldn't have any more responsibilities. I could just… not exist."

"This isn't the end. I know you're feeling pretty bad right now, but that doesn't mean things won't get better. When I'm in the hospital, in the psych ward and it's Christmas Eve, or a few days before that, I can't see any hope. I can't see any light at the end of the tunnel, just darkness in every direction. What would you tell me?"

Tyrrell sighed. "That things would be better after Christmas. You'd start feeling better again and be able to go on. But there is no Christmas for me, Zachary. There isn't one magical day when I'm going to start feeling better again. I'm just going to keep feeling bad, and keep fighting the cravings, and keep giving in. And then feeling worse for giving in. There is no getting better."

"You were doing better. You were sober for a year. Longer than that. You were seeing the kids, and working, and you had your own place. You had me and the others to talk to."

"It's all temporary. It never lasts. The longest I ever lasted was when I was at college. That's some kind of joke, isn't it? Most kids go away to college and binge drink. I go to college and stay sober. Some kind of backward. But in the end... what did that matter? I can't use my degree. I can't even stay sober when I know all the stuff I learned about addiction for my degree. I should be able to overcome this."

"Knowing what addiction is doesn't change what you went through as a kid. It doesn't change your genes. It doesn't change the cravings to go back to—" Zachary cut himself off, realizing that he was talking about his own addiction rather than Tyrrell's. "You need help. You need to get into a program. Do you go to AA? Do you have a sponsor?" Zachary hadn't seen anything in his email that seemed to indicate a sponsor in the wings.

"No. We studied that in school. There are a lot of different programs that can help; AA isn't the only one. Not everyone believes in abstinence. People have been successful with moderation."

Zachary resisted asking how that approach had worked for Tyrrell. "Maybe you need more than that. A support network. Instead of hiding your drinking from everyone, be honest and talk about how hard it is, and how you're doing, and what is or isn't working. Just dropping out of sight like that... deciding you couldn't handle it and going to drink with Berk instead of fighting it anymore... it wasn't just hard on me. Mason was crushed. Alisha too. They need their dad. Even if you're not perfect. Even if you screw up sometimes."

"Screw up sometimes," Tyrrell snapped. "You have no idea. Screw up all the time. You think you know what it's been like, but you don't. You don't know what it's like to be a dad, and to see that you just can't do it. That you're a failure at it and just end up hurting your kids."

Tyrrell held his head. Zachary had picked up a bottle of Tylenol at the nearby convenience store, and nudged it in Tyrrell's direction. There was a glass of water waiting on the nightstand beside it. Tyrrell shook his head.

58

T yrrell just stayed there, hunched over, his hands over his face and fingers pressed into his temples for a long time, not moving or saying anything.

"He's a good guy, Zachary," he protested, as if Zachary had been lecturing him on how he needed to stay away from Berk. Which Zachary wished that he could do, but he knew only too well how Tyrrell would receive it. Like Rhys, Tyrrell wouldn't take Zachary's advice as to whom he should stay away from. "He really is. He's a lonely old man, and I like being with him, and the way he talks about how things were when we were young."

"I know you remember them fighting."

"But everyone fights. You and Bridget fought."

Which didn't exactly recommend the practice.

"How much do you remember?" Zachary tried to keep his voice neutral. To invite Tyrrell to tell him about it rather than suggesting he would confront Tyrrell over any detail he got wrong, that he was just looking for an opening to jump all over him because of his choices.

"I remember…" Tyrrell's brow furrowed.

For a long time, he was silent. Zachary looked down at his phone and waited. They had all night and into the next morning if they needed it. Zachary could wait until Tyrrell was ready to share.

"I remember things differently… when I'm with you than when I'm with him."

"Which one do you think is right?"

"When I'm with you, or with Heather or Joss, then I know what happened and how abusive he was, and I remember specific things. And that makes me feel *worse*. I don't want to be like him. But I can't help it. It's built into me. All of his shortcomings. I see myself and the way that I treat my kids, and I know that I'm a monster on the inside, just like him."

"You're not a monster. And you're not like him."

"He's an alcoholic."

"Yes."

"Just like me. And he was… he was abusive."

Zachary nodded.

"And I am too. You think I don't see the hurt and fear in my own kids' eyes? The way that they look at me and expect me to explode and to get after them, maybe even to hurt them. I can see that in their eyes."

"But you haven't. You haven't hit them." If Tyrrell was telling the truth about that part. "Nothing we could ever do would stop him from hitting us. You're not like that. You care about your kids."

"He does too. You haven't heard the way that he talks about us, about how he loved us when we were all at home."

Zachary searched his memory for any recollection of tenderness from his father. There had been the occasional happy interlude when Berk had decided to teach him how to make a paper airplane or lift a candy bar from the store. But tenderness? He couldn't remember Berk ever tucking him into bed. Or telling him he had done something well. Maybe that was just Zachary. Maybe he was the only one who couldn't do anything right.

"T… I don't know. I don't think he's telling you the truth. He might like hanging out with you and drinking, but when we were kids…" Zachary trailed off. "He says he loved us?" He shook his head. "I don't know, I don't think he did. We were in the way, and he said so plenty of times. When I was in foster care, I wondered why they'd had so many kids. Why they didn't just stop at one or two, and maybe that wouldn't have been so hard for them to manage."

Tyrrell frowned at Zachary, unsure where he was going with it.

"I think it was the money. Claiming more dependents. Being able to qualify for food programs, get lower taxes, and get into city programs that were subsidized. I think… the only reason they kept having children was to take advantage of the financial programs."

"That doesn't make sense," Tyrrell said.

Zachary shrugged. "I don't know. I never had any kids that I could make claims against. I don't know how it all works."

Tyrrell shook his head stubbornly. "No. You're wrong. He cared about us."

"Like he did Jason and his sisters? Dropping in on them every now and then, beating on their mom, and then taking off again? Molesting the girls?"

"That's not what happened. You need to listen to him tell about it."

"You can't believe what he says. He's just trying to make himself look better."

"Jason and the girls are the ones making up stories."

"Why would they? What do they get out of telling you about it?"

"Sympathy. They just want… they didn't want me to have anything to do with Dad, so they made up stories about him."

"What they said about the abuse *weren't* stories. Ask Joss and Heather if you don't believe me. They remember more than I do."

Tyrrell rolled his head back, banging it into the wall. Zachary winced in sympathy. Tyrrell rubbed his forehead slowly, the headache obviously bothering him. But he still didn't take the proffered Tylenol and water.

"You said that when you're around us, you remember," Zachary said. "So you know it's true. You know he wasn't the kind of dad who was just happy to be home with his kids at the end of the day. He was the kind of dad who wanted his beer and his easy chair and the remote, and if anyone got between him and one of those things…"

"I know," Tyrrell moaned. "I know you're telling the truth. But… I like the way he talks about it better. It's like… he had a family that meant something to him. That I was his son and he was proud of me."

"You know it's all lies. That what you remember when you're with us is the truth."

"A person can have too much truth," Tyrrell said, his tone angry. "There are times when it's just too much. When we were in that cabin, and I remembered what he was like, and I saw how I was with my kids... I just couldn't take it."

Zachary swallowed, feeling guilty. They had invited Tyrrell to the Lodge. He and Kenzie had no idea that being with Zachary stirred up negative memories and emotions in Tyrrell. He had never mentioned it before.

It was Zachary's fault that Tyrrell had started drinking again.

His fault that Tyrrell had been in a cabin stocked with alcohol.

His fault that Tyrrell could not be around Zachary without thinking about their past and comparing himself to their father. Thinking himself a failure because he was not patient enough. Not perfect.

"T... I'm sorry. Neither of us meant for that to happen. It was just supposed to be a nice family vacation."

"I know. I'm the one who wrecked it. Not you."

But Zachary couldn't help but see his own fault in it. "We need to get you dried out. Get you back in recovery again," he told Tyrrell. "You want to be able to see the kids again, don't you? To be a part of their life? No matter what our dad chose to do, you can still choose for yourself. Don't abandon them like our parents abandoned us."

Tyrrell started to cry again. Not the messy, loud weeping he had done when drunk to the gills. But tears ran silently down his cheeks and he stared at the wall opposite him, looking hopeless. He sniffled and his breaths shuddered.

"I love my kids. I do."

"I know. That's why you need to do what you can to get your life under control again. I'll help you all I can. But you have to let me know if what I'm doing is making things worse, because I don't want that."

"The best thing for them is if I just stay out of their lives."

"No. You know how much that hurts."

"They still have their mom. They can grow up to be normal. Not *damaged* like me."

Zachary shook his head, frustrated. He knew he couldn't talk a drunk into sobering up. He shouldn't even be trying. Tyrrell had to decide for himself if that was what he wanted.

"How about we order in something to eat?" he suggested. "How long has it been since you ate something solid?"

Tyrrell snorted. "Look at yourself before asking that question."

"I'm going to eat too. Come on, let's just relax for a while. No pressure. No lectures. Let's just be together for a while."

"Okay," Tyrrell agreed with a sigh. "We could just go downstairs. There was a restaurant..."

"No." Zachary wanted to keep Tyrrell away from alcohol as much as he could.

But if Tyrrell didn't see the light pretty soon, Zachary was going to lose his chance.

59

They ordered pizza. Tyrrell would eat and seem fine and cheerful for a few minutes. Then he would break down again, holding his head, weeping, rocking back and forth and explaining to Zachary how horrible he felt about everything he had done, both to his kids and to Zachary and the rest of his family and friends when he had disappeared without telling anyone what was going on. Eventually, the tears would wind down again. He would be calm, blow his nose, maybe even laugh at himself in a sad, regretful way, and then have another slice or a few more bites before breaking down again.

Zachary watched and listened patiently, wondering how much was emotional and how much was the result of the alcohol and maybe other drugs he had taken and the effects of withdrawing them from his body.

And then Tyrrell slept.

He was clearly exhausted by all the crying and emotion and, since he was in a safe place with a full stomach, his brain decided it was time to shut off and just let Tyrrell heal for a while. Zachary watched the TV with the volume low. He texted with Kenzie and a few others, rotating from one conversational thread to another.

His phone started to buzz and, looking down at the screen, Zachary saw that it was a call coming through rather than a text.

Lindsey.

He connected the call. "Lindsey?"

"Zachary. Umm… hi. Is it a good time?"

Zachary nodded. As long as he kept his voice low, Tyrrell would not be disturbed by their call. "Sure. He's asleep."

"I know I was short with you when you called, and I'm sorry about that."

"It's okay. He's put you through the wringer just as much as he has me. More so; this isn't the first time that you've had to deal with it, and you have the kids to worry about too, and their feelings and reactions."

"Yeah. It's hell. Christmas this year was…" She sighed. "More tears than I can remember for any other Christmas. They didn't want anything except their dad."

"I'm sorry about that. I wouldn't even have called you, because I know you don't want to have to deal with his stuff, and it isn't your responsibility to make sure that he is safe or that he isn't drinking or anything like that. But I thought… you deserved to know that he was safe. And for the kids to know that he was… still alive."

"I appreciate that. I know I was a grouch with you. When you came here to talk to me too. It's just that this keeps coming up over and over. It isn't something that we can ever leave behind, and it wears me down so much."

"Yeah. I can believe it." Zachary himself was exhausted. Worse than when he was fighting his own demons. At least then, when his body finally gave in, he could sleep. But he didn't want to go to sleep while he was looking after Tyrrell, in case Tyrrell woke up and decided to go down to the lounge or to disappear again. Zachary had to be vigilant and watch over his brother. Even though logically, he knew he couldn't stay awake forever and couldn't actually stop Tyrrell from doing anything if he put his mind to it. Tyrrell was bigger than Zachary and his desperation would make him stronger than ever. There was no way for Zachary to physically overcome him. He just hoped that he could keep talking to Tyrrell and get through to him.

"Okay, well... I just wanted you to know that I appreciate what you've done and letting us know that he is okay. I'm sure that Tyrrell appreciates it too." Then she seemed to reconsider what she had said and laughed. "Or not. He isn't exactly appreciative when someone tries to change his mind or tells him he is drinking too much."

Zachary chuckled. "No. He hasn't exactly thanked me."

She laughed again, rueful.

"Lindsey... I hope you don't mind me asking, and if you don't want to answer, that's fine. I'm just wondering if you can tell me anything about his drinking. When it started, or when you figured it out. If his relapses are triggered by anything in particular."

"He tends to get triggered by the kids," Lindsey sighed. "And trust me, you do not want your kids trying to take responsibility for their dad's alcoholism. They think that if they just do everything right, he won't start drinking again. And, of course, that's not true. He'll always go back to drinking, whatever they do. But it is true that it's usually something to do with the kids, their behavior, home stresses, that triggers him."

"That's not their fault. He has a lot of family stuff he's trying to process. From when he was a kid."

"I know. You know, when we first met, I didn't know about any of that stuff. I thought that the Millers were his real parents and that he'd had a normal childhood, a brother and a sister, and that everything about his past was normal. I didn't know anything about the abuse and the fire and his other siblings until after we got married. Even that he'd been in foster care. He kept it all away from me."

Zachary tried to picture that. "Wow. I don't know how I would ever do that."

"He's a master at covering things up. I didn't know anything about the drinking for the first few years we were married. I knew that he had mood swings, that he went through these dark periods when he was thinking about his past, but I had no idea he was drinking."

Zachary had assumed from what Tyrrell had said and his cheerful disposition that the alcoholism he'd mentioned was years in the past,

something that he had suffered with as a teenager and long since overcome. Tyrrell had fooled him too.

"When did you finally find out?"

"When Mason was born."

Zachary knew there was more and waited for the story.

"I had a lot of problems with the pregnancy and Mason was
premature. We almost lost him. He was born so early and they didn't
know if he would make it. I was sick and sore and trying so hard to
hold on to that tiny little baby. And Tyrrell just disappeared."

They both breathed for a few seconds, thinking about that.
Zachary tried to picture it. He'd been in the NICU with Bridget's
twins in December, so it wasn't hard to visualize Lindsey beside an
incubator with a tiny baby struggling to live. How much she had
needed Tyrrell's help and support, and instead, he had taken off.

"He said he needed to go to the restroom… and then he never
came back. I was frantic. I thought he'd had a stroke or something.
Got mugged, maybe, or hit his head. I couldn't wrap my mind
around the idea that he would just walk out of the NICU and walk
out of the hospital and disappear, leaving me there to deal with
Mason's care and the doctors. Everything on me."

"That must have been awful."

"It was. I already had a toddler at home; my mom was looking
after Alisha. Here I was with a second baby in the NICU and a
missing husband. I reported him missing, and the police believed it.
They didn't believe that a young husband with a brand-new baby
struggling to survive in the hospital would just take off. We all
thought that something horrible must have happened to him."

"It did," Zachary pointed out. "Just not what you thought. Or
when you thought."

She blew out her breath in a whistle. "I suppose so. I never
thought about it that way. But at the time, we had no idea about his
alcoholism or all the stuff from his past. I knew by then that he'd had
some challenges as a teenager, but that's all. The rest didn't come out
until later… after he reappeared."

"He came back on his own?"

"He always has, sooner or later. There's really no point in trying to short-circuit the process. Sorry." She obviously knew that was exactly what Zachary was trying to do. "I think he just has to go through it. Travel through the darkness to wherever it is he can find some peace for a little while."

"Yeah." That had been Zachary's experience with his cyclical depression as well. No amount of new medication or therapy seemed to be able to cut it off. Certainly no amount of wishing or arguing about it. His brain was just going to keep putting him through the process over and over again, year after year.

"The police couldn't find any sign of him. They were really ticked when he showed up again. More than I was, even. I was so relieved, because I'd thought that something had happened to him. He was dead in a ditch somewhere. I was just so relieved that he was back in one piece. I was happy to take him back and pick up where we had left off. Pretend that it hadn't happened and that we had weathered the storm together. That was probably a mistake. I should have had a big blow-up with him then. Laid it all on the line and told him that wasn't an acceptable response to stress. Instead, I made it okay, and so he kept doing it."

"I doubt it made any difference whether you accepted it or not," Zachary disagreed. "He's not an alcoholic because he chooses to be."

"He chooses his actions, no matter what his genes or his traumatic past are. Where were you this December?"

Zachary was startled by the question, which seemed to come out of left field.

"Uh... in the hospital."

"Voluntary, right?"

Zachary nodded, his mouth dry, and managed to make a noise of acknowledgment that she could hear.

"When you have your problems, you know to go to the hospital and they'll help you. He could do the same thing when he wants to escape and is thinking about drinking again. He could go to AA or a treatment program or to the hospital. He's had a dozen therapists in the time we were married. He could go to any one of them and get help. But he doesn't. It's easier to run away and hide. Have his little fantasy and pretend that he doesn't have any responsibilities."

"Did you have any idea that he'd been drinking with his—our—biological father?"

There was a pause as she processed this. "Are you kidding me?" she asked in disgust. "Talk about dysfunctional. That's just sick. Why would he?"

"I guess because Berk likes to drink and likes to hang out with Tyrrell and tell him about how much he loves his kids and that back when we lived at home, everything was hunky-dory."

"And Tyrrell needs to hear that he wasn't rejected."

"I guess so." Zachary wouldn't mind hearing from one of his parents that he wasn't a total failure, wasn't incorrigible as his mother had told him all those years ago. But at the same time, he wouldn't want to be around either one of them. Just seeing his father had been creepy and uncomfortable.

But however much Tyrrell needed to hear that he was loved and accepted by his father, he also needed to know that he wasn't Berk, that he wasn't doing the things his father had done to traumatize them in the first place.

"Well... I'm glad he has you," Lindsey said. "There probably isn't anyone who can understand him better."

60

When Zachary hung up after talking to Lindsey on the phone, he just sat for a long time staring into space. He didn't look down at his phone when it buzzed as responses from his various conversations arrived. After a while, the alerts ceased, and he was alone with his thoughts and Tyrrell sleeping on the bed.

He knew now what had triggered Tyrrell to start drinking again and what had triggered this disappearance. What had made him go running again, not even able to wait until after Christmas so that he could see the kids and have a nice holiday with them.

And both were Zachary's fault.

Tyrrell had started drinking because they had thought that it was a good idea to stay at the cabin together for Thanksgiving. Tyrrell had been forced to sit in the same cabin and the same room as Zachary, reliving his traumatic childhood memories, while at the same time trying to deal with his own children's increasing demands in the middle of a power blackout.

And as if starting him drinking again after a year of sobriety weren't enough, Zachary had triggered his escape response by placing Tyrrell back in the NICU. Zachary had unintentionally pulled his own disappearing act when he left psych and went down to the

NICU to keep watch over Bridget's twins. And when Kenzie had figured out where he was, she had brought Tyrrell with her. They had left him to watch over and protect the babies while Zachary went down to the cafeteria with Kenzie to eat and talk things through. All of the responsibility for not just one tiny, vulnerable infant landed on Tyrrell's shoulders, but for two of them.

Tyrrell had done well. He should have been proud of himself. But being in the NICU with the twins must have triggered flashbacks to Mason's life hanging by a thread in the NICU when he had been born. Tyrrell felt all of the responsibilities and his inadequacies closing in around him and did what he had done then—run away and hidden from them.

And that was all on Zachary.

Just as the break-up of the family had been Zachary's fault when his ill-considered decorating of the tree and lighting the candles had resulted in the devastating house fire. He couldn't blame that on anyone but himself.

Zachary watched Tyrrell breathing, his chest rising and falling rhythmically. Zachary's heart hurt and he wished that he were home with Kenzie and didn't need to think about all the bad things that had happened not just to Tyrrell, but to all of his family because of what Zachary had done. Even Berk being free of his first family, able to hook up with Jason's mother and to have a second family and wreak havoc in their lives.

All harm caused by Zachary's choices.

61

Zachary hadn't been thinking about clothing appropriate for a memorial service when he had gone looking for Berk, nor when he and Tyrrell had picked up clothes from Tyrrell's car before going to the hotel. And of course, a suit wasn't something packed in his go bag in the car. Come to think of it, he probably didn't even own a suit. He couldn't remember the last time he had worn one. If he'd been thinking about the memorial service, he would have at least packed a nice button-up shirt and something other than blue jeans.

But by the time he could get Tyrrell out of the hotel and hit the road, he was already worried about making it to the memorial service on time. Tyrrell had slept heavily and been difficult to waken, even late in the morning. And he'd been in a foul mood when he'd gotten up; grumpy, with a hangover and plans to start drinking again as soon as possible to combat these conditions.

It took a while to talk him down and get some food and water in him. He explained about going to the memorial service being put on by Pat and Lorne. He coaxed Tyrrell into going as a show of support. Lorne had said that Tyrrell was family, and Zachary did his best to use Tyrrell's hunger for another family to get him to agree to go to the memorial with Zachary rather than just heading back to the pub where he knew his father would be drinking.

But they were finally headed south, Zachary keeping one eye on the time and the other on the speedometer.

He had hit the edge of town and was only a few minutes from the house when Kenzie called. Zachary glanced at the phone screen and answered on Bluetooth.

"Zachary." She sounded relieved that he had answered. "I was getting worried. Are you going to make it?"

"I'll be there within five minutes. I'm in town."

"Oh, good. I'll see you in a few minutes, then."

Zachary said goodbye and hung up. Tyrrell was wearing sunglasses, but he rubbed his forehead like he was still getting a headache from the sun.

"How long is this going to be?"

"I don't know. I suspect an hour or something like that. And then we'll have a break before supper. If you want to get in a nap."

He couldn't see why Tyrrell would need a nap after how much he had slept since leaving the pub but, if he was withdrawing from the alcohol, maybe he would just want to sleep.

"Don't want a nap," Tyrrell growled.

He didn't say the other part of the equation that Zachary heard in his head. All Tyrrell wanted was a drink. And if Tyrrell was determined, there wasn't anything Zachary could do to stop him. He had agreed to attend the memorial out of consideration for Lorne and Pat. Zachary wasn't sure whether he could prevail on Tyrrell to stick around the rest of the afternoon and have dinner with them as well. Tyrrell's car was still back in Riverbrook, but that wouldn't stop him from walking or catching an Uber to whatever watering hole was closest.

Zachary glanced sideways at him but didn't say anything.

In a few minutes, they were at the Peterson home. Zachary couldn't park as close to it as he usually could. There were a lot of unfamiliar vehicles parked along the curbs, which meant that they had a good number of people for the memorial. He was glad that they would have a lot of support.

He couldn't help remembering the protests, the media attention, and the window broken by a rock when word of Jose's disappearance and the possibility of a serial killer targeting gay men had hit the news. A horrible note had been wrapped around the rock, ranting about how people didn't want a gay couple living in their neighborhood. Even though Mr. Peterson and Pat had lived there happily for over a decade already. Mr. Peterson had told him that it was just hate mail from a stranger, that he knew it wasn't from anyone who actually lived there. And he seemed to have been right. There didn't seem to be any lasting bad feelings against them from the neighbors. Zachary just hoped that the memorial for Jose would not cause a backlash.

They were met in front of the house by Mr. Peterson, who smiled broadly upon seeing them and gave Zachary a hug. "Glad you made it! Cutting it a little close."

"Sorry, we got away late."

Zachary was glad to see that Mr. Peterson was not dressed in a tux or something fancy or formal. He knew that the group of men had attended musical performances together, some of them very classy, and he'd been a bit worried that all the guests would be dressed formally except for him. But Mr. Peterson was in slacks and a polo, with a warm coat thrown over top. No tie. No tails.

Mr. Peterson offered Tyrrell a hug too, and the two men clasped, murmuring to each other. Mr. Peterson directed them around to the backyard.

Zachary knew Pat was a gardener and kept up the flower borders in the front yard, but he had never spent time in the backyard. It was Pat's space, and Zachary usually spent time indoors with Mr. Peterson. They talked, looked at each others' photography, and ate.

He had expected the backyard to be plain and bleak in the winter. Yard and trees decked with snow. But the yard was very large and looked almost like a fairyland with ornate arches, winding paths, decorative rock piles, and trees cut in topiary shapes. The trees and branches, the bones of the yard, all seemed to work together. There were a couple of circular areas that he thought must be ponds or water features during the warmer months. Although it was only mid-afternoon, the clouds and shorter winter days meant that the daylight was already fading, but the yard was not dark and gloomy. White twinkle lights were wrapped around every tree, fence, and arch, and the pathways were lighted by lines of tiny lanterns.

"Whoa." Zachary stopped and stared at the yard, spellbound. He felt like a child seeing his first electric train set. After a moment of Zachary standing there, frozen on the path, Tyrrell tugged on his arm.

"Let's keep moving. We don't want to block anyone behind us. Looks like everyone is gathering over there."

There was an open area where chairs had been set out. Not cold metal chairs, but cushioned, and the snow on the ground had been partially cleared so that people wouldn't be sitting with their feet in the snow.

"Go ahead," Zachary told Tyrrell. He patted his pockets until he located his camera. He was oblivious to anyone around him while he checked the settings and started snapping photos, capturing each part of the yard before the light changed. As he finished up and headed back toward the seating area, his path was blocked by a large, broad-chested man.

Zachary blinked, looked up, and focused on Pat's face. Pat smiled and gave him a brief hug. "We're getting ready to start."

"This is beautiful. It must have taken you hours."

Pat nodded. "Thank you. I'm so glad you could make it. Thanks for making the time."

Thinking of Jose, the man he had sacrificed so much to find, even if it was in death, Zachary gave Pat another hug, patting him on the back. "Of course. Tyrrell is here too, and Kenzie got here ahead of us..."

Pat nodded, eyes twinkling. He pointed out Kenzie and Tyrrell in the seated audience. "Kenzie's right there, saving you a seat."

Zachary quickly joined her, feeling a little embarrassed that he was one of the last few stragglers to make it to his seat. But he'd had to get some pictures before the light faded.

"Isn't it beautiful?" Kenzie whispered as Zachary sat down next to her. "Who would ever have thought a garden could be so beautiful in the middle of Vermont winter?"

"Pat is amazing."

"He really has a knack."

Pat stood in front of the audience, Mr. Peterson at his side, and welcomed everyone out. Zachary's focus quickly drifted from Pat, taking in the whole of the garden once more and then looking around at the audience. He recognized Eric Naylor from the clothing store and a few other people that he thought were neighbors he had seen around before but, on the whole, he didn't know Pat's and Lorne's friends. Kenzie tilted her head toward a couple of women on the front row, one close to Pat's age and one older. His sister and mother. Zachary was glad that they had come to support Pat, especially considering the number of years he had been an outcast from the family. But things had changed after his father had died, and he had been able to recommence a relationship with Suzanne and Gretta. Gretta good-humoredly referred to Zachary as her grandson, and he didn't object. Pat really had been like another father to him from the time he and Mr. Peterson had started seeing each other when Zachary was a teenager.

"Glad they're here," Zachary whispered.

He tried to catch the thread of what was being said about Jose, but couldn't focus on it.

His eyes were pulled back to Naylor, and he remembered interviewing the man in his store, confronting him with his relationship with Jose. But Naylor hadn't been the killer. He wasn't the one who had kidnapped and tortured Jose. And Zachary.

Zachary's breath caught in his throat as he was pulled down into those memories. He closed his eyes to shut them out, but that never worked. He floated, anchorless, above his body as Archuro worked over him.

There was a hand on the back of his neck, a light touch, bringing him back to himself.

"You okay?" Kenzie whispered.

Zachary nodded. He leaned forward with his elbows on his knees, staring down at the frozen ground. Kenzie rubbed the back of his neck and ran her fingers over the short, stubbly hair at the back of his skull. She knew he liked it, that it was a safe touch. He put one hand on her knee and she put her other hand over it, warm and comforting.

Zachary didn't hear much of what was said. It was too hard to listen to them talk about Jose without picturing what had been done to him. Archuro had described his rituals to Zachary in graphic detail, so Zachary knew. He breathed slowly, trying to keep nausea at bay.

It was definitely getting colder as the memorial drew to a close, despite the padded seats and cleared ground. Zachary was getting stiff from sitting there in the cold and holding himself tense.

He lifted his camera as Pat opened a small container the size of a perfume bottle and sprinkled it in front of him slowly, so that the contents were caught by the wind. The fine powder sparkled in the lights. Zachary wondered whether ashes always did that, or whether Pat had mixed glitter in with them. The effect was magical, and everyone seemed to be holding their breaths until it dissipated. There was music and there might have been a prayer. Eventually, everyone was standing up, talking and preparing to say their goodbyes.

"Do you want to go inside?" Kenzie suggested. "We'll have the chance to visit later when it's just us."

"Yeah. Let's do that," Zachary agreed.

He and Kenzie and Tyrrell retreated to the house to let the rest of the mourners finish paying their respects.

62

Pat and Mr. Peterson seemed worn out after the memorial and decided on naps before supper. Kenzie asked if she could get supper together for everyone.

"No, no," Pat told her. "I made everything ahead. I'll just warm it when I get up. I won't sleep for long. It's just been… a very emotional day. I need some time."

"I'm quite capable of warming up," Kenzie persisted. "If you just point me at what you want me to do, I'm happy to help."

Pat shook his head firmly. "You guys could probably use some time to decompress too. Don't worry about it." Closing the conversation, Pat turned toward the bedroom where Mr. Peterson had already retired. He stopped and turned back to Zachary. "Zach… did you get any footage of me sprinkling the ashes? The videographer said that the light was too low for him to get anything clear."

Zachary nodded. "I'll borrow Mr.—Lorne's computer and see how it looks. I can play with the lighting and contrast and see how much I can bring out."

"No rush. But that would be great if you were able to get anything."

That gave Zachary something to do while the others napped. Even Tyrrell said that his head was killing him and he hoped a nap would help. Zachary directed him to the guest bedroom and was glad not to have to babysit him to keep him from looking through the cupboards for anything to drink. Kenzie curled up on the couch and was snoring softly within a few minutes.

The aroma of creamy chicken soup and what smelled like fresh garlic toast eventually tempted Zachary away from fine-tuning the video on Mr. Peterson's computer and back out where the others were gathered.

The table had been set, probably by Kenzie, and Pat was setting out the serving dishes. He grinned at Zachary. "Was it the garlic bread?"

Zachary looked at Kenzie, feeling himself flush. "Are you telling all my weaknesses now?"

"To Patrick? Yes. Definitely."

They all laughed. In a few minutes, they were seated around the table, hungrily inhaling the savory smells. Zachary looked surreptitiously at Tyrrell, remembering the night before and how Tyrrell kept breaking down as they were eating the pizza. He seemed much more stable today, and Zachary hoped that was a good sign. Tyrrell didn't show any signs of breaking down in front of the others.

He was good at hiding his feelings.

Mr. Peterson raised a water glass—there wasn't any wine on the table as there usually was—and waited for silence. "To family," he said simply. "Even if none of you around this table are related to me by blood, you are still my family. Thank you so much for sharing this day with us."

Zachary nodded. They all raised their glasses, then drank.

Tyrrell set his glass back down on the table and looked at it. His gaze was so intense that everyone around the table was drawn to look at him. He noticed their gazes and tried to laugh it off, leaning back in his chair and looking away.

"How can this be a family?" he asked after a minute, while everyone sipped spoonfuls of the soup. "None of us grew up together.

The only ones related are Zachary and I, and we've only known each other for a year. How can this feel more like a family than the people I was raised by or people who share my DNA?"

"Because we care about each other," Pat offered. "No one here expects anyone else to be perfect or to carry the full load. We all... choose to be here and to support each other."

Tyrrell dragged his spoon through his soup, but didn't raise it to his mouth. "I don't think you'd feel the same way if you knew all the stuff that I've done."

"We all have regrets."

Tyrrell shook his head. "I'm not talking about 'regrets.' I'm talking about really bad stuff. Hurting people. Disappointing everyone. Abandoning all my responsibilities. And more. If you knew... I don't think you would feel the same way."

Pat looked at Mr. Peterson. He was the one who had experience as a foster parent. Experience dealing with hurt kids. Mr. Peterson took a few sips of his soup, pondering on it.

"Tyrrell... I'll bet that no one is harder on you than you are yourself."

"No one else knows everything," Tyrrell pointed out. "So how could they be?"

"Even if we knew all of the details, we wouldn't be as hard on you as you are."

"I know what I deserve. And it isn't to sit around a table like this and be counted as family."

"You don't have to earn it. You're family just because you are who you are. And because of the kindness you have shown to Zachary and to us. Look... I dealt with a lot of kids in the years Lilith and I fostered. And they were always hard on themselves and didn't believe they were worth anything. Being discarded by your family or being taken away from them causes a wound. They all came to us broken. Not a single one was untouched by it. What you went through was traumatic." Lorne's gaze shifted to Zachary. "We had hoped to be able to do something for Zachary, but he was one of the most traumatized kids we ever took, and we couldn't keep him. It was too much for my wife and she was concerned about possible danger to the other kids in the home. We just didn't have the resources to help him."

Tyrrell nodded, already aware of this history. "Yeah."

"You came from that same home. I doubt if you were any less traumatized than he was."

"He was ten. I was only six. He'd had to go through a lot more than I did."

"You came from the same place. You were both harmed."

"Vinny and me are only two years apart. And he's just fine. He grew up just like a normal kid in a normal family."

"He probably has a number of issues too. Maybe better hidden. But even kids as young as he was when he was removed are likely to have issues. Did you ever get any treatment?"

"Like therapy? My mom and dad didn't really believe in it. I went through other programs. Like boot camps and addiction treatment programs. I was usually doing pretty good when I graduated from them. But once I was back with the family again, things just fell apart." He pushed the soup bowl away from him, the soup untouched. "That just goes to prove that I was the problem. Not the Millers. Not the home that I came from. Me. Because whenever I was on my own, things went sideways."

"You need support. It's not too late to start therapy now. And AA or another addiction program."

"They've never stuck."

Mr. Peterson sighed and looked down at his meal, brows knit together.

"And maybe they never will," Zachary said. "Am I ever going to stop being depressed? Getting suicidal before the anniversary of the fire? I don't know. I'm not counting on it." He looked at Kenzie, who seemed ready to argue the point. "I'm getting more engaged in the therapy now. Choosing to go instead of being forced to. Going as a couple. I think... I don't know if it will ever change my brain, the way I think. But it's given me some more coping strategies. More ways to talk to Kenzie and have a better relationship."

Tyrrell rolled his eyes and let out a puff of air. "I don't have anyone. It's too late for me and Lindsey."

"Yes, but… some family sessions might still be a good idea. You're still a family, even if you're not together. You still want a relationship with the kids. And you still have to talk to Lindsey and work things out with her, even if you don't live together."

"She wouldn't."

"I think she would. I've talked to her a couple of times, and I think she'd be willing to try."

"I don't know. We've never talked about it. And that wouldn't stop me from drinking. Or messing up with the kids."

"One step at a time. It *might* help with the drinking. And it would help you deal with the kids and co-parenting." Zachary knew he was overstepping his bounds. He didn't actually have experience overcoming alcoholism with therapy or with family therapy and parenting. But he knew Tyrrell needed to try something new. Something other than just running away.

Tyrrell shook his head and picked up a piece of the golden, buttery garlic bread and took a bite. He looked surprised. "This is *really* good. Why haven't I tried this before?"

Kenzie looked from Zachary to Tyrrell and back again. "Oh no, we've got another one. We're going to have to make a loaf each if anyone else wants any."

Pat laughed. "Noted!"

Zachary helped himself to another piece of garlic bread, even though he'd been trying to be polite and eat more of the chicken soup rather than just pigging out on the bread. "Sometimes… trying something new can be good," he told Tyrrell, around a mouthful of bread.

63

K enzie had taken a day off work so they could sleep over at the Petersons' and to give Zachary a chance to see Joss before they headed for home.

He met Joss and Luke at the little coffee shop in the bookstore, where he had met with her once before. She seemed to prefer meeting him away from home, maybe so that she didn't have to worry about making sure the house was presentable, or maybe because home was her sanctuary and she didn't want it invaded any more than necessary. Zachary wasn't really sure. But if she felt better meeting him for coffee, that was fine with him. Anything that would smooth Joss's rough edges a little.

Zachary didn't for a minute think that Joss was a bad person or that she was willfully rude or hurtful. She'd just been through so much that she didn't see the point in sanitizing or sugar-coating what she had to say. People could take her at her bluntest and most acid, or not at all. It was probably a defense mechanism. Show people the worst and hope that it would scare them away, and she wouldn't have to deal with hurt feelings or put all of that effort into maintaining a relationship.

Kenzie had suggested before that it was probably easier for Zachary to deal with Joss if he were by himself than if she went along.

Zachary knew and understood Joss's background. Kenzie's privileged upbringing was obviously an irritant to Joss, and she didn't hesitate to throw out barbs about it. It was a lot easier for Zachary to talk with Joss if he weren't constantly trying to defend Kenzie—even though she was a big girl and could defend herself. That fact wasn't going to stop Zachary from jumping between them.

Luke had come along for coffee. Zachary wasn't sure why. He had expected that Luke would have his own interests and better things to do than to talk to his guardian's brother. Luke greeted Zachary with a friendly, familiar smile. They sat for a few moments in awkward silence after placing their coffee orders, looking at each other and trying to decide where to start.

"So, you found Tyrrell?" Jocelyn asked.

She was one of the people that Zachary had texted about it. She hadn't responded, even just to acknowledge his text. "Yeah. He's safe and sound. He and Kenzie are at the Petersons'."

"So he *did* just disappear because he wanted to."

"Yeah… I guess so. But it could have been something else. He could have been hurt or sick."

"But that wasn't likely."

Zachary shrugged. He'd had to track Tyrrell down. They had both known that from the moment he contacted her to find out if she knew anything. There hadn't been any question of it.

"Glad he's okay," Joss conceded. Then, after a pause, "Is he?"

"Is he okay? Yeah. I think so. For now. But it's been so difficult for him… do you know where he was…?"

She shook her head.

The waitress returned with their coffee order and handed them their cups, speaking in a bright voice, her movements quick like a bird's. Joss drank a couple of swallows of her coffee, even though Zachary's, when he tested it, was still boiling hot.

"No," Joss said. "Where was he? Some dark tavern somewhere."

"He was living out of his car. Drinking in a pub with Berk."

Jocelyn's brows rose up her forehead.

"Who's Berk?" Luke asked.

"Our father," Joss told him.

"Oh." Luke shrugged, not finding this to be as interesting an answer as he'd hoped for.

But Jocelyn was clearly as shocked about this as Zachary had been. "Drinking with Berk? Why would he be doing that?"

"I don't get it. He runs away because he's afraid he's becoming like Berk, but then he runs *to* him. Drinks with him. Listens to his lies about how everything was fine when we were kids and he loved us."

Joss's eyes looked intense enough to burn holes right through Zachary. Luke tilted his head, listening.

"Loved us," Joss repeated in disbelief.

"Apparently. Or at least, loved Tyrrell. I don't know if he's said that he loved all of us."

"Blech." Joss spat like she was trying to get something bitter out of her mouth. "You've got to be kidding me."

"You guys didn't get along with your dad?" Luke teased, his eyes dancing.

"I'll tell you how I'd get along with him if *I* met him again," Joss told him. "I'd like to get my hands on a nice PKM, and then I'd use the full one-hundred rounds to cut him in half both directions and reduce him to a pile of hamburger meat."

She sipped her coffee.

"That's what I would do."

Zachary widened his eyes at the graphic violence. He looked at Luke, who appeared to be only mildly surprised at this suggestion.

Luke shrugged. "It's probably a good idea if we don't give her one," he told Zachary.

"Yeah."

"I would *not* sit down with the man and drink with him," Joss clarified, in case they had missed her point. "Unless it was to toast his last remains."

Zachary nodded. "Okay. I wouldn't either. But I don't know about the machine gun."

"You use your weapon of choice; I'll use mine." She tossed her hair. "It's all fantasy anyway. I'm never going to meet him. He'd know better than to contact me."

"You were only thirteen when we... left."

"Too young to get my hands on a machine gun then," she said with regret.

"You felt that way then? Before the fire?"

"It's been a longstanding fantasy."

Zachary thought about Margot and Celia and sighed. He supposed he had his answer about whether Berk had always been predatory.

"How do you... put that aside and just... carry on?" Zachary asked, unsure how to put what he wanted to know into words. Despite the horrors that Joss had been through, she blended well. She worked a regular job and owned or rented a little house, and seemed just like anyone else in the quiet suburbia around her. As far as Zachary knew, she didn't suffer from any crippling mental illness as he did and had overcome her drug addiction. He didn't think it was just because she was a few years older than he that she seemed so mature. He wanted to know the secret.

"I... compartmentalize," Joss said. "I just put all of that 'dad' stuff in a box, and I shut it away. And I don't think about it unless someone like you brings it up. And now that you have, I'll close it up and put it away again."

Zachary was not unfamiliar with stuffing his feelings. He had forgotten a lot of what had happened to him as a child and teenager. He thought about Tyrrell, about how he said he could forget unless he were around Zachary or one of the others, and then it would come back to him. Joss made it sound easy. She was well-practiced, but even she said that things could bring it back to her.

Luke was nodding at Joss's explanation. "Separate yourself from it," he suggested. "Like it happened to someone else. That's the best thing to do."

"Is that what you do?" Zachary asked.

Luke shrugged. "Sure. I don't want to think about it if I don't have to. Avoid making memories in the first place if you can. If it's too late, then forget about it. Rewrite it. You can *change* what you remember."

Joss pointed at Luke. "That's what you've been doing. Rewriting what happened when you were with the organization."

He blinked at her, saying nothing.

"I won't rewrite what happened to me," Joss said strongly. "I'll remember what Berk did to me. And what the traffickers did to me. That's what keeps me from ever going back. If you rewrite it as a fairy tale, you'll end up going back because all you remember is the good stuff."

Luke took a long sip of his coffee, thinking about this.

"Compartmentalize," Joss reiterated. "Don't rewrite it. Just put it away in case you need it again later." She shook her head. "Don't be like Tyrrell, drinking with the enemy." She snorted in derision.

"Yeah," Luke agreed. He rubbed his upper lip, giving it some more thought. Then his gaze shifted to Zachary. He had another swallow of his coffee. "What's up with Rhys, do you know?"

Zachary raised his eyebrows, wondering what Luke had heard from him. That he was angry at Zachary? That he was going to leave his grandma's and run away from home? "Why? What did he say?"

"Nothing." Luke turned his hands palms up, demonstrating that they were empty. "He hasn't been messaging me. And when I message him… he doesn't answer."

"Oh?" Zachary gave it a few beats. He was happy to hear that Rhys had pulled back on communications. Maybe their talk had made Rhys reconsider. "Maybe he's been grounded and his grandma took away the phone."

Of course, Vera would never take away Rhys's phone, an integral part of his communications system. She understood many nuances of Rhys's facial expression and gestures that Zachary couldn't, but they still used the phone for some of the more complex subjects.

Luke shrugged and nodded. "Yeah, that's probably it," he agreed. "It's good he's got a grandma to look after him."

He turned to stare out the window, away from Zachary and Joss. Probably remembering his own grandma, the only person who had really cared for him and tried to keep him safe from harm. It was after she had died that he had been left floundering, anchorless, abusing alcohol and drugs, and getting into other trouble. Until he'd been scooped up by the trafficking ring that had put him to use. Something that, despite his attempts to rewrite history, he wouldn't want to subject his new young friend to. But if he did give in to the temptation to return to that life, he would bring whoever they told him to into the business.

Zachary was glad Rhys had stopped answering him and hoped that Luke would do as Joss suggested, and not pine after the life he'd had in the syndicate.

64

B
ack at the Petersons', Zachary lounged on the couch with Kenzie and recounted parts of the visit with Joss to Kenzie and to Lorne in his easy chair. Pat was off running errands, maybe buying ingredients for his next culinary creation. Tyrrell sat by the window, a book in his hand. Still, he didn't appear to be putting much effort into reading it, mostly staring out the window into the distance. Zachary had only seen him flip pages once or twice and thought it was just for show rather than that he'd actually finished reading those pages.

Zachary recounted Joss's comments about compartmentalizing old memories, but not the part about how she'd like to make mincemeat of Berk if she ever saw him again.

Mr. Peterson shook his head. "We dealt with a lot of kids over the years, and the ones who were able to deal with what had happened to them and work through it in therapy were the ones who had the best outcomes. The ones who just stuffed all their feelings and memories and pretended that everything was fine... it eventually catches up with them at some point. Sooner or later."

"Joss has been pretty successful with it."

"I don't claim to know all of what happened to her. But from what I saw of her… I assume she has spent most of the intervening years *self-medicating.*"

"Well, yes," Zachary agreed.

"That's not exactly a healthy coping mechanism."

Zachary glanced over at Tyrrell. "No."

"She may find, one of these days, that those memories won't stay in their compartments anymore and she has to deal with them."

Zachary's own box of memories had been opened during the assault by Archuro. All those experiences that he had been so careful to push down and hide even from himself had surfaced and couldn't be stuffed away again. Dr. B said that was actually a good sign. A sign that he was healthier mentally and ready to deal with them, as he hadn't been equipped to do as a child. But that hadn't made Zachary feel much better about it. Even after a year, he still fought to keep those resurfaced memories from affecting his focus and daily activities.

"Zachary, can you help me pack? I don't want to forget anything."

Zachary looked at Kenzie, frowning. She rarely asked him for help on anything. Certainly, she had always packed her own bags, whether for a weekend trip to the Petersons' or the holiday at the Lodge. She jerked her head toward the bedroom.

"Oh. Sure, of course." Zachary followed. "It's always those charge cords…"

They retreated to the guest room and Kenzie shut the door. Her packed bag was already on the bed. Zachary looked around the room, but it was clear she hadn't forgotten to put anything in it.

"I wanted to talk to you about Tyrrell," she told him.

Zachary was feeling pretty talked-out about Tyrrell. She already knew all of what had happened and what was on his mind. Going over it again seemed more stressful than helpful.

"Okay," he agreed. "What did you want to discuss?" Dr. Boyle would be very proud of him for engaging with Kenzie without whining about it.

"I wanted to offer him the guest room for a few days while he gets back on his feet. And I can help find a program for him. Maybe something a bit different from what he's done before. But I didn't want to do it without talking to you first, in case you feel like it would be a problem, the two of you getting in each other's way."

Zachary felt a rush of warmth and gratitude toward Kenzie. While he had thought about bringing Tyrrell home, he knew he couldn't do it without asking Kenzie first. It was her house, after all. But he didn't want to ask, in case she might feel obligated.

"Are you sure? That would be great, if you're sure it's what you want to do."

"Yes. I want to do something for him, and I don't think that a few days in our guest room would be too difficult for any of us. I'm worried that if he just goes back to Riverbrook, he's going to go straight back to drinking with your father again. If we can get a little distance between them, then at least there's a chance he'll work toward sobriety again."

"What if it doesn't work out? He doesn't want to get into a program and won't get out and look for work?"

"Then I'll be the bad guy. You can tell him that I've had enough and am kicking him out."

Zachary chuckled. "I couldn't ask you to do that."

"You absolutely should. I don't want to be tripping over him for a year while he sits on the couch and drinks. But I don't think he'll stay long. If it isn't working out like expected..."

"He'll run away."

She raised her brows and shrugged. "That's his pattern."

Zachary nodded. "Okay. Let's go tell him."

He grabbed Kenzie's hand, and they walked together out to the living room.

Did you enjoy this book? Reviews and recommendations are vital to making a book successful.

Please leave a review at your favorite book store or review site and share it with your friends.

Don't miss the following bonus material:
Sign up for mailing list to get a free ebook
Read a sneak preview chapter
Other books by P.D. Workman
Learn more about the author

UNLOCK ACCESS TO
ZACHARY GOLDMAN'S CASE FILES!

Get a peek inside Zachary's case files and see what other intriguing tales are in store!

SCAN TO UNLOCK OFFER

books.pdworkman.com/sign-up-zg

PREVIEW OF THEIR WALLS WERE EMPTY

ZACHARY GOLDMAN MYSTERIES #12

A simple robbery

Back in the saddle, Private Investigator Zachary Goldman is hired by Kenzie's father to investigate the heist of valuable memorabilia from his favorite sports bar.

Kenzie did say that it was a bad idea.

Maybe Zachary should have listened.

Because nothing is as it appears. As Zachary digs deeper, it becomes apparent that there is far more at stake here than just some sports memorabilia.

Just what has Walter put him in the middle of?

CHAPTER 1

Zachary sat bolt upright in the bed, gasping for breath. The room was dark and he was disoriented. He felt around him for something that he had lost, desperate to lay hold of whatever it had been. A key? A coin? A baby that had slipped out of his grasp. It was important that he find it before it was lost to him forever. He slid his hands under the covers, under the pillow. He encountered Kenzie beside him, but it was a minute before he knew who it was and that she wasn't the thing he had lost.

"Zachary?" Kenzie's voice was sleepy. "What's wrong? Are you okay?"

"It's... no... I lost it..."

"Lost what, hon'?" Kenzie stirred. She turned over to face him, reaching out to touch him in the dark. A hand on his side, then his chest, which was still heaving from his gasps, his heart pounding so hard and fast he was sure she could feel it right under her fingers. "Hey. It's okay. You had a dream."

"I know, but I needed... I needed to hold onto..." He couldn't even remember what it was, that wisp of a dream that had become concrete in his hands that he had been determined to hold onto this time. Not to let it fall from his grasp and dissolve into nothingness again.

"Shh. It's fine," Kenzie murmured. "Try to go back to sleep."

"No. It's here somewhere. I just have to find it..."

He again slid his fingers under his pillow, looking for it. Frustrated, he reached over to the nightstand and turned on the lamp. Kenzie fell back, covering her eyes with her arm and making an irritated sound.

"Sorry. It's here. It's here somewhere." Zachary lifted up his pillow and looked underneath. He slid out of the bed and pulled back his blankets, looking underneath. There was nothing there. No sign of the precious thing he had lost.

What had it been?

He was anxious. How could he have lost it so quickly? It had been in his hands.

Kenzie lowered her arm slowly and was watching him. "It's just part of the dream," she assured him. "It just left you disoriented. That happens sometimes. It might be a side effect of your sleep aid."

Zachary sat back down on the mattress, feeling bereft. What had he lost?

"I hate this feeling. It can't just be the dream."

"Have you had it before? I know sometimes I have part of a dream that sticks with me for a few extra seconds, and it can be a little freaky."

"Yes."

"Just take a few minutes to calm down."

Zachary looked around the room, still sure that he must have missed something. He looked down at the floor to see if something had fallen off of the bed, trying not to let Kenzie see that he was still searching for the lost thing.

"Is everything okay?" he asked her. Though he had woken her up, so she probably didn't know any better than he did. "Did something happen that woke me up? A noise?"

Kenzie appeared to be listening, trying to catch any stray noise that might have startled Zachary awake. A siren in the distance. A tree branch rubbing against the side of the house in the wind. They both listened, but didn't hear anything unusual. Just the usual noises that houses made. Hot air vents. The occasional creaks and pops. Nothing unusual.

Zachary rubbed his eyes.

"Tyrrell," he said suddenly. He turned his head, looking around the room, as if Tyrrell might be there. But he hadn't slept in the same room as his younger brother since he was ten and the house had burned down, and he and Tyrrell had been sent to separate foster families. But Tyrrell was back in his life now, had been back in it for just over a year. And Zachary had brought him home to stay with them while they tried to help him get into a treatment program.

But of course he wasn't in the bedroom. He was in the guest room, where he had been staying for a few days.

"I have to go see if he's okay."

Kenzie didn't object, just sat there rubbing her eyes. She probably knew better than to argue with him. Knew that when he got into this mood, she couldn't tell him anything. He needed to see Tyrrell, to know that he was okay. To know that he wasn't the thing that Zachary had lost and was still searching for.

Zachary pulled on a pair of pajama pants he had left crumpled on the floor and went to the guest room to make sure that Tyrrell was still there. What if he had left? What if that was what had woken Zachary up, his subconscious brain alert to the fact that if Tyrrell left, he might be in danger. From himself, if not from out outside threat.

He tapped lightly on the guest room door but knew that Tyrrell wouldn't answer it. He would either be gone, or he would be deeply asleep. Not sitting there waiting for Zachary to check in on him and make sure that he was okay. He turned the door handle slowly to try to keep it from squeaking or making any other noise, and then it had turned all the way, pushed it slowly forward.

The room was dark and still. If Tyrrell had left, he hadn't left a light on behind him to draw attention to the fact that he was gone. Zachary tiptoed into the room, trying not to awaken his brother, if he was still there. His eyes had to adjust to the dark again after having turned on the lamp in the master bedroom.

There was a lump on the bed. Tyrrell? Or a couple of pillows and some blankets shaped to look like he was still sleeping in the bed? A juvenile trick, but one that Tyrrell might have used anyway, if he didn't want Zachary to know if he had left.

Zachary reached out and touched the blankets. He expected to fill it all give under his fingers, squashed flat by his touch, but he encountered resistance. Someone was curled up under the blankets. Tyrrell had not snuck out.

Zachary breathed a sigh of relief. For the first time since he had gasped himself awake, his breathing started to slow and settle. More convinced now that no one was in danger, and that the feelings of loss and dread were just that, feelings, artifacts of the dream, and Kenzie had suggested.

"What? Zachary?" Tyrrell turned over in the bed to face him. "What's wrong? What is it?"

"Nothing. Nothing wrong. Sorry. I heard a noise. Wanted to make sure you were okay."

"I'm okay, bro. Just sleeping. Like you should be."

"Yeah. Sorry. I'll go back to bed. You go back to sleep too."

"I plan to," Tyrrell agreed dryly.

Zachary gave his arm a little squeeze, to reassure Tyrrell and himself that everything really was okay, then retraced his steps, closing the guest room door behind him and rejoining Kenzie.

She was dozing even with the bedroom lamp on. Zachary felt bad for waking her up, especially on a work night when she should be able to sleep all the way through and get all of the rest that she needed to be fresh at work.

He sat down on the edge of the bed again, easing down slowly in an effort not to jar her awake again. She made a murmured sound, not really awake, but knowing that he was there.

He probably wouldn't be able to get back to sleep again. And even if he could, he would probably have another nightmare and another waking where he couldn't fully separate himself from the sticky stuff of his dreams. If he stayed in bed, he would probably keep waking Kenzie up again, and she needed her sleep more than he needed his. He was used to operating on just a few hours of sleep.

He turned off the lamp and waited for a moment to see whether that had woken her up again.

"Everything okay?" Kenzie murmured.

"Yeah. It's fine. Sorry. I didn't mean to wake you up again."

"Don't worry about it. Tyrrell is okay?"

"He's sleeping. Shouldn't have woken him up."

"Mmm."

Zachary rubbed Kenzie's shoulder for a minute so that she would think that he was also settling in to go to sleep and would drop off faster. Then, like after putting a baby to sleep, he got back to his feet very slowly so that she wouldn't be aware of the shift in the mattress and wake back up again. Her breaths continued, long and slow and even.

CHAPTER 2

Z achary adjourned to the living room, which operated as his office and central hub. He sat down, turned on the TV, found a movie to provide some low background noise, then opened his laptop on his mobile desk. He had checked his email before going to bed, so he knew there wouldn't be much more there. Mostly spam. Not a lot of people emailed him overnight.

After glancing over the subject lines, he closed the email inbox and started to go through his project folders, seeing what he could find to keep him occupied for a few hours. There was a backlog due to the amount of time he had spent in the hospital and then searching for Tyrrell. Zachary had only been back at it again for a few days, so there was plenty for him to catch up on.

It was the first year that he had worked with Heather, his older sister, and she had kept things running while he had been in the hospital. She was a remarkably efficient manager. She had conducted skip tracing and the easier computer work, had sent out bills, collected on some of the delinquent accounts, and generally kept clients happy while Zachary had been unable to tend to his business. He had thought that his PI business would forever be a one-man business, but it was nice to have someone else helping out. He probably wasn't paying Heather enough. He might have to task her with researching how much he should actually be paying her. Her husband was a bookkeeper and probably had sources for that kind of thing. Heather mostly liked having something to do, since she didn't really need the money as much as she did something to fill the empty hours while her husband was at his own job.

The movie playing on the TV helped to cover up any night noises the house was still making but was not interesting enough for Zachary to pay any attention to it as he did some deep research and looked at the insurance investigation files that Heather had opened for him. He didn't really like trying to catch people defrauding their insurance companies. Still, it was, at least, better than chasing after errant husbands. Or wives. He had made a significant shift away from adultery investigations in the past two years, and he was glad of that. Less surveillance, fewer lives ruined by his pictures, and more time spent on more constructive investigations and might actually make someone happy.

By the time he heard Kenzie up using the shower, the movie had ended. Or maybe two movies; he wasn't sure since he hadn't actually been watching or listening to any of the action. He got up from the couch, where he had been sitting in the same position for too long, stretched his shoulders and back, and wandered into the kitchen. He put coffee grinds in the hopper, set the carafe under the spout, and started the coffee brewing. He helped himself to a cup once it was finished and went back to his computer, where he checked out his social networks and email again until Kenzie was out of the shower.

She smiled at him, her bright red lipstick looking particularly kissable and dark curls bouncing around her head. "How long have you been up? I didn't hear you get up."

Zachary shrugged. "A few hours."

"You didn't get up after that dream, did you? You got back to sleep for a couple of hours?"

Zachary shrugged and didn't answer to confirm or deny. "There is coffee in the kitchen."

"I can smell it. Thanks."

He followed her into the kitchen, where they worked side by side for a few minutes to prepare their breakfasts. Nothing fancy. A granola bar and yogurt for Zachary and toast with marmalade for Kenzie. And coffee. Then they sat down for their morning visit.

Zachary hadn't realized until they had brought Tyrrell back just how much he valued those quiet breakfast visits. The mornings that Tyrrell woke up early and was prowling around the house and getting his own breakfast or chatting while they were getting theirs, Zachary tended to feel flustered and crowded and just wanted their space back again. But that was selfish. Tyrrell needed them. So Zachary said nothing, but still felt irritated by Tyrrell's presence if he got up for breakfast and much preferred the quiet start with Kenzie when he could get it.

Kenzie watched Zachary open his chocolate chip granola bar in preparation for his breakfast. She smiled, nodding her approval. "So nice to see you eating again. This med cocktail is better for that reason, for sure."

Zachary nodded. It was nice not to be so nauseated in the morning. Much easier to eat if he didn't have to fight his own body to get the food down. And while his appetite still probably wasn't where it should be and he didn't feel hungry most of the time, it was better than it had been with the meds he'd been on the last few years. Which should help him get up to a healthy weight much faster than usual and make his doctors happy.

"It's working okay in other areas too, I think." It was impossible to tell whether it would help him get less depressed before the next Christmas, but that was almost a year away, so he didn't have to worry about it yet. One of the open questions was whether it would help with his obsessive thoughts about Bridget, his ex-wife, and the compulsions to check in on her or follow her. He knew that he had disappointed Kenzie by giving into those compulsions again when Bridget had been pregnant, convinced that she could not take care of herself and the twins and that she would need him there, close by. He had been the one to call for help when she had collapsed in the garden the day she had gone into labor, so he hadn't been wrong.

Since getting out of the hospital, he had been able to keep those obsessions reined in. But he had been trying to find Tyrrell, so he'd had something else to occupy his anxious brain. Whether he would be able to keep those thoughts at bay as he got back into the normal routine was still uncertain. He was hopeful that the new cocktail would help. And yet worried that it wouldn't.

Their Walls Were Empty, Book #12 of the *Zachary Goldman Mysteries* series by P.D. Workman can be purchased at pdworkman.com

ABOUT THE AUTHOR

P.D. Workman is a USA Today Bestselling author and multi-award winner, renowned for her prolific output of over 100 published works that span various genres. With a knack for crafting page-turners, Workman captivates readers with everything from cozy mysteries like the Auntie Clem's Bakery series to gripping young adult and suspense novels.

A prolific reader and writer since childhood, P.D. Workman crafts emotionally powerful stories that don't shy away from hard topics. Her books tackle mental illness, addiction, abuse, and trauma with raw honesty and compassion, giving voice to the often unheard. If you crave authentic, character-driven page-turners that hit deep and stay with you long after the final page, you're in the right place.

With each new release, fans eagerly anticipate another thrilling blend of thought-provoking storytelling and relatable characters that define P.D. Workman's brand as an author of unforgettable page-turners—gripping tales that leave a lasting impact long after the last page is turned.

P. D. Workman, does not shy from probing the deep psychological scars of childhood trauma, mental illness, and addiction. Also characteristic of this author, these extremely sensitive issues are explored with extensive empathy, described with incredible clarity, and portrayed with profound insight.

— —KIM, GOODREADS REVIEWER

Some of Workman's titles have been translated into Spanish, French, Portuguese, German, and Italian.

Workman began writing at an early age and is a prolific reader as well as writer. She is also passionate about teaching and learning, expresses her creativity through art and cooking, and loves exploring the Calgary parks and green spaces where the Parks Pat Mysteries are set. She was a legal assistant for many years and has done extensive charitable work.

Workman was born and raised in Alberta, Canada, and is married with one adult son.

Please visit P.D. Workman at pdworkman.com to see what else she is working on, to join her mailing list, and to link to her social networks.

If you enjoyed this book, please take the time to recommend it to other purchasers with a review or star rating and share it with your friends!

tiktok.com/@pdworkmanauthor

facebook.com/pdworkmanauthor

x.com/pdworkmanauthor

instagram.com/pdworkmanauthor

amazon.com/author/pdworkman

bookbub.com/authors/p-d-workman

goodreads.com/pdworkman

linkedin.com/in/pdworkman

pinterest.com/pdworkmanauthor

youtube.com/pdworkman

Find P.D. Workman's books at

PDWORKMAN.COM

Scan the QR code below